PEARL HARBOR DESTROYED . . . AGAIN!

There were thirty-four U.S. Navy ships at anchor in Pearl Harbor on Sunday morning. Eight destroyers, five frigates, four battle cruisers, plus numerous patrol vessels and rocket boats. Biggest of all were the five megacarriers, each nearly a mile long and half a mile wide. The ship's company for each megacarrier topped 25,000 men, not counting the pilots and air crews for the aircraft on board. While many of the airplanes were up on the decks of the carriers, like the ships themselves they were in the midst of major reconditioning. None were ready for action.

There would be no air raid sirens. No alert Klaxons. No warning at all for Pearl Harbor. The attacking bomber force came out of the west, thirty airplanes aligned into two long rows. They swept over the anchored ships, one massive bomb under each wing.

The lead airplane let loose its pair of bombs and with a great scream of jet engines, turned wide and began climbing again. Both bombs hit a megacarrier midships. A gigantic plume of fire rose high above the ship, flames spilling out for miles around. The ship was blown apart, along with the dock works and the repair facility. All that was left was a massive crater, filling with tons of seawater.

It would take less than ninety seconds for the attacking bombers to destroy the rest of Pearl Harbor.

THE WINGMAN SERIES
by Mack Maloney

Return of
Sky Ghost

Mack Maloney

Pinnacle Books
Kensington Publishing Corp.
http://www.pinnaclebooks.com

PINNACLE BOOKS are published by

Kensington Publishing Corp.
850 Third Avenue
New York, NY 10022

Pinnacle and the P logo Reg. U.S. Pat. & TM Off.

First Printing: May, 1998
10 9 8 7 6 5 4 3 2 1

Printed in the United States of America

Part 1

One

The small Navy patrol boat USS *Neponset* was two hours out of Oahu, Hawaii, when it happened.

It was a cloudless day, a Sunday, and very hot for December. The seas were extraordinarily calm. There was no wind. The commander of the vessel had stopped and allowed his crew a 10-minute cool-off and swim.

Half the men were in the water; the others were sunning themselves on deck. They were just kids mostly, the oldest among them was twenty-two. World War II had ended two months before, and all the fighting had taken place in Europe. The crew of the sleek, wood-and-plastic *Neponset* had been half a world away from the hostilities. None of them had ever seen combat.

Nor had their commander, Lieutenant A. J. Noonan. Compact, rugged, with a friendly face and a lightning-quick mind, at twenty-four, he was barely older than his men.

It had started out as a routine patrol. The *Neponset* was a TPB, a torpedo patrol boat. It had made this trip every other day for the past six months. Basically two hours out and two hours back, these voyages were always uneventful. Occasionally the crew would help civilian boats in trouble, or serve as navigation beacons for off-course aircraft. But the guns on the patrol boat had never been fired except in training. Same with its air torpedoes.

So the crew was swimming and Lt. Noonan was in the chart room below, rechecking his navigation plots, when the world suddenly turned upside down.

The first indication of trouble came when Noonan heard his men gasp—all at once. Then the shouting began. Then came cries of disbelief. He hurried up to the deck and the first thing he saw was a wall of water heading for his vessel. One word flashed into his mind: *tsunami*. A huge tidal wave was coming right for them.

Noonan reacted instantly. He yelled for the men in the water to get back onboard fast. None of them needed further prompting—they were already scrambling up the access ladder onto the foredeck. Noonan hit several buttons on his control panel at once. The boat's powerful engines immediately roared to life.

Then he spun around and activated the boat's Main/AC battle management computer, the "thinking machine" which was aboard every U.S. Navy vessel, big and small, as well as every Air Corps airplane, every Army tank, jeep, and helicopter. Noonan hastily typed two words into the keyboard: *tidal wave*. When he looked up again, the wall of water was just a mile away.

But there was something else too—something more frightening than the tsunami. For now, Noonan could see beyond the wave. And what he saw just didn't seem real.

It was a submarine. Yet it was enormous. Bigger even than the largest Navy megacarrier—and that was one mile long!

This ship, this monster, was longer than a mile, and wider by half. It was flat, squat, like a huge, metallic hammerhead shark. Still, it was at least ten decks thick. The whole thing seemed so unnatural; like a huge floating city had just popped up from beneath the waves.

In a second Noonan knew what had happened. This tidal wave bearing down on them had been caused not by an undersea earthquake or some other natural event, but simply by the monstrous ship breaking the surface.

It was that big.

As soon as all his men were safely on board, Noonan hit the ship's throttle and the TPB took off like a rocket. The vessel could top 100 knots, but he knew he could not outrun the tidal wave. No ship was that fast. His only option was to face the tsunami head-on.

He turned the TPB hard to port and pointed the nose right at the coming wall of water. At the same time he shouted an order for all his men to get below and strap down.

The wave was 750 feet away now and seemed to be growing by the second. Noonan increased throttle to 100 percent and locked his steering column down. He pushed a button which sealed every window, bulkhead, and weapons port on the ship. This was called cocooning. Another lever lowered a glass canopy, which fit snugly over the open bridge, sealing him in with just his navigator and boatswain.

Now the wave was just 250 feet away. The TPB was heading for it at nearly ninety-five knots. Noonan had time to yell *Hang on!* just one more time.

Then it hit . . .

And then everything went black.

The thirty-five-foot patrol boat collided with the wave with such force, it was lifted two-thirds of the way up the side of the 100-foot wall of water. Only then did its forward momentum kick in and knife the bow through the swell, popping the boat out the other side. The *Neponset* plummeted down sixty feet, nose over and straight into the ocean, hitting the surface hard and going completely under.

But Noonan had performed well. He'd done everything

right. The vessel was watertight and thus buoyant. It popped back up to the surface almost immediately, and though battered and woozy, was still afloat.

More important, everyone on board was safe.

The TPB stabilized, the engines coughed a few times, but then came right back on line. Noonan heard the Main/AC beeping and when he turned around he saw the computer was advising him to meet the tidal wave head-on. He even smiled a bit—his quick thinking had beaten the thinking machine by several crucial seconds.

But now Noonan and his crew had other problems. Bigger problems. There was no great wave blocking them from the huge ship anymore. It was just 2500 feet away, in all its monstrous glory. Noonan immediately called his crew to battle stations. Those men running to their deck guns just stared in utter disbelief at the gigantic ship.

Noonan had never seen anything like it. No one in the crew had. The sub was not of U.S. military design, that was for certain. First, it was dark green, not the usual drab Navy gray. And it just didn't look "Navy." It was sharper, more extreme than any current Navy design, with many angles and attachments. It really did look more like a mechanical creature than a ship, especially with its wide mouth, expelling steam, and the four-stories-high multi-window bridge. Its aqua-tinted Plexiglas windows looked like a set of giant green eyes.

Noonan cut back all speed, and hastily called the boat's cameraman to the bridge. The man arrived a few seconds later, wearing a bulky battlesuit complete with flak jacket and helmet, and lugging a large insta-film movie camera. He took one look at the floating monster and almost went right over. Noonan steadied him and told him to shoot the length of the ship twice, and then concentrate on the bridge. Meanwhile, Noonan punched the Main/AC options panel and began the process of sending a secure message back to his home port at Oahu.

He had to tell someone about this.

The cameraman had just started rolling when something else happened. About five miles beyond the first ship, another monstrous sub had surfaced. This one in a gentler fashion, causing little of the tsunami effect. But this sub was just as big as the first monster and it too opened a giant mouth and began belching steam as soon as it surfaced. Then three miles beyond that one, another giant broke the waves.

Noonan and his crew were astonished at what was happening. One moment they'd been enjoying a leisurely, peaceful patrol. Now it seemed as if some hell beneath the ocean had opened up and its worst creatures were coming to the surface.

The cameraman ran out of film or courage or both, and quickly scrambled below. Noonan put the TPB into a 180-turn, not quite sure what to do next. He was still a minute away from getting a secure line back to base. Until that happened, he felt his duty was to stay where he was and report back what he was seeing.

His headphones began buzzing. It was his radar man. An aircraft was approaching from the northwest. Noonan saw it a moment later. He recognized the plane right away. It was CB-201, a huge twelve-engine maritime cargo airplane. The crew of Noonan's vessel saw this particular aircraft frequently while patrolling these waters. It was an island-hopper, delivering supplies, food, and mail to far-flung U.S. Navy posts.

Now it had blundered into this nightmare.

The airplane was flying at 6,000 feet, but its pilots, obviously not believing their eyes, were descending to get a better look at the three giant ships. Suddenly one section atop the first ship opened and an array of antiaircraft muzzles appeared. They turned toward the CB-201 and fired at once. Each shell contained a tiny radi-seeker nose cone. Each one scored a direct hit either on one of the airplane's twelve engines or on its cockpit, the hottest places on its airframe.

The mammoth airplane simply disintegrated in flight. One moment it was there—the next, it was just a huge cloud of tiny debris. No fire, no smoke. Forty-five lives and a gigantic aircraft gone. Just like that.

Suddenly, the steam stopped belching out of the great ships. A tremendous roar was heard—so loud it stung Noonan's ears. He would later discover this was the sound of many jet engines revving up at once. A few moments later, an airplane came roaring out of the mouth of the first monster sub. There was another one right behind it. Then another, and another.

The airplanes were huge! They had long slender fuselages, swept-back wings with eight jet engines per side. Each airplane was carrying a huge bomb under each wing. The bombs were so big, they were nearly one-third of the length of the airplane.

Now planes began flying out of the other two great ships as well. They, too, were huge. They, too, were carrying enormous bombs under their wings.

Noonan took only a few moments to decide his next course of action. These ships were alien to him, as were the airplanes. They were obviously taking off to bomb something, somewhere, and the only likely targets around were American military or civilian sites. Plus, they'd just shot down an American plane.

So there really was only one thing he could do . . .

He keyed his microphone.

"Prepare for action," he told his crew.

If the crew was astonished by his order, they did not show it. Bells began blowing and Klaxons screaming. Yet the men stayed calm. Noonan soon had twice as much power at his disposal as before. The TPB's double-reaction engines were now kicking up to 150 percent.

He turned his bow toward the first big ship. It was about

half a mile away and still disgorging the huge bombers. The TPB had sixteen air torpedoes on board, plus ten triple-fifty machine guns on deck. But this ship was the size of a small city. It was bristling with guns and radar dishes and missile launchers. David had had a better chance against Goliath.

Still, Noonan knew his duty.

He put on his helmet, hit the throttle, and made sure his vessel's battle seals were still tight and in place. Then, at 2000 feet out, he ordered the first air torpedo launched.

It went off the front rail clean, displaying its characteristic yellow plume of smoke. The fifteen-foot-long silver tube rose steadily, leveled off at exactly fifty-five feet and began its target run. Noonan watched the torpedo's progress on his weapons management screen. The Main/AC computer behind him was buzzing about something, but he had no time to attend to it now.

The torpedo gained speed as it neared the huge ship. Noonan took over manual steering at 750 feet out and turned the weapon toward the control window of the monster sub. At 500 feet out, the torpedo's impact motor clicked on, and suddenly the weapon and its substantial warhead were streaking up toward the sub's eyelike control bridge at more than 300 knots.

Impact came three seconds later. The missile smashed through the window and exploded. A good hit!

But Noonan was already turning the TPB hard to starboard and booting all power. They had barely scratched the huge ship—and now it knew they were here.

He ordered a second air torpedo launched. Like the first, it rose in a cloud of yellow smoke, leveled off, and began looking for an impact point. Noonan steered its nose toward the end of the giant ship—maybe he could hit a crucial propulsion component and at least disable the behemoth.

But this was not to be. Just as the air torpedo's impact

motor was turning on, an antimissile missile shot out from the foredeck of the sub and in a burst of amazing speed, hit the torpedo and simply vaporized it.

Noonan was astounded at the gigantic ship's lightning-quick defenses. This thing really did act like it was from another world!

Still, he ordered a third air torpedo launched. For this one, he would swing back around and try for a hit on the sub's huge mouth, which was still expelling huge bombers at a rate of one every ten seconds.

The third torpedo went off the rail and made it to within 200 feet of the sub's bow before another antimissile missile materialized from the foredeck and blew it up.

Noonan swung the TPB around a fourth time—he was running on pure adrenaline now. The engines were screaming, the chatter in the ship's radio was deafening as his men shouted out targets and defenses on the side of the nearest mystery ship. They were within 500 feet now and the thing looked like a huge floating skyscraper lying on its side. By comparison, they were like a gnat trying to take down a buffalo—or more appropriately, a minnow trying to stop a whale. The dreamlike quality of the whole thing was the strangest of all. Noonan kept asking himself over and over: *Is this really happening?*

Then he started picking up puffs of red smoke coming from the bottom two levels of the ship. Then the air around him literally began shaking.

"Disruption shells incoming!" his sea defense officer's voice shouted in his headphone.

Those three words were enough to make anyone's stomach turn. If a disruption shell made a direct hit, it would destroy the TPB in two seconds. Or even if a DS hit the water near the ship, its disruption waves could fry all the electronics onboard, blow up the engines, and leave them powerless and unarmed.

Three disruption shells went screaming over the TPB

and landed about 1000 feet beyond. Their shock waves still shook the vessel from stem to stern, but no permanent damage resulted. It would have been prudent to withdraw.

But Noonan would have none of that—he was furious that such a huge ship would dare to destroy his own and hurt his men. He turned the TPB back toward the front of the sub and ordered another air torpedo be fired.

At that moment, all defensive fire from the big ship suddenly ceased. It was so quick, so strange, Noonan took it as a bad omen. Behind him the Main/AC had been buzzing wildly—only now did he turn around and hit its "reveal" function The Main/AC spit out a ticker tape that said just one thing: *initiate evasive action.*

But it was too late for that. Noonan looked beyond the computer to the rear of the ship and saw another amazing and frightening sight. Another vessel, smaller than the aircraft-carrying subs, but just as terrifying and alien, had surfaced off his stern and was coming at full speed right at them!

Noonan initiated the Main/AC advice and began to twist the little patrol boat out of the way—but it was not soon enough. The sharp bow of the enemy vessel sliced right through the middle of the patrol boat, killing seven of his men instantly and tearing the little vessel in two.

The engines blew up a second later. The next thing he knew, Noonan was flying through the air, his hair on fire, the combat gloves burning right off his skin.

In his last conscious moment, he saw many things: His men in the water. His vessel in two pieces, smoking and sinking. The wake of the strange ship that had split them in half. And beyond, the big, bombed-up airplanes still flying out of the mouths of the huge submarines. And in that last blink, he saw a flag flying above both the huge aircraft carrier sub and the ship that had just destroyed his own.

The flag was white with a huge red ball in the middle.

The Rising Sun symbol—the emblem of the Armed Forces of Japan.

Two hundred and fifty-five miles to the southeast, a B-17/52 superheavy bomber was about twenty minutes away from landing.

The crew of the gigantic aircraft, forty-four men in all, were strapping down equipment, securing weapons, and stowing away all loose gear.

The airplane was a cross between a B-17 Flying Fortress and a B-52 bomber. The nose and fuselage were reminiscent of the famous Fortress; the swept-back wings and high tail came from the '52. The monstrous airplane had sixteen engines; six of them were now shut down for the landing approach. There was a total of twenty-six gun stations up and down the fuselage, each one bearing a triple-.50 caliber machine gun. Each of these weapons now had to be locked down and their ammunition belts secured.

The giant bomber was heading for Hickam Field, the sprawling if sleepy air base located on southern Oahu, near Honolulu. The airplane was on a training mission. More than half the crew were making their first flight. The primary flight crew were all veterans of the recently completed fighting in Europe. Now they and their much-patched slightly battered airplane would spend a six-week tour of duty in the friendly environs of Hawaii.

Or at least that's what was supposed to happen.

The plane was now fifteen miles out from Hickam. The navigation section was bringing up a TV image of the air base; they would be putting down on Runway 5-Left a six-mile-long asphalt strip built to handle the Air Corps's largest bombers like the B-17/52. The radio section had made contact with the base; the skies were clear; there was no air traffic in the area. The B-17/52 was cleared to come straight in, which was good. Just to turn the huge bomber in a ninety-degree bank could take more than fifteen minutes and an avalanche of new navigation plots. For an airplane as massive as the B-17/52, a straight-ahead landing was definitely preferred.

At ten miles out, two more engines were shut down; now the aircraft was flying on eight, the minimum required for safe landing. The nonessential crewmembers—the gunners, the oilers, the radio engineers—were strapped in, preparing for touchdown. At the moment, the major concern of the plane's four pilots was one of postflight maintenance. As it was Sunday morning, they wondered if a large enough ground crew would be on hand to service the big plane once it was down.

They were five minutes out when the lead pilot called Hickam for final landing clearance, a mere formality. But instead of granting the OK the tower personnel sent a rather odd message: "Hang on . . ." the shaky voice told them. "And prepare to go around."

Now this was a problem because the huge bomber was already descending, losing altitude from its cruising height of 65,000 feet. It was so big, that to be waved off now would be a major operation. The plane would have to restart its eight dormant engines, halt its descent, and claw for some altitude. A new flight plot would have to be calculated and a long, slow turn initiated.

Why then wouldn't Hickam air control give them the OK?

Just on a whim, the lead pilot punched the "Situation Inquiry" button on his Main/AC computer. Why, he was asking the battle management machine, couldn't they land at Hickam?

The answer that came back was as puzzling as it was startling.

It read: "Impending Enemy Action."

A moment later the pilot's situation awareness display began blinking. The air defense computer was suddenly going berserk. The TV screen popped on and instantly the bomber's pilots were staring mouths agape at a huge airborne force heading for the same field they were—but from the opposite direction!

There were at least fifty airplanes in all, flying in ten chevrons of five each. These airplanes were enormous, bigger than the B-17/52 itself. They were about to make landfall over Keahi Point. They were heading northeast, toward Hickam Field and the huge Navy base nearby. The place called Pearl Harbor.

The American bomber's pilots began evasive action as directed by the Main/AC. At the same moment, Hickam Field air control told the B-17/52 to abort its landing, do a slow turn, and go into a holding pattern at 35,000 feet.

The pilots complied, hastily restarting the eight turned-off engines and yanking back on the control column to get some height. The second pilot called back to the crew compartment and ordered the gunners back to their stations immediately. The gunnery officer unsealed the recently stowed ammunition feeds. Confused and more than a little anxious, the plane's gunners dashed to their triple-.50s.

Meanwhile the bomber climbed to the prescribed altitude of 35,000 feet and went into a long, looping circuit high above Hickam field.

From this height, they were about to witness a devastating action that would go down in history.

The approaching bomber force split in two just after making landfall.

Half the number turned slightly east, their noses pointed toward Hickam Field. The remainder continued northeast, toward Pearl Harbor.

There were thirty-four U.S. Navy ships at anchor in Pearl this Sunday morning. Eight destroyers, five frigates, four battle cruisers, plus numerous patrol vessels and rocket boats. Biggest of all though were the five megacarriers. They were the USS *Detroit*, USS *Boston*, USS *Cleveland*, USS *Las Vegas*, and USS *Chicago*.

Each carrier was nearly a mile long and half a mile wide. Their immense decks contained twelve separate launching and landing zones each, complete with twenty steam catapults, rocket-assist rails, and massive arrays of arresting cables. The ship's company for each megacarrier topped 25,000 men, not counting the pilots and air crews for the aircraft on board. Each ship weighed more than 200,000 tons. Their displacement was nearly sixty-five feet.

The *Cleveland* was the only megacarrier permanently assigned to Pearl Harbor. The other four had transitioned from the Atlantic six weeks before, after the European War had ended. Their crews were in need of hard-earned rest; the ships themselves in need of major refurbishment. Pearl Harbor—with its proximity to some of the world's most beautiful beaches and its vast ship repair yards—offered both.

Each megacarrier had its full complement of aircraft on board this dreadful morning. More than 250 Navy bombers—fourteen-engined B-332 Privateers mostly—were aboard each ship, along with five complete air wings of Navy fighters, a mix of F-J14Y Sea Furys and F-9F-265 SuperPanthers.

Many of these airplanes were up on the decks of the carriers; but like the ships themselves, they were in the midst of major reconditioning. None of them were ready for action.

There would be no air raid sirens. No alert Klaxons, no warning at all about what was to fall on Pearl Harbor. The attacking bomber force came out of the west, thirty airplanes now aligned into two long lines of fifteen each. They swept over the anchored giants, one massive bomb under each wing. These bombs, it would be later determined, were a variation of the DG-42, a German-produced super-blockbusting weapon containing nearly 200 tons of high explosive. Three such weapons had obliterated Paris about a year before, beginning the last brutal phase of the European War. Though the Germans eventually lost the war, the designs for their huge bomb, as well as some bombs themselves, had been floating on the black market for months. Now they were hanging from the wings of the attacking airplanes.

The first two planes peeled off and came in low and slow. Their target was the *Las Vegas*, docked in the first repair slip of the Pearl Harbor facility. The lead airplane let loose its pair of bombs and with a great scream of jet engines, turned wide and began climbing again. Both bombs hit the *Vegas* midships—but neither one exploded. They passed right through the carrier's hull, traveled the width of the ship, and exited the other side. More than 100 men were killed by the pair of tumbling bombs, but their warheads did not explode.

The second bomber came in and did a bombing run that duplicated the first. Two massive bombs fell from its wings as the bomber turned left and began to climb. The first bomb hit the water 100 feet from the side of the *Vegas* and sank. The second bomb went right through the deck however and detonated.

The explosion was so bright dozens of people within a mile of the blast were blinded permanently. It was so loud, it deafened hundreds more. The great ship was literally picked up out of the water and slammed back down again, creating a massive blow-back wave. A gigantic plume of fire, in the characteristic shape of a flower, rose high above the ship, petals of flame spilling out for miles around. Once this firestorm dissipated, there was nothing left. The ship had been utterly blown apart, along with all the dock works and the repair facility. All that was left was a massive crater, half of it now filling with tons of seawater.

In a flash, 28,761 people had been killed and three times as many wounded.

Just like that, the USS *Las Vegas* simply ceased to exist.

Meanwhile two more bombers were heading for the *Cleveland*. As with the previous attack, the first two bombs from the lead airplane were massive duds. One went through the deck of the megacarrier, the other simply bounced off. The second plane's weapons did not malfunction however. Both went through the *Cleveland*'s hull, traveled deep inside, and detonated.

The explosion two seconds later was twice as massive as the one that had destroyed the *Vegas*, twice as bright, twice as loud. The *Cleveland* was blown apart so completely, no piece of wreckage was more than a foot long. The ship did not sink per se, simply because there was not enough wreckage to constitute a sinking. Pieces of the *Cleveland* would later be found as far away as Molokai, some forty-five miles to the southeast. More than 25,000 sailors and airmen were blown apart with her.

The *Boston* and the *Detroit* shared similar fates. Both were hit by two massive DG-42 bombs each; both were blown to kingdom come along with their crews. Only the USS *Chicago* was spared. It was hit by no less than six DG-42s—all of which failed to explode. The bombs themselves caused severe damage plowing into the ship, killing more than 1000 people, wounding many more, and starting dozens of huge fires. But the *Chicago* did not sink, and its airplanes were not destroyed.

Even in this dark hour, it was apparent it had lived to fight again.

The second group of DG-42-carrying bombers attacked Hickam Field and the city of Honolulu beyond.

Eight DG-42s fell on Hickam—four exploded, but this

was enough to obliterate the place and the surrounding countryside for ten miles around.

Eight more DG-42s were dropped on Honolulu itself—five detonated, vaporizing just about everything within a twelve-mile radius and killing nearly half a million people in the process.

With the bombs dropped and their sneak attack complete, the enemy bombers linked up again and headed northwest, leaving behind death and destruction on an unprecedented scale. High above, the B-17/52 continued circling, its crew members in a collective state of shock at what they'd just seen. The pilots were too stunned to even make a Mayday radio call. They simply did not believe what their eyes were telling them.

The American bomber would later be forced to crash-land on a sandbar near Ewa Beach; it was a tribute to the pilots that only a handful of their crew were killed in emergency touchdown. When the survivors finally made it to where Hickam Field should have been, they found nothing but four massive craters, each one nearly a mile across and a quarter mile deep.

Later on, it would be determined that in all, the twin attacks on Pearl Harbor and Hickam Field/Honolulu had lasted less than ninety seconds.

All of the attacking bombers returned safely to the surfaced aircraft-carrying submarines which had remained in a holding pattern some 250 miles northwest of Oahu.

The bombers split into groups of ten each and with great precision began landing back on the monstrous subs. The pilots, aided by a bevy of automatic navigation and control systems, flew their huge bombers into the gaping mouths of the subs, recovering on massive arresting wires located inside.

Once each ship had recovered its squadron, the huge

front doors began belching steam again and then started to close. It took about five minutes for the ships to seal up. Then, along with their coterie of seven submersible cruisers, they began to dive. Inside, their commanders were radioing back to their supreme headquarters in Tokyo. The sneak attack on Pearl Harbor had been a huge success. Four of the five megacarriers had been destroyed, along with the airfield at Hickam and the city of Honolulu itself.

Best of all, surprise had been preserved for a second phase of the overall operation because the attack had gone off completely undetected. No one had seen the ships surface, launch their aircraft, or recover them, the ship commanders reported. No one left alive anyway.

But this was not entirely true.

For two miles away from where the huge Japanese ships were now slowly sinking into the waves, there was a small island called Buku-Buku. On this island, hidden in the thick underbrush, were the sixteen survivors of the USS *Neponset*, the TPB cut in half by one of the Japanese cruisers.

The American crew had reached the small island by sheer determination alone. Many were injured, two severely. These men had been carried to safety by Lt. Noonan, who lashed them together with pieces of rope and wire and then swam slowly and surely to the island, towing the two wounded men behind him.

It would be seven days before the crew was rescued from Buku-Buku.

But when they were, they would tell their superiors just how the Japanese had been able to carry out their vicious attack and then disappear, as if into thin air.

Two

The Panama Canal
Pacific Side

Rear Admiral Eric Wolf was relaxing.

It was the first time in a while—at least a few years—that he had actually kicked off his shoes, removed his thick sunglasses, leaned back in his chair, and done nothing.

The feeling was quite alien to him. He was a very stoic man, a highly professional naval officer and consummate loner. Things like kicking back and taking a nap in the middle of the day hardly came naturally to him.

But here he was, sitting in a chair on the veranda of a ten-story building, looking out on the vast expanse of the Panama Canal and the lush green jungle beyond. The air was thick and sweet, a breeze off the Pacific just two miles away made the scorching temperature bearable. Wolf fought to keep his eyes closed and let his mind wander. After all, he *was* supposed to be taking it easy.

There were some who said that Wolf was one of a handful of individuals who'd won the European War for the United States. He did not agree with them. There was only one person who could rightfully make that claim—and it was not him.

However, he *had* been instrumental in overseeing the American Forces' defense in the Atlantic during the bleak fall and winter months of 1997, back when it seemed certain that Germany was about to invade the United States and finally win the fifty-eight-year-old conflict known as World War II. Both in his command of a sub-hunting destroyer and later as overall commander of the Atlantic Wartime Command day-to-day operations, it had been Wolf's meager forces that had held the German Navy at bay until the war could be won, far away in Europe.

When the war was finally over and all the celebrations had died down, Wolf's superiors ordered him to take two months R and R. He refused. Admiring his pluck, his superiors did the next best thing. They assigned him to the combined Army-Navy station at Fort Davis, astride the Gatun Locks. This was a very lazy base where many veterans of the hardest-fought battles had been sent after the war. Little was expected of the men here. Routine drills, occasional musters. But that was about it.

In Wolf's section there were three companies of Sea Marines and Naval Infantry. In his first month here, he'd come to know just about all of them by name. Like him, most were lifers in the Navy. Just about every one of them was a hero of some sort too, or had endured wounds above and beyond the call of duty. Wolf had become close to many of them, because he'd been there himself. He knew how tough it had been in those very lean months. Now they were all getting their sunny reward.

Still, it was just not like Wolf to sit around all day, soaking up the sun and letting his mind and soul drift away. But he'd been dozing for almost a half hour now and even he had to admit it felt damn good. So good, he'd even loosened his tie and undone his shirt collar—minor violations of the uniform dress code that Wolf had never ever broken before.

But there was a first time for everything.

Sweet cooking smells drifted up from below. It was Sunday afternoon, and the base cooks usually laid out a massive meal at 1700 hours. This aroma was proof that the meal was not far away. Wolf was sleepily looking forward to the feast. After that, the base saloon would open. Tonight, Wolf told himself, waving a fly off his nose, he might even have a drink. Or two.

Things were that peaceful. . . .

It was strange then when it happened. Wolf thought he'd fallen asleep—a first on duty!—and that the noise that so suddenly pierced his ears was actually part of a dream he was having about riding a surfboard to the Moon.

It was a high-pitched squeal, both mechanical and unearthly. It seemed to go in Wolf's right ear and come out his left, at least that's what it felt like in his dream. But then the noise seemed to get caught in the back part of his skull, and there its high-pitched whine turned into a full-throated scream.

He opened his eyes a split second later. What he saw looked to be still part of his dream—a dream that had quickly turned into a nightmare.

The scream was coming from sixteen jet engines. They were attached to a huge jet that was directly overhead but coming down fast. It looked very odd at first, especially to Wolf's sleepy eyes, because the plane was coming straight down, very fast, its engines howling as they worked with gravity to hasten this dive.

A million thoughts ran through Wolf's head in those few seconds. This airplane was not of any kind he'd ever seen. It was painted green and was larger even than a Navy B-201, the largest airplane in the U.S. inventory.

It was coming down so steeply, Wolf knew its pilots would never be able to pull up in time. This meant it was going to crash, and in just a few seconds.

Wolf felt the panic instantly rise up inside him. It was just a question now of where the huge airplane was going to crash. Would it hit the building he was in? Or the nearby barracks where he knew 300 of his men were lounging, eating a late lunch, or attending afternoon Sunday services?

Or would it hit the canal locks themselves?

The canal stretched nearly five miles wide at this point and the Gatun Locks Station which held it in place was a massive structure of concrete and steel. Bombproof, Wolf had once heard someone claim. In the next split second, he wondered if that claim was about to be put to the test.

For instinctively he knew two things even as the screaming jet spiraled madly toward the ground. This plane was not crashing—at least not by accident. He could tell that it was under some kind of control, because it was moving slightly to the west and away from him now. He also knew it was heading not for his building or the barracks, thank God, but for the locks themselves.

It hit five seconds later, slamming into the main control station and blowing up immediately on impact. The force of the explosion threw Wolf back through the plate glass window of the veranda, across his living quarters, and against the outer door. Through some miracle he survived all this with nothing more than a broken finger, a dislocated nose, and two busted front teeth.

He got to his feet somehow and staggered back toward the porch. All the windows had been blown away and the wind was howling madly through his living quarters. He stumbled out onto the balcony and beheld yet another scene from a nightmare. The huge locks had been destroyed and now water was pouring in with a great gush from the Pacific. All the support buildings on both sides of the lock station were either on fire or simply gone. The remains of the crashed airplane were scattered for more than half a mile in every direction.

Wolf reached to his forehead and came away with a handful of blood. There was a cut above his eye, but this did not matter to him now. He was slipping into shock.

His brain simply couldn't accept what he'd just seen. He grabbed his radiophone and started dialing madly. His addled brain somehow believed he could call down to the barracks next door and tell his men . . . well, tell them what? To take cover? It was already too late for that.

No, he must have them assemble, and they would aid in the rescue effort. Yes, that's what they would do!

But now there was another strange sight. His men were already assembling. They were running out of the barracks and lining up on the parade ground right below his veranda. Wolf felt a surge of pride run through him. His men were already one step ahead of him.

Still bleeding heavily, Wolf ran back into his quarters, grabbed his combat pack, and started toward the door. But then he heard yet another sound, one that went right down to his toes and back up again.

Airplanes. More of them. Coming this way.

He turned on his heel and made his way back out to the porch. His guess was right. There were three airplanes approaching from the west. They were nowhere near as big as the airplane that had smashed into the lock station, but they were still substantial in size. The thought ran through his head that they were cargo aircraft of some kind. He could clearly see the national markings on their wings and fuselage. White field with a big red ball in the middle.

Japanese? Wolf asked himself. *Really?*

The three aircraft flashed by him a moment later. Each plane was trailing a plume of faint yellow smoke. Wolf watched in horror as this mist quickly settled all along the edge of the overflowing canal, coming down right on his men assembled below.

The stink hit his nose an instant later. Suddenly Wolf was doing two things at once. Two crazy things. He was simultaneously screaming down to his men to get their gas masks, while pulling out his own mask from his combat pack.

But it was way too late for his men. They began dropping

even before the mist settled on them. Many had been looking skyward at the three airplanes going over and thus the
fast-moving smoke entered their noses and mouths very
quickly. Many were dead before they even hit the ground.

Wolf barely had time to save himself. He got his mask on
just before he was about to inhale a large quantity of the
gas. Still the stink filled his nose and he knew what it was
right away: Cyanide-sulfate. Poison gas. Lethal chemical
weapons.

The Japanese were covering this part of the canal with
it like crop dusters dusting a huge cornfield.

Thousands would die before the air around Fort Davis
was breathable again.

The Japanese paratroopers began arriving about ten
minutes later.

Jumping from huge lift planes flying very high above
Fort Davis, they drifted to Earth by the thousands, gas
masks in place, weapons ready to be fired as soon as they
hit the ground.

But they needn't have worried. Their landing would go
off unopposed. Most of the 3,500 men assigned to Fort
Davis were already dead. Those who lay dying were bayo-
neted to death by the first-arriving Japanese troops. It was
all over in a matter of minutes. Nearly 7,500 Japanese paratroopers had landed around the damaged locks and more
were coming ashore in large LSTs, landing craft disgorged
by three huge troop-carrying submarines which had surfaced offshore.

A similar operation at the opposite end of the canal had
gone off just as flawlessly. The major lock system there had
been destroyed, too. But those in the middle of the vast
waterway had remained untouched—just the ends had
been sealed. No one could get in, no one could get out.

Which was just the way the invaders had planned it.

* * *

By sunset that terrible Sunday, the entire canal was in Japanese hands.

Watching all this from the top of a heavily shrouded hill, Wolf felt tears mixing with the blood on his cheeks.

How could they have been caught so unawares? Was it his fault? Out of the thousands of Americans killed, why was he the only one to survive?

He watched from the hill now as the sun dipped below the watery horizon and more Japanese troop-carrying subs surfaced offshore. It was like a bad nightmare starting all over again. The U.S. had just defeated Germany after a titanic fifty-eight-year struggle, only to be hit from the rear by the formerly docile Japan. . . .

It just didn't make sense to Wolf; it didn't *feel* right. As if some higher hand was actually pulling the strings. He looked up into the bloodred sunset and saw a huge fist, pulling on what looked to be millions of long, slender silver strings.

Yes, he thought, what happened here was something beyond human control . . .

Wolf shook his head and the strange vision went away. He realized he was probably becoming delirious, and after that, shock would set in, and then he'd be no help to anybody.

Taking one long last look at the incoming Japanese troopships and the enemy displacement around the canal locks, Wolf memorized the scene.

Then he plunged back into the jungle.

Three

The water off the coast of Lima, Peru, started bubbling just as the first rays of dawn hit the surface of the calm Pacific Ocean.

The Japanese aircraft-carrying submarine—they were known as *Kawishee-ma*—broke the surface with a huge gush exactly one mile off the beach at Callao. No sooner had the waves settled down around the huge ship, when a second Kawishee-ma came up just 1000 yards away. Then, a quarter mile from this monster, a third gigantic submarine surfaced. Then a fourth. And a fifth.

Warned in advance, Peruvian troops were rushing to the beach. In trucks, jeepsters, tanks, cars—they were using anything that would carry them. A full division of special operations troops, the famous Peruvian Quinto Division, quickly took up positions along the dunes and inlets lining the five-mile-long beach. They'd been practicing this deployment for weeks. Now they were finally doing it for real.

By 0700 hours, the horizon was dotted with twelve Kawishee-mas and sixteen other support ships. All of them were huge. All of them submersibles.

There were now thousands of citizens lining Callao Beach as well. Gaping at the vast armada which had so

suddenly materialized off their shore, all of them knew
that from this day forward, Peru would be changed forever.

At 0715 hours exactly, the fronts of three Kawishee-mas
opened and with a great roar, aircraft began flying out.
These were attack planes and fighters—dozens of them
were suddenly shooting from the mouths of the great
ships. Their numbers grew so quickly, they looked like
huge mechanical bees leaving a hive. A gasp went up along
the shoreline; soldiers and civilians alike were astonished
at the number of airplanes that were so suddenly in the
air. Soon reaching into the hundreds, the aircraft climbed
and began forming up into intricate holding patterns high
above the sea.

Meanwhile, the mouths of the other nine Kawishee-mas
had opened and begun disgorging combat troopships.
These huge landing craft were filled with soldiers, as many
as 500 per craft. Like the airplanes above, the landing craft
went into intricate holding patterns, interlocking ovals
running rings around the giant troop-carrying subs.

It took just twenty minutes for all the airplanes and all
the soldiers to be out of the ships and circling. Again, the
crowds onshore just gasped. The display of military power
and projection was simply frightening.

At 0745 hours, there was another great roar. As one, the
landing craft stopped circling the motherships and began
a mad dash for the shoreline. At precisely the same moment, the circling aircraft all turned as one and headed
toward the beach as well.

Now a great cry went up from those onshore. There
were at least 20,000 Japanese troops heading for the five-
mile-long beach. No less than 500 aircraft were speeding
inland too. There were barely 4,000 Peruvian troops on
hand to meet them, and no Peruvian planes in the air. If
a battle was to be fought here, it would be terribly one-
sided.

But that was not going to happen. . . .

For as the approaching Japanese landing craft reached a point one-half mile off shore, the Peruvian commanders shouted an order to their troops. Quickly the Quinto soldiers began running down to the beach itself. Their weapons up, they stood at rigid attention as the first Japanese landing craft reached the waterbreak. Another order was shouted and the long line of Peruvian troops went into present arms.

That's when it became obvious: This was not a combat force waiting for the Japanese—it was an *honor guard*. The citizens lining the sand dunes had not come out to meet their end. They were waving flags—of both Peru and Japan.

The first wave of Japanese landing craft hit the beach just a few moments later. Overcome with emotion, many citizens broke from the sand dunes, ran past the honor guard, and swamped the incoming troops with flowers, hugs, and kisses. Somewhere a band began playing. The gaggle of Japanese aircraft roared overhead, their formation now in the shape of a huge Japanese flag.

A silver landing craft disgorged from the first Kawisheema finally made it to the beach. From it stepped a small man in a big uniform, his baggy shirt weighed down by several pounds of war medals.

A hush came over the beach as the man reached the shore. He was Supreme Commander General Hilo Wakisaki, the highest-ranking officer in the Nipponese Imperial Forces and its main strategist. It was he who had masterminded the twin attacks on Pearl Harbor and the Panama Canal. It was he who had negotiated this massive unopposed landing.

A phalanx of Peruvian officers was on hand to greet him; they too were in awe of such a powerful man.

Wakisaki grunted at their barrage of salutes. Finally one Peruvian general stepped forward. General Ramos Lamos, the highest army officer in Peru, bowed deeply before

Wakisaki and, in very halting Japanese, said "The forces of Peru are at your disposal, sir."

For the first time, Wakisaki actually smiled.

In halting Spanish, he replied, "Thank you, and greetings to your people. This is a great day for us. A new day. A new beginning."

The crowd cheered lustily.

"The people of Japan wish to thank the people of South America for the opportunity to come here for the good of all. . . ."

More cheering.

"And at a future day," Wakisaki continued, "we will all march together. . . ."

Even more cheering. Now some tears of joy too.

"And together," Wakisaki concluded, "we will defeat the *norteamericanos*. . . ."

To this, the crowds along the shoreline—both military and civilian—gave out the loudest cheer of all.

The Japanese occupation of South America had begun.

Four

The place was known as Summer Point.

It was an ironic name because the weather here was usually anything but summerlike. Cold, wind, rain, and snow were more the norm. Located on the northeastern edge of West Falkland Island, it was a tiny settlement built onto a cliff which overlooked the frigid, frequently stormy South Atlantic.

This cliff was so windswept, its trees grew sideways. The scattering of buildings located near its edge also boasted a pronounced lean to the east. The rocks on the cliff and on the beach below were as smooth as pearls, so long had they been battered by the raging winds roaring off the ocean.

The largest building at Summer Point was the Government Hall. It was a combination post office, fire station, health clinic, and grocery store. Two members of the British Royal Administration Corps manned this facility. The three other main buildings at the Point were related to the area's only visible means of support: fishing. One structure held a deboning operation. Another was a fish-drying and packing building. Beside it, and right next to Government Hall, was a warehouse for storing nets, spare engines, and sundry equipment. A few small stone houses surrounded these structures. In all, less than a dozen people lived at Summer Point year-round.

One-half mile up the main road was a large rugged farm surrounded by a sheep pasture. This place was known as Skyfire Downs. The farmhouse itself was rather unspectacular. It too leaned to the east, even more so than the buildings in town. The farm was actually higher in elevation than Summer Point, so the winds were even more acute.

Only two stories of the farmhouse could actually be seen. Its roof had been patched over so many times, the shingles formed several nonsensical multicolored designs. Its windows were so loose they shuddered in their casements day and night. The front porch was so creaky, it actually whistled when the wind hit more than thirty-five knots.

It was what surrounded the farmhouse that made it unusual. A squadron of six SuperChieftain tanks lay hidden in the small woods nearby. These huge machines carried enormous firepower, including two 188-mm guns, four triple-.50 caliber machine guns, plus various rocket launchers including ones adapted with antiaircraft projectiles. Each vehicle held a twenty-two-man crew, members of the elite Special Tank Service of the British Royal Army. The tank crews rotated in twelve-hour shifts. Those not at work could usually be found sleeping in the basement of the Government Hall downtown.

The farmhouse was also surrounded by many strands of barbed wire, most of which were hidden in the overgrown brush ringing the place. Five TV cameras also stood sentinel on various parts of the property, perpetually sweeping the nearby fields, woods, and cliffs for intruders. Should one be found, the men in the tanks had permission to shoot on sight.

A separate mobile radar station, towed by another huge armored vehicle known as a Roamer, was located behind the farmhouse itself. It continually swept the surrounding skies for 150 miles around. At all times two men inside each SuperChieftain tank had their eyes glued to the readout from this radar. The main danger to the farmhouse at Skyfire Downs was an air attack. That's one of the things the rocket-firing SuperChieftain tanks were on hand to prevent.

The interior of the farmhouse was unremarkable, at least the top two levels. On the first floor was a kitchen, a dining room, a living room, and a den, all small, but cozy. The floors were wooden and covered in several layers of rugs, as was the west wall. The other three walls were covered with photographs and other framed pieces.

One photograph was a split-screen image depicting a small Cessna airplane. The left visual showed the plane intact; the right showed it battered and broken, as if it had plunged from a great height onto a hard surface. Next to this picture was a watercolor portrait of a young boy. Blond hair, bright face, quick eyes, a hint of the devil above the left eyebrow. If one looked closely at the painting, one would see several teardrops splattered in the lower right hand corner where the female artist had signed her name. The teardrops had dried along with the painting, and now were simply part of it.

Next to this painting was a diploma of sorts. It was handwritten, in pencil. Each letter had been printed very meticulously, though some of the Latin words had been misspelled. The diploma claimed to be for a doctorate in advanced aeronautical theory given by the Massachusetts Institute of Technology. No such school existed in this world, but the person who had written out the diploma knew that. In fact, *that* was precisely the joke.

He now sat at the kitchen table, sipping tea with his wife. She was the artist in the family. Only a checkerboard separated them, and the woman was laughing a bit. Her husband, despite his "diploma," was easy pickings at this game. She beat him at checkers regularly, yet he kept coming back for more. It was a lopsided contest that had lasted more than ten years. In all that time he'd prevailed only twice.

That was how long the couple had lived in the farmhouse; they'd always been surrounded by tanks and barbed wire. They'd always played checkers. They'd been together just about every minute of every day in all that time and still they could not get enough of each other. Such was love in a very isolated place.

It was a dark afternoon as usual, and the couple had whiled away the hours playing game after game, sipping tea, laughing and conversing in thick Boston accents. Despite all appearances, this was a typical day for them.

It was about 4 P.M. when the knock came at the door. The man got up and answered it to find one of the STS tankers standing on the porch. He was bearing a yellow piece of paper known as an EMS, for electronic message sheet. The soldier looked worried, but was trying hard not to show it. He passed the EMS to the man, had a few friendly words, then saluted and disappeared.

The man stood in the doorway, and as the wind howled, read the message. It was a direct burst from Washington D.C., transmitted to him from the British Foreign Office through a staggering array of scramble systems and decoding stations and finally to the lead SuperChieftain tank. The words the message contained made his jaw drop. He read it three times over, just to make sure he understood it correctly.

Somewhat staggered by the news, he walked back into the living room where his wife took one look at him and let out a little cry.

"My god, what is it?" she asked him.

He handed the EMS to her. She read it and felt the breath catch in her throat.

It was a simple message. It said that two huge American

bases in Hawaii had been attacked by Japanese military forces, as well as the city of Honolulu itself. Furthermore, Japanese forces had apparently attacked and taken over the Panama Canal.

But it was the third part of the message that the couple found most startling. It told of an "unopposed" landing of Japanese troops in Lima, Peru, as well as other coastal cities. This was relatively close to where they were.

"What does this mean?" the woman asked her husband, all thoughts of checkers gone now.

"It means the United States is at war again—I guess," he replied.

"But Japan?" the woman said. "I didn't even know they had an army. You always hear how peaceful they are."

"Well, something has apparently changed in that area," the man said, sitting back down and sipping his tea, trying his best to act normal.

But acting normal would prove difficult. This message had many ramifications for them here, none of them any good. What were the chances the Japanese would make it all the way down to the foot of South America, unopposed or not? he wondered silently. From there it would only be a 600-mile leap over to the Falklands. Would the Japanese eventually invade here as well?

He really didn't want to think about that.

He checked his watch—his only nervous habit. It was 0415 hours. He drained his tea then stood up again.

"I think I'll check the doughnuts," he said.

She laughed. He always made her laugh when he said that.

"OK, dear," she replied. "I'll start dinner. We'll eat early tonight."

He leaned over, kissed her lips, a little longer than usual, then gave her a hug.

Then he walked over to the kitchen closet, stepped inside, and closed the heavy wooden door tightly behind him.

He was now in a tiny, dimly lit hallway. Before him was another door. Beyond it was an elevator which went down sixteen levels, right into the heart of the small mountain on which the farmhouse sat.

The man stepped into the elevator, pushed the button for the bottom level, then endured the painfully slow descent. Thoughts of the secret message he'd just received were still burning in his mind. How far away *was* Lima, Peru, from here anyway? He promised himself he'd check a map the first chance he got.

The elevator finally arrived at the sixteenth level—the man was now 250 feet below the basement of the farmhouse. The door opened and he saw two familiar faces staring back at him. They were British STS commandos, part of the permanent guard for the well-hidden underground facility.

They gave him a friendly salute, asked about the weather and his wife—it was a daily conversation between them. The man replied in a friendly manner but then hurried down the long metal-encased corridor the men were guarding. At the end was another thick, reinforced door. The man reached it quickly, and unclasped the intricate lock. The door opened with a squish of hydraulics and a whoosh of air. A laboratory lay beyond. It was of ample size and contained many pieces of exotic scientific equipment. This had been the man's workplace for the past ten years.

There were eighteen men inside the Level 16 lab at the moment. Most stopped working when the man came in, and either nodded or voiced a greeting. He politely waved them back to their work. The man then walked the length of the lab, eventually finding the lead scientist on duty.

The man handed him the secret message he'd just received. The scientist read it, his eyebrows arched, his forehead wrinkled in worry.

"The Japanese Army in South America?" he murmured. "What does this mean for us?"

The man just shrugged.

"Maybe nothing," he replied optimistically.

The man looked around him. This laboratory probably contained more secrets than any other place in the world. Weapons, materials processing, communications. Power generation. By its very isolation, below this hill on the windbeaten spit of land known as West Falkland, it was a highly secure facility.

Or it had been. Now, with these new events in South America, that security seemed a little less certain.

The man looked into the glass-enclosed room nearby and saw four men leaning over a table on which a bomb had been placed. The black-painted bomb was thin and about thirty inches long. In most respects, it looked like a typical aerial-delivery weapon. But the man, the scientist, and everyone else down here knew the bomb was anything but typical.

"How's our progress today?" the man asked the scientist, nodding toward the glass enclosure.

"On the Z-project you mean?" the scientist asked. "Slow but steady."

"That's always good to hear," the man replied.

There was a short silence between them, each one still wondering exactly what the secret message might portend for them. Finally, the scientist asked the man a question.

"Do you want to do a security check in Room One?"

The man nodded. "Yes—even though it's a little early, I do."

They walked to a huge iron door located at the far end of the lab, behind which was Room One. Within it lay the greatest secret of them all.

The scientist went through the complex series of security systems and finally managed to open the door. The man stepped inside and the scientist closed the door behind him. Once again he was in a small, dark room with only a faint red light for illumination. At the far end of this small chamber was yet another door. Nearby was a control panel containing a myriad of blinking lights. The man scanned each one of them and was heartened to see that all was normal, all was safe. A smile creased his sixty-year-old face. Thank goodness for that, he thought.

He walked over to the door itself, put his ear to it, and smiled again.

He could hear the wind rushing on the other side.

Five

The waves no longer broke along the shore of Callao Beach.

There were no more seabirds. No more fish or crabs, sea otters or seals. The whales no longer visited the inlets and bays dotting the mid-Peruvian coastline. The water itself was no longer blue.

The coastline was now blocked off by a miles-long artificial harbor. Made of aluminum planking, huge rubber inner tubes, and miles of rope and steel cables, the harbor, complete with immense off-loading machinery, fueling berths, and repair facilities, had been fouling the waters off Callao since the first Japanese soldier had come ashore back in December. So much oil and grease and waste water had been dumped into the faux harbor, the sand was now black as coal, the water as thick as the worst of Prudhoe Bay.

The city of Lima, just a mile away, had changed as well. Gone were the slums, the narrow streets, the neighborhoods teeming with the poor. Now the city was a magnificent example of new urban sprawl. High-rises, business towers, trading halls filled the municipal landscape. Downtown Lima was not a place where people lived anymore—at least not the native Peruvians. The former citizens had been driven back into the jungle long ago. The new city-dwellers were all Japanese, and the design of their architecture was definitely Pacific Rim. Just about all the new structures—made almost entirely of pearl-white cement—had a pagodaish look to them. In many places it was as if an entire section of Tokyo, Osaka, or Yokohama had been picked up, carried across the vast Pacific, and plunked down into the South American jungle. Nearly a quarter of a million Japanese citizens had emigrated to the city and the outlying areas.

Even the name of Lima had changed. It was now called *Sukiwishi-mi.* Roughly translated: *It belongs to us.*

This term could have been applied to most of the South American continent as well. The Japanese invasion—peaceful, but not benign—had been a monstrous success. Brief but brutal battles with Paraguay and Colombia had quickly brought those countries into line. Chile, Argentina, and Ecuador immediately accepted provisional status. Brazil agreed to a nonaggression pact with Tokyo, but relations were still very shaky. Bolivia was in a constant state of anarchy, as was Venezuela. But for the most part, the Japanese digestion of America's southern hemisphere was on schedule.

The Japanese were still in firm control of the Panama Canal as well. Repairs were in full swing and expected to be completed within a month. With the canal reopened, Japanese access to the Caribbean and the Atlantic would be solidified. After that, there were secret plans among Japan, Argentina, and Peru for a three-pronged invasion of Brazil.

If successful, then the entire continent would truly become a colony of Japan.

* * *

This particular day was a special one for the new inhabitants of *Sukiwishi-mi*, Peru.

A celebration was being planned in honor of the one millionth Japanese soldier to come ashore. On hand for this event was Supreme Commander General Wakisaki, the godfather of the Japanese occupation of South America. Wakisaki's appearance in downtown *Sukiwishi-mi* the day before had set off waves of hysteria, so revered was the high general. The small, toadlike man who seemed to have a slight slump to his left shoulder due to the pounds of medals he constantly wore, was close to deity status among the new South Americans these days. In their eyes, and in the eyes of the million troops under his command, Wakisaki could do no wrong. He was considered infallible.

He had a specially built aircraft, a huge ten-engine SuperKate transport which had been designed to look like an airborne palace. Wakisaki had taken an aerial tour of the new South America the previous day and what he saw would have made Buddha cry. Where once stood thick rain forests, now cities were being built. Oil rigs by the thousands—from the Bolivian plain to the Chilean lowlands—grew higher than the trees. Seven of the great South American rivers had been dammed extensively and now the western portion of the continent positively crackled with electricity. On thousands of acres of newly cleared land, tens of millions of cattle now grazed.

The sight-seeing flight had brought a slight grin to Wakisaki's face—the only hint of the delight hiding within the stone of a man. Even the most famous samurai warriors had not accomplished what he had. He was certain to go down in history as the most successful soldier ever to come out of Japan, or anywhere else.

So the general was in a good mood when the ceremony on Callao Beach began. The millionth soldier had been carefully selected from a new division of engineering troops that had arrived off the Peruvian coast two nights before. The man bearing the magic number had to be well-groomed, well-indoctrinated, and of the correct political stature, and many hours had gone into this. A reviewing stand had been erected near the beach, a huge ornate affair located up on the highest dune, with the new city of Lima as a background. Every Japanese officer of any import was on hand for this ceremony, nearly 300 in all.

An honor guard of no less than 10,000 troops had also been mustered. Six thousand of them were Japanese; the remaining troops were made up of native regional allies, Argentines, Chileans, Bolivians, and of course Peruvians.

It was a bright sunny morning. The waters off Callao were sparkling like coal. The temperatures had already started to climb. At precisely 0900 hours, the ceremony began. The special boat carrying the special soldier crept toward shore. General Wakisaki grinned slightly as he got caught up in the moment. Never had a deployment of troops gone off as successfully as this, he thought for the millionth time. The boat arrived. The special soldier stepped off. Trumpets blared. Dozens of twenty-one-gun salutes were fired. A cheer went up from all those assembled.

No wonder then that no one heard the dull roar of aircraft coming from the north.

The first plane to come out of the sky was an enormous B-17/52.

It was bright silver, with long, swept-back wings bearing eight engines per side. Its thick body carried no less than four separate bomb bays. As many as forty triple-.50 machine guns poked out of gun stations up and down the aircraft's fuselage. The roar from its engines was simply deafening.

It came in low and slow, and flames could be seen shooting from its engines as it passed over the Tower of the New Sun, the combined temple, government center, and military officers' club located in the middle of the city. The airplane was so low and moving so slowly it looked like a gigantic prehistoric bird; this is why the native Peruvians, who had seen this thing before, called it *ala del muerte*, roughly translated, "The Death Wing."

The plane roared over the Temple of the Sun and opened all four of its bomb bays. In seconds, long streams of black sticks began falling from the great plane's belly. The black sticks were incendiary bombs—explosives designed to start fires. Much of the new Lima was built of flammable materials: wood, hemp, plastic, rubber. Even some of the properties inside the pearl-white cement were flammable.

The huge plane began dropping 40,000 pounds of fire-bombs along a one-mile strip in the center of the city. In seconds the main avenue was awash in a horrible yellow glow. Fire was suddenly everywhere. Stores, cars, trees, people burst into flame. The mechanical screams overhead were as terrifying as the human ones below. The plane unloaded its final bay of ordnance, then with a great explosion of energy and power from its sixteen engines, sped up and roared away.

But no sooner had it departed when two more B-17/52s arrived above the city, roaring over the mountains to the north and dropping down just as low as the first plane. They headed for the eastern edge of the sprawling metropolis, opening their massive bomb bays and letting go thousands of more powerful incendiary devices.

The target of these bombs was a huge barracks located on the outskirts of New Lima. Guided by the flame caused by bombs dropped by the first aircraft, this pair of attackers laid a carpet of yellow fire and smoke across the long line of military housing units, incinerating soldiers and civilians alike.

As soon as they departed, two more huge bombers appeared and began dropping their fiery loads on the city's central marketplace. More death. More screams. More unspeakable horror. Behind them came two more—their target was the city's waterworks. Behind them, two more, aiming for the city's power station. Without water and electricity, the fires raging throughout the city could not be put out.

All this was happening so fast, the people on the beach stood aghast, not quite knowing what they should do. It was High General Wakisaki who acted first. As the fifth pair of bombers swooped in low and unloaded their fire weapons, Wakisaki pulled out his pistol, put it against the head of his chief Air Defense officer, and pulled the trigger. The man immediately collapsed to the platform floor, blood spurting out of his forehead. His second-in-command, the assistant air defense officer, got Wakisaki's message right away. He grabbed a radiophone and made a very urgent call to the air base located in the Lima suburb of Costa Camu.

But the people at the air base, where five squadrons of Mitsubishi SuperZero jet fighters were stationed, needed no warning about what was happening. Their radar sets had picked up the incoming bomber force as soon as the first airplane came over the mountain. This was way too late to prevent the bombs from falling on New Lima, but still enough time to scramble aircraft together, to attempt to shoot down the attackers. The problem was, the air base itself was being attacked. Not by the gigantic B-17/52s, but by a single, much smaller aircraft.

The officer on the other end of the radiophone was in such a state he could barely speak—not a good situation for the newly appointed air defense officer. With panic breaking out among those on hand for the One Millionth Soldier ceremony, the air defense man wanted action quick from his newly acquired charges at the air base. But it seemed as if a single enemy airplane was keeping them all pinned down.

"How can this be?" the air defense chief demanded of the air base commandant.

"This pilot, he is crazy," the air base commander was saying. "He is everywhere at once. We thought at first there were four or five of them. But it is only one!"

The air defense officer was getting very angry—and nervous. Wakisaki was not two feet away from him, broiling him with his laser eyes, even as the city of New Lima began to burn just a mile away. The next bullet from Wakisaki's gun would surely wind up in the new air defense minister's head if he didn't get action very very quickly.

"You have antiaircraft rockets!" the air defense man was screaming into the radiophone. "And antiaircraft guns. And more than fifty airplanes. Are you saying that one airplane—a fighter—is preventing you from taking any measures?"

The air defense man hit the receive button for his answer—but there was no reply.

Startled, he sent the message again, his voice rising a full octave and five meters in volume for the benefit of Wakisaki, who was again fingering his pistol.

But again, there was no reply from the air base commander. A third try produced the same result.

The line from the air base was dead.

Wakisaki shot the new air defense man anyway and then turned to his ministers of ground troops and security. Unfortunately, both men were diving for cover under the review stand at that moment, an action Wakisaki first interpreted as cowardice but was actually done out of self-preservation. For now there was a new growl in the air. Wakisaki finally looked up and saw two more airplanes coming over the mountain.

They were big. They were silver. And they were heading right for the ceremony on Callao Beach.

Wakisaki himself just barely made it under the platform as the two huge airplanes roared overhead. The troops on the beach scattered at first sight of them too—the civilians had already fled the area in panic. Some soldiers simply hit the ground where they stood, covered their heads, and hoped for the best. Others darted into patches of jungle nearby. Some even jumped into the filthy water of the artificial Callao Bay. Everyone expected to have a heavy rain of firebombs come down on them at any moment.

But that did not happen. Dropping firebombs on human targets was usually a waste of weaponry. Besides, these airplanes—they were B-24/36s, mammoth aircraft which embodied the look of a B-24 Liberator and a B-36 Peacemaker—were not bombers per se. Rather their fuselages were thick with gun blisters up and down the length of them, and dozens of triple-.50 machine guns had been installed in these stations. They were then a rarity in this world. They were flying gunships.

Now, as the two planes roared over, they both went into a long, slow turn above the beach, one plane placing its nose on the other's tail, almost forming one, nightmarishly huge gun platform.

Their first targets were the gaggle of warships anchored and vulnerable about one mile offshore. The airplanes went into a very tight circle not 500 feet above one of the huge, submersible troop ships. Suddenly, all at once, every gun on the right side of both airplanes opened fire. It looked like a sheet of flame pouring out of both giant airplanes. In seconds, the huge sub was shrouded in a cloud of fire and smoke as the planes went round and round like a devilish aerial merry-go-round.

When they finally backed off sixty seconds later, the big sub was burning in hundreds of places, stem to stern. So sudden was the attack, and so awesome in its sheer power, not a shot was fired in return from any of the many guns aboard the hapless warship. Soon the entire upper deck of the sub was consumed in flames.

The pair of gunships moved on to their next victim: a battle cruiser which served as Wakisaki's floating command station while he was in South America. The gun crews on this vessel did send up some defensive fire. But their aim was so shaky, due to simple fright no doubt, that they missed both planes by a wide margin.

As with the troop-carrying sub, the gunships rained a storm of fire and lead down on the cruiser, and soon it was burning ferociously too. The planes moved on to the next target—another big sub, this one an aircraft carrier. They mimicked their earlier attacks, tearing up the top deck of the sub while successfully wending their way through weak streams of AA fire. This ship caught fire very quickly, its pathetic defenses soon disappearing altogether.

By now, the rest of the anchored fleet had finally sprung into action. There were fourteen other ships in harbor at the moment. None of them dared to return fire or flee to the open ocean. Instead, they simply dived—whether their crews were on deck or not. They began going down quickly, creating ripples of small tidal waves as their oxygen displacement systems expelled great amounts of air while sucking in seawater for ballast. The ships disappeared so quickly, the pair of giant gunships were able to set only one more on fire before they had no more targets to shoot at.

General Wakisaki watched all this from his hiding place beneath the ceremony platform, shaking with fright along with 300 or so of his best officers. The city of New Lima was burning behind him; the prize of his navy was burning in front. His troops were scattered and hiding their heads in the sand like ostriches. Wakisaki was quite nearly in tears. How could his world have turned so upside down so quickly?

Perhaps I didn't pray hard enough this morning, he thought.

* * *

The bombing of New Lima and the fleet offshore had come so suddenly, the city's air raid sirens had not even sounded.

But the attack was not unexpected. Rumors that a mysterious air force had been seen operating way up in the mountains had been circulating in New Lima for weeks—though they never reached General Wakisaki's ears.

Just who this mysterious air force was—and who was flying the Deathwings—was simply not known.

But the fortunes of the Japanese seemed to suddenly reverse when the tenth pair of bombers appeared over the city. Nearly one-third of downtown was aflame by now and these two airplanes seemed bent on adding to the conflagration. But they were both flying so low and so slow, it seemed impossible for them to stay in the air while they dumped thousands of pounds of firebombs down on the city below.

And as it turned out, one of the bombers was indeed flying too low.

It had just discharged all of its weapons when its pilots began a sharp pull out to the right. But the big plane was now over the center of the new city and trying to negotiate its way through a virtual forest of skyscrapers. Suddenly its left wing clipped one spire. The force of the collision cut a quarter of the wing off, taking two engines with it. The impact caused the pilot to yank the big airplane to the right, where it hit another tall building, taking off about one-quarter of its right wing. The plane was in grave trouble now. It roared over the southern part of the city emitting huge quantities of smoke and flames. Those on the beach hiding beneath the platform saw this, and suddenly a huge roar gurgled out of them. Their new city was burning, five ships in the harbor were in the process of sinking, and yet the sight of one airplane in trouble gave them occasion to cheer.

Now the officers were crawling out from their hiding places and watching the big plane struggle to stay airborne. Its pilots did a good job of keeping the huge bomber trim and steady as it passed over the city and headed toward the thickest part of the jungle, to the south.

But it was obvious to all those watching that the airplane was too severely damaged to stay aloft much longer. Indeed, about a minute after the twin collisions, and thirty seconds after it passed out of sight, it dipped down and crashed into a thick canopy of trees about ten miles south of the city limits. A cloud of smoke—but not too much flame—was seen rising over the forest. Another cheer went up from the Japanese officers on the beach.

Even General Wakisaki was letting out a guttural cheer. Then he turned to the man next to him, who just happened to be the officer in charge of security for the city, and shouted an order directly into his ear.

"Go, hurry to the crash site," Wakisaki told the man. "And bring back any survivors to me!"

As it turned out, there was a large contingent of Japanese troops already near the crash site.

They were a combat engineering group located in another suburb of New Lima called Cucucha. This put them only four miles from where the huge bomber went down. The unit, 300 men strong, was equipped with heavy-duty earth-moving supertanks, mobile weapons that had huge shovels and blades on their front ends and towed assemblies for moving dirt on their backs. They would be ideal for making their way through the dense undergrowth and get to the crash site.

The phones started ringing at the engineering unit's HQ not a minute after the big plane went down. The en-

gineers needn't have been told there'd been a crash. The
burning airplane had gone right over their base camp and
shaken it from top to bottom before finally plowing in.

But now the phones were ringing and the messages were
coming directly from High General Wakisaki himself. The
engineering unit was being told to get themselves to the
crash site immediately. They were to bring back any survivors to Wakisaki personally, plus any pieces of wreckage
which would help identify where the mysterious bomber
had come from in the first place.

Knowing that the price of failure was death, the engineering unit's commander managed to muster 200 of his
troops in a matter of minutes. Within a quarter hour of
getting the first call, twenty tanks of the unit were moving
up the road toward the crash site, 200 heavily armed soldiers hanging from them.

After just ten minutes, this column was able to get within
one mile of the crashed bomber, which was in a small ra-
vine on the edge of the Simpacoo Hills. They could clearly
see the smoke from the roadway. The column's commanders laid out their maps and saw what was ahead of them.
About 150 feet of thick jungle was right off the roadway.
Then there was a bare field which ran up to a wide but
shallow river. Then more jungle, then the crash site itself.

The task facing the engineers wasn't so daunting then.
They would plow through the first strip of jungle, quickly
reach the field, and make short work of crossing the river.
After that, only several hundred more feet of jungle
needed to be covered before reaching the aircraft itself.
Confident in the ability of their men and their machines,
the commanders radioed back to High General Wakisaki's headquarters and reported they would be at the
crash site within twenty minutes.

Sending that overly optimistic report was their first mistake.

The first pair of tanks crashed into the thick undergrowth, their bulldozer blades cutting and slashing trees, rocks and thick vines alike. Behind them, another pair of tanks flattened the destroyed fauna into a makeshift roadway. Behind *them*, the majority of the column followed, two tanks remaining on the road in reserve.

The lead tanks reached the open field in just five minutes. From here they could see the shallow river and the thicker forest beyond. A large column of smoke was rising right above the next line of trees. The first tanks went into high speed, the troops draped all over their exteriors, holding on for dear life.

It was these troops who first heard the strange noise coming from high above them.

It was not a typical jet-engine whine. This sound was deeper, almost echoing. A definite *chop-chop-chop!* Times eight.

They saw it a few moments later, coming out of the north. It looked like a prehistoric monster. It was almost as big as the bombers which had just set many parts of New Lima ablaze. But it had no wings. Instead, it had many spinning rotors—eight of them. And it was gangly. It was all wires and wheels and engines and noise. There was a huge bubble of glass on its front which gave it an insect look. Yet its eight legs and rotors made it more resemble a flying octopus, which was close to its official name: Octocopter. It was loud, and scary, and it was coming down right on top of them.

The tank drivers saw it and out of sheer panic stomped on their brakes and brought their huge vehicles to a screeching halt. This served to throw many of the hitching soldiers to the ground, their weapons and helmets flying. The strange air beast descended on the field and went into a hover. Several dozen portholes opened all over the aircraft's convoluted body, and just as many gun muzzles appeared. The Japanese soldiers looked up, and many of them saw their last sight: thick smoke and flame coming from those muzzles.

The noise from the guns was almost loud enough to drown out the roar of the aircraft's eight rotors. The first two tanks were destroyed in a matter of seconds, so intense was the Octo's high-caliber barrage. The second pair of tanks, and all those behind them, had just arrived in the open field—a big mistake, as they soon realized.

Some of their soldiers, getting over the shock of the bizarre aircraft's sudden appearance, began firing back. But this was also a foolish gesture. It simply turned the attention of the people in the weird aircraft toward them and now these soldiers were being perforated just like their colleagues in the lead two tanks.

By this time the rest of the Japanese column had gone into hard reverse and backed up into the jungle, hoping the dense undergrowth would offer them some protection from the weird flying death machine. And it did. The jungle was so thick, and the engineering tanks so well camouflaged, that they blended right in, almost disappearing from view.

The strange machine stayed hovering, though—as if it was waiting for something.

About thirty seconds later, another scream came from the sky. This was from a very strange plane—and compared to the Octocopter, a small one. It had a long slender fuselage that appeared to have been cut off right behind the cockpit. It had an oddly crooked pair of swept-back wings. It had a very strange set of tails and a very powerful engine.

It was also loaded with bombs. The wings and fuselage were so laden with huge, teardrop-shaped weapons, the weird little plane's wings were actually drooping a bit.

This new airplane seemed to have come from nowhere as well. It went right over the pair of burning tanks and dropped two teardrop-shaped bombs into the thick jungle beyond. Instantly there were two huge explosions, followed by two balls of orange fire and smoke. The swift little fighter had to veer off dramatically in order not to get caught in these fiery mushrooms. It did so, but just barely.

The fighter climbed now, flipped over, and came back down at twice its escape speed. It roared over the jungle again, letting loose two more firebombs. Its engine screaming, the airplane twisted away again as another pair of gigantic fireballs erupted from the thick forest. Above the roar of this jet, the racket of the eight rotors of the Octocopter, and the four fiery explosions, a new sound could be heard: the screams of the Japanese soldiers being incinerated by the firebombs.

The little fighter twisted over and was coming back again. Meanwhile the Octocopter had moved off and was now hovering above the spot where the huge bomber had crashed. Rope ladders were cascading from the bottom of the weird aircraft, and soldiers were being lowered on them. Within seconds, these ladders were being raised again, each one bearing a rescue soldier and a survivor from the crash.

The fighter kept sweeping over the jungle, plastering firebombs on the hapless tanks leading all the way back to the road itself. Many of the Japanese soldiers that had somehow escaped the conflagration had scattered into the thick jungle, getting tangled up in the many vines and roots that twisted in a nightmarish patchwork along the jungle floor. The heat was so intense by this time that the leaves were actually melting off the trees, in some cases dripping a burning, rubberlike substance onto the panicking soldiers.

All thoughts of reaching the wrecked bomber were long gone now.

Those few soldiers who did survive saw the Octocopter raise up a total of thirty-two people from the crash site, along with six bodies. The little fighter, its wings expended of firebombs, was still strafing the jungle where the column of burning tanks now lay. Only after the Octocopter began pulling away from the crash site did the little plane go into a steep climb and take up a position above and to the rear of the strange eight-rotor craft.

Together they moved off to the north, leaving behind barely twelve survivors of the column of 200 men and twenty tanks.

In all, the one-sided battle had lasted just ten minutes.

In the basement of the main military government building in New Lima was a small hospital used for officers of the Nipponese Occupying Armed Forces.

There was only one patient being treated here at the moment, though; while nearly two dozen army and navy officers lay dying in the waiting room, no less than seventeen surgeons were praying over High General Wakisaki.

The general had been hurt in the attack on Callao Beach. Not by enemy action per se—the reviewing stand under which he and many others fled at first sight of the bombers had collapsed, giving the general a slight cut on his nose.

The wound required not even half a dozen stitches, but still the top doctors in New Lima were working on closing the cut, and trying their best to reassure the general that no scar would remain, or if one did, it would look rather "manly."

But Wakisaki wasn't really listening to them at the moment. Laid out on the operating table, lights and masked faces staring down at him, he was simply too busy crying.

The tears had been flowing for almost an hour now. They'd started soon after the mysterious bombers had left New Lima ablaze, and had continued unabated through the general's evacuation to the basement hospital.

The very unmanly waterworks had little to do with the general's nose wound, though it did sting anytime his salty tears found their way into the cut. No, the majority of tears were the result of shame—*his* shame—and from his hurt feelings.

He just couldn't understand what had happened. Why would anyone want to bomb New Lima? Or his troops? Or his ships offshore? What was the point of it?

For his army and navy to be attacked was an affront to his own personal honor, and no blade could go deeper into Wakisaki than a disgrace of his good name. That's why what happened to the general this day became a scar that would last much longer than the cut on his nose. This day, he knew, would live on inside him and haunt him right to the core.

Such a compulsive obsession was a result of his psychological makeup. Unbeknownst to anyone, Wakisaki actually regarded his occupation of South America not so much as a conquest, but as a thing of beauty. Like a pearl vase or a sculpture, he'd shaped it, he'd executed it, he'd dreamed of its every detail. And for the first six months, this thing of beauty had grown, had been nurtured by him. Had taken on an extra beauty. In his hands, he'd crafted no less than a new kind of culture. He had projected the Asian way of life to another continent, half a world away. They might as well have been on another planet!

And now, this thing had been ruined, had been fouled. *Why?*

This was why there were tears rolling down his cheeks and sometimes getting into his nose wound. His perfect record had been besmirched. His pure white soul was now stained. His heart was now ringed with filth.

But the real question ran even deeper than why. The real question was who. *Who* could have done this?

And just as these words were on his lips, there was a

knock at the treatment room door. A very shaky officer in a very sweaty uniform stepped in. He was not a military officer, rather he was the police chief for New Lima, a sacrificial lamb if there ever was one. In his trembling right hand was the report on the action from the bomber crash site; in his left hand, a small pistol with one bullet in it.

The police chief handed the report to the high general, who was eating him alive with his teary eyes. Then, calmly, the police chief raised the pistol to his own head and pulled the trigger. There was a crack, a splash of cranial matter hit the far wall, and the man slumped to the floor, bleeding profusely. The seventeen doctors ignored him, of course. They were too busy tending to the last stitch on Wakisaki's wounded nose.

The report was stark in its details. Twenty tanks and 189 men had been lost to enemy action in attempting to reach the bomber crash site. All survivors of the bomber had been rescued; even the bodies of those killed in the crash had been carried away. The wreckage had by now burned away to nothing, destroyed by time-delayed magnesium bombs left behind by the mysterious rescuers.

Wakisaki felt his spirits plummet even further. What a difference a day makes! Now there was no wreckage to be recovered, no survivors to torture. No way to find out where they all came from.

He let out another gush of tears, and thought he saw a few of the doctors laugh at this girlish display. But two words in the report were beginning to burn their way into Wakisaki's brain. *Enemy action.*

Yes, Wakisaki realized, forcing back the tears. He suddenly had an enemy on his hands. But who were they? Certainly not the Colombians, or the Brazilians. Neither of those troublesome states would dare attack New Lima. Nor did they have anywhere near the military technology Wakisaki and thousands of others had seen during the bombing raid. Huge bombers, huge gunships, small swift fighters, strange hovering aircraft bristling with guns. Wakisaki knew aircraft, and he knew that no one on this continent flew the kind of airplanes he'd just seen.

Then where did they come from? Even the most obvious choice—the *norteamericanos*—made no sense. Wakisaki had seen the heavy bomb loads these aircraft had been carrying. There was no way they had flown all the way down from North America carrying such heavy loads for this sneak attack. And from the reports of the survivor-rescue, the strange eight-rotor flying contraption certainly could never have made such a long trip.

Yet Wakisaki was sure there were no American megacarriers on either coast of South America. In fact, in the six months since the Japanese takeover of South America, there had not been one peep from the North Americans. Not one. They were exhausted, the conventional wisdom went, from their very draining, very close-run victory over Germany after fifty-eight years of war. It was a keystone of Wakisaki's plan that North America would not lift a finger when Japan invaded South America, or took over the Panama Canal. The attack on Pearl Harbor had taken care of the aircraft carrier fleet, they had nothing left to fight with, even if their citizenry wanted to.

Yet logic dictated these attackers had to be North Americans. So then, where was their base? How could the *norteamericanos* hide an entire air base anywhere on a continent that was so firmly in the grip of Japanese hands?

Wakisaki didn't know.

But as the tears continued to roll down his face, he made a vow right then and there to find out.

Six

Two days later

The all-black airplane set down at the New Lima airport just after sunset.

It was a troop transport, an eight-engine miniknockoff of the infamous *Spruce Goose*. It came in easily and took the full three miles of runway to slow down.

The airport itself was cordoned off to all but the highest level of security troops. The damage from the freak air attack two days before—one small airplane had knocked the base out of action at the height of the bombing raid—had been repaired by now, or simply covered over. The entire security detail and air traffic control staff for the air base had paid the price for the single plane attack. All of them had been quietly executed earlier that day.

The huge plane rolled over to an isolated hangar and finally came to a stop. Its rear clamshell doors opened and slowly but surely a long ramp extended from its rear. No sooner was this platform down than two long lines of dark figures began disembarking.

Black uniforms. Black helmets. Black face masks, gloves, and boots. Even their weapons were black. No surprise then that they were known as *Brigata de la Noche,* literally, the Night Brigade.

They were Argentine commandos, special-ops troops

who had terrorized the Argentine population and those in neighboring countries for years before the Japanese ever came ashore. Each man was more than six feet three inches tall and many were a half a foot taller than that. They lived on raw meat—and literally drank cow's blood at least once a day. The Night Brigade, 1,200 men strong, were experts at both jungle warfare and urban combat. They could kill a man with a twig; crush his skull with a pebble. They had made torture an art form. They sometimes ate babies.

The Japanese had been very concerned about dealing with the Night Brigade, that's why the unit had been paid 2 million dollars in gold before the Japanese invasion even took place. Now they were beholden to the Nipponese High Command and especially to General Wakisaki. He'd called on them several times since the occupation to take care of particularly nasty holdouts in Colombia and the forests of Brazil. On all occasions, the Night Brigade resolved the problem quickly, if brutally.

Wakisaki was expecting no less from them this time.

The bombing raid on New Lima was now firmly implanted in the combined psyche of the Japanese occupation forces. The first six months of their invasion had gone so smoothly, the troops had begun to think of themselves as agents of destiny and of Wakisaki as being divine. Now the jewel city of the New Japan lay half in ruins. The other half was soaked in water and muddy ash. A foot thick in some places, it was the lasting result of fighting more than a thousand fires.

Wakisaki knew that whoever was responsible for the fire-bombing raid had to be found and had to be punished in a very public manner. That's why he'd called on the Night Brigade. Being home troops, they would be able to handle any terrain on the continent to get at the perpetrators. This was something the imperial Japanese troops could not do as well. The Night Brigade also knew how to deal with native populations, something else the occupation troops weren't too good at.

This is what Wakisaki knew had to be done. The mysterious bombers had to have come from within a 150-mile radius of New Lima—this figure from analysis of several insta-films that had been made during the raid. The huge bombers—definitely of North American design—had been so weighted down with bombs, Wakisaki's aeronautics people told him the planes couldn't have been carrying very much fuel, and thus a 300-mile round-trip would have been their limit. There were only three directions from which the bombers could have come: north, east, and south—west was simply the ocean, and the planes definitely did not come from an American megacarrier. There was only one left, the USS *Chicago*, and it was still in dry dock in San Diego.

Another clue: The raiders had come from the northeast and departed in that same direction. Japanese and Peruvian airplanes had been overflying the area northeast of New Lima for forty-eight hours straight, looking for any sign of a secret air base, but with no luck. This was not unexpected, though. The area the planes were canvassing was among the most rugged on the continent, all mountains and thick jungle and valleys so deep, reports persisted that dinosaurs still lived in some of them.

The suspected area was also sparsely populated, but some tribes still lived in the region, and again, that's why the Night Brigade's talents would be needed. It would be up to them to question the local tribesmen by any means necessary as to what they might have seen along the lines of a secret installation or airplanes flying overhead. Through these native peoples, Wakisaki was certain, the mysterious air raiders would be found.

A line of tracked vehicles rolled out onto the runway just as Wakisaki was reviewing the dastardly Argentine troops. There were no speeches, no ceremony. Wakisaki simply looked over the gigantic soldiers, nodded a little, and rubbed his bandaged nose. Then, with his vast entourage in tow, he jumped into his heavily armored limousine and left the air base.

Once he was gone, the Night Brigade climbed aboard their huge tracked vehicles—there were thirty of them in all—and their long column departed.

Across the airfield, toward a highway just recently built, they headed north.

Northeast Peru

The place was called *Exuxuci.*

Loosely translated in the dialect of the Intez Indians, it meant the Two Mountains of the Gods.

And indeed there were two mountains here. Both more than 8,000 feet above sea level, both enshrouded in perpetual mist. They were known as Xne and Xwo. Ringing them on all sides were thick forests, the trees of which reached about two-thirds of the way up both mountains. After that, they both wore crowns of stone and snow.

Like Xne and Xwo, the forests were considered holy by the local Intez Indians. Stories passed down from the Ancients, the distant ancestors of the Intez, told of beings from the Heaven landing on Xwo thousands of years before and living there for a very long time. These beings made friends with the Intez, even though they never really spoke to them. After a while, the Intez came to revere the beings, and in turn, the beings protected the tribe. When the beings finally returned to space, they asked the Intez to watch over Xwo, as it was now a holy place to which they might someday return.

One family of Intez, the Xuzu, lived in the forest between the two mountains. Their warriors had protected these holy lands for nearly five millennia. It was the duty of the family chief to make a pilgrimage to the top of Xne Mountain at least once a week, to check on things on the top of Xwo, the second mountain nearby.

The current family chief was a man named Xaxmax. He was 253 years old by Intez time, and considered a very noble and brave leader. He'd been head of the 145-member family for nearly forty-five years, taking on the traditional role his father had passed to him.

Xaxmax had made the weekly pilgrimage to Xne to look over at Xwo every week for the length of his tenure. This involved sitting on the peak of the first mountain and gazing for one whole day and one whole night on the flattened-off surface of Xwo, which was approximately half a mile away.

This weekly trip had been a mostly ceremonial journey for the past 5000 years, yet it had remained unchanged in all that time. There was no reason for it not to be. After all, this area of Peru was so isolated, the world's anthropologists weren't even aware of the existence of the Intez. It was accurate to say that very little ever happened in this part of the continent, either down in the jungles or on the tips of the holy peaks.

At least, not until a month or so ago.

That's when Xaxmax had first seen them. Three weeks ago. The lights. The fire.

The gods themselves.

Now, he was preparing to make his weekly climb up to the top of Xne once again. He hoped this trip, like the last three, would prove to be very exciting.

He'd already eaten his mescal flowers; the ingestion of the powerful hallucinogenic was part of the weekly ceremony. He'd also drank from the waters of the nearby River Ugu. He'd hugged his wife good-bye and all of his twenty-seven children, saving the last embrace for his oldest son,

Itax. Then, as the mescal began to kick in, he set out on the path to the top of Xne, starting as always when the sun was highest in the sky.

The trip up usually took six hours. The first three were relatively easy. The path Xaxmax followed had been worn down for thousands of years by his ancestors making this same journey. It was as smooth as glass in some places, its texture feeling cool to the bottom of Xaxmax's bare feet.

At the beginning of the fourth hour, however, the path got steeper, rockier, the jungle less dense. By the fifth hour, there were no more trees, just the rocks and the wind whipping everywhere. When the trees dropped away, the mescal flowers really began to take effect, and usually Xaxmax could see the stars and planets, even though the sun was still out. The constellations took on new shapes in the daytime and whenever he saw the animals of the jungle in the star formations—the jaguar, the snake, the condor—then Xaxmax knew it would be a good journey up.

One month before, on his 2,334th trip up to Xne, the chief had seen a strange, new star formation. This was of a huge bird—long wings, a long silver body, with a mighty hooked beak and huge talons. Xaxmax was frightened by this image at first. The stars looked strange enough in the daytime; this particular vision had been slightly terrifying.

But he'd continued climbing that day, knowing it was the proper thing to do. But thoughts of his family, his wife, his children, his oldest son, and the rest of the tribe had saturated his brain with every step he took. When he'd reached the top, his body had begun vibrating, though he wasn't sure why.

This journey had been easy compared to that one.

This day, the sun was not so bright, and he saw the stars through the sunlight very clearly. They formed the large silver bird again, but he no longer feared it. This would be the fourth time he saw it; and each time, he grew to like it even more.

The mescal was at full peak when he reached the top of Xne. His brain was spinning in a million different directions as usual. From here, he got his first good glimpse of Xwo, half a mile over. The peak of the sacred mountain was obscured in fog, but that was not unusual. Xaxmax found his favorite rock and sat down on it. He ate his last mescal flower, drank his Ugu water, and sat back. Slowly his eyes gained in power and clarity.

Just like that trip one month ago, strange sounds began to reach his ears. It was not the wind, not the jungle below. Not the symphony of the planets. These sounds were very unusual and so different from anything Xaxmax had ever heard before.

They were very high-pitched, the sound of metal and fire mixed together. Xaxmax sat on his holy rock, the flattened piece of stone where he would spend the night and the next day and tried his best to make his eyes burn a hole through the fog. Sometimes, this would take a while.

As before, his nose began picking up the strange odor; he'd smelled it the last three times he was here as well. But what was it? Something was burning . . . over on Xwo. But still, he could see nothing but fog.

So Xaxmax sat on the holy stone, peering through the mist, smelling the smell, and hearing the strange sounds until night fell and the stars came out for real.

That's when it happened again.

The fog had blown away from the top of Xwo, but Xaxmax could still see nothing unusual. The flattened-off peak looked the same, though his vision was getting blurry from the afterglow of mescal.

But then, the noise! It came again. Like a thousand children screaming at once. It was so loud Xaxmax fought the temptation to put his hands to his ears. With all his willpower he fought to keep from closing his eyes. Soon his mouth was open, but he could not scream.

Above him, as if it had suddenly appeared out of the thin air itself, there was a huge flying machine. It was much bigger than Talaz, the mythical bird of creation. It had silver wings and a giant glassy head, there was fire coming from it, and the noise it made nearly caused his ears to bleed.

It went right over his head. Screaming, burning, filling the air with fire and smoke.

Then suddenly—it was gone.

Just like that.

Xaxmax shook his head, cleared his eyes, and stared over at the nearby mountain peak. Just like the past three times, it seemed as if the giant silver bird had simply disappeared as soon as it had reached Xwo. But how could this be? Even under the influence of the mescal, Xaxmax knew that things like a giant silver bird could not simply disappear. That was just not the way of the world—or at least this part of the world.

So, what had happened?

Like before, Xaxmax, still frozen in place, tried to wrack his brain for anything in his teachings that might give him a clue as to what he'd just seen. Then, he heard the sound again—and an instant later, another gigantic silver bird appeared over his head! It too was sprouting fire and smoke. It too was screaming with the voices of angels. It too disappeared into nothingness.

Then came another. And another. And another!

They were flying over his head, with fire and smoke and noise, and the smell, descending onto Xwo, where suddenly they simply vanished.

This was madness, and again for a moment Xaxmax feared that he'd ingested too much mescal. What should he do? He'd asked the same question the last three times he'd journeyed to Xne. Those times he'd fought the temptation to flee back down the mountain after seeing the silver birds. He'd fought to keep his courage and his sanity and had laid on the rock all night long, shaking with fright, but knowing that to be brave, he must stay. And each morning he woke up and the sun was shining and all seemed normal again. And he'd gone back down the mountain and told not a thing to his tribe.

But now the silver birds were being very loud, very fiery, and very terrifying. Xaxmax wasn't sure he could take it. He cried out. He prayed. He beseeched the gods for an answer. But he heard nothing in reply.

Now more of them went over his head and simply vanished. His ears sounded like they were full of bells, he knew he couldn't take it anymore. He got up and gathered his things, making ready to run down the mountain and face the disgrace that would bring.

Then he heard another sound. This one was not a scream. Rather it was like many wings flapping at once. He turned around and saw that another kind of flying monster was hovering right above him! It was just as big as the others, but very different. This one was flying in place, right over his head.

And then suddenly, a line fell from it, and smaller monsters came down these lines. And the whirring things on top of the flying beast—there were eight of them in all— were kicking up dirt and dust and little bits of snow, and Xaxmax found it hard to breathe and keep his balance.

This might be the end of him, he knew. The monsters had spotted him and now they might tear him to shreds. The first few reached the end of their lines and now they were coming toward him. He drew his only weapon, a small, sharpened stick which held some small magical powers, and tried to stand tall. If he was to die, he had to do it with dignity, so at least the gods would not show displeasure on his surviving family members.

But these monsters were huge! And they were dressed

in strange blue skins and had strange bubblelike heads and their belts were full of weapons and wires and things. They were carrying long magic sticks which Xaxmax knew could destroy him in a second.

So this is how I will die, he thought . . .

But then something very odd happened.

One monster stopped, looked at Xaxmax, and slowly removed his headgear. His face was very white, his hair long, and Xaxmax realized he was not a monster but a human being like himself. The man smiled at him, and Xaxmax smiled back. Above them another silver bird went over and quickly disappeared from view.

The man smiled again.

And somehow, Xaxmax finally understood.

Later that day, when Xaxmax went back down the mountain, he gathered his family around him and told them of his adventure. He'd watched the huge silver machines—yes, that's what they were—go over his head and simply disappear. He had made friends with the ones he had first thought were monsters. Before he left, he waved to his friends inside the silver machines and they waved back to him as they went over and disappeared into the fog of Xwo.

What Xaxmax now understood, and what he told his tribe, was that these men were here to save the people of the forest just as the people from Heaven had come 5,000 years ago to do the same thing.

He told the people of his tribe that these strangers were their friends too, and that some evil ones were now ravaging the jungles for many miles around.

Someday soon, the Intez and the strangers might have to fight these evil ones.

And when that day came, they would all have to be ready to die.

Seven

The first village the Night Brigade reached was called Oxapi.

It was located about eighty miles northeast of New Lima, on a small mountain which looked out over a vast river valley. To the Oxapi people, the mountain and the valley beyond were considered sacred ground. The plants, the animals, the water, and the earth it contained were gifts to them from the gods above.

The long column of trucks and armored vehicles pulled into the very isolated settlement around dawn, waking many of the 300 inhabitants. The sight of the trucks was startling to the Oxapi—many had never seen a motorized vehicle before, and certainly never an Argentine soldier. The Oxapi were peaceful people, prone to singing most of the day and coloring their hair and faces with red berry paint at night. Small in stature, some were not even half the size of the massive Argentine commandos.

The commanding officer of the Night Brigade column was a colonel named Juis Ganganez. His nickname was *El Bruto* and it was one well earned. He was a pathological killer who just happened to be a soldier. He was known for such ruthlessness that even his superiors had had to rein him in on occasion.

Ganganez was a charming killer however. His face was solid and handsome, his features always ready to break into a disarming smile. He gave most people a queer sense of reassurance upon first meeting, a grave error for many of them. Ganganez also knew how to speak many of the languages of the jungle tribes.

As it turned out, he was fluent in the language of the Oxapi.

Ganganez's soldiers rounded up the tribe's leader, a small elderly man with a smile so wide he was called Cizi, or "Toothy One." Ganganez had Cizi brought to his command vehicle, a fifty-ton tracked behemoth which was a combination tank, assault gun, and mobile headquarters for the Night Brigade. Ganganez gave the man a package of candy, a delicacy among the natives. He also gave him a baseball cap and a pair of very cheap sunglasses.

A brief conversation established that the Toothy One was in close contact with the other tribes in the area. If anything happened anywhere within a fifty-mile radius, Toothy would usually hear about it, though he rarely had anything to report back to them. This was exactly what Ganganez wanted to hear.

He asked the chief if he would like to take a ride in the command vehicle; the elderly man heartily agreed. Ganganez ordered the driver to pull out of the village and head for a nearby ridge. The villagers cheered as the command vehicle left their little settlement. The Toothy One was laughing and waving to his people. Hat on, sunglasses in place, this was the greatest day in his life, he was shouting to them.

The huge tanklike vehicle rumbled up a dirt path, breaking trees and fauna as it did so. Finally they reached the crest of the ridge. From this elevation, the huge river valley stretched out before them.

Ganganez took Toothy from the back of the vehicle and stood him at the edge of the cliff. They could see for miles from here, and Toothy began pointing out places of interest to Ganganez: the river, the fields where his people hunted, the sacred mountains beyond.

Ganganez asked Toothy if he or his people had seen any strange things in the sky lately. Toothy answered the only way he could: that he and his people *always* saw strange things in the sky. Their religion was based on the sun spirits. But they could not speak of these things as it was a very private thing within each individual. In fact, it was forbidden to discuss such things with anyone who was not an Oxapi.

This upset Ganganez, but not very much. He stood Toothy closer to the edge and asked him again: What had he seen in the sky recently?

Toothy stopped smiling for the first time. He explained again in his odd click-clack language that he could not say. It was against his religion to speak to outsiders about these things. Ganganez nodded to one of the guards who'd accompanied him to the ledge. The man immediately made a radio call back to the village.

Then Ganganez took Toothy's new hat and threw it off the cliff. The chief nearly began crying. Ganganez asked him a third time: Tell me what you've seen. But again Toothy refused.

Ganganez nudged him closer to the edge. All pretense was gone now. A fourth time he asked what Toothy had seen lately. A fourth time, Toothy refused. Ganganez flipped the sunglasses from his face and threw them off the cliff as well. Toothy was in tears by now, so sure he was going to die at the hands of this huge strange man.

But Ganganez surprised him.

He pushed Toothy, not over the ledge, but back into the command vehicle. Then he joked with the man, saying he was testing his manhood and that he was glad the man did not break his religious convictions.

Toothy began laughing again.

The command vehicle returned to the village, but all

was very quiet. Ganganez lowered the rear ramp and led
Toothy out. He found a horrible sight. Everything in his
village was dead. Every man, woman, child, pig, duck, and
goat. Slaughtered. Blood was everywhere; the air smelled
of death.

Toothy stopped smiling; he would never really smile
again. Ganganez and his men were laughing at him as they
started their vehicles and began to move out of the village,
leaving the chief alone with the dead.

Ganganez's last words to him were: "Now you have
something to tell the other tribes about."

New Lima

General Wakisaki was smiling.

It was the first time in a while, but he could feel the
corners of his mouth start to crease and his eyes start to
squint and then, at last, he fell victim to it. He was happy,
an experience he hadn't felt in more than a week.

He was sitting in his penthouse located atop the military
government building in downtown New Lima. This was
the tallest building around, and with its four glass walls, it
gave a fantastic, sometimes startling view of the city surrounding it.

This was not the New Lima he'd stared out at for the
past six months. No, many parts of the city were now just
burned-out wrecks, the result of the vicious firebombing
a week ago. The intelligence building, the television broadcasting center, the communications center, and the indoc-
trination building, all within one square mile of Wakisaki's
penthouse, were just smoldering shells of what they once
were. Hundreds of buildings beyond were in the same
sorry shape.

Off shore, the hulks of four warships still lay flounder-
ing, further fouling the waters and making it even more

difficult to navigate in and around the artificial harbor of Callao. The enormous vessels were total losses, their bombings and the fires that resulted being so complete.

No matter. Wakisaki had finally managed to put all of these negative thoughts out of his mind and again concentrate on the future. He'd been able to do this as a result of three things.

First, he'd spent the previous day meditating. The object he'd concentrated on was a priceless Hintu vase. It was a 16th-century piece of art, delicate, like a pearl, with tiny cherry blossoms painted on its neck and base. It was one of Wakisaki's most prized possessions, and absolutely priceless. He'd discovered great comfort in the past by simply staring at it, turning it over and over and over in his hands. Feeling it. *Being* it.

It was in front of him now, sitting on the low table, glistening in the morning sun.

Wakisaki's second object of resurgence was right next to the vase. It was an empty bottle of grape sake. High in alcohol and extremely sweet to the taste, grape sake was considered rather low class back in Japan. But Wakisaki simply couldn't get enough of the stuff. With the correct combination of meditation and grape sake, the high general could achieve a mental state close to cosmic. He would actually hallucinate sometimes, so inebriated he would become. On these occasions, his staff knew it was best to leave him alone.

The third part of his passage from depression was all around him. Young girls, mere teens, were always a key to Wakisaki's revivals. There were five of them scattered about his penthouse now. They were all Asian, all beautiful, all barely one-quarter his age. He had used them all, had watched them with each other, had ordered them to do many vile and erotic things and they had complied after ingesting a lot of grape sake themselves.

One who lay nearby was a particular favorite of his. She

was of undetermined age, but Wakisaki had grandchildren older. She was sweet, small, innocent. It was her performance around midnight that had finally broken his grand funk. He barely remembered it, so drunk he'd been. But he recalled the smile returning to his face just as he reached his release—and the grin had remained ever since.

She was passed out beside him now, but he stroked her partially clothed body and stared at his vase again.

Yes, life was good for the conqueror. After all, life was simply how one looked at it. Setbacks were actually opportunities in disguise. The burned-out buildings downtown? They could always be rebuilt, bigger and better. The four gutted warships in the harbor? Their scrap could be used to build a statue honoring him. The 2,391 people killed in the firebombing? That many fewer mouths to feed.

Yes, High General Wakisaki was smiling again. He felt vital again. Strong. *Invincible.*

It was a great feeling.

It would last all of five minutes.

The knock at his penthouse door was very light.

The general sensed right away the timidity of the person on the other side. He knew immediately this was not going to be pleasant news.

He grumbled a reply and the person entered. It was the new police chief of New Lima, the designated bearer of bad news for the Japanese military commanders. He was carrying with him an insta-film cartridge and a combination radio/TV/film player, the device everyone on the planet called a Boomer.

"What is it?" the general yelled, loud enough to awaken the young girls. "Why are you here?"

"News, sir," the man said, his voice trembling so much he could not speak above a whisper. "From the front . . ."

Front? Wakisaki thought, the word burning a hole right through his stomach, to the acidy juices beyond. *What front?*

The chief set the Boomer down and inserted the insta-film cartridge. It began playing right away.

"This just arrived from Ayacucho," the police chief whispered. "Your staff felt you should see it immediately."

Ayacucho was a military district capital about 200 miles southeast of New Lima. It served as a major logistics center for men, ammunition, and equipment for both Japanese and native forces on the continent.

At the moment, it was in flames.

Wakisaki watched in horror as the film played out. It was a disturbing case of déjà vu. Gigantic silvery airplanes, flying so impossibly low, dropping tons of incendiary devices on the burning city below. The smoke alone was thicker than cumulus. The flames seemed to be reaching higher in altitude than the attacking airplanes themselves.

Through it all, Japanese SuperZeroes were screaming through the sky above the burning city—not attacking the bombers, but trying their best to get away from a lone airplane that was attacking them. Even as the city burned below, Wakisaki could clearly see this lone enemy airplane darting this way and that, seemingly shooting down his fighters at will.

It seemed unreal; it seemed impossible for one pilot to fly this way. Yet it was happening, right before his eyes.

"When?" Wakisaki mumbled, stunned. "When did all this happen?"

"This morning," the chief replied. "The film arrived here less than ten minutes ago. There are reports that the airplanes also attacked La Paz and Cosnipata."

Wakisaki felt his face go hot. His eyes began to bulge. He looked up at the police chief, who was now crying.

"You know what to do," he said.

The chief nodded sadly, walked over to the balcony,

calmly stepped over the railing, and jumped off. It was forty-three stories down.

Then Wakisaki rose, picked up the priceless Hintu vase, and hurled it against the wall. It smashed into hundreds of little pieces.

Then the general broke down and began crying himself. "Why?" he blubbered. "Why is God doing this to me?"

Eight

Colonel Ganganez was gamboling with one of his men when he got word about the attacks on Ayacucho, La Paz, and Cosnipata.

He was furious, yet not at all surprised. After having reviewed the films of the first attack on New Lima, he knew that whoever was responsible for the massive bombing would not likely stop with just one raid. These mysterious fliers had much in the way of firepower and aircraft. In fact, Ganganez had never seen airplanes as big as the ones that had attacked New Lima. He knew being in possession of such military might didn't exactly lend itself to sitting still and not using it. These people would continue attacking major Japanese installations for as long as they could.

That's why Ganganez had to find them—and quickly.

He kicked the young soldier out of his quarters in the back of the command vehicle and pulled out his maps. His column had been making its way through the jungles northeast of New Lima for three days now. In that time they'd destroyed five villages and killed more than 1,000 natives. But still, they were no closer to their goal.

Ganganez knew there were really only two locations from which the huge bombers could be flying from. The most likely would be a low, hidden valley, perhaps with elaborate camouflage on both the aircraft housings and the runways themselves. This valley would need access in and out for supplies and fuel. That told Ganganez it would have to be close to the sea, or at least a river which flowed out to the sea.

The problem was, there were no such valleys, at least not on his current maps. This left the only one other option: that the secret air base was located on a mountaintop somewhere.

But this too was very unlikely, and in Ganganez's mind, judging by the size of the aircraft involved and their numbers, nearly impossible. Japanese recon aircraft had been scouring the terrain within a 500-mile radius of New Lima for a week, concentrating on mountains and highlands. They had all come back with absolutely nothing.

Ganganez was really stuck on zero. Though he and his troops had slaughtered hundreds of innocents in the past few days, they had not received one piece of helpful evidence from any of them. And while Ganganez knew that word of the natives' deaths would spread through the countryside like a wildfire—after all, that's why he'd bothered to kill so many—he was finding the natives in this region tough nuts to crack.

But for a man like Ganganez, that just meant he had to hit them a little harder.

The Night Brigade's column continued winding its way through the vast Pasco region, slowly moving toward the northeast.

At about noon on this, the fourth day of their trek, they came upon four girls bathing in a tributary of the Tisqui river. They slaughtered the girls, ate them, and moved on. By midafternoon, the lead vehicles had topped a series of hills known as the Uni. From here the next region of

Huanuco stretched before them. The column remained at rest as a passing thunderstorm went overhead, then resumed when the late afternoon sun reappeared.

They went through the village of Ytapti around 1700 hours. The place was deserted except for two elderly women who were too frail to move. Ganganez shot them and ordered the village burned. The column then skirted the main section of the Tisqui River, coming upon two more deserted villages, looting them of their meager possessions, and then burning them and pressing on. Obviously word of the advancing Night Brigade had traveled very fast through the jungle as the next three villages were also empty. The soldiers burned them anyway and poisoned their water supply.

They came upon a field of cattle around 1730 hours and shot them all. Then they came to a fish pool and poisoned it. Then they came to a large forest and set it afire.

By 1900 hours, the sun began to dip. The scouts up ahead reported another village. It was a small one at the base of two mountains. Only one person was there.

His name was Xaxmax.

The message back to New Lima was so optimistic, General Wakisaki almost smiled again.

He successfully fought off the feeling though, knowing it would be a crush to be disappointed once more. But the news was so good, it was hard to resist. Finally, after several tense days, the report from Colonel Ganganez said that he'd located the secret enemy air base.

As Wakisaki expected, it was located on a mountain peak about 200 miles northeast of New Lima. The mountain, which was barely on the map, was constantly enshrouded in fog, according to Ganganez. This was how the enemy fliers had apparently been able to appear and disappear at will.

Ganganez's secret report indicated that he and his men would soon have the situation in hand, but that air strikes might be needed and reinforcements would probably be required for the mop-up. The entire operation was expected to take less than a day.

Wakisaki grinned slightly now, rereading the report over and over. It had been slipped under his penthouse door just a few minutes earlier, no one on his staff daring to face him, no matter what the news was. Not that Wakisaki could blame them. He'd been locked up inside his penthouse headquarters for nearly five straight days now. Discarded grape sake bottles, hypodermic needles, blood on the rug in many places, young girls' clothes. The place was a mess!

All this, of course, was the result of the deep funk he'd plunged into after hearing about the triple air raids two days before. But now the Night Brigade had come through, allowing him to at least beat his chest again. He really was an extraordinary commander, he told himself. It had been pure genius on his part selecting the bloodthirsty *Brigata de la Noche* to root out these mysterious airmen. With that one little act, his place in the history books was probably restored.

That's when he almost smiled again.

He walked out to his balcony and tried to think of something else. There were some details he had to attend to. He had just the airplanes in mind to send to Ganganez when needed. They were the elite 1029th Battle Squadron, attack pilots known for their ruthlessness. Once the secret air base was destroyed, Wakisaki planned to have his best ground troops kill everything and everyone within a 100-mile radius, as a warning to the natives that any aiding and abetting the enemy—whoever the hell they were!— would not be tolerated.

Wakisaki sipped the last few drops of a grape sake bottle and stared out on the water as the thick alcohol did its work on him. The hulks for the four burned-out warships were still in evidence—the cutting crews would begin work on them today. Other ships were coming and going in the artificial harbor, plying the filthy water, bringing troops and supplies in and taking raw materials and foodstuffs out for shipment back to Japan. Everything looked as it should.

You see? a small voice in Wakisaki's head began saying. *This is the way it was supposed to be. Everything is right again.*

He picked up his radiophone and called down to his staff room. They were to muster the 1029th Battle Squadron immediately and prepare them for air strikes at Ganganez's request. Then he ordered a huge celebration planned for downtown New Lima within two days' time.

He requested that the following message be sent to the Night Brigade: *Destroy enemy base and aircraft. Bring all top enemy officers to New Lima for torture and public execution. Congratulations on a job well done.*

Wakisaki hung up the phone and sipped the last few drops of sake from yet another nearly depleted bottle.

The sun was just coming up, and the water before him was beginning to sparkle black. Below him New Lima was coming to life too. Tanks rolling through the streets, airplanes flying overhead, port docks getting busier by the second. Wakisaki felt an odd feeling on his lips and cheeks. It startled him, it came so quickly.

He looked at his reflection in the balcony glass door and saw a brightened face staring back at him.

That was when he finally cracked.

He just couldn't help it. He *was* smiling again.

Nine

At the bottom of Xwo Mountain

Xaxmax loved his new sunglasses.

They were a great invention, he thought. With them, he could shield his eyes from the burning sun and yet still see. He imagined they would be extremely helpful while hunting for monkeys in the high trees of the forest. They might also help in catching fish.

He loved his new hat, too. It was blue with a wide brim and it fit over his matted hair nicely. Again, he was sure that it would help him during the hot days and maybe even the cool nights. After all, what spirits he possessed were in his head, and it was up to him to keep them comfortable.

The huge mechanical war machine he was sitting in didn't impress him that much, though. He'd seen greater things atop of Xwo mountain. Sure this vehicle, with all its guns and smoke and fire and lights and bells and noises and things, was interesting—but could it fly?

He didn't think so.

Could it drop bombs? Or fire guns from the clouds?

No. . . .

It was big and mighty, yes, but Xaxmax had seen mightier things.

He'd drawn a map of the easiest way to get up Xwo, to where the airplanes landed and launched from. There were 700 men in Ganganez's army and most of them would be going up the mountain with him. The path had to be wide enough for them to walk three abreast but not so wide as to attract attention. The path should also be shaded, Ganganez said, so the men didn't lose their energy too soon. But it shouldn't be completely covered, so the men would be able to see where they were going.

As the climb would take at least six hours, Xaxmax knew it was best to bring them up on the southeastern side, so the sun would be on them during the late morning, when it was most important.

So Xaxmax was drawing a map of a trail he knew would fit the bill perfectly. He'd taken it several times to the top of Xwo himself recently. In fact, he knew just about every step of it by now.

He'd spent the night in the back of the command vehicle, watching Ganganez and his officers plan the ascent up the mountain and the battle which they believed would take place once they arrived. He heard them talk about what weapons they would bring and how they would talk back to those few soldiers they would leave behind, here, in Xaxmax's deserted village, with their extra equipment.

He heard them brag about bringing in their own airplanes to help in the battle—small ones, from what Xaxmax could determine, which was funny because he had never really seen an airplane of any kind until a few weeks ago. Now, suddenly, he was an expert!

He watched the soldiers eat their morning meal—all red bloody meat, from what Xaxmax could tell. They drank a premission liquid which Xaxmax thought smelled of spirits.

He watched as the soldiers applied green paint to their faces and hands, for reasons Xaxmax could not understand. They took great care and time looking over their weapons, too. Cleaning them, loading them, and praying to them—or at least that's what it looked like to Xaxmax.

Finally, the soldiers were ready to go. They lined up in formation, ten deep, seventy across, and listened as Ganganez went over their plan. Climb up the mountain, reach the top, attack the air base, destroy the airplanes, capture as many officers and pilots as possible, and kill the rest.

With Xaxmax leading the way, the column should reach the summit in plenty of time to win the battle while there was still plenty of sunlight.

It seemed simple enough to Xaxmax.

The column started out at midmorning.

The soldiers were quiet as they began the climb up the trail. The animals were quiet, the wind too, as the hundreds of boots commenced the trudge upwards.

Xaxmax was in the lead, Colonel Ganganez and his personal bodyguards right behind him. Ganganez carried just a pistol and a sword; his bodyguards carried heavy bulletproof armor shields, not for themselves, but to protect their leader with, should it come to that.

The trail was thick with fauna the first hour of marching. The column, which had started out with much enthusiasm, began almost imperceptibly to slow down thirty minutes into the hike. Ganganez didn't realize it, his men didn't either. But Xaxmax could tell. It was very obvious to him.

The second hour brought more heat from the sun and more silence from the jungle around them. The column stopped once for a water break and again, just twenty minutes later, to allow those at the rear to catch up. This took ten minutes, and while those at the front of the column waited restlessly, they drank more water, depleting their rations needlessly.

Xaxmax, on the other hand, was enjoying the march, his new hat, and his new sunglasses. Moreover, he was enjoying the warmth and the scenery and the cosmic amuse-

ment of no animals growling, no birds singing, and no
wind blowing.

The delay was prolonged when two of the men at mid
column collapsed from the heat. Ganganez angrily sent
them back down the mountain, taking their water and
weapons from them and casting them adrift on the winding, confusing mountain trail. Xaxmax doubted they
would reach the bottom of the hill alive, but that didn't
seem to be a concern to Ganganez.

The column began again. They were now approaching
the end of the tree line, maybe 4,000 feet up the side of the
mountain, and entering a stretch of brush, thick bushes,
and vines. Xaxmax stepped lightly over and around these
obstacles, but the soldiers, marching three across, had a
harder time of it. The column slowed even further.

Another half hour passed. The sun became brutal. The
air absolutely still. Suddenly, there came much shouting
from the rear of the column. Ganganez called his men to
a halt once again and watched in growing irritation as a
runner from the back of the column approached.

"Twenty men are missing, sir," the man told the colonel.

"Missing?" Ganganez asked, more confused than anything. "Well, just wait for them to catch up."

But the man was shaking his head no.

"They are *gone*, sir," he was saying. "One minute they
were there. The next—*vamoose!* We went back to where we
last saw them. We found their guns at the trail's edge. Their
boots too. But the men themselves are gone."

Ganganez just stared back at the man. He was talking
crazy. If his men had fallen off a cliff, or if they'd deserted
or given up the hike, surely they wouldn't have left their
boots behind. Or their guns.

"Take a count," Ganganez ordered his lieutenants.
"Quickly!"

But taking a count of a 700-man column was not a thing
that could be done quickly. The men began sounding off,

but it was time-consuming. The column was so stretched out by now, it took runners several minutes to move up to Ganganez's position with updates on the counting process. But when the final tally reached him, things were more confusing then ever. Now forty-three men were missing. All of them from the end of the column, all of them inexplicably leaving their boots and weapons behind.

Ganganez was now more confused than ever. He ordered all his men to prepare arms, then made a call back to the base camp in the village, to see if the forty-three missing men had been spotted below.

But there was no reply.

That's when Ganganez pulled Xaxmax down off a rock and held him tightly around the throat.

"What is happening here, bird-head?" he asked him in the ancient Intez language.

Xaxmax had his answer already prepared.

"Your men will meet us at the top of the mountain," he said.

He pried himself loose and began running up the trail again, beckoning Ganganez to follow him.

"Come on," he called back to the Brigade commander. "You'll see. . . ."

It was the men at the rear of the Night Brigade's column who were the most nervous.

Several times in the past thirty minutes they had turned around and found dozens of their colleagues suddenly gone. Vanished, without a trace. When they went back for them, cutting their way through the dense brush, all they found were their boots and their guns. No footprints. No bloodstains. No last cries. They were just gone, as if swept away by ghosts.

Now these men—they were part of the Night Brigade's explosives squads—were suddenly on the tail of the column.

They were so frightened, some were actually wetting themselves.

One man, a sergeant named Aswalo, was trying to keep his courage up by chanting under his breath. To the sun god, the moon god, the earth god, the water god. To any god who might hear him, he chanted and sweated and gulped, while wiping the fluid from his nose and eyes. He was trying his best to keep up with the main column, but felt himself being slowed down, and losing sight of the man in front of him for long periods of time.

The vegetation was so thick, his eyes were suffering from green-out, a condition that made him see just about everything in shades of green only. Even his skin looked green to him now. Or maybe that's what happened when a man lost his courage for good, he thought.

He was almost running now, trying like hell to keep up with the man in front of him, but slipping and sliding on the liquid pathway and falling further and further behind. He should never have slaughtered that family of innocents back in Bolivia several months ago, he cursed. He should never have blown up that church in Chile with so many women and children inside it. He should never have killed his own father in a dispute over two pesos. And he should never have . . .

Aswalo was sweating so much now his boots were hard to keep on. In that frightening moment, he became convinced *this* was the way his missing colleagues had lost their boots!

Aswalo looked down at his jungle shoes and saw they were coming undone. A new streak of terror went through him. He knew he would have to stop and retie them—but this meant he would fall further behind the column. But not to do so would be even more foolish. If he walked very far in the squishy untied boots, he knew from experience he would develop sores and blisters which would make it impossible for him to walk at all.

He quickly stopped, laid down his rifle, and hastily began to restring his boots.

When he looked up again, he found himself staring into the eyes of one of his colleagues.

It was Sergeant Pedro Petro, one of the company's cooks and a friend of Aswalo. But in the microsecond that Aswalo recognized his old chum, he also knew something was very, very wrong. Pedro's eyes were staring at him unblinkingly and his head was cocked in such a way as to look very unnatural. A moment later, Aswalo knew why: It was Pedro's severed head he was looking at.

It was tied through the ears with hemp twine and looped around the neck of the man who was standing over him, watching him tie his boots. This man was wearing Pedro's severed head like a ghoulish necklace, even though Aswalo had spoken with Pedro not five minutes before he'd disappeared.

Aswalo tried to cry out, but even then he knew it was useless. This person standing over him, he was a native— just like the one who was leading them up this mountain of hell. But his face was painted with bloody red liquid. And his eyes were fierce and burning. He had a double-barrel machine gun in one hand and a huge machete in the other. And he was looking down at Aswalo like a hunter looks down on a calf before slaughter.

In his last seconds on earth, Aswalo saw another strange thing. It was a gallery of faces staring out at him from the bush. Same blood-painted faces, with the heads of his friends hanging around their necks. Same fierce look in their eyes.

We should never have come here, Aswalo thought as the machete came down on his neck. *We should have all just stayed home. . . .*

There was real trouble now, Ganganez could taste it in the air.

The men at the rear of his column were running toward

the safety of the middle, thus bunching the majority of his force in a small clearing about halfway up the side of the mountain. Despite his efforts, both yelling into his radio and at the top of his lungs, Ganganez could not calm his men down. Something awful was happening at the rear of the column. Unseen, unheard, but terrifying enough to make his highly trained soldiers panic.

Ganganez looked up ahead of him, at the trail as it left the small clearing, and saw the native guide Xaxmax standing on a tree stump, waving at him. The native was tipping his hat and laughing, too. Ganganez raised his pistol and fired twice at the man—obviously he'd led them into this trap. But the bullets missed the grinning native by a mile.

Ganganez directed his men to shoot at the gap-toothed man too, and they did. But somehow the man was able to dance his way out of the line of fire. Now more soldiers were firing at him, but the native continued his dance and managed to dodge the fusillade being directed at him.

By this time the column of panicky soldiers was flowing into the clearing, accordionlike, dangerously bunching up in clumps of ten or more. Ganganez turned his attention away from the native and back to his men. He began screaming at them again, ordering them to go back down the trail so they all wouldn't be so woefully exposed. But no one was listening to him. And no one was going back down that trail either. That was very evident now.

The gunfire aimed at the native, the sounds of the panicky 600-plus men pouring into the clearing, and the sound of Ganganez's own voice drowned out another, deeper, more ominous sound riding on the wind.

It was the groan of sixteen jet engines, flying very high, but coming down very, very fast.

The gunship arrived overhead at precisely 1100 hours. It had been airborne for ninety minutes, circling very high above Xwo mountain, tracking the progress of the ascent of the Night Brigade via its long-range monitoring array.

The timing of this aerial operation had to be exact for several reasons. It would have been a mistake to attack the Night Brigade while they were still in the village below. Thousands of years of heritage were represented by the Intez settlement and it simply could not be destroyed. Besides, an attack on the ground would have given the Brigade a means of escape.

But up here, halfway up the mountain, they had nowhere to go.

Taking out fifty of the Argentine soldiers at the rear of the column had been a ritualistic exercise more than anything else. It was the Intez way to instill fear into their enemies before destroying them. Lopping off the column's tail had certainly filled that bill.

It had also served to drive the rest of the column into the open area known as Axaz, or "flat place, halfway up."

This was the only place on the mountain trail in which the gunship would have a clear shot at the column. It was here that the airplane—and its forty-four high-powered guns—would do their bloody work.

The pilots of the aircraft got a message from the control hut on top of Xwo at 1110 hours. The native chief, Xaxmax, was clear of the enemy column. The Axaz plain was now a free-fire zone. The controllers were giving total fire control over to the big airplane's pilots. They in turn radioed back to their small army of gunners in the hold of the aerial giant: Load weapons and get ready for action.

The airplane itself was rather frightening just to look at. It was nearly 300 feet long, with an enormous wingspan. Sixteen engines adorned its wings. All of them jets, all of them spewing thick, gray exhaust and emitting a scream that sounded like a thousand people crying at once.

There were more than 600 soldiers caught on the Axaz

Plain. They saw the airplane, saw its muzzles, saw that they were, in effect, trapped before its gun sights.

The engines screamed as the airplane dipped down closer to them. Many men simply stood frozen and looked at it.

The fusillade came two seconds later. Thirty-eight triple-barreled machine guns, two small howitzers, and four 20-mm cannons all fired at once. Some of the soldiers pitifully turned their rifles toward the flying monster, but that was immensely futile. The stream of gunfire hit the field like a wave on a beach. In ten seconds, half of the soldiers simply ceased to exist.

The airplane pulled up, its size so immense it seemed impossible for it to fly, and came back around again. Those soldiers not already killed or horribly wounded were still frozen in place. Or at least most of them were. One man had just a little bit more of his wits about him. It was Colonel Ganganez. He'd somehow escaped the initial barrage and was watching the airplane come around again.

A fleeting notion went through his mind. In this moment of tragedy, he should be with his troops, he thought.

But he quickly dismissed that notion.

Screw his men—he wanted to live. Just before the airplane's guns opened up again, Colonel Ganganez turned around and began crashing through the jungle.

With the cries of his men ringing in his ears, he simply ran away.

Back in New Lima, a flight of SuperZeroes from the 1029th Battle Squadron was taking off.

They'd been dispatched by General Wakisaki to aid in the Night Brigade's destruction of the secret enemy base on Xwo Mountain. The problem was, the pilots weren't sure where Xwo Mountain was exactly. They were aware of the Night Brigade's general vicinity, about 250 miles

north of New Lima, and they were fairly certain of which
mountain range Ganganez and his men were now scaling.
It would just be a matter of the Brigade marking their
position with smoke for the pilots to determine the correct
combat area. After that, the plan called for a combined
land-air attack on the secret mountaintop base. One, two,
three, and out, a very easy operation. So easy, the pilots,
Japanese officers all, expected to be back at their home
field by noon.

The SuperZeroes were fierce airplanes. Jet-powered yet
retaining many of the innovative and lightweight characteristics of the old Mitsubishi Zero, these aircraft carried
six machine guns, plus twin cannons—and up to five tons
of bombs. The SuperZero pilots were as famous as their
airplanes. In the Imperial Japanese scheme of things, they
were regarded as highly skilled, combat-hardened, and absolutely without mercy for their opponents. They were
known to unforgivingly strafe the wreckage of planes
they'd downed, always making sure the pilots were dead.
They routinely bombed villages that were miles from any
military activity, seemingly for the sport of it. Their favorite
pastime was strafing hospitals and orphanages. It was said
that no flight of the SuperZeroes went up without detailed
maps of all the enemy hospitals and orphanages that would
be within their day's area of operations.

There were eight planes on this mission. They were flying in two flights of four. They foresaw bombing the secret
air base first, then coming back and strafing whatever help-
less enemy troops they could find on the ground. The only
opposition they could think of possibly encountering was
small arms fire, or at most, a cannon or two. Neither fazed
the SuperZero pilots. Their planes were heavily armored
on the bellies, wings, and tails. While a well-placed cannon
shell might put a nasty dent in the body, machine gun
bullets usually just bounced off.

The flight up from New Lima took but twenty minutes,

the SuperZeroes bumping up their double-reaction fuel-burners and streaking to the combat area at nearly 600 knots. Soon after arriving they spotted a column of smoke rising up from a mountain located deep inside the range. This particular mountain was about 8,000 feet high; the smoke was coming from a spot about halfway up. This was obviously the marker being sent up from brigade ground troops.

Or so they thought.

The airplanes lowered their speed and went down to 5,000 feet. If they assumed this was the target mountain, then they assumed the secret air base was at its summit. The flight leaders told their men to fuse their ordnance and begin to line up for initial bombing runs.

But the pilots saw something that was fairly odd. There was another smoke plume rising up from the side of the mountain. And another. And another. This signaling method was a little extreme by the Night Brigade. A simple smoke flare would have done the job. The pilots *knew* something was wrong, so they stopped their bomb fusings and prepared their machine guns and cannons instead.

As they drew closer to the mountain, they found their intuition proved correct. There was a battle raging on a flattened-out piece of terrain 4,000 feet up the side of the mountain. It appeared the Night Brigade had run into some trouble. No problem. The 'Zero pilots simply test-fired their weapons and reconfigured their formation from prebombing to ground support.

But as the planes got closer, they beheld an even more confusing situation. It appeared as if one section of the mountain had been literally blown away. A huge smoking crater was the source of the large plume of smoke spotted by the pilots. Many parts of the jungle were on fire as well, causing the other half dozen smoke trails. People could be seen on the ground—but were they Brigade troops or enemy soldiers, or both? It was impossible to tell from the

'Zero pilots' point of view exactly who they'd be shooting at.

But this was not a big deal for the fliers. They wouldn't really have to change their plans all that much. The SuperZeroes would just go in shooting.

They would leave it to the Night Brigade soldiers to sort out the bodies afterward.

Colonel Ganganez was hiding.

He was laying low in a tuff of snake grass, so called because of its long, slimy appearance. Before him was the horribly scorched plain of Axaz. It looked like a scene from hell. Fire. Smoke. Bodies. Pieces of bodies. The occasional cry on the wind.

The gunship had circled for just three minutes and had left a hole in the ground bigger than a soccer field. The fusillade had perforated anything within that area, and Ganganez's men couldn't have made a more convenient target for the aerial slaughter. As their commander, he had made a blunder of enormous proportions in leading them up the mountain in the first place.

But life was strange, and the cosmos stranger. Though it seemed impossible to him now, somehow, some way, some of Ganganez's men had actually lived through the three minutes of horror.

He could see some of them now through the snake grass. A few were trying to crawl into the bush, some were attempting to help others. Many were horribly burned. Many were missing arms and legs. One man was actually dragging his shorn-off leg behind him. Still others were lying still, occasionally twitching among the dying fires and thickening smoke. These people wouldn't be going anywhere.

Beyond all this, Ganganez spotted a larger clutch of men gathered on the periphery of the huge, smoldering crater.

These soldiers, maybe fifty in all, seemed less injured than the rest. They even appeared to be regrouping a bit, finding weapons and checking their mechanisms.

Ganganez could hear them. First one voice. Then two, then many. They were calling for someone. He listened harder, his heart pounding. They were calling out a name. *His* name.

"Colonel? Colonel Ganganez! We are here. . . ."

The soldiers had spotted him, were waving to him, even laughing at the fact that they were still alive, that they had somehow managed to avoid getting killed in the gunship's attack.

Ganganez's spirits soared. He still had an army!

But then, as he began waving back, he saw from the trees behind his men gangs of painted natives with huge machetes emerging. They began overwhelming this small pack of laughing, waving soldiers, stabbing them, or chopping at them as calmly as a man chopped a tree. Ganganez's men were just standing there! They were not fighting back. They were not running away. Some even calmly sat down and waited for the approaching natives, almost as if they'd been expecting them to come and slice their throats.

Not one scream, not one cry came up, as the soldiers simply submitted to being killed. Ganganez's head was about to explode. The scene was so grotesquely sheeplike, Ganganez vomited all over himself. What madness of war would make men act like this? If there was ever any time they needed his leadership, it was now.

But Ganganez stayed frozen. He was not moving, not one iota. He couldn't. He was petrified with fear so thick, he could taste it. For the first time in his military career, his ruthlessness was no help to him whatsoever. Even worse, he realized it was just a matter of time before these natives found him too.

He had to get away, had to get further into the jungle. But he was just too sacred to move. His legs wouldn't work;

neither would his arms. He felt as if his body was made of stone. All was lost then, he thought, and he would probably die here, of fright if not a slashed throat, on this haunted mountain, all alone.

But wait . . . there was another noise on the wind now. Not the sound of the still-burning forest nearby or the screams coming from the slaughter of his men.

No, this was a different sound.

Ganganez looked up and was pleasantly stunned. It was a very hopeful sight: eight SuperZeroes of the Japanese Occupation Air Force were coming right toward him. Ganganez's heart soared. What providence this was!

His mind began buzzing madly. The SuperZeroes could easily mow down the enemy troops now engaging what was left of his column. After that, the planes could bomb the secret enemy air base on top of this damned mountain as well. This meant that the day still might still be saved for Ganganez. He took a deep breath and inhaled a mouthful of smoke. He'd just gone from hell to heaven in a split second. Now, not only did he believe that he could still make it out alive, he was actually thinking he could claim credit for what was about to happen on top of the mountain!

But he still had to stay alive and he was at the moment too close to where the 'Zeroes would be coming in. Ganganez finally managed to get his arms working and crawled to an outgrowth of rock nearby. It would provide perfect cover for him during the impending air strike. He huddled behind it, eyeing the eight SuperZeroes as they peeled off into their attack profiles. Across the field the one-sided battle continued going badly for his men. They were still proving little match for the strange enemy, falling calmly to the razor-sharp machetes of the bizarre natives.

Ganganez was certain the upcoming air strike would take care of the enemy, even if he knew many of his own men would be killed in the process. He was sure there were still plenty of his troops hiding in the woods and it would be with them that he would ascend the rest of the mountain and emerge triumphant at its peak.

So he took one last look at the eight incoming jet fighters and then cowered behind the outcrop of rock, hiding his eyes again and waiting for the ground to shake.

But just then, he thought he heard yet another, higher-pitched screech. Then he felt not a ground tremor but a disruption in the air around him. He opened his eyes and saw two SuperZeroes crashing into the fires already burning on the plain.

He felt another concussion and saw a third 'Zero plow in. Behind it was a fourth. Then a fifth. The jet fighters were coming down in pieces—many pieces, as if they'd been shredded by something from above. But how? The flying monster gunship was certainly nowhere to be seen—its screaming engines would wake the dead at twenty miles.

Ganganez dared to look up and saw the seventh SuperZero disintegrating before his eyes as a very unusual-looking airplane attacked it. The plane was very small, looking like it had been cut in half just behind the cockpit, where oddly enough its propulsion unit was. But this plane was acting very strangely as well; Ganganez could tell just in the first few seconds. It seemed to be able to flit back and forth across the sky, more like a hummingbird than a normal aircraft. Herky-jerky, turning, twisting, at times it seemed to come to a complete halt as it sprayed gunfire into the hapless number seven 'Zero.

The 'Zero came down not 200 yards away from him just seconds later. Even through blocked ears and closed eyes Ganganez could tell what was going on above him. The last 'Zero was being executed by the strange airplane. Fire on metal, explosions above his head. Maybe even a long human scream. Inevitably the crash came. Number eight augured-in nearly on top of the wreckage of number seven.

The flight of SuperZeroes had been shot down by one

little airplane in less than forty-five seconds. Their bullets never reached the spot where the last of his men were being slaughtered.

Now came a dreadful silence.

No more airplane engines, no more wind. No more crackling of nearby flames. Just the faint screams of his men as they continued to get their throats slashed.

Something inside Ganganez's mind snapped. It was an actual snap—he heard the noise as plain as the scream of a jet engine or a cannon round going off.

Snap! Just like that. And after that, he knew he would never be the same.

That's when he jumped up and started running. Running like death itself was on his tail. Running away from the fire and the smoke and the pleading cries of his men.

Running, up the path, toward the top of the mountain.

Ten

It took Ganganez less than thirty minutes to scramble up to the top of Xwo Mountain.

He made the trip quickly, fueled by the pure, unadulterated adrenaline of a madman. Breathing wildly, drool running from his mouth and nose, by the time he reached the summit, he could no longer feel his feet or his hands. Still, he became oddly calm. At least he was far away from the madness of the killing field at Axaz.

But what he would find at the top of Xwo would seem more insane, more unreal than what he'd seen below.

At first, he saw nothing. He reached the end of the steep path and found himself looking out over the vast Peruvian forests, stretching all the way to the sea. Ganganez was not interested in the scenery, as awesome as it was. He was actually quite startled. The flattened-out peak was deserted, barren, empty. There was nothing up here except windswept rocks and a few patches of snow.

How could this be?

Had he been suckered in and led to the wrong mountain to begin with?

It seemed that way. But that was not the case. There *was* something up here. Ganganez thought he could hear it: engines, generators, radio static, humans moving about. He thought he could smell it. Fumes. Gas. Exhaust. Thick as the night.

No—there was a secret base up here all right.

He just couldn't *see* it.

Ganganez let out a long, chilling scream. He'd gone insane for sure, his worst fear since childhood. The next thing he knew, there was blood running from his ears, and a sound like the ocean was pouring over his head. He looked down at his feet and felt a great trembling. It was not him; he was too frozen to move a muscle. It was the ground that was shaking beneath him. Everything got black. The sun was blotted out. He could no longer see his shadow.

That's when he was able to turn and see the monstrous gunship coming right at him.

He wet his pants. He couldn't even breathe. Yet somehow he realized he was not totally insane. Not yet anyway. Because at least he could see this thing. He could hear it. It was there. Bearing down on him like death itself.

But instead of tearing him to pieces with its multitude of guns, it went right over his head, all noise and fire and smoke—and then it disappeared.

Ganganez, near the edge of the cliff, considered just jumping off right then and there. At last, his insanity *had* gotten the best of him. Why not just complete the trip and get it over with?

Then came another huge roar. He looked up just in time to see another gigantic airplane roar over his head— and disappear. Then another. And another.

Ganganez sank to his knees and held his head and knew at last that yes, he was going, going, gone.

With the last of his strength he reached into his belt, came out with his pistol, cocked back the double hammers and pointed it at his head.

He began to squeeze the trigger . . .

. . . but then, he stopped. . . .

He looked up. Another plane went over his head and disappeared seemingly into nothingness. But Ganganez had seen something. Another plane came in, and instead of watching it, he watched the rugged, barren terrain in front of it.

Sure enough, he saw something move.

It was like a rip in the fabric of reality, a slight appearance of a spark. Something was quickly drawn back only long enough for the airplane to go through, and then was instantly drawn closed again.

Ganganez slowly rose to his feet. Maybe he wasn't insane after all.

Another plane came in—they were obviously bombers returning from a raid somewhere over Japanese-occupied South America. Ganganez saw something move again, this time much more distinctly. It was an enormous curtain! One that was so highly reflective, it was nearly a mirror. It was being opened and closed so quickly, it gave the appearance that the planes were disappearing into thin air.

In fact, they were flying into something.

Ganganez began scrambling over rock and bush, his knees scraping badly, his face tearing from the thorns. It was about 500 feet to this thing, but Ganganez made it quickly and soon he was able to see it up close, and when he did, he knew immediately what it was.

It was called an LSD—Light/Sound Deflection. It was an electrically charged curtain, a device that could block out light, radio waves, TV waves, even human voices and mechanical sounds from the inside, while allowing those inside to look out.

Ganganez had heard of these things. The *norteamericanos* had placed them up and down their shorelines during the last years of the war against Germany to alleviate the need to black out their major coastal cities. But until this moment Ganganez never realized just how effective the damn things were.

The barren topography helped the illusion. The LSD reflected light, like a huge, flexible mirror. Just like a magician's box, if the mirror's angle is just right, appears empty, when in actuality, one is simply staring at a mirror's reflection of an empty space.

Ganganez found the strength somehow to get to his feet and walk over and actually touch the thing. He got a medium-sized jolt of electricity for his trouble, but still he was fascinated with it.

He heard another huge roar behind him and he turned around to see another gigantic airplane bearing down on him. It was so big and moving so fast, he didn't have a chance to move. The flying monster went right over his head, no more than fifteen feet from the top of his singed hair and blew through the sudden opening in the LSD. The afterdraft was so powerful, and the screen opened and closed so quickly, the vacuum served to suck Ganganez right in with it.

It was like falling into a dream. On the outside, the mountain's peak looked like it was part of the moon. Empty, cratered, craggy. . . .

But inside the LSD, the brigade officer found himself in a whole new world.

There *was* an air base up here—buildings, runways, airplanes and all. Ganganez saw at least twenty bombers, lined up wing to wing. All of them were huge and frightening looking. There were dozens of smaller airplanes too.

But what was most astounding was the number of people on top of the mountain. Ganganez could see at least a couple of hundred people, walking around, going about the business of running airplanes off the mountain. It was just amazing!

Dazed as he was, Ganganez knew it was only a matter of time before someone spotted him. He tried to take a mental photo of this strange place. If he could somehow escape and return to New Lima with this piece of news, then maybe he could still prevent this mission from being a complete catastrophe.

In addition to the twenty bombers and the dozens of smaller aircraft, he saw two enormous, straight-ahead runways, plus a smaller, angled one. Four hangers, an administration building, a set of barracks, four watchtowers, a fuel dump, an ammo dump, a generator plant and a projection maintenance facility for the LSD.

The LSD itself was just about invisible. Looking out of it was like looking through a fine screen mesh. Several hundred feet above him, the screen was sagging a bit, almost like a circus tent. Now Ganganez knew how the Japanese recon airplanes had missed spotting the hidden base from the air. This place actually had a roof on it!

The LSD also served to seal in a lot of heat, he realized. It was hot in here—very hot.

That's why it was so strange to feel something cold touch him on his neck. Cold steel. Like the barrel of a gun.

He turned around slowly and saw there were actually five of them. Double-barreled machine guns.

And they were all pointing at him.

Ten minutes later, Ganganez was sitting in a dark room located somewhere inside the base's operations center.

His hands were not bound, he was not gagged or blindfolded. He had not been beaten or whipped or prodded by his captors. Indeed, it was almost as if they'd been expecting him to show up.

A woman and a man had come into the room first and like the insane fool he believed he was, Ganganez gave them a twenty-minute dissertation on all of the atrocities he'd committed in his career. Next, two other officers came in with a map and asked him to show them every Japanese Occupation base and weapons facility between here and New Lima. Again, Ganganez told them everything.

The third and last person to come in was a very strange-looking individual. He was a pilot, he was still in his flight

uniform, all black with a black crash helmet adorned with
yellow lightning bolts on its sides. The man was handsome,
his hair long, his features distinctively hawklike.

But he looked so strange. Insane though he was, Ganganez knew this and stared at this man for a long time,
trying but failing to determine exactly what was odd about
him.

This man only had one question for him.

"Do you know who I am?" he had asked Ganganez.

Ganganez studied him. His face seemed familiar, but he
just could not place him.

"No," the Night Brigade commander finally replied. "I
don't."

The man was obviously relieved. He finally said: "Good."

Then he left.

The people who came to take Ganganez away were not
soldiers protecting the base, but the grotesque natives who
were still wearing the severed heads of his men around
their necks.

The natives took him out of the LSD-shrouded base and
back down the mountain. The long trip recounted the steps
Ganganez had taken earlier that day. He saw the plain of
Axaz, where most of his men had died. He saw the headless
bodies of those men at the end of the column who'd been
so cunningly attacked as the Brigade had climbed its last
hill.

Finally they reached the village where the Brigade had
jumped off. Here he remet the native chief who had so
completely fooled him.

Xaxmax.

In his hut there were representatives from all the tribes
who had suffered the Night Brigade's rampage during
their search for the secret base.

With each face, Ganganez sank deeper into his malaise.

Yet he was still too far gone to feel anything deeply, like guilt or responsibility.

"You have committed great crimes against our families and our lands," Xaxmax told him. "However, we will not kill you. We will give you the gift of life back, something your people did not give to us."

Ganganez let out a long sigh of relief.

"Thank you," he whispered, knowing he'd just dodged a very big bullet. "Please, tell me. What can I do for you?"

The natives all looked at each other, and several had to fight off a smile.

"What can you do for us?" Xaxmax asked. "You can deliver a message back to your gods."

One week later

High General Wakisaki had just woken up when he heard the pounding at his door.

He ordered the two young girls out of his bed and padded over to answer the door himself. He was badly hungover. This was the sixth day of a sake binge that had begun the day he'd received word that the Night Brigade had been wiped out on some unknown mountain northeast of New Lima. Several search parties had been sent out to look for them. None of them had returned either.

Wakisaki opened the door to find three of his highest officers looking back at him. They were pale. Wakisaki felt a chill go through him.

"How bad will this news be if you've come to tell me yourselves?" he asked them.

"You must come with us," one of the officers replied, absolutely petrified.

Wakisaki didn't protest. He was the highest military man in the Occupation Forces, yet he was going to obey, simply because he knew that what waited for him transcended military protocol.

They took the elevator down to the lobby of the head-quarters building. Here a squad of dirty, dusty soldiers awaited. They were Peruvians, the last search party that had been sent out to look for the Night Brigade.

They had found something.

There was a stretcher in the middle of the lobby and on it was the body of a man. It was very bloody, but some-how this person was still alive.

Wakisaki just stared down at this figure. It was a human being—but just barely.

This man had no hands, no feet. His ears had been cut off, his eyes had been gouged out, his nose had been sewn shut. His tongue was gone, and bloody spittle was drooling from his lips. A bloody stain around his groin told of other things that had been removed as well.

"What is the meaning of this?" Wakisaki finally burst out.

One of the Peruvian officers stepped forward.

"It is an *espectro vivo,* sir," he said. "A man who cannot speak, or hear, or see, or walk, or touch, or smell. The natives of the highlands used to do this to the last enemy soldier they could find—as a way of telling the other side who won the war. But that was thousands of years ago, back in the days of the Nazcas."

Wakisaki looked back down at the pathetic figure, twitch-ing on the stretcher. In all his years as a combat man, he'd never seen anything quite so disturbing.

"But . . ." the High General began to stutter. "Who is it?"

The Peruvian took a step closer to Wakisaki and said something so low, only the High General could hear it.

"It is Colonel Ganganez, sir," he whispered. "Of the Night Brigade."

Part 2

Eleven

The storm had grown during the night.

The wind was whipping in from the south pole at nearly eighty knots. It was blowing so hard, the heavy snow accompanying it was moving sideways. As a result, very little of it was reaching the ground on West Falkland Island.

The fishing boats at Summer Point were in, of course. Their crews had known this storm was coming for three days just by sniffing the air. The small fleet was now in safe harbor, its crews warm and dry inside Government Hall.

Up the road a mile, the crews inside the squadron of SuperChieftain tanks ringing the small farmhouse were trying their best to stay warm as well. Running their vehicles' small double-reaction engines on low kept the heat fairly consistent. Still, the howl of the wind outside their tanks seemed to bring an even deeper chill.

Inside the small farmhouse, the man and woman were asleep. But in the secret laboratory sixteen levels below the house, amazing things were happening.

The elevator leading up into the farmhouse arrived at the top floor at exactly midnight.

A scientist stepped out, turned on his flashlight, walked

through the door facing him, then through the closet and finally into the living room. All the lights were turned off and the wind was howling madly outside. The scientist felt for all the world like a burglar, an intruder on sacred ground. But he tiptoed softly into the couple's bedroom nevertheless and gently nudged the man awake.

"Sir, we have found something," he told the man. "You must come and see it."

The man needed no further prompting. He quickly put on his trousers and his bathrobe and boots. Quietly closing the door behind him so as not to wake his wife, he followed the scientist to the elevator and rode the sixteen floors down into the cold Earth.

One minute later they were inside the hidden lab itself. Five other scientists were inside the separate glass-enclosed room, standing around the operating table. As always, the scientists were dressed in long blue gowns and wearing rubber gloves and surgical masks.

But the patient laying on a white sheet on the table before them was not a human being. It was an atomic bomb.

At present it was in six different pieces.

The bomb's background—and how it got to be here—was so secret even the man from the farmhouse didn't know the exact order of events. This he did know: Right before the end of the recent war with Germany, an American agent was dropped into the Rhineland and somehow managed to steal six atomic weapons from the Germans. Five of these bombs had been dropped by the U.S. on occupied Europe shortly thereafter, wiping out the core of the German military hierarchy, and thus ending the war.

This was the sixth bomb. It had been transported back to the United States and after much examination, was sent down here, to this very secret place in the South Atlantic. A place where all the strange things—and strange people—in this particular world eventually seemed to wind up.

The scientists had been studying the sixth bomb for nearly a year now. The U.S. government had sent it here because no one in the regular U.S. military knew exactly how it worked. Nuclear power was a totally alien aspect in this world. In this place of huge airplanes, huge tanks, huge ships, the double-reaction process provided the power by fusing two atoms together and draining off the residue energy.

This bomb though, this queer thing, seemed to work on the exact opposite principal: It gathered energy by splitting an individual atom down the middle, not by combining the bodies of two.

The scientists had seen aerial recon photos of the destruction the first five bombs had done in Europe. Each bomb blast was exactly twenty times greater than one of the double-reaction warheads used by the Germans to destroy Paris in late 1997. Just who was responsible for building the six atomic bombs—or rather who was the person who *instructed* German scientists in how to build the bombs—was not known to them. The rumors were that he was dead.

All that was left of his handiwork now was this last remaining bomb. After nearly a year, the scientists were aware of its basic principles. But being scientists in this extremely inquisitive world, they'd set about not just to dissect it and duplicate it, but to make it larger. To increase its power. To make it bigger.

On this night, with a storm raging full gale overhead, they believed they had reached that goal.

Now the man from the farmhouse put on his own surgical gown and radiation protection suit and went into the glass-enclosed room.

The bomb's warhead was being examined via manipulator in a transparent safe box. What the group of scientists had done was to saturate the warhead with trillions of "mute-quakes," the passive castoffs of the double-reaction process. It was hoped these odd little things would attach themselves to the uranium atoms inside the nuclear warhead, increasing their charge while not perceptibly increasing their mass.

This idea came from a separate experiment the scientists had conducted a month earlier. They had set off a minuscule atomic explosion by splitting a mute-quake clustered atom. The result was an explosion, which had been expected to be the size of a firecracker, blowing apart a reinforced steel and lead chamber. Since then the scientists had been trying to figure out just exactly how many times larger that explosion had been compared to one using a uranium atom that had not been reinforced.

In other words, how much bigger, how much more powerful would this atomic cluster bomb be?

This stormy night they had reached that conclusion finally, and that's why they'd summoned the man.

He now read the data spitting out of the Main/AC computer and at first was convinced it was a misprint.

"Gentlemen, this report must be in error," he said, rereading the report. "You must mean that we've made the bomb *three* times more powerful than before—not *three hundred* times."

The scientists looked back at him, their faces all weighted by the same worried expression.

"No sir," one finally said. "That is no misprint. This bomb, clustered with mute-quakes, is now three hundred times more powerful than those dropped in Europe."

The man was stunned. He just stared at the scientists, then at the bomb, then back up at the scientists again. Three looked like they wanted to laugh; the other three like they wanted to cry. The man felt exactly in between.

The significance of what they'd just discovered here was slowly sinking in.

Before them was a single bomb that could, quite literally, blow up a sizable part of the planet.

"God help us," the man heard himself whispering. "God help us all."

Twelve

The crippled B-24/52 had two engines on fire when it came in.

Its pilots had expertly slipped through the massive LSD screen even though their steering program was down to just forty percent and the landing gears were knocked out.

They had no choice but to bounce the plane in on its belly. It skidded and screeched its way along the hidden base's longest runway, leaving small pieces of fuselage and wing and a lot of dust and smoke in its wake.

It sounded bad, looked worse, but finally the gigantic airplane came to a halt. The crash crews were quickly on hand, hosing it down, but there was little danger of fire now. The pilots had long ago disengaged their double-reaction power units and had glided the big bomber in, using momentum, gravity, and then a final burst from its wingtip-mounted rocket-assists to reach home.

The rear doors were opened and the twenty-three-man crew staggered out. Some had cuts and bruises, one had a broken leg. But they were all alive, and that's what counted up here.

The crumpled bomber was hauled off the runway to allow the next-in-line B-24/52 to come in. There were six more behind it and they were bunching up high over Xwo Mountain. The planes were returning from bombing runs over southern Peru and northern Chile. Twelve bombers had gone out—twelve had come back. Two had been shot up badly: this one and the first to come home. They were good examples of the increased Japanese reliance on antiaircraft flak, especially low-area stuff. The bombers had been facing clouds of it for the past eight weeks.

The battle for Xwo Mountain, and its result, had changed the face of the Japanese occupation of South America. The Nipponese Occupation Army was still in control of the continent; there was no doubt about that. But the bombers atop of Xwo had forced the Asian invaders to devote many of their precious resources to defense: air defense, fighter protection, AA sites, bomb shelters, and the million other things one side must do when its enemy is attacking it from the air.

Stopping the momentum of the Japanese conquest of South America had been the intent of the hidden base all along—and the people here had accomplished their mission. But the price also had a direct result: The flak over the target cities was now thicker, the home-defense fighters were more numerous, and many key enemy installations were being moved underground, making some previously available targets somewhat scarce.

But if they were the victims of their own success, it did little to bother the pilots and crews of the hidden air base. The important thing for them was that even though the Japanese knew the location of the base, since the battle down on the plain of Axaz, no further attempt had been made to destroy it. No Japanese pilot would fly anywhere near it for fear they'd be shot down. No Japanese or home troops dared approach it on the ground, for fear they'd be beheaded, or eaten alive, or worse.

For the first intention all along had been to spook the Japanese, and in that, the people at the hidden base had succeeded grandly. Things were tougher over the target areas, but the bombers were able to come and go from their base with virtual impunity.

The losses to increased enemy fighter activity had been surprisingly small in the past two months, but that had little to do with luck, or spooking the Japanese.

Rather it was the fighter escorts the bombers relied on now whenever they went up for a mission.

There were a total of thirteen escort fighters at the Xwo base. Twelve of them were Mustang-5s, an enormous combination of two airplanes, the P-51 Mustang and the F-86 Sabre jet. The Mustang-5 was a formidable weapon. It had the distinctive nose, fuselage, and tail of the famous P-51, but shared the air intake, the swept-back wing, and the cockpit of the equally famous F-86. More important, it combined the best handling and aerial combat characteristics of both classic airplanes, plus it could hit Mach 2.5 while carrying 1500 pounds of ordnance and featured no less than four machine guns and one huge cannon for firepower.

The thirteenth fighter at Xwo looked nothing like a Mustang or a Super Sabre. It was a Super Ascender/Phantom. Carrying strange, upturned wings and very long of nose, the Super-A looked like an aircraft that had been cut in half, midway down the fuselage. Here sat a powerful turbo prop engine which gave the airplane bursts of speed unheard of in bigger airplanes. The aircraft could climb and dive with hellish precision. It could turn, it could stall—some said that it could actually stand still for seconds at a time in midair. But like many things this particular plane did, that maneuver was partly an optical illusion.

As always, it was this airplane which landed last from

any bombing mission. Only after everyone else in the flight
was back down safely did the Super-A come in. Once down,
it rolled to its own special parking area at the far end of
the flight line, where it was greeted by its own special
ground crew.

This day, its guns were as empty as its fuel tanks. The
ground crew could tell just by the way the airplane taxied
up to its hardstand. The quicker it went, the more spent
it was. Oddly, that was also a good description of its pilot.

He pulled the small plane up and killed its engine just
before his tanks went dry. The air crew came out. Though
they were all under eighteen, all three were veterans of
the war against Germany. They knew this small plane inside and out, and had been selected personally by its pilot.
Of the 100 ground personnel at the base, only they could
touch the Super-A. This was something they were very
proud of.

Their nicknames were Dopey, Sniffy, and Sneezy.

The pilot popped his canopy and climbed out, jumping
down from the high cockpit without the benefit of an access ladder.

Dopey appeared, took the pilot's helmet, and gave him
his ever-present baseball cap.

"Good flight, Major?" Dopey asked.

"Ran great," the pilot replied. "I'm empty on ammo,
so you can align the gun sights if you want."

Another member of the ground crew appeared. He had
a can of paint and a small brush on hand.

"How many today, sir?"

The pilot had to think a moment.

"Six for sure," he said finally.

The kid checked his can of paint.

"I might run out," he told the pilot.

They both walked around to the snout of the strange
little airplane. On both sides of its nose, and all the way
down to the cockpit, there were dozens of tiny pictures of

yellow airplanes with little red balls on their wings—the symbol for a downed Japanese SuperZero. There were so many of them, they threatened to cover the entire fuselage.

"Sir, if you keep going like this, you'll have to get a new airplane," Dopey said.

The pilot just smiled and saluted them off.

"I don't know about that," he said. "It would be hard to give this baby up."

He was Hawk Hunter. Fighter pilot extraordinaire, secret agent, infiltration expert, military strategist. More than anyone else, he was the brains behind this secret base.

He walked into the administration building to find the base's operations officer, Major Eddie Payne, planted as always behind a very disorderly desk.

Hunter and Payne had most recently served together flying bombing missions from Iceland against the Germans. Payne was middle-aged, balding, solid with a slight paunch. He was a highly professional combat officer whose main concern was always getting his men home safely.

That was a tough order up here, atop Xwo Mountain, but Payne was trying his best.

Hunter put his mission recorder down on Payne's desk and gave his fingers a snap.

"The group nailed the target absolutely," Hunter told him. "The fighter opposition was . . ."

But Payne wasn't listening. Hunter looked down at him and saw that the operations officer was pointing across the room with one hand and holding a finger over his mouth with the other.

Hunter turned and saw there were three other people in the room with them. One man was holding a camera, one man was holding a set of lights. The third person was a very attractive female. She seemed familiar to Hunter, not an unusual occurrence for him. She was wearing a

very short skirt, a lot of makeup, and holding a microphone.

"Hello, Major Hunter," she cooed. "We're from *CNT World News*. . . ."

Hunter looked back at Payne as if to say, *You've got to be kidding me.* . . .

Payne just shrugged.

"Sorry, Hawk," he said.

It was a strange thing in this world that even though the U.S. military was running an operation as secret as this one atop of Xwo Mountain, they allowed the press almost unrestricted access to whatever they wanted. Why? Because it was in the Constitution and the American public was rabid for news from the front. But it was also Freedom of the Press at its most extreme.

"They've been waiting for you all day," Payne said under his breath. "Flew in just after the group took off. Why don't you just do a quick interview and maybe we can get rid of them."

Hunter felt the adrenaline of the mission quickly drain out of his body. Due to circumstances beyond his control, Hunter was a big hero back in the U.S. Though never officially confirmed by the U.S. Government, it was he who had infiltrated Germany, found the six atomic bombs, se-cured their smuggling out to U.S.-controlled territory, where five of them were re-fused and then dropped on Nazi Europe, ending the fifty-eight-year-old conflict known at one time as World War II.

Thus he was known to many as "the Man who won the War," though he loathed that title. More than a million American soldiers had died fighting fifty-eight years of World War II; in Hunter's opinion, they'd had more to do with winning the conflict than he had.

When Japan attacked Pearl Harbor, the Panama Canal, and later invaded South America, the U.S., still reeling from the war against Germany, had been deliberate, some said *too* deliberate, in taking action. It took months to gather enough forces just to secure the border of Texas and Mexico; after all with the Japanese in Panama, and a constant state of anarchy in Mexico, a potential invasion force was just a few hundred miles away.

Only then could the U.S. start thinking about taking the war right to the Japanese. Hunter had been a spearhead for this, parachuting alone into the jungles of Peru just two weeks after the Japanese landed. Operating from a small ultralight aircraft, the man some people had taken to calling "The Sky Ghost" did target identification, defensive assessment, and forward base scouting.

It was he who had found the mountains of Xne and Xwo about a month into his mission. Reconnoitering them extensively, he had made certain they were big enough, wide enough, and remote enough for the secret base to be set up. The first problem was making sure enough portable electricity could be airlifted up to the mountaintop to run the high-voltage LSD screen. Once this problem was solved by the construction of a superpower, air-portable double-reaction generator, the base began to take shape. Late-night flights down from Texas gradually dropped enough supplies on the peak to build the base, construct the runways, and most importantly put up the LSD screen, including the unique LSD "roof," which covered the secret facility from the air as well.

The bombing campaign had begun soon afterwards.

So far it had been a great success, for what it was intended. That was, to put the Japanese on the defensive whenever and wherever possible.

All of this was more or less known back in the U.S. due to the wide-open relationship between the Pentagon and the media and the American people's endless fascination with war heroes. In addition to Hunter, many of the other pilots on Xwo were celebrities back in the States as well. Their exploits had been recounted over and over in the press back home, as a way of building morale, which in the end Hunter knew was vitally necessary.

But Hunter was the most famous of them all. He was the one everyone wanted to talk to, get a glimpse of, get an autograph from. And now, with the appearance of the Network TV crew, it looked like all that was going to continue.

Hunter walked over and shook hands with Kate Kalloway, the beautiful familiar-looking female reporter.

"So, Major," she asked, "Do you have a few minutes for us?"

Hunter shrugged.

"A few, I guess," he replied.

With a roll of the eyes from Payne, they all filed into a private office off the main ops room.

Hunter took a seat across from the reporter. The lights came on; a microphone was put in front of him. Ms. Kalloway fixed her hair. Hunter started going over his usual responses in his head. He knew by now what to say and what not to say to the media. If these press people were no different from the thousands he'd met before, they would ask about his early days in the jungles of Peru, the building of the hidden base, the first missions against the Japanese, the battle on the mountain plain of Axaz.

But the reporter had a surprise for him.

"Major Hunter, exactly where did you grow up?"

The words froze Hunter. He looked over at Payne, whose face began to pale. This is not what they were expecting.

"I . . . I believe that is actually classified information," Hunter was finally able to mumble.

This much was true. All information about Hunter's personal background was classified top secret.

"But there are rumors . . ." the reporter persisted.

Again Hunter paused. Yes, there *were* rumors. Where did

Hawk Hunter come from? The real answer was, no one knew for sure.

Not even Hunter himself.

He'd been picked up by a U.S. warship in the middle of the Atlantic Ocean on August 15, 1997. How he got there was still a mystery. Hunter had total amnesia at that point, but some memories began draining back to him soon afterwards. He soon remembered he was a pilot, an extremely good one, and that he'd come from a different place. It was a place exactly like this one, with the United States and all the other countries of the world, and 6 billion people and the daily conflicts of life—but a place much different too. The only explanation Hunter or anyone else privy to all this had come to was that he'd somehow passed into an alternate universe somehow.

Gradually, just about all his memories came back. "Back There," in the place from where he came from, Hunter had been the world's best fighter pilot ever. He'd been an officer in the United American Armed Forces, who protected the American continent after their version of World War III went against the U.S. Five years of civil war and foreign invasions followed before the United Americans finally freed their country again.

Then the UA found itself involved in several wars overseas, and gradually, it became known that one person was behind all of this misery and war: A superterrorist named Viktor Robotov.

When Hunter discovered Robotov had managed to go into orbit in an old Russian-made space shuttle and take over a secret orbiting space station, Hunter stole the shuttle and went into space after him. But the Earth learned it was in the path of a huge comet which would destroy the planet in one gigantic collision. This disaster was averted—Hunter assumed—when he used the space shuttle to tow a string of nuclear weapons directly into the path of the comet, the explosions from which deflected the gigantic snowball away from the Earth.

Robotov was in the space shuttle with Hunter for this suicidal mission, as was a close friend of Hunter's named Elvis Q. All Hunter could recall was watching the bombs detonate in space—and then falling . . . falling . . . falling into the Atlantic Ocean, where he was eventually picked up.

Elvis had been picked up too—by the Germans. He had turned against the principles of the United Americans, single-handedly revitalized the Nazi cause, and in the end, killed himself over it shortly before the war was over.

What had happened to Viktor, who'd also fallen into the water, was not known. At least not by Hunter.

But all this—where he came from and how he was found—was still very top secret, simply because the U.S. military didn't know where the hell Hunter came from either—or at least they claimed they didn't. True, they'd recognized Hunter's special abilities in ending the war with Germany and now they relied on him very heavily in light of the new Japanese threat. But there was still a certain element who hadn't quite figured him out yet—something Hunter himself could sympathize with. He hadn't figured out a lot of things either.

One reoccurring event since he'd arrived here was an overwhelming feeling he had at times that the people he was talking to were vaguely familiar. He'd theorized these déjà vu-like events were leftovers from his previous life. It stood to reason that if he was here, then people that he recalled from his previous place would be here, too. Though just to what extent these familiar ones were his friends or enemies was sometimes pretty hazy, as well as where he had met them or why.

But again all this was top secret and he couldn't possibly

get into it with the TV reporter, as he wasn't even sure what was going on himself.

Thus his current dilemma.

"I really can't say very much about the subject," he tried again—but the woman wasn't letting go.

"Look, Major," she began slowly. "You are a hero. You are known to millions of people around the world. *Billions*, in fact. Even the Japanese have offered cautious praise for you. During the war with Germany, the Germans held a memorial service for you when they thought you were dead. They even gave you your nickname, the Sky Ghost.

"Now, you must see that with all these admirers, many people would be curious about your background. . . ."

Hunter was trapped. He looked over at Payne, who could only shrug back. Even he didn't know the circumstances of Hunter's arrival in this place. He only knew that those circumstances were highly classified.

"As I said," Hunter tried again, "the information you are asking me for is classified. I'd be committing treason if I told you."

"Classified?" the reporter huffed. "Your birthplace? Who your parents are? Your whereabouts before August 1997? Why would these things be top secret?"

Finally Payne spoke up.

"I believe the answer to that question is also top secret," he said, the absurdity of his statement slowly sinking in among those gathered. Even the technicians looked at him bemused.

Payne sought to recover.

"Look, Miss Kalloway," he began, "Major Hunter just returned from a long mission. I'm sure his mind is, well . . . in other places. Why not give him some time to get back to Earth, so to speak? Then we can all get together again real soon."

The newswoman frowned at this suggestion, but knew

it was one she would have to take, mainly because Hunter was already on his feet and leaving the room.

"OK, Major," she called after him. "But tomorrow morning. Bright and early. We begin again."

Thirteen

Night fell and the jungle beneath Xwo Mountain finally quieted down.

As always, several squads of Air Guards—the U.S. Air Corps's infantry division—went outside the LSD screen for their nightly patrols. Between these soldiers, the hundreds of electronic detection devices scattered about the mountain, and help from Xaxmax's extended family, as well as all the neighboring tribes, the mountain and the area around it were virtually impenetrable.

Any time any Japanese airplane came within 100 miles of Xwo, fighters were scrambled and the enemy was either shot down or chased away. After a while, the Japanese and their allies knew better than to approach the area from land or air. In many ways, Xwo Mountain was probably the safest place on the South American continent.

Still, every other night, whenever the sun went down and the jungle got quiet, Hawk Hunter would find a pang of concern begin to well up in his stomach. As the hours grew to midnight, this feeling would grow no matter what he was doing or where he was.

By 2300 hours, he would usually start walking down to the flight line, and this knot in his stomach would grow until it felt like it was the size of a small boulder.

There was a reason behind this seminocturnal bout of stress. The 2001st Fighter Squadron flew the Mustang-5s off Xwo. Twelve aircraft in all, the squadron was made up exclusively of women pilots.

Hunter had served with them during the last days of the war against Germany, first in Iceland, and later off one of the Navy's megacarriers. He'd gotten to know all of the female pilots, and had come to admire them greatly for their courage, skill, and openness.

The fact was, though, he'd come to know one of them very well.

She was Captain Sara James, the squadron's CO. She was smart, funny, and drop-dead gorgeous. A brunet with big blue eyes and lots of curves wrapped tight in a compact body, she and Hunter had grown close since their first meeting.

Very close. . . .

More than once they had broken regulations about officers sleeping together in a combat zone. But with Hunter's stealth skills being what they were, he'd yet to get caught sneaking in the window of her billet to spend the night or sneaking back out again before the crack of dawn. Their romance was not exactly a top secret though, despite all these high jinks. Sara served with eleven other women and, like men, they talked.

He cared for her deeply for many reasons. She was there during the coldest days of his service in Iceland, when he was battling the Germans with one hand and trying to figure out just who the hell he was with the other. She was with him during his rise to superhero status after the war. She stood beside him at every celebration, at every boring speech, at every boring party that followed. All this while never asking him a question about who he was, or why he seemed to be able to fly an airplane like no one else in this place.

She was a very important person in his life now. What's more, the skills of her squadron mates and their ability to adapt made them perfect for this strange mountaintop

duty. When Hunter requested they be assigned to the secret air base, the Air Corps heartily agreed. Their romance
simply went south of the border after that.

The problem was, Sara flew the midnight patrol mission three times a week, and it was this that caused the
stress bubble to grow in Hunter's stomach. Though he
knew she was a great pilot and tough as nails in the air,
Hunter was still afraid for her every night she went up.
He couldn't imagine what he would do if she went off
on a mission and didn't return. He would be lost without
her.

So he would walk down to the flight line every night she
was going up and help her do her preflight walkaround.
He wanted to make sure for himself that her plane was in
optimum condition to fly. If he didn't, and something happened, he knew he'd never be able to forgive himself.

This night, they met at her plane as usual and stole a
brief hug in the shadows. She was letting her hair grow
long and with each day she grew sexier, if that was possible.
The preflight went quickly and without a problem. Hunter
then accompanied her into the ready room.

"I hear a reporter has sunk her hooks into you," Sara
said, as she began climbing out of her duty overalls.

"I just don't get it," Hunter told her. "We're here, in a
top secret operation, and yet the press is here as well. I'm
not sure that's how it should be or how it was back . . ."

He caught himself before he blurted out the next sentence.

She stopped dressing for a moment and just looked over
at him. She knew exactly what he'd been about to say.

"Well, you should be used to talking to the press by
now," she said, changing the subject slightly. "I've seen
you give the same song and dance a hundred times my-
self."

But Hunter was only half listening to her. Instead he
was intently watching her dressing process. She had

slipped out of her duty overalls, wearing only underpants and a bra beneath. Then she'd slipped out of the bra, giving him an all-too-fleeting glimpse of her pert breasts. Finally she'd slipped into her skintight flight suit, zipping it up like a cocktail dress.

In all, the process took just twenty seconds or so, and Hunter had seen it many times before. But his breath never failed to catch in his throat when it happened.

She laced up her flight boots, grabbed her helmet, her survival pack, and her gun, a massive double-barrel Colt .45.

That's when Hunter's stomach began tossing at full throttle.

They embraced, as always, and kissed, once, twice, three times. It was a ritual now after three months, and again he was loath to break it. She'd come back every time since beginning it; he wasn't about to break that streak now.

He walked her back out to the flight line. The three other pilots going up with her were already in their cockpits warming their birds up.

They would be flying a patrol route which would take them 300 miles to the south, 250 miles to the east, and then back on the northwest line for about 400 miles. They would fly this route three times; the mission would take five hours. Barring any unforeseen circumstances, he would meet her for breakfast at 6 A.M.

She climbed into the cockpit and he helped strap her in. They kissed goodbye—again three times. Sara looked up at him and smiled.

"Listen, if that woman reporter is too hard on you," she said with a wink, "just leave her to me. I'll take care of her."

Hunter smiled, saluted, and went back down the ladder. He watched her taxi away; she was waving and smiling as if she were going no farther than the corner store for a quart of milk. Hunter felt his chest heave again. It was very strange. He'd only known her a short time, yet he felt like they'd been together for years.

The four black Mustang-5s roared off into the night, expertly slipping through the hole in the LSD screen. Hunter watched them disappear into the starry abyss. He checked his watch. It was five minutes past midnight.

Now the real waiting began.

Ten minutes later, Hunter had made his way up to the highest point on Xwo's peak, a place where the LSD screen gave way to the stars overhead.

There was a ledge here on which he could perch and watch the constellations march across the sky. This was where he usually wound up on a night Sara was on patrol.

It was usually his only time to think as well. *Really* think— about his present life as compared to his previous one. There were still many things he couldn't remember about the other place. He knew he was called the Wingman back there, and he remembered how he'd gotten that name and what battles big and small he'd fought in. But other things weren't so clear. He had a hard time remembering individuals, friends, lovers, enemies. This was especially frustrating considering the never-ending sense of déjà vu he experienced anytime he met a person he thought he might already know back in the other place.

This had happened twice for real so far. The first example was the man known here as Agent Y. He was an OSS officer, an intelligence agent who had engineered Hunter's assignment to Iceland from where he had led the air war against Germany. Back in the other place, Hunter knew Agent Y as Stan Yastrewski. In fact, "Yaz" and Hunter had fought many times together and were close friends "Back There."

The Yaz here and the one Back There were exact duplicates of each other, in physical description, age, and so on. They were exactly the same in temperament, courage, and professionalism, too. The only real difference was that in this world, Yaz was an OSS agent; Back There, he was a liaison officer for the United Americans.

Hunter and Agent Y had become good friends since the end of the war against Germany; in a way, Y was Hunter's guardian angel. The OSS agent knew that Hunter was an extremely valuable commodity on an almost cosmic level. It was his entry into the war against Germany which had provided the defining moment that turned the tide back in favor of the U.S. Y also knew that Hunter was from somewhere else, which for various reasons was highly classified information. So Y acted as Hunter's shield. Sure, the American people knew Hunter as a mysterious hero. But only Y and a very few others knew just *how* mysterious he was.

The other example was Captain PJ O'Malley of the 99th Bomber Squadron, one of two units presently operating off Xwo Mountain. Hunter had known O'Malley as "Captain Crunch" back in the other place, and, like Y, this man was in fact the same person. Back There, Crunch had also been a close friend of Hunter. He'd run an outfit called the Ace Wrecking Company, had fought many battles along with the United Americans and had drained just as many whiskey glasses with them too. In this place, Crunch was still hard drinking, still absolutely fearless. Except here, he was a superheavy bomber pilot. Back There, he flew fighters. Just like many things, the difference between Here and Back There was usually very small.

The reporter today looked fairly familiar to Hunter too, as had dozens of people he'd met since coming here. He just assumed these were people he might have had a passing acquaintance with Back There, and thus would cross paths with them infrequently here. Still, he couldn't help but feel a pang of regret when he thought about people who he'd been close to Back There and who he would *never* see again.

Unless, somehow, he got back home . . .

He shook these sad thoughts away, and looking back up into the heavens, tried to recall more from his previous existence. He knew he dropped into this place after detonating the string of nuclear bombs which diverted the comet from smashing into his old Earth. This meant he'd been in space, of course. But oddly enough, he couldn't really remember what it had been like up there. This was strange, because in his heart he felt a deep urge to fly in space. It was a dream, a vision—and Back There, he'd obviously done it. But, curse of curses, he could not remember any of it. Liftoff, orbiting, weightlessness—it was all a blank. His memory banks as far as space travel was concerned had been deleted, a particularly cruel joke that the cosmos had played on him.

What made it worse, there *was* no space travel in this world. No satellites, no high-velocity rockets, nothing. The decades-long World War II here had made the notion of spending money to travel in space both ridiculous and unthinkable. In fact, it just wasn't something the people here even had in their consciousness.

That's what fifty-eight years of constant war could do.

So Hunter could only stare at the stars and wonder what it had been like and what his lost memories had been.

He watched the stars spin across the sky for another two hours.

The concern he'd felt for Sara was still there, but it was gradually replaced by another emotion—one of growing relief that the long night would eventually end in a couple of hours, and that he was over the hump, and that he would see her again soon and that she would be safe.

He was just starting the climb down from the ledge when suddenly his body began shaking. He knew what it meant right away: An aircraft was approaching the base. His internal psychic-radar usually gave him advance warning of such things. But this wasn't an enemy aircraft coming in. The vibe was all wrong. Yet something about it gave him a tinge of dread.

He scrambled down from the peak just in time to see the faint red light approaching from the north. The noise arrived a second or two later. Engines misfiring, the sound of the air being chopped through. He watched as the LSD technicians opened a hole in the screen not at one end of the runways, but in the roof. This was not a fixed-wing aircraft that was coming in. It was one of the monstrous eight-rotor aircraft known as Beaters.

It came down through the LSD hole like a sack of bricks, standard landing profile for the ungainly thing, bouncing twice before settling down on solid earth. The crew immediately shut down all engines and the base ground personnel routinely hosed down a few of the aircraft's side-mounted engines, power plants which always seemed to be catching on fire.

The access ramp was lowered and Hunter saw the aircraft had only one passenger aboard.

It was Agent Y.

Hunter met him at the bottom of the ramp. They shook hands heartily. They hadn't seen each other in a couple of months.

"Hawk, how are you?" Y asked.

"Doing good," Hunter replied. "This is an unexpected visit, isn't it?"

They began walking away from the smoldering Beater.

"Unexpected and quick," Y replied. "Per order of our friends in Washington."

"I don't like the sound of that," Hunter said.

"See for yourself," Y said.

He handed Hunter a mission viewing pad, or MVP. This was a flat screen device about the size of a hardcover book. It had a six-inch-square screen on it surrounded by a series of buttons and dials. Animated films could be back-projected onto this small screen, either by inserting an insta-film cassette tape, or via radio waves sent from just about anywhere in the world. MVPs had about a million different uses. This was how many combat pilots were briefed on their upcoming missions. The MVP would contain all elements of the mission, play them out as little cartoons on the screen, and then go with the pilots as a kind of guiding light throughout. It was the same with Army officers in the field, and ships' captains at sea. The OSS in particular relied on the MVPs to keep their agents updated, in touch, and safe.

Hunter switched this one to Play and saw a map of South America materialize on the screen. Two-thirds of it was painted orange. The remaining part, Brazil and several smaller nearby countries, were painted blue.

Hunter knew exactly what the map meant.

"Brazil is finally coming into the war on our side," he told Y.

"Good guess," the agent replied. "Negotiations have been going on in Washington for two months, and they've reached what the diplomats call 'the fruitful stage.'"

"What's the timetable?"

Y shrugged. "Six weeks, maybe eight," he replied. "We began shipping them shitloads of stuff even before the secret talks started. They've got enough materiel now to field ten divisions. In a month that number will triple."

Hunter did the math. "Three hundred thousand guys—plus force of our own I assume?"

Y nodded. "We've got twenty divisions in an expeditionary force ready to sail. The Brits are sending five divisions. The Italians will do air support for the Brazilians. We might be looking at a pretty even-up situation down here in not too long."

Hunter had to agree.

"Interesting . . ." he said.

"Go to the next page," Y said, "if you want interesting."

Hunter found himself looking at a close-up picture of occupied South America. The mountain ranges were highlighted in topographic relief and there were blue cartoonish stars above six of them. Hunter pushed the Continue button. The cartoonish mission film then showed six of the peaks being flattened off and tiny airplanes arriving. Once in place, the airplanes took off again and began bombing dozens of sites all over Japanese-held South America. Little flames and plumes of smoke appearing above the targets boasted future successes.

Hunter smirked. MVPs always ran like this—like a cartoon. It was a strange way to get briefed. All that was missing was the music.

"The Air Corps figures they can have six more LSD-protected air bases operating down here inside of four weeks," Yaz explained. "Following your model here, they're very optimistic."

Hunter was getting mildly excited. Big things were happening in South America. The Japanese were already on the defensive. An invasion from Brazil, coupled with bomber strikes, carrier strikes, and insurgency actions could prove to be a hell of a fight, one the Americans and their allies just might win.

Hunter was glad that he was going to be a part of it.

But Yaz saw the look on his face and stopped walking. He took the MVP from the pilot and lowered his voice.

"I know exactly what you're thinking," he told Hunter, "so I'll just be straight with you: They're calling you back to the States."

Hunter shook his head, as if this would somehow unclog his ears. He had to have heard Y wrong.

"Excuse me?"

But Y looked too grim-faced to be kidding.

"It's true," the OSS agent told him. "They've got something for you up north. I have orders to bring you back."

Hunter was absolutely bowled over. Why in the world would they be recalling him now, just when things looked like they were about to pop in the U.S.'s favor?

Again, it was not hard for Y to read his mind.

"I don't know why, Hawk," he said. "And I couldn't tell you if I did. You're needed up north. That's all I know."

Hunter had to take a few moments before the news finally began sinking in. He looked around the base, and in a flash realized he'd actually miss it.

He checked his watch. Sara would be back in two hours. He'd have to tell her of course, hopefully spend some time with her, then he'd pack his things and check with the Super-A's ground crew and . . .

"OK," he told Y. "If I got to go, I can leave by noontime—or midafternoon would be better."

But Yaz was shaking his head. At that moment Hunter noticed that the Beater crew had never shut down their main power plants. Nothing was being unloaded or loaded onto the Octocopter. It was suddenly obvious the aircraft wasn't staying on the mountaintop for very long.

"We got to go now, Hawk," Y was telling him. "And I mean, *right now.*"

Now a new feeling came over Hunter. He was getting pissed.

"Wait a minute," he said with rare sternness. "I got loose ends to tie up here."

Y was shaking his head. "Sorry, man. No can do."

Hunter felt his temples flush. "These people in Washington. They realize I've been busting my ass down here for almost a year now? That I was eating snakes and bugs and wearing the same undersuit for six weeks at a time?"

Y was nodding. He was obviously in a bad position. On

the one hand, Hunter was his friend; on the other, he had his orders from the highest levels of the U.S. government.

"They all appreciate your contribution, Hawk," he replied. "Obviously they do. The whole upcoming air campaign is based on your work here. This counteroffensive would never be happening so soon if you hadn't done all the grunt work. And they know it."

"So?"

"So," Yaz went on slowly, "there's something maybe even bigger they want you to do. And to do it, we've got to go now. There's a rocket plane over in Brasilia that's already heating up its engines."

Hunter began to say something—but stopped. What was the use of arguing?

He felt the weight on his heart double in size. He'd have to leave his airplane behind. His colleagues. And Sara. He wouldn't even be able to say good-bye to her.

That hurt the most.

"We'll leave a message for her," Yaz said, reading his mind again. "Now . . . ?"

He indicated the waiting Beater.

Hunter just shrugged and together they started walking toward it.

Off in the distance he heard a jungle bird begin its morning song. The dawn was just an hour away; another day on the mountain would begin. And he wouldn't be here.

As it turned out, he would miss Sara by less than fifteen minutes.

Fourteen

The Beater flight over the predawn Peruvian jungle was, as always, a white-knuckle affair.

The Octocopter—any Octocopter—seemed to defy every major law of aerodynamics. It looked too big, flew too big, usually had a couple of engines out, or even in flames. It was gangly, loud, uncomfortable, slow, smelly, and forever unstable.

But it got the job done—at least this time. The light green hue of the Peruvian countryside gradually gave way to the dark emerald color of the Brazilian rain forests. The constant bucking and broncing and Hunter's deep funk prevented him from enjoying the scenery. He found himself checking his watch every few minutes and thinking, *She's just turning back to base now. She's just beginning her prelanding checks now.*

She's just landing . . . now.

Finally he just slumped deeper into his seat, and closed his eyes. Surprisingly enough, he fell asleep. He dreamed he lived on a farm, somewhere back in the U.S.

It was on the edge of a cliff. With a little house. And a hay field. And the great blue Atlantic beyond.

Brasilia was a city in the middle of the jungle.

It was a futuristic design, from the eyes of someone forty

years ago. Lots of strange-looking buildings, wacky statues, wide-open roadways. Stadiums. Weird globular structures that served little or no purpose. It was a place built to be people-friendly and was anything but.

The Beater swooped low over the center of the city and set down at the huge military air base on its eastern fringe.

Hunter and Y got off the noisy aircraft only to have their ears assaulted by the thunderous roar of jet engines. Gigantic unmarked C-919 Super Flying Boxcars were landing at the air base at a rate of one a minute, lugging in the materials of war for the upcoming Brazilian offensive. The staging area was thick with military equipment, from supertanks to artillery guns to rocket launchers to mountains of ammunition. There were also many troops in evidence. Brazilians, British, Dutch, Icelanders, and Americans. No one was wearing any insignia, though. Like the jumbo cargo planes, everyone was playing a game of deniability.

"Quite a show," Hunter told Y as they walked along the very busy tarmac. "Isn't anyone concerned that there might be a few eyes here in the employ of the Rising Sun?"

Y chuckled a little.

"There's more than a few, I'm sure," he replied. "But that's the point. It's no secret what's going on here. I mean the Japanese would have to be complete idiots *not* to know. It would be impossible to hide all this—plus everything that is happening at seven other bases like this. So why not let them know just how big the punch is going to be? It will just put them more on edge—or at least that's what Washington thinks."

They walked by a parking area containing no less than two dozen huge jets, each one belonging to a major network or media outlet. ABC, NBC, CNN, CBS, CNT were all there as well as many international services. There were many long-distance, insta-film signal senders in evidence, thicker than trees in a forest. Battalions of media pretty boys, all in freshly pressed camos, were strutting around like herds of roosters. So many technicians were moving, their numbers rivaled those of the combat troops.

"This will be the biggest story in a while," Hunter observed.

"Sure, if these guys can stay out of each other's way long enough to cover it," Y replied. "My personal opinion is most of them couldn't cover a fire."

Again Hunter felt like he'd been punched in the stomach. Even these weeny media guys would be closer to the action than he would.

It took them nearly thirty minutes to walk the length of the air base. Finally they reached the rocket plane station.

Hunter was still foggy on many things that existed back in his time, but he was fairly certain they didn't have a lot of rocket plane travel Back There. Quick travel by aircraft burning rocket fuel was fairly commonplace here.

These "R-planes" essentially were passenger carriers. They did not employ jet engines to fly, but rather rocket motors, which were fed a continuous, but finite amount of fuel, usually just enough to get from point A to point B. The rocket planes were inherently more dangerous to fly, especially with all that volatile rocket fuel aboard. But they were smoother, could fly higher—and most of all, much faster.

The X-1, the first aircraft to break the speed barrier back in Hunter's world, was a rocket plane. But after that, for whatever reason, the vast majority of airplane technology Back There had centered on the jet engine. Here, it was a little bit of both.

Hunter had ridden a few rocket planes since arriving in this world. He regarded them as oddities. They weren't especially maneuverable. They couldn't carry much in the way of weapons. Or carry much of anything at all. But there was one thing he couldn't argue with: They were usually the quickest way to get someplace. And in military situations, they were especially useful because they went so fast that no jet aircraft could keep up with them.

He and Y went through the pretenses of booking themselves onto the rocket plane. The rocketport was run by an air service company called Global Airways, a poor attempt at a front company for the OSS. The plane itself was roughly one-quarter the size of a gigantic B-17/36, still a substantial size. It had been painted to look like a regular cargo carrier, but it would fool absolutely no one who was looking for it.

Hunter and Y were both weighed and assigned a seat. The inside of the R-plane was small and cramped, not dissimilar to the Concorde SST. Hunter got a window seat, of course. There were only three other passengers on board, Air Corps officers all.

Y had a word with the pilots and then sank into the seat facing Hunter.

"We got about four thousand miles to go," he said, strapping in. "So if the winds hold true, our time to destination will be about fifty-five minutes. The pilots promise some interesting scenery about halfway through the jump."

Hunter sat back and looked out the window, thoughts of Sara and Xwo Mountain momentarily overwhelmed by the sheer excitement of the upcoming rocket jump.

He loved flying—any kind of flying. Every time he strapped in or belted down, the sheer joy that ran through his body was indescribable. Even if he was taking off on a combat mission—even a very hazardous one—he always felt that way. An almost orgasmic rush simply at the anticipation of flight. He couldn't have prevented this feeling if he'd tried. That's just the way he was.

After a few minutes, the doors were closed and the engines began to warm in the rear of the R-plane. Two seconds later they were moving very fast down a long rail which angled skywards at its terminus. Three seconds later they were going off this scoop, the increase in elevation being spiked by the first-stage solid fuel boosters being lit. Then the primary rocket motors kicked in and off they went.

They climbed, wickedly, and nearly straight up. Past 5,000, 10,000, 15,000 feet. The g-forces were pressing Hunter's body deep into his seat. His face distorted to the point of curling his eyelashes. Fighting to keep his eyes open, his mouth stretched back into a wide grin as he let this extremely pleasurable feeling wash through him.

The R-plane hit 30,000 feet, 40,000, 50,000, and still it climbed. The idea was to get as much elevation at the beginning of the flight as possible and then dump the booster rockets, turn the plane over, and use the liquid-fuel engine to power you through the thinner air to your destination.

Finally they topped out at a nose-bleeding 98,000 feet. All of it nearly straight up. They were barely seventy miles downrange at the end of two minutes. Finally the plane turned over, the boosters were discarded, and the primary liquid-fuel motors went throttle up.

That's when the real fun began.

Suddenly they were going just as fast but in a horizontal mode. The R-plane was doing Mach 3 at the turnover. Now it was passing Mach 4. Then Mach 5. Then Mach 6. Outside, the clouds seemed like water flowing past. The light blue of the Caribbean was soon in evidence. The pilots made a slight right-hand turn and now the top of South America could be seen.

Hunter checked his watch—they'd been up for only five minutes and already they were leaving South America behind.

Y leaned over and gave him the heads-up sign. The area the pilots had promised for some good sight-seeing was coming up.

A minute later they roared over the eastern edge of the Japanese-occupied Panama Canal zone.

Even though they were at 95,000 feet, Hunter could clearly see the Japanese construction crews still rebuilding after so many months what it had taken their bombers just minutes to destroy.

He could also see much military activity in evidence—at least a couple of dozen warships protecting this end of the canal, with at least a half dozen air bases ringing its edge.

But what was most interesting was that the pilots were flying right over enemy-held territory, and doing it so brazenly. Rocket planes were not at all stealthy. Whenever an R-plane went overhead, everyone on the ground below was well aware if it. They made a lot of noise, burned very hot on radar screens, and produced sonic booms that were simply tremendous.

So the Japanese knew American rocket planes were going over Panama and doing so on a routine basis. There was simply nothing they could do about it. They had no aircraft that could break Mach 2.5, never mind Mach 7 or 8. The R-plane pilots could routinely thumb their noses at the Japanese and there wasn't a damn thing the occupiers could do about it.

No surprise then that just about every Global Airways rocket plane jumping between South America and the States carried recon cameras in its nose.

Y leaned over to him.

"It's a great way to say *fuck you*, isn't it?" he asked Hunter.

Hunter watched as the last of the Japanese zone passed from view.

"Yeah," he replied. "I can't think of one any better."

They soon passed over Mexico, and then finally crossed the U.S. border.

It was uncharacteristically cloudy here, and the R-plane flew the last few minutes totally enveloped in clouds. When the visibility cleared again, the plane had slowed to a relatively poky 500 knots and was losing speed and altitude very quickly.

They were over a large city, but this was strange: Even though it was barely midmorning, the glare of neon lights below was startling, almost blinding.

Hunter stared down at the city in some disbelief. This place was the opposite of Brasilia, the place they'd just left. This place was *very* people-friendly. It was a collection of barrooms, eateries, saloons, dance halls, strip clubs, and what could only be brothels. The strange thing was that each building had a sign on its roof which loudly proclaimed whatever wares were available inside.

Some of these garish billboards featured huge TV screens, on which digital women danced naked above the vast urban sprawl. The streets below were alive with vehicles, crowded with people, and slightly above, traffic jams of sky bikes. Though it would have seemed like an impossibility, Hunter could have sworn he heard music rising up from this neon heaven below him.

It really was a very different place.

The rocket plane got lower and slowed even further. Now they passed over apartment buildings, again their roofs crowded with X-rated signs. They went over vast swimming pools, each one with an army of topless women sunbathing around it. They passed over dozens of street parties, and more saloons, and more brothels, and more swimming pools. . . .

Finally Hunter turned to Y and asked: "Where the hell are we?"

The OSS agent smiled.

"Boy, you really *are* from another place," he said. "Below us, my friend, is the city of Dallas, Texas."

Fifteen

The rocket plane finally set down and Hunter and Y quickly deplaned.

The airport, called Love Field, was actually in Fort Worth, right next door to Dallas. It was an enormous place, bustling and incredibly crowded. Y and Hunter made their way through the throng, Hunter embarrassingly obliging several people who recognized him with some quick autographs.

Finally they made it to the curb, where Y was able to hail a jeepster cab. The driver squealed to a stop, Y and Hunter quickly climbed in, and the cab squealed away again.

Y had been consulting his MVP throughout the trip, constantly receiving updated instructions on the handheld screened device. This was for security reasons. Wherever he and Hunter were headed, it was so secret, the OSS brass in Washington were taking them one step at a time. Plus, as Y had pointed out to Hunter several times, OSS agents were always prime targets for assassins. The Japanese were known to have several hit squads roaming the U.S., looking for OSS and top-level military people to kill, just as the OSS had agents in Japan and occupied South America, looking to whack high-level Nipponese officials.

So security, both for the upcoming mission and personal safety, had to be at a maximum. That's why Y's instructions were being doled out to him just a little at a time. The reasoning was, if he didn't know where he was going, how could a potential assassin?

So far, the MVP had brought them from Brasilia to Dallas. Now Y asked it what they should do next.

The instructions came back with the address of a hotel in downtown Dallas, where they were to check in. After that, they were to "AFI,"—"await further instructions."

Y yelled the address to the cabdriver, who nodded and made his way out of the airport. The cab was very long and black and had its convertible top down. Its driver was a stone-cold silent type, hat and sunglasses hiding most of his features. He seemed to have trouble lighting his cigarettes.

The trip toward the center of the city quickly turned into a real slow-boat affair. Apparently there was a never-ending street party going on in Dallas. People were simply everywhere—on the streets, on the sidewalks, in the alleys. It made driving extremely slow.

The big limo wound its way through the celebrating, the drinking, the carousing. Past the hoariest of whorehouses, the loudest of dance halls, and the largest barrooms Hunter could ever imagine. Their cab was soon caught up in a traffic jam of limo cabs, all of them black, all of them with convertible tops down, and all of them going painfully slow.

Rarely moving at more than ten miles per hour, this was closer to what Hunter recalled of New Orleans during Mardi Gras. Actually, what was happening here made Mardi Gras look like a kids' birthday party.

They reached an intersection that was only slightly less busy and congested. Here the parade of limos came to a complete stop. The driver in the lead car got out and talked to a pair of policemen standing on the corner. Quite brazenly, the limo driver pulled a few bills from his pocket and handed them to the cops. Then he ran back to his car.

The policemen climbed onto their motorcycles and fired up their engines. All of the limo drivers put their cars in gear and got ready. It was obvious they'd been through this drill before.

The motorcycle cops pulled out in front of the cabbies and then with the wail of their sirens, took off in a screech of smoke and rubber. All the limo drivers did the same, and soon the string of cabs was gaining speed very quickly. This was good old police work, Texas style. A few bucks in the right palm, and boom!

With a high-pitched wail cutting a path through the partygoers on Main Street and then Delmont, the twelve convertible limousines now had a police escort to downtown Dallas.

The partygoers had seen this type of thing before too.

Whenever the wail of the motorcycle sirens first appeared, the boozy citizenry would scramble to either side of the street and wait for the police escort and its entourage to plow through. Once the people got to the curb, they would usually wave wildly as the police and their special party roared by, and then retake the street and resume their revelry. Hunter saw hundreds of people lining both sides of the street, waving and cheering wildly. Many of the other passengers in the other limos were waving back to them, as if they were heads of state ceremoniously waving back to the peasantry.

Hunter and Y just sat back and enjoyed the ride. It was a bright blue November day in Dallas. The crowds seemed very happy, if spirited.

"Is it like this all the time?" Hunter yelled over to Y.

"It can get worse," Y yelled back.

But Hunter really wasn't sure what he meant.

Up ahead the motorcycle cops had decided to take a right hand turn toward Congress. The parade of limos slowed down a little bit as each wide-body car had to make the turn at less than top speed.

This brought the caravan past a few buildings, then to another left turn, which would carry them by a grassy knoll, under a railroad overpass and then onto the freeway. It would be much quicker traveling up there.

The limo that Y and Hunter were traveling in made the left very slowly, but now was picking up speed again. There were fewer people standing on the sides of the road here, but those that were, were waving enthusiastically. Some were even taking pictures.

They were just passing the grassy knoll when Hunter turned to say something to Y. But before he could say a word, there was a loud *pop! pop! pop!*

And then everything went into a freeze.

This sort of thing had happened several times to Hunter since arriving in this new world. He wasn't sure what had caused it exactly, or under what circumstances this sensation came over him. But to his eyes, strange as it seemed, everything appeared to stand still.

He looked over at Y, who was looking back at him, absolute horror in his eyes. His head had been blown apart and he was actually holding a bloody piece of his own skull in his hands. He was staring over at Hunter as if to say *why?*

Blood was everywhere. And yellow gelatin-like matter too. Then Hunter could hear screams, and maybe a few more pops. And then . . .

And then, Hunter blinked and everything went back to normal. Yaz's head was back in one piece. There was no blood, and the limo driver had finally lit his cigarette with his very noisy butane lighter.

Hunter felt one last quake go through him then he relaxed again. Y saw that his eyes had just come back from some faraway place; he actually asked if Hunter was OK.

The pilot replied in the affirmative and then asked Y: "Do you like politics?"

The agent thought for only a half second.

"Hate it and love it," he replied as the car roared under the overpass. "I've actually thought of running for something someday. Why?"

Hunter considered this for a moment and then just shook his head.

"Take my advice," he told Y. "Don't ever run for President."

They finally reached downtown Dallas and the parade of limos dispersed. The police went on their way and the twelve limos headed in twelve different directions.

Y was consulting his MVP again and directing the driver which way to go. The crowds were no less numerous down here, traffic was simply moving better because the streets were wider.

Finally their cab arrived in front of what had to be the largest brothel/saloon/casino complex in the whole wide world. It was six blocks long, four deep, with several huge marquees and a gigantic TV screen on its roof displaying dozens of images of beautiful naked women dancing. The neon glare from this sign alone was so blinding Hunter yearned for sunglasses.

The name of the place was *Happy Valley*.

"You sure about this place?" he asked Y. "Not exactly the subtlety I expected."

Y rechecked the MVP and confirmed the address.

"Yep, this is it," he declared. "Our home, for a little while anyway. Those are my orders."

Ten minutes later, Hunter was sitting in a room on the twenty-sixth floor. The place was clean, not too small, and, thank God, soundproofed.

The entire casino/brothel mall was actually first-rate.

The first two floors were devoted entirely to gambling; floors three through six could only be described as a department store of sex. Anything could be had for a price. From the seventh floor up, the place resembled a four-star hotel. And the staff was superb. They were all female, all built for action, and all just dripping with Texas charm.

Happy Valley was as far away from Xwo Mountain as one could get. Maybe that was the point, Hunter thought, looking out the window at the ocean of neon beyond. Deep inside, a small voice was telling him this might be a sort of planned distraction, a way to allow him to decompress before whatever was about to happen happened. Or maybe the OSS just fucked up and booked them into the wrong place. Either way, as far as their quarters were concerned, they would have little to complain about.

There was a bundle of clean clothes and toiletry items waiting for him, courtesy of the OSS he guessed. Hunter showered, shaved, and climbed into the new duds. It was an all-black combat suit, freshly starched and pressed, with a baseball cap, a pair of spiffy new combat boots, and cool sunglasses for keeping somewhat anonymous. Everything fit Hunter perfectly, making him think that maybe being at Happy Valley was not a mistake after all. Once dressed, he realized he was famished, and thirsty as well. A moment later the phone rang. It was Y. He had read his mind again. He was ready for chow too.

Hunter met Y in the casino ten minutes later. The agent was standing near a blackjack table, one fifty-dollar chip in hand.

"I've got to get some funds," Y told Hunter.

With that he walked over to the blackjack table and sat down. Hunter scanned the table. There were four other players; each with a huge stack of fifty-dollar chips in front of them. The stakes at the table were very high.

"You any good at this?" Hunter asked Y.

"Never played it before in my life," the agent whispered back. "But this is what the MVP told me to do."

Y threw in his single chip ante and the dealer began dealing. The OSS agent was soon looking at a pair of sevens.

"Double up?" the dealer asked Y, but the agent just shook his head. Instead he told the dealer to hit him.

The dealer dealt—it was another seven. Y had just doubled his money.

The dealer dealt again. Y was now looking at the king of hearts and the nine of spades, a total of nineteen. Common sense dictated that Y should stay pat. But he pushed his second chip forward, betting a total of one hundred dollars.

"Hit," he said.

There was a chuckle from the other players; the dealer arched his right eyebrow. He threw the next card.

It was the two of diamonds. Y had just doubled his winnings again.

It went this way for the next ten minutes. No matter what hand Y was dealt, he always called for the third hit and he hit twenty-one every time.

Finally he stopped, at $2000. He collected his chips, tipped the dealer, and cashed in. As he stood counting out the bills, Hunter wondered exactly what he'd just seen. Was Y so incredibly lucky that he could hit on nineteen and win? Or had the OSS somehow rigged the game? Both choices seemed highly improbable, if not impossible. What was the truth then? Hunter didn't know, and part of him believed that Y did not know either.

"I guess you're buying the drinks tonight," Hunter finally told him, as the agent stashed the bills into his wallet.

"I guess I am," Y mumbled in reply.

* * *

They hopped into a jeepster cab and headed for the south side of town.

According to the Happy Valley doorman, this was the best place in the hectic city to grab a meal and a drink in relative peace.

Their cab got into a traffic jam almost immediately, and their progress became agonizingly slow in short order. As with their ride in from the airport, the streets were filled with people partying, and, Hunter was realizing, many street entertainers. They passed musicians, magicians, jugglers, dancers, and people hawking everything from moonshine to machine guns. More than once, Hunter saw someone getting their palm read by curbside fortune-tellers.

Their cab eventually reached an intersection where an enormous sports stadium was located. Literally thousands of people were pouring into this place. Like everything else here in Dallas, it was huge. It reminded Hunter of one of the Navy's megacarriers. The mile-long ships were so high, it was impossible to see their decks from dockside. This stadium obviously housed something sports-related, but Hunter had no idea what it was.

As seemed to be the case always, Y read his mind.

"It's the new Dallas Cowboys stadium," he told Hunter as the cab crept by. "The pro football team. They're the biggest thing in Texas. Have been for years."

Hunter studied the sheer size of the stadium. The enormity of the place, plus the crowds and the hoopla surrounding it, caused him to ask Y an odd question.

"Do they play in there twenty-four hours a day, seven days a week?"

Y looked at him like he was nuts.

"What are you asking me?"

"Do they play a football game that just goes on forever and ever and people can bet each quarter?" Hunter was saying, the words coming out of his mouth almost involuntarily. "You know, like a nonstop game, day and night? Three hundred and sixty-five days a year?"

Y just stared back at him.

"Are you crazy?" he finally replied. "They play four quarters of fifteen minutes each. It takes three hours, tops."

Then he lowered his voice.

"Why would you have a crazy notion like that?" he asked Hunter. "Is that how they play football back . . . well, back wherever you're from?"

Hunter looked up at the huge stadium and finally just shook his head.

"I don't know," he said finally. "Maybe . . ."

They wound up at a place called the Tip Top Club.

It was a relatively subdued establishment, a private club located in a slightly more upscale part of town.

Hunter and Y walked in and no sooner had they ordered a drink from the bar than two blonds attached themselves to them. Both were tall, buxom, beautiful, and dressed to kill. "SuperBlonds" in the local vernacular.

They chatted with the girls and drank some fine bourbon, but the timing was just a tad early. Hunter wanted to talk to Y about their upcoming secret mission, something that would be impossible to do in front of the two gals.

With Hunter's urging, Y gave the bartender a small stack of bills and told him to keep the girls watered.

Then he and Hunter retreated to a corner table. Soon enough, Hunter was looking at a steak that seemed the size of an entire cow. A giant goblet of red whiskey was set beside his plate. It was more food and booze than Hunter had seen in nearly a year.

Y needed no prompting, he dug right into his slab of meat. Hunter did too, and soon he was trying to talk between mouthfuls of prime steer and gulps of Kentucky mash.

"I know you can't reveal anything to me," he said to Y. "But can't you give me a hint as to what's up? You know, 'off the record?' "

" 'Off the record' or 'on the record,' they'd still shoot me if I told you," Y replied. "That's if I knew anything—and I swear I don't. But I think we can deduce a few things."

"Such as?" Hunter asked with his next mouthful.

"Well, I think whatever it is would have to be some kind of airborne mission," Y said. "That's your forte."

"Let's hope so anyway," Hunter told him.

"And some people in the War Office—the few enlightened ones—realize that you should be used only in the most critical situations."

"Nothing like adding to the load," Hunter said, swigging his drink.

Y shrugged. "Would you rather sit on the sidelines?" he asked the pilot. "I mean, the War Department has many secret weapons at their disposal. God knows what kind of airplanes, ships, rifles, rockets they are working on. But you are a secret weapon, too. A *human* secret weapon. So at the very least, they understand that everything you do should be high priority. So I think we can be reasonably sure it will be a high-priority airborne sort of thing."

Hunter considered this and filed it away. Then he brought up a topic he'd been reluctant to ask Y for many reasons.

"Have you ever seen anything or talked to anyone at that country club of yours that has any idea how I dropped into this world?"

Y stopped his vigorous chewing for a quick moment. Still he betrayed a small secret.

"Not exactly," he replied slowly, trying to cover his tracks with a sip of whiskey.

Hunter smirked. "You mean no? Or not exactly? Or they'll shoot you if you tell me?"

Y never stopped chewing.

"Two out of three," he said.

Hunter downed another huge bite of beef. It was tender, flavorful, intoxicating.

"Look," he began again. "Let *me* go off the record: While I try to keep all things in perspective, I have to say that I can't be accused of not putting my butt on the line when needed, correct?"

Y just nodded. "Correct."

"And I have helped the cause for a country that I'm sure is like mine, but isn't exactly . . . right?"

Again the OSS man just nodded and continued chewing.

"So if there was some secret project somewhere delving into all this stuff," Hunter said, "don't you think I could be at least prebriefed on it?"

Finally Y looked up and stopped chewing.

"Again, let's use our powers of deduction," he said. "If such a project existed—and I'm not saying it does—but if it did, you could see how it would have to be the deepest, darkest secret this government could keep. I mean—where *did* you come from? Are you from outer space? Are you from another dimension? Another universe? You don't even know yourself. It's just as fundamental a question as anyone with a normal life could ask themselves—and still come up empty."

"You make it sound almost Biblical in proportions," Hunter told him.

"And do you blame me? It's almost the question of 'what is life' itself."

Hunter had to agree.

"Now such a project would have to be extremely top secret," Y went on. "However, if it existed, and if these theoretical scientists were going to want to ask someone some questions—I think it would be you on the top of their list, don't you?"

Hunter shrugged.

"Sure . . . I guess," Hunter replied. "Are you telling me I should wait for a phone call or a bolt out of the blue? I mean theoretically, if I'm all classified as well, how would these scientists know I was even here?"

Y stopped chewing again just for a second. But now it was time to smile.

"They know," he replied.

And that was all he would ever say on the subject again.

They finished their meals, polished off the whiskey, and linked back up with the pair of SuperBlonds.

The night then turned into one long march from one bar to another. Large quantities of alcohol were consumed. More food was inhaled around midnight, and again at three. Somewhere along the way, they lost sight of the SuperBlonds, only to meet up with a pair of SuperRedheads. When they got lost, the SuperBlonds somehow found them again. At least Hunter thought they were the same two gals. He wasn't sure. After a while, it all became one big blur.

When Hunter woke up the next morning, there was one of each in his room. Half expecting a message from Y that they would be leaving that day, Hunter shooed the girls out and quickly cleaned up.

But no such message came. Y monitored his MVP all that day as they lay recovering next to the vast swimming pool, but no orders appeared. They ate dinner that night and drank cautiously. But again, there was no word from Washington.

As it turned out, Hunter and the OSS agent were planted in Dallas for a week. Seven days of sleeping late, by the pool, eating dinner, meeting girls, and then drinking the night away.

Slowly the memories of South America began to fade. All but those of Sara. . . .

The adventure was funded in a very curious way: through Y's gambling. Every morning the OSS man would hit the same blackjack table and play exactly seven hands. He would bet outrageously, he would take outrageous hits—and he would win every time. Always in the area of $2500, always in less than ten minutes. It never failed.

Was it a fix? Or was Y just incredibly lucky? Did the MVP, which ordered Y to gather their spending money this way that first day, know something they didn't?

Hunter never asked and Y never offered any further explanation.

So it was six days of booze, women, and great food. Hunter couldn't help but enjoy himself. He found himself sleeping eight hours a day for what felt like the first time in his life.

But no matter how much partying they did, he always managed to steal a few moments to go up to the roof of the Happy Valley, away from the storm of neon waves, and look to the southeast. He imagined he could see Xwo Mountain from here, and depending on the time, he knew Sara was either sleeping, or doing combat reports, or just returning from night patrol. He hoped she was safe, and that she understood.

On the fifth night, after he'd just completed this ritual and had already turned to go, he found himself looking off toward the northeast. He stayed frozen in that position for the longest time, a strange feeling washing over him. He suddenly had the notion that someone—someone he cared about very deeply—was way off in that direct as well.

Someone warm. Someone beautiful.
Who was she?

On the sixth night, something *really* strange happened.

Hunter and Y were out on the town as usual, bar-hopping the exclusive gin joints on the south side of Dallas.

They were crossing the street, moving from one place to another, when Hunter felt a tug on his arm.

He spun around, expecting yet another admirer asking for yet another autograph. He'd given out many in the past six days.

But this was not a fan waiting for him. Not a typical one, anyway. It was a woman, she was probably in her midtwenties, attractive, but with a definite air of mystery about her.

The first thing Hunter noticed after her looks was her perfume. It was sweet, earthy, pungent. Hunter would not soon forget that smell. Her clothes were odd. Long skirt, loose blouse, big hoop earrings, a bandanna on her head.

"Read your palm?" she asked him.

That's when Hunter's alcohol-soaked brain put things together. She was a street performer, a psychic.

Hunter just shook his head. He didn't really believe in that stuff. At least, he didn't think he did.

"No thanks," he said politely, bolting across the street in Y's wake. "It would be a waste of time."

"But you need it," she called after him, but Hunter barely heard her above the noise.

He and Y drank another place dry and moved on to a strip club in the company of two more SuperBlonds. This place was actually closer to the center of town; the cab ride took about thirty minutes to go ten miles. Leaving this place an hour or so later, Hunter was surprised to run into the same female psychic. She seemed very far away from where he'd first seen her.

"I think you should reconsider," she told him after pulling him aside again. "I think you should know what awaits you."

Hunter gave her a good look this time—and felt a jolt go through him.

Damn—that very familiar feeling of déjà vu began washing over him. He stared at her. Pretty face. Long brown hair. Big brown eyes. Almost academic-looking.

"Do I know you . . . ?" he heard himself ask her in a mumble.

But then, he felt himself being dragged away—this time by two more females he and Y had met.

By the time Hunter was able to turn back toward the psychic, she was gone, lost in the perpetually crowded street.

That night continued as had the previous five. More drinks, more food, more trafficking with SuperBlonds.

But Hunter saw the psychic again. He was going into his hotel just about dawn when he spotted her standing in the crowd out front, staring at him. Her eyes seemed to burn a hole right through him.

That feeling would stay with him a long time as well.

On the morning of their seventh day in Dallas, there was a knock on Hunter's door.

The two showgirls who had stayed over answered the door just as they were leaving.

It was Y. Two girls were just leaving his room across the hall as well.

Hunter was in the process of washing his face when the OSS agent came in.

"Where's breakfast today?" Hunter asked him.

"At the airport coffee shop," the agent replied.

Hunter stopped in mid splash.

"You got the orders?" he asked.

Y was looking at his MVP and nodding.

"Sure do," he replied.

Hunter dried his face.

"Where are we going?"

Y shook his head. "Still can't tell you," he replied. "We just have to be out at the airport inside thirty minutes. We better hop-hop."

Hunter told him he'd meet him downstairs in five minutes. The OSS man left and Hunter took a quick shower, jumped into some clean clothes, gathered his meager belongings, and left, leaving his last fifty bucks behind for the maid.

He took the slow elevator down to the first floor, where he expected to join Y at his favorite gaming table. Instead, he found someone else was waiting for him.

It was the psychic.

"You really should see what awaits you," she told him. "Many consequences hang in the balance."

Hunter couldn't take his eyes off her now. He *knew* her just as sure as he knew he knew Yaz and Crunch O'Malley. He just couldn't recall her name, or how he had known her.

Finally he decided to submit.

"OK," he said, holding out his palm. "Read it. What do you see?"

She took his hand and rubbed it. But she never took her eyes off his.

"You will soon be very cold," she began, slowly, in a whispered voice. "A loved one will surprise you. You will meet old friends again. They will build something to come apart. You will fight a stupid enemy. You will fly that way and this, and this way and that. Then . . . you will be asked to die."

Hunter felt a chill go through him. The woman was very

pretty, but there was insanity in her eyes. He was so entranced by her, he'd barely heard what she had said.

"What's your name?" he asked her.

She smiled. "My name? You know me," she finally replied. "It's Elizabeth. Elizabeth Sandlake."

Then she laughed, turned around, and disappeared into the crowd, leaving Hunter frozen to the spot, staring blankly at his hand.

Hunter eventually found Y leaning over his favorite twenty-one table.

He came up beside him just as the dealer was laying out the seven of hearts and the five of clubs before him. Y had a small pile of chips in front of him, three hundred dollars left over from the night before.

He told the dealer to give him a hit. The dealer complied—and the King of Spades flew out of the deck and landed atop the two previous cards. Seven and five and ten make twenty-two.

Y went bust. For the first time in seven days.

He looked up at Hunter, his face partially drained of color.

"Not a good way to start the day," he said.

Sixteen

Hunter and Y got to the airport in time and began searching for their assigned departure gate.

It was located at the far end of Love Field, Gate 99, a place isolated from just about everything else. And what they found was not a typical passenger terminal but a storage barn for Global Airways, the poorly concealed front company for the OSS.

Both Hunter and Y groaned upon arrival as they saw a Beater was being pulled out of the hangar for them.

"Do we *always* have to fly in these things?" Hunter asked the OSS man, his exasperation finally breaking out.

Y was not happy about it either. But he was checking with his MVP, which was now absolutely burning with information after seven days of virtual silence.

The screen was filled with instructions as to what they had to do next. Apparently travel by the Beater was mandatory.

"I guess where we are going," Y said, "this is the only way to get there."

They took off thirty minutes later, the Octocopter fighting its way into the air, as they all did, with a disturbing clanking sound.

Once it reached a shaky altitude of 2,500 feet, they

turned northwest and began crawling through the low clouds. Hunter and Y strapped down in the forward observation compartment, and were soon fighting off nausea from the engine fumes and the sudden shifts in altitude.

Over the saloons, over the brothels, and over the casinos they flew. Hunter looked down at the party capital of the world and felt a slight tug in his chest.

Something told him that wherever he was going, it would not be one-millionth as exciting as Dallas had been.

It would be a while before he realized how wrong he was.

The Beater flew on for what seemed like hours.

Hopping over mountains, skirting valleys, jumping across entire deserts. Hunter dozed most of the way, his face pressed up against the chopper's forward observation window, as if he was trying to sleep and watch the earth go by beneath him at the same time.

The trip lasted six long hours. When Hunter finally woke again, Y was nudging him with a cup of coffee. He wiped the sleep from his eyes and looked out at what he'd been missing.

They were still over a desert; Hunter recognized the slightly red tinge to the sand and dust as being indicative of Nevada.

"Good guess," Yaz told him, routinely reading his mind.

The Beater came up and over one particularly barren mountain range and before them was a vast valley, white as salt. The heat was rising off the desert floor, distorting everything into wavy liquid lines. It looked like a huge lake in the middle of nowhere.

But Hunter could see through this mirage. And what he saw was a collection of low, white buildings located next to a series of mammoth runways. There was nothing else around for miles. By its sheer isolation it was obvious this was a very secret place.

The Beater took another fifteen minutes to slow down, hover, plunge a few terrifying feet, right itself, hover again, and finally set down, with a spine-jarring bump. Hunter just shook his head as he climbed out of the beast. Why the hell did people insist on flying in these pieces of crap?

He and Y left the Beater crew to hose down their smoldering engines and began walking toward the cluster of buildings about a quarter of a mile away. A jeepster approached, squealing to a stop in front of them. A man in a plain, unmarked uniform was at the wheel. He introduced himself as the security officer for the base, then he and Y exchanged clearance information. Once everything was checked out, Hunter and Y climbed into the jeepster and the officer squealed away.

Soon they were speeding along the rock-hard white surface, leaving a storm of white dust in their wake. The officer passed Y a book full of codes and a map. The codes were the electronic combinations for all the doors on all the hangars at the secret base; the map showed where everything was.

In effect, the man was giving Y free run of the place. Not that there was much happening here. Tumbleweeds had literally gathered on the massive runways. Everything looked slightly overgrown. Y expressed surprise at this.

"Where is everybody?" he asked the security man.

"Most of the people stationed here have been called to active duty," the officer replied. The jeepster's accelerator was pressed all the way to the floorboard by now. "As for everyone else, we were told to give them the day off."

They arrived at the cluster of buildings. Hunter and Y climbed out and thanked the man for the ride.

"Let me know if you need anything," he said with a salute.

They returned the salute and the jeepster squealed away, leaving them in a tiny storm of the powdery sand.

Hunter and Y dusted themselves off and studied their new surroundings.

"So, is this place familiar to you at all?" Y asked him.

Hunter scanned everything. The buildings. The mountains. The obvious top secret status. But most of all, it was those big runways. There were five of them, all were very, very long.

Then it hit him. Of course he knew this place. Back in his world, it was supposedly the most secret air base in the world.

"Area 51," Hunter blurted out. "Groom Lake . . ."

Y laughed.

"As usual, you're right, but all wrong," he said.

He pointed to a sign hanging on the side of a nearby administration building.

It read: "U.S. Air Corps. Bride Lake. Area 52."

Hunter laughed too.

At least the cosmos had a sense of humor.

There were six streets in all. Most were lined with hangars and support buildings. Several bore pump houses, radio receivers, and long-range radar stations. In an odd way, the alignment of the streets and buildings was similar to the air base up in Iceland from which Hunter had fought the war against Germany, a place nicknamed "Dreamland." That too had been a secret place of sorts.

Y consulted the map, then punched a few things into his ever-present MVP. A message was soon beamed back to him: *Proceed to Hangar #19.*

It was about a two-minute walk to the designated air barn. Y had a little trouble at first punching the long combination number into the electronic lock, but eventually he got the access door to spring open. He and Hunter stepped inside.

Hangar #19 wasn't too big, but it had high walls and a high ceiling. It was also very dark inside. Hunter took a deep sniff. Aviation gas. Oil. Hydraulics fluid. Spilled coffee. Just like every other hangar he'd ever been into. The thickness of the combined odor told him there were about half a dozen airplanes in here.

Y somehow found the lights. He flicked the switch and suddenly Hunter was looking at a room full of aircraft. There *were* six of them and they were stacked wing to wing in such a way that there was very little room to move about.

And what strange airplanes they were!

"A couple of these were actually built more than ten years ago," Y said consulting the MVP. "The others much more recently. One thing they did here at Area 52 was test new aircraft designs. A few of these airplanes were being evaluated when everyone left to go fight against Germany. Then the others were being tested when the war with Japan broke out. So now, here they sit."

One airplane looked to Hunter to be a cross between an old prop fighter he recalled as being named the P-39 Aerocobra, and a much more updated design for a swing-wing attack jet. The result was a big and bulky, complicated-looking airplane, one that managed to look fast and slow at the same time. Its name, painted on its side in fancy lettering, was Z-5.

"Did this thing ever really fly?" Hunter asked Y.

Y checked the MVP.

"Yep," he replied. "Exactly twice. Both times it clocked in at more than 2,200 miles an hour."

Hunter just shook his head. That was more than Mach 3, yet the airplane itself looked like a flying can of crap. Even Y noticed that.

"Think it's still airworthy?" he asked Hunter.

Hunter just shrugged.

"I hope I don't have to find out," he replied under his breath.

Two more planes nearby were even odder. They were very small, diminutive, no bigger than a jeepster. No tail wing, barely a bubble for the canopy. Yet they were jet fighters, with wings loaded down by air-to-ground rockets, and three cannon muzzles sticking from the nose cone.

"Flying hot rods," Y said. "Official name Z-4 Bantams. Old-timers here. They were one of the original Z-planes."

"Z-planes?" Hunter asked.

"Sure," Y replied. "You know, that's the designation given to planes that are prototypes. Experimental planes. . . ."

Hunter scratched his head.

"Yes, but why wouldn't you call them X-planes then?"

Y thought for a moment.

"I don't know," he finally replied. "Never occurred to anyone, I guess."

They moved on.

The next four airplanes were very eye-catching. They were smallish, and at first glance, of simple design. Wings, fuselage, normal tail. But their two engines were lined up on either side of the nose, almost parallel with the cockpit. What Hunter quickly realized was that these were actually movable jet nozzles. They were attached to a pivot which could swing down and provide the jet with a powerful blast toward the ground.

"VTOL aircraft?" Hunter exclaimed. "Very cool."

Y checked his MVP.

"They can take off vertically and fly horizontally," he said reading a designation statement. "Is that what a VTOL is?"

But Hunter didn't reply. It was not out of rudeness; he was simply too fascinated with these bizarre aircraft. Like a lot of things in this world, they looked both old and new at the same time. They weren't fighters; they were too gangling and unstreamlined for that. They were perfect insurgency airplanes. Ground supporters. Mudmovers. Things for which the VTOL aspect was ideal.

The sixth and final plane might have been the most unusual of all. It was bigger that the rest of the others combined. Very long wings—so long they drooped to the hangar floor. Otherwise the plane was normal, or as normal as one in this strange world could be.

"That is a Z-16, prototype for an ultralong-range recon plane," Y explained, via the MVP. "Apparently it's absolutely crammed full of long-range navigation gear. The idea was to fly it high over one spot for days at a time and take pictures of the bad guys."

"Interesting stuff," Hunter said after they finally reached the other side of the hangar. "Unusual, too."

Y looked back at the strange gang of airplanes. "That's an understatement, I think," he said.

"But now," Hunter continued. "The question is, what are we supposed to do with all this stuff?"

"Let me find out," Y said.

He immediately clicked on his MVP. Another screen appeared and Y read it with a shrug.

"It's telling us to proceed to another area," he reported. "Not here at Bride Lake. Somewhere farther out in the desert. This thing says the answer will be out there."

They got ahold of a jeepster and, using directions provided by the MVP, started driving north.

They were soon roaring down a barely paved roadway marked Highway 6. For the next thirty minutes, the road carried them through miles of open desert, around several buttes, and through a few dry washes. Then they went up and over a small mountain. On the other side, off in the distance, they could see their destination: an enormous hangar nuzzled into the side of a blind canyon. The jagged ledges above it made it nearly impossible to see from just about any direction save south.

It was the perfect place to hide something. Something very big.

They made for this place, per instructions from the MVP. But Hunter soon realized that the long, straight-as-an-arrow road they'd picked up at the bottom of the mountain was actually not a road at all. It was a runway. One that was at least ten miles long and ended at the front gate to the huge hangar.

"If whatever is in that barn needs ten miles to take off, I don't even want to see it," Hunter said.

"This time I tend to agree with you," Y replied, looking at the MVP. "But that's exactly what we've been told to do."

They finally reached the main gate, where they were met by a pair of sentries. These men were attached to the Air Guards, the Air Corps's infantry wing. They were a bit surprised to see them.

"Are you lost, sir?" one asked Y. "We don't get many visitors out here."

Y showed his OSS pass plus one for Hunter and then displayed his orders on the MVP screen. The sentries saluted and they were waved in. Up close, the hangar looked like a gigantic cigarette box. No windows. Two doors. Another pair of guards was stationed at the front door. They too checked their passes and the MVP orders and directed them to a small parking area. Here they left the jeepster.

Y punched the combination into the hangar's side-access door and this time it opened on the first try. He and Hunter stepped inside, closing the door behind them. The inside of the barn was cold, dark, and extremely dusty. The sentry had been right. This place didn't get many visitors. Judging by the musty odor, it seemed like no one had been inside the hangar in years.

They walked into the main room and Y somehow found

the light switch. Like before, he fumbled a bit and then finally turned it on. The lights flickered once and then stayed on for good.

What stood in front of them now was both startling and slightly unreal.

It was an airplane—and it was a huge one all right. Huge wasn't the right word—this thing was way bigger than a B-17/36, way bigger than a B-24/52. It was even bigger than a Navy CB-201.

It was enormous. Immense. *Colossal.*

"Wow," was all Hunter could say.

Y was speechless.

The monster had wings at least three hundred feet long *each*. Ten giant reverse contra-prop engines adorned each wing, with an additional four-jet array down near each tip. The fuselage was about 1,000 feet long, and the tail wing assembly probably ten stories high. The giant plane most closely resembled the B-17/36; it bore the nose of a '36, as well as the wings. Its fuselage actually looked closer to what Hunter knew as the B-29 Superfortress, a late-entry long-range propeller-driven bomber from his version of World War II. But this airplane was a hundred times bigger than what he remembered a B-29 to be.

In this strange world of big, bigger, and biggest aircraft, this one was simply the largest airplane either one of them had ever seen.

"Who in the world built this?" Hunter asked, astounded. "And why?"

Y was already punching buttons on his mission pad to find out. But he read the next set of orders and again was simply left shaking his head.

"It says we have to climb into this thing and look around before we can find out," Y said.

They did.

If possible, the airplane was stranger inside than out. It was so immense, it actually had a little shuttle car to carry crewmembers the length of the fuselage. The flight deck looked better suited to a battleship. There were seats for six pilots above which the commander of the aircraft sat like a king lording it over his court.

The flight chamber was encased almost totally in Plexiglas. It sat above the nose of the airplane like the huge glassy pupil of a monstrous one-eyed bug. A four-stop elevator was used to get from this lofty position to the lower chambers.

The fuselage itself was as cavernous as a subway tunnel. It was pockmarked with observation blisters and four sets of catwalks for traveling the sides of the great airship. Once at mid fuselage, Hunter was astonished to see one could walk *inside* the wings. There were actually small living compartments inside the wing roots, complete with bunks, sinks, heads, and even observation windows.

The long ride to the end of the airplane revealed mountains of tubes and wires and switches and more wires. Sitting in the tail, protected somewhat by a wire mesh enclosure, was a larger than usual Main/AC Battle Management Computer. The interconnected "thinking machine" could be found in one form or another aboard every U.S. Navy warship, Air Corps aircraft, Army tank, jeep, and mobile gun, as well as inside many noncombat sites, from the office of the highest general in the War Department to the cubicle of the lowliest supply clerk.

The Main/AC was everywhere—even in the back of this enormous airplane.

They walked the length of the aircraft again, still astonished at its size. But could it fly? Y didn't know and Hunter wasn't asking.

But once they'd reached the forward compartment again, Hunter took another long glance down the interior of the ship and then turned to Y. "OK, I'll ask again: What exactly do they want me to do with this thing?"

Y pushed some buttons, retrieved his next set of instructions and immediately frowned again.

"Sorry, I can't tell you yet," he said. "We've got another place to go."

The MVP had them driving back out into the desert ten minutes later.

The heat was searing now, beating down on them in their unprotected jeepster. But Hunter's mind was not so much on the sweaty conditions, as it was on what he'd seen here already and the surprise he knew the OSS was laying for him.

The monster airplane was intriguing to him at least—as all things aeronautical were. Back There, if he recalled correctly, the usual process for building military aircraft began in the design stage, then advanced to building several prototypes. The best performing prototype would be selected, and soon, factories would be turning out the new airplane based on this design.

Here, in this place, the building process was more specialized. Instead of 5,000 copies of one design being produced, there might be 100 copies of *fifty* designs. It seemed to be the less efficient way of doing things, but it did have one positive aspect: It made for a world that was rich in different airplane designs and capabilities. Back There, Hunter could count on one hand the number of airplane designs a typical military pilot might fly in a typical career. Here, that number would be doubled, maybe even tripled.

But even this, that he might have dozens of cool airplanes to fly, wasn't enough to lift the suspicion that the OSS was about to use him, rely on him, entrust him with something way out of proportion to what he could really do. It was a very uneasy feeling.

Strangely, he accepted the premise that he was a "secret weapon," as much as a human could accept such a thing.

He *was* an anomaly here in this world, and he couldn't argue with the thesis that he did have an effect on the outcome of the last war. But was that because he was not from here, and just by his transference to this place alone caused the war to end once he jumped into it? Or would it have ended anyway?

It was a strange but important question and he didn't have the answer and that's what bothered him the most. It was not long after he found himself in this world that he had made one important discovery: that the people here had no conception of the idea of "coincidence." Everything that happened Here just simply happened, and if two events seemed to coincide, the people here just accepted it as the way it was supposed to go. They did not appreciate the irony of the coincidental event because they had no concept of it.

Hunter's insertion into the war against Germany and the fact that the conflict finally came to an end shortly thereafter could not be labeled a "coincidence," no matter how mystical or cosmic or strange it might be. Here, it was just accepted as the way things were.

But now, with these new burdens being placed upon him, what would be their result? Would Hunter's simple presence in the OSS's future plans actually guarantee them to work? Or did they depend more on his skills, his reasoning, his derring-do to pull the fat out of the fire at the end?

He just didn't know. But one thing seemed certain: He felt he was used to doing these things—leading desperate missions, fighting against the odds, and trying to win big. The vast majority of his memories were still hazy. But back where he came from, Back There, he knew he must have been quite a hero.

They drove for about half an hour, again staying on the barely paved roadway, passing enormous buttes, dozens of small canyons, and innumerable dry washes.

Finally they reached their next destination: It was another hangar simply plunked down out in the middle of nowhere. It was ringed with concertina wire and had the requisite pair of guards watching the front gate.

Y flashed their OSS passes and again, they were waved in.

The size of the hangar was interesting, because it was normal. Something built to house just one, normal-size airplane. This was another oddity here. In this bigger-is-better world, it was the small things that were special.

Y got them by the second set of guards and they soon gained access to the small hangar. Like the one before, it was dark in here, and musty. The air stank, telling Hunter that the door to this place hadn't been opened in a while either.

But when Y flipped on the light, what Hunter saw next made him forget the stink, the heat, the dirt, the dust, and the fact that the OSS was counting on him to win a major war—again.

What he saw gave him such a jolt, all these things were suddenly washed away. A spark in his memory turned to flame. Years ago. Back There. He'd walked into a hangar and seen his beloved F-16 revealed to him. It would be his plane for the next five years, through many air battles, many wars, many memories.

Now that identical feeling was running through him again.

Before him was an airplane. A jet-powered one. Those were the only two things he knew for sure.

It was sleek. Sleek to the nth degree. It was so sleek in fact, it looked like a flying hypodermic needle. Its nose was so sharp it did indeed look like it could puncture skin. Its fuselage was extremely long and thin, so much so that the canopy blended right into the airframe. Its wings were short, stubby, almost nonexistent. The fuselage ended, quickly, with a small tail section positioned slightly above the twin exhausts. It was painted all white, with silver and chrome trim.

Quite frankly, Hunter had never seen a more beautiful plane in his life.

"Jessuzz, what is it?" Hunter heard himself exclaim.

Again, Y checked the MVP.

"It's called the Z-3/15," Y said. "Nickname, 'Stiletto Deuce.' First flight, October 1972. Reason for being: a high-speed transsonic fighter, capable of near-space flight. Development off and on until 1991. Top speed attained: Mach 6.1. Highest altitude climbed: 111,000 feet. Wow, that *is* the edge of space. Armament: two cannons, two antiaircraft missiles. Only one model exists. This is it."

Hunter was slowly nodding his head as if he was paying attention to every word Y was saying—but he wasn't. He couldn't. His ears weren't working. Neither were his knees.

This plane looked so . . . well, *cool,* he really couldn't do anything else but stare at it.

"What . . . is it for?" he finally managed to ask Y.

Y check his orders. And at last he saw something that didn't make him frown.

"What is it for?" he replied. "It's for you. It's yours. This is your new mode of transportation. To do with what you like."

Suddenly, with those words, everything that had been weighing on Hunter's mind simply ceased to exist. Suddenly everything had changed. Suddenly he was more one with Here than ever. Because now, he had something that he'd had Back There. He had an airplane. His airplane. Sure, the Mustang-5 of his European war days was a great plane. And the Super Ascender was also a neat little bird.

But they weren't like this.

Y consulted the MVP, then walked over to a utility deck which was on wheels next to the sleek airplane. He rummaged through the top drawer and came out with a silver-plated card with many numbers displayed on it. It was an activation card, the thing that was needed to plug into the cockpit's Main/AC computer extension and start the airplane

With no ceremony at all, he simply handed the card to Hunter. It was like giving him the keys to the Kingdom.

As soon as that card touched his fingers, Hunter knew his world Here would be different. No more doubts. No more questions. He was suddenly complete. Stay tight. Stay cool. It was time to do the impossible.

His seduction by the OSS was now complete. And he knew it.

"I've got to hand it to your bosses," he said to Y. "They really know how to pull a guy's string."

Seventeen

They returned to Area 52 and after tracking down the security officer, were given the use of an office, a telephone, and a place to plug in the MVP for recharging.

Hunter lay sprawled on the couch in the small office. Its only window looked west, out away from the runways and the rest of the base, and into the mountains beyond. He was drinking coffee and watching the sunset as Y, seated behind an ancient oak desk, fiddled with the power-drained MVP.

A number of thoughts drifted through Hunter's mind, as was his wont at the end of most long days. As the sun was going down, the desert was turning golden. His thoughts went backwards from there. Seeing all the strange planes at Bride Lake. The wild nights in Texas. Xwo mountain. The battle at Axaz. The Super Ascender. Sara.

His brain rewound itself, and then took a right turn. Stranger notions began streaming in. Eating bugs on the ground in the Peruvian jungle. Trying to stay invisible atop of Xwo. The strange feeling that night on the roof of the Happy Valley when his psyche had him staring off to the northeast. Then, earlier this very day in Dallas, and the strange fortune-teller.

Hunter laughed a bit to himself. It seemed like ten years ago now. It was strange: He could picture the psychic right down to her dimples and her deep brown eyes. But he could hardly recall what she had told in her prediction.

You will soon be very cold—he remembered that much intact. But that was hardly true. It was ninety-six degrees inside the office right now, even though the sun was going down and the huge windowframe air conditioner was blowing cold at full tilt.

What came after that? *You will meet old friends again,* she had said. Again Hunter chuckled. Not out here, he wouldn't.

They will build something to come apart. What the hell did that mean?

Hunter frowned. What was the rest of it? *Then you will be asked to . . .*

"Holy shit. . . ."

Y's soft exclamation broke Hunter out of his trance. The MVP was repowered and reconnected. Their new orders were streaming in. Y was reading them—and swearing in amazement with each line.

"Son of a bitch," he was mumbling. "Are they kidding?"

"Jessuzz, break it to me gently," Hunter told him, staring now up at the ceiling, as if he was waiting for it to fall in on him at any moment.

"Well, first off," Y began, "by a presidential order you have been officially designated a 'secret weapon' by the War Department."

"You're kidding. . . ."

Y shook his head no.

"I'm quoting here: 'A panel of the senior Psychic Evaluation Officers have recognized that for whatever reason, Major Hunter's presence in a tactical or strategic situation will probably have an effect in the overall outcome.' Therefore, Major you are valuable. Therefore, you are now a secret weapon. It also means you can be cleared for some of this."

Hunter just shook his head and went back to staring at the ceiling.

"Point Two," Y went on. "The U.S. and its allies are going to attack the Panama Canal."

Hunter stopped looking at the ceiling for a moment. "Really?"

Y nodded. "That's what it says. They're looking at a two-pronged assault simultaneously on both entrances. The Navy is taking the Pacific side, the Army and Air Corps are taking the Caribbean end. If they can gain both approaches to the waterway, all the Japs left in the middle will wither on the vine."

Hunter turned this concept over in his mind a few dozen times in the space of about five seconds. "Hey, a plan like that just might work," he said finally.

"Maybe," Y replied. "But here's the real bombshell: It says that the whole Canal attack is just a diversion. For something bigger . . ."

"Bigger?" Hunter asked. "Bigger, like the Brazil operation?"

"Nope," Y replied. "Bigger than that even."

Hunter was stumped. "What the hell could be bigger than a full-scale invasion?"

That's when Y just handed the MVP to Hunter.

"You should see this for yourself," he said.

What the screen showed was, to Hunter's surprise, a huge mushroom cloud. It was an image not seen very often in this world—at least not until the five H-bombs he'd stolen were dropped on Occupied Europe to end the war with Germany about a year before.

This image faded into a long text detailing the mission statement, which had the words *classified* and *top secret* written all over it.

Hunter hit the "Fast" button on all this. He wanted to see the MAS, the "mission animation sequence." It would tell him not in words but in pictures what lay in store for him.

What he saw was almost comical.

It showed a group of men entering an animated version of the huge hangar they'd visited in the middle of the desert earlier, the one that housed the colossal airplane. Once the tiny figures were inside, the building started spewing smoke and literally shaking at its foundations—this was the animation-briefers' way of telling him that work was going on inside the big hangar.

Then, after a while, the doors to the big hangar opened, and he saw an animated version of the colossal airplane taking off, using the entire ten-mile runway to do so. Even as a cartoon, this sequence looked a little scary. The plane just appeared to be too gigantic to ever get airborne in real life. It just barely made it off the ground in the animation! Again, this was the briefers' way of telling him that they expected the takeoff to be a bitch of an experience.

Once airborne, the airplane flew very, very high and very, very slowly, and began a long journey around the world via the polar route. Flying south, the giant aircraft went over the south pole, up the other side of the planet, over the north pole, and back down again.

Toward the end of this long, long journey, the plane was shown being attacked by dozens of smaller airplanes and antiaircraft rockets. The big plane plowed through all of this, only to be attacked again and again. Finally, still in one piece, it arrived over an island land mass, where it was attacked even more fiercely than before.

The view changed and the plane's enormous bomb bay doors opened—and a single bomb fell out.

The plane speeded up, but just a little—it couldn't go that fast. When the bomb went off, the resulting mushroom cloud was so enormous, it immediately engulfed the colossal aircraft.

When the smoke cleared, the animation showed the spot of ocean where the land mass used to be. Most of it was gone—exploded into the sea. Only the barest outline remained, but it was enough to provide the only clue needed as to exactly what the target had been: The Home Islands of Japan.

The animated briefing ended.

Hunter just looked over at Y and numbly shook his head.

The point of the cartoon briefing was clear: The OSS wanted the colossal airplane to go on a very secret bombing mission. There was no doubt exactly where the OSS wanted this mission to go.

Even why this big airplane was being asked to carry one tiny little bomb was not that mysterious. Obviously the plane needed both surprise and the ability to fight off masses of enemy aircraft to get to the target and drop what had to be the only available copy of the diminutive bomb.

But who did the OSS expect to fly this thing? It would take a crew of at least a dozen or so, Hunter surmised. Probably three or four times more.

"Well, I only have about a million questions," he finally said to Y. "Number one being, do they expect me to fly that thing alone? I mean not even the OSS is crazy enough for that . . . are they?"

"No, they're not," Y was saying, going back into the mission statement itself and reading the text set of instructions.

"It says here that you have to gather a group of 'associates,' " Y revealed. "And again I quote, 'Individuals who are known intimately to you, who can be trusted, who have flight experience, and who can clear security. And be assembled in a week's time.' " Y looked up at him. "Now that's a tall order. . . ."

Hunter was just shaking his head. "I only know about twelve people here intimately," he said. "And half of them are SuperBlonds back in Dallas."

Y just shrugged. It did seem like a strange order.

But Hunter's mind was already on to the next question. The MVP made it quite clear that this plane was to drop a bomb that would produce a mushroom cloud, obviously

the sixth and remaining H-bomb from the cache he stole
from the Germans near the end of the war.

But now, as they watched the tail end of the animated
briefing again, obviously this sixth bomb had been altered
somewhat. Because according to the cartoon, the version
this plane was to deliver was so powerful, there was no way
the giant bomber could get out of the way of its own blast.

Once this had sunk in, they both just looked at each
other.

Y had to say it for both of them.

"From the looks of this," he said, "it's a suicide mission."

Hunter just went back to looking out the window. The
psychic's last words were coming back to him loud and
clear now.

You will be asked to die, she had said.

How could he have ever forgotten that?

Eighteen

It was the night-shift maintenance crew who first became suspicious.

The three-man cleaning team who regularly swept, mopped, and buffed the floors of all the offices inside the massive OSS main building had not been able to gain access to Room 222 in nearly a week.

Knowing that the men who used this room were among the highest intelligence operatives in the country, the cleaning crew wasn't about to ask around as to their whereabouts, not after just a couple of days anyway.

But by Day 3, the cleaning crew grew concerned. Room 222 was probably the hardest office for them to clean simply because the two agents who used it smoked more cigarettes, drank more coffee, and missed the wastebaskets more often than the rest of the people working inside the entire OSS complex combined. In other words, the OSS's two top agents were also its sloppiest.

There were visions of a nightmare rising then by Day 4 as the cleaning crew, assuming the agents were working during the day and just not leaving the door unlocked at night, feared a powerful mess was building up inside. Four days without a sweep-out meant a colossal job for maintenance once access to the room was reestablished, and that would wreak havoc on the entire cleaning schedule. And that was one thing the maintenance men did not want.

So, by Day 5, their concern had grown to the point that they finally asked the building's superintendent to please look into it for them. The superintendent asked the building's night operations officer about the situation, and he expressed surprise that the men in Room 222 weren't following the common procedure on building maintenance, which was, you left your office door open every night. The officer then turned to his Main/AC computer and asked it to locate the men from Room 222 for a message transfer.

The computer churned and chugged for a while, but then came back with an unsettling response: *Not enough input for evaluation.* This meant the computer didn't know the whereabouts of the two agents, a highly unusual situation.

This is what prompted the strange delegation of the night officer, the superintendent, and the three-man cleaning crew to journey up to the twelfth floor and unlock Room 222 with a pass key.

The door swung open and it was the maintenance guys who gasped first. The room was spotless. No discarded coffee cups, no small mountain of expended cigarette butts rising from the ashtrays, no sea of litter around the wastebaskets.

Both desks were clean, as was the floor, the windowsills, and the adjoining bathroom.

This was all highly unusual. The office was just as the cleaning crew had left it six days before.

The two agents who used it—men also known by their code names X and Z—had not been here in all that time.

Nineteen

Above Bride Lake
Nevada Desert

It was just a blur really.

A streak through the sky. A flash, like a lightning bolt. White-hot, no exhaust, moving faster than seemed possible.

Above the barren desert it went, riding a sonic wave that was causing dishes to rattle as far away as Las Vegas.

It was the Z-3/15 *Stiletto Deuce* with Hawk Hunter behind the controls, going out for a morning spin.

He'd been at Area 52 for nearly a week, and this was his twelfth ride in the Z-3/15. Without question, it was the ballsiest airplane he'd ever strapped into, in this world or the last. Its needle-nosed appearance, its absolutely clean lines and its incredibly powerful double-reaction engines all conspired to make it so fast, some of its flight characteristics seemed to defy explanation.

For instance, with its nose being so very long, turning the airplane should have been a problem. But it wasn't. And with its wings being so short and stubby, radically maneuvering the aircraft should have been difficult. But it wasn't. And the thing could move so goddamn quick, it would have seemed that the whole package would be unstable and prone to stalls. But it wasn't.

The truth was, the Z-3/15 had been built too well, and made to perform so far beyond the envelope, that a pilot had never been found who could fly it properly.

Until now.

Five days, twelve flights. Each time, Hunter didn't want to come back down.

But he hadn't spent all his time flying the *Stiletto,* although he certainly would have preferred to. Per his updated orders, he had devoted many hours to flight-checking each member of the small squadron of rogue planes found in Area 52's Hangar #19. These airplanes were old but in surprisingly good shape, the major problem being oil sludge which had built up inside their engines simply from lack of flying time.

With the help of some Bride Lake flight mechanics, Hunter had put each airplane through a thorough washing and engine test. As each plane was put back together again, Hunter would take it up, climb to 10,000 feet, roll it over, and come back down in a screaming spiral. Pulling out only at 2,000 feet, he would do a series of rolls, stalls, and wing inversions, then climb back up to 10-angels—and shut the engine off. Letting the airplane plunge back down to 2,000 feet again, he would do an engine restart and pull out of the heart-stopping dive.

If the aircraft survived all that in the span of ten minutes, Hunter deemed it airworthy. In the end, all six planes—from the diminutive Bantams to the ultrawinged Z-16 recon plane—had passed the test.

Once the rogue planes were checked out, Hunter's next concern was the mammoth bomber.

His orders called for him to get this ultramonster airworthy as well, but he knew he could only accomplish ground testing on it. To actually get it airborne and fly it would take a crew—a large one.

And that came to the strangest part of his orders from OSS headquarters. The MVP had said he was to assemble a group of "previous associates" with which to crew the monster airplane. But who were these people supposed to be?

Y's attempts to have OSS Command clarify this particular order had not been fruitful. The OSS Command was working closely on this with its Psychic Evaluation Corps. Essentially psychics with officer rank inside the military, these swamis-in-medals were saying that for the mission to be a success, Hunter and *only* Hunter, could divine who these mysterious "previous associates" could be.

He'd been thinking about this queer aspect ever since. What the hell did the "previous associates" order mean? The usual suspects—such as Sara's female fighter pilots, or a select crew gleaned from the bomber gangs now operating off Xwo Mountain—were quickly discounted by him. That solution would have been way too easy.

It was the term "previous" which obviously held the key. But who would his "previous associates" be if not the people with whom he'd fought the Germans out of Iceland or those atop Xwo Mountain?

Hunter had found himself dwelling on this question nearly every hour of every day and very late into every night. Now, as he was roaring along not 200 feet above the desert floor and reaching speeds close to Mach 4, he was working on a new theory.

Back in the other place, he had known Agent Y as Stan Yastrewski, the man nicknamed "Yaz" who was part of the United Americans' inner circle. In strict terms then, he certainly qualified as a "previous associate."

The same was true for the bomber pilot currently serving on Xwo Mountain named PJ O'Malley. Back There, Hunter knew him as "Captain Crunch," president and CEO of the Ace Wrecking Company, a private fighter-bomber outfit. He too could be accurately described as a "previous associate."

And then the third clue: When Hunter was first being

shipped up to Iceland, he'd met a man briefly on the way who was being sent to another front. This man's face had been extremely familiar; his Irish brogue had been too. Hunter eventually realized who this guy was. Back There his name was Mike Fitzgerald and he'd been as close a friend to Hunter as one could get.

But while some of Hunter's memories of his previous life were still foggy, there was one of which he was quite sure: Mike Fitzgerald was dead, killed at the Battle of Football City, the turning point in the war, which threw the Fourth Reich out of America.

This had brought up a tough question: If there were people who existed in two places—Here and Back There—and one of them was dead Back There, was there a possibility they could still be alive Here?

That thought opened up some rather unnerving possibilities—frightening in their implications. Because if people Hunter both loved and hated and had passed on Back There, they could still be alive Here . . . well, every time he'd gotten to that point before, he'd had to literally shut his mind off. The ramifications of such a thing were just too broad.

But this day, he willed his mind to stay open and was determined to let it all flow. At the same time, he started climbing. Up from 200 feet to 50,000 in less than sixty seconds. Up to 75,000 in just twenty seconds after that. Then up to 85,000, then 90,000, and then finally topping out at 100,000 feet. From here he could see the curvature of the earth, the edge of space, and the stars beyond. He was high, man. Almost twenty miles high.

And it was up here that he did his best work.

He started from point one. He had apparently been handed a suicide mission by the OSS, but did it really need to be a voluntary death sentence? He had been told to assemble a crew of "previous associates," but did finding them really have to be so difficult? He had to get the monster bomber in the air in order to drop a bomb so powerful, it couldn't possibly escape the blast. Or was there some way he could solve this dilemma as well?

He goosed his throttle and pulled back on the stick and began climbing even higher. Up to 105,000 feet, 110,000, 115,000 . . .

He flew higher and higher, and faster and faster, and allowed his mind to spring wide open and let everything in.

Around 118,000 feet, and Mach 6.6, it began coming to him. . . .

Twenty

Area 52

It was strange how Agent Y got the message.

He was sitting in his new office at Area 52, eating a sandwich and slurping coffee when his MVP began blinking.

He lazily sat up and punched the activate button. Because he'd just downloaded a ton of mission updates a half hour before, he was thinking this indication was nothing more than the goose the Main/AC would run through the mission pad every so often to make sure he was still "on the system."

Usually just turning the MVP to full power was enough for the diagnostic scan check to be run, with any errors found instantly corrected. Then the pad's screen would go dark again.

But this time, there was actually another message beaming on screen. It had been coded, recoded, and decoded a total of nine times already, extraordinary security for what Y still assumed was a routine transmission.

He worked the MVP's buttons and was finally looking at the very unscrambled message. It would turn out to be anything but routine.

It was a simple inquiry really: Had Y had any recent contact with two of his OSS colleagues, Agents X and Z?

It was a strange question, because even though Y had

worked closely with X and Z in the past,OSS Command as well as every Main/AC in the country knew that he was not working with them on this Area 52 project. In fact, he hadn't worked with them in some time.

But if this was common knowledge within the odd world of the OSS, why this message?

Y answered truthfully that he hadn't heard or talked to or had any kind of communications with his two erstwhile partners in nearly four months.

The mission center accepted his reply and began to break transmission. But Y stopped it at the last moment. He was curious. He asked the MVP a question: Why did OSS Command want to know this? The answer took about a minute to churn out, but when it did, it shook Y right down to his feet.

It seemed that the exact whereabouts of Agents X and Z was unknown at the moment.

Y had to read the stark message several times before it began to sink in. X and Z missing? How could that be?

These two were among the high cadre of the highest-clearance agents in the U.S. Someone *always* knew where the hell they were. So how could their present location be unknown to the all-knowing OSS and its mechanical partner in crime the Main/AC? The Main/AC had the ability to find just about anyone in the world. How could it lose track of two of the OSS's highest agents?

Putting his sandwich away, Y asked the Main/AC that very question.

But no matter how many ways he phrased it, no matter what kind of verbiage he used, the thinking machine replied the same way, over and over again: "Not enough inquiry input."

In other words, the all-powerful computer simply didn't know. . . .

* * *

It was exactly noon when Hunter walked into Y's office.

The OSS agent barely looked up when Hunter came in.

"Just getting a new mission update," he said as Hunter flopped onto the couch.

"The OSS is canceling all this nonsense?" Hunter asked hopefully.

"Far from it," Y reported. "It has to do with the bomb they want you to drop."

"What about it?" Hunter asked with a yawn.

"They want you to pick it up and bring it back here for loading."

Hunter immediately began paying attention. It was strange, because at that moment, the prospect of a trip out of Area 52 was appealing to him.

"Where is it?" he asked, sitting up.

Y laughed as he read the MVP screen.

"Well, this is something," he said. "They don't know. At least they're saying they don't know. Supposedly the bomb's location is so secret, it doesn't exist. At least according to the guys typing on the other end of this thing."

Hunter reflopped himself back onto the couch. *Alice in Wonderland* made more sense than the OSS did sometimes.

"So, if it doesn't exist," he asked Y, "how the hell am I supposed to find the damn thing?"

Y kept reading from the MVP: "You are to proceed to a certain air coordinate, and receive further orders once you get there."

Hunter nearly burst out laughing. Maybe he was dreaming all this.

"Are you saying that before they send me on a suicide mission, they're sending me on a wild-goose chase?"

"It says you should launch tomorrow at midnight," Y continued. "The mission requirements call for you to carry long-range drop tanks on your new bird. They want you to go up with about two thousand gallons of gas."

Hunter did the math. The Z-3/15 carried 1,000 gallons

of gas internally. With its superefficient engines and that much fuel, he estimated its range to be about 4,000 miles. The OSS brain trust wanted him to go up with another 1,000 in gas and, he assumed, be expected to rejuice at his point of return departure. Either way, it was obvious they were sending him someplace out of the local neighborhood.

"Where is this coordinate?" Hunter asked him. "Or is that top secret too?"

Y shook his head and wrote down some numbers. Then he changed screens and came up with a world map on the MVP. He punched in the numbers and had the coordinate on the map in five seconds.

"Sixty degrees latitude, twenty degrees long," he said. "That puts you right above Bolivia somewhere. Once there, you'll get your next vector point and the final go orders."

Again Hunter just shook his head. The OSS was looking at him as some kind of superman now. He was sure that back where he came from, Back There, he had done similar things. But he was also certain that the United Americans had never loaded so much pressure on him, in such a robotic, faceless, impersonal way.

"You know, I don't even get paid," he grumbled suddenly to Y.

"You don't?"

"No, I don't," Hunter told him. "I went from flight officer to major after the war. I got my pins and my new uniform, but I never got a paycheck. Not then. Not down in South America. Not now. The least they could do is pay me."

Y just shrugged.

"I guess now that they consider you a secret weapon," he said, "they feel they don't have to pay you. You're considered priceless, invaluable. Beyond mere monetary compensation."

"Well, that's comforting," Hunter replied, again with a grumble.

There was a short silence between them.

"Is everything about the capabilities of the Main/AC computer classified?" Hunter asked.

"Just about," was the agent's reply. "Why?"

Hunter hesitated a moment before asking the next question. If he didn't have a crew to fly the monster bomber, then he couldn't go on the suicide mission. Was it a dereliction of duty if a man refuses to dig his own grave?

He didn't know.

So he pressed on.

"Would it be accurate to say that the Main/AC has a file on every member of the U.S. military, past and present?"

Y actually smiled at that one.

"Confidentially," he said, "I happen to know the Main/AC has a file on every person in the United States—military or not."

That reply sent an unexpected chill down Hunter's back. Suddenly he was back on the roof of the Happy Valley casino again, his psyche pestering him to look north, his mind's eye trying to find someone else close to him.

Someone other than Sara.

If the Main/AC could find anyone, then . . .

But he quickly shook these thoughts away and went back to the matter at hand.

"So, in theory," he went on, "I could give you a list of names, and if they were put into the computer, it would locate them?"

"I guess so," Y replied. "Why?"

Hunter lay back down on the couch and began staring at the ceiling again.

"Because," he answered slowly, "I think I've found our bomber crew."

Twenty-one

Somewhere in the mid Atlantic

The aircraft was called *Nacht-Sputnik*.

It was a bastardization of German and Russian. Roughly translated, it meant "Night Traveler."

In a world of huge aircraft, the NS-1 was a fair oddity. It was about one-tenth the size of a B-17/36, which made it about as big as a Boeing 727 airliner from Back There.

It was powered by six double-reaction engines, again a small power-pack for a plane these days. Its cabin could support a crew of only a dozen or so, and it had only a single galley, a single head, and just a few foldout bunks. Again, small accommodations for an ultralong-range airplane.

Long-range capability the *Nacht-Sputnik* had, though. It was relatively small for a reason: efficiency. Its engines had been finely engineered in Germany during the last days of the war. Its airframe had been crafted of lightweight but sturdy aluminum taken from downed U.S. aircraft. The smaller the plane, the less it weighed. And the less it weighed, the more efficient its engines could be, especially in saving fuel. This plane was very efficient. As a result, it could stay aloft for three weeks, or even more.

It was originally built for the most senior officers of the German High Command as a kind of escape pod, an airplane that could have left Berlin just minutes before the collapse and stayed aloft long enough for the heat to cool down and a deal to be made for it to land somewhere hidden or neutral or both. Because the planet was 70 percent water, and the preferred hiding place might be a deserted island somewhere, the airplane had been adapted for sea landings and takeoffs as well.

The plane never got to take off on that mission, though. It had been spirited out of Germany by the OSS after the war and brought back to the United States, where it had sat languishing in a hangar in Maryland until recently.

The mission it was on now did not exactly pale in comparison to the original, however. Truth was, in some ways it was even more intriguing.

There were thirteen people on board at present. Two pilots, three navigators, a flight engineer, and a guy to grease the Main/AC. Four other crewmembers were high-priced call girls pulled into duty at the last moment for the two men who were presently acting as Commanders of the Aircraft.

These two were OSS agents: code names X and Z. At the moment, just about the entire U.S. intelligence community was looking for them.

They were sitting in the flight compartment's top tier, looking down over the pilots' workstation. Both agents were glum, exhausted, and hungover. Not accustomed to being airborne for more than twelve hours at a time, they were now enduring the fifth day of this trip. It was ironic that while many people were searching for them, they in turn were searching for someone else.

They'd been flying knit patterns over the mid Atlantic for four of the five days. Back and forth, up and down, looking for a ship, a boat, even a small uncharted island on which a man who had been lost in this area more than a year ago might be found. This person was considered officially to be dead by drowning, his body never found.

But, as the rumors went, he'd been picked up and made to crew a ship that regularly plied the waters in this area.

But four days of looking had turned up nothing. No islands, no ships fitting the description of the rumors, no fishing boats or pleasure craft. No nothing.

This was frustrating for the agents. They'd been secretly planing this unscheduled, totally unauthorized mission for some time. They were so used to getting their way, the OSS way, that to look for something for so long with no good result was tough.

Plus the bad food, the bad sleeping conditions, the smelly toilet. It was not to do for this pair, used to a certain amount of luxury. Drinking heavily at night had been the result.

Still, inside they knew that if they ever did actually find who they were looking for, it might all turn out to be well worth it.

They knew him only as "Number 3." Eighteen months before, three men had been found floating in the middle of the Atlantic. One was Hawk Hunter, fighter pilot and hero, the one everyone now called The Sky Ghost. The second man was a guy named Elvis Q, who had been picked up by the German navy and gone on to engineer the remarkable if brief resurgence of Iron Cross Germany before its final defeat by the United States.

The actions of these two men and their influence on the outcome of a war that had lasted fifty-eight years would be debated for eternity probably. Yet the evidence pointed to these facts: that these two men—who apparently dropped in from another world or universe or whatever—had had a huge effect on the conflict's outcome simply because of their presence in it.

These men then might be angels—literally *angels*—sent from another place and possessing powers that while subtle were undeniable. Agents X and Z were aware that the War Department had classified Hawk Hunter as a secret weapon. Even in defeat, the Germans, what was left of them, still honored Elvis Q like a messiah.

This was why X and Z were looking for the Third Man, Number 3. They had to believe that he would have the same powers and talents as the first two men. And once found, the agents were arrogantly self-assured that they could make him do their bidding.

But they had to find him first.

And that had become a problem.

The automatic command system aboard the *Nacht-Sputnik* was called *Uebertinker*—very roughly, "the over-thinker." It was the German version of the Main/AC.

The rogue OSS agents had been taking advantage of this time on board the airplane to run every piece of evidence they had through the *Uebertinker*'s minitubes to see if it could divine exactly where they should look for their elusive quarry. Already the computer had told them that the Third Man was probably still alive, had probably been picked up eighteen months before by a passing ship, that there were only a certain number of ships that regularly sailed these waters, and that the majority of them never went to port. Therefore, there was a high probability that the missing man was aboard one of them.

But beyond these predictions—basically a list of probabilities in disguise—the German thinking machine had not been too helpful. Thus the interminable search patterns.

Strictly out of boredom, the pair of rogue OSS men began asking the computer other questions. If the Third Man was never found, would he still have an effect on the outcome of life on the planet? (The computer's response: *Maybe.*)

If the Third Man was found by the U.S., would his presence override that of The Sky Ghost, or vice versa? (The computer's response: *They would probably be equal.*)

But there was only so long they could play this game and not get bored. So after a while, they began to run out of questions. Then X in a drunken blur, asked the *Ue-bertinker* what turned out to be a rather fateful question: If the Third Man *was* in the hands of either the U.S. or Japan or even themselves, and if he was affecting events, what would those events be?

The computer started churning that question nearly three days ago. It was churning still. In all that time then, the agents didn't know if the thing was broken, or if it was actually thinking of an answer.

It would be another few days then before they found out that the reply to their question had implications that could literally change the world and the course of human events.

Until then, they kept flying square patterns over the empty, tempestuous Atlantic, getting drunk, getting sick, looking for an angel.

Twenty-two

It was just a few minutes after midnight when the control tower atop Xwo Mountain received the radio call.

It came in the highest code. It was from a pilot approaching from the northwest. He was requesting the LSD screen be opened.

The code words matched those of the day found inside the Main/AC battle management computer, so the control tower called down to the LSD techs, who opened the screen as requested.

It was a cloudy night, so it looked like the strange, unidentified aircraft came out of nowhere. No sooner had the LSD screen parted when the aircraft zipped through, at first appearing only as a blur.

But those who actually saw it would later describe the mysterious aircraft as being long and white and very, very sharp. Like a hypodermic needle, with wings.

Very few people were out on the flight line this time of night, so just a handful saw the airplane come in. Still, those who did, watched as the strange aircraft taxied up to a familiar parking area. It was the one at the far end of the flightline, the one that had formerly been used by the base's only Super Ascender fighter aircraft. The place where the man they now called Sky Ghost used to park his airplane.

Prewarned of its arrival, the ground crew of Dopey,

Sniffy, and Sneezy was on hand, waiting as the needle plane finally came to a stop in front of them. They watched the Z-3/15's knifelike canopy rise up. They were surprised, despite clues to the obvious, when the pilot climbed out and took off his helmet. It was Hawk Hunter. Back on Xwo Mountain after an absence of nearly a month.

Hunter greeted the ground crew warmly, then asked that they get the *Stiletto* under wraps quickly. He really wanted his presence here to be a secret, at least for the moment. He would eventually have to report to the operations building and say hello to Payne. But before all that, he had something else to do.

His airplane secured, he began walking toward the main part of the base. The trip down from Area 52 had been uneventful; even streaking very high over the occupied Panama Canal had been anticlimactic. The Japanese could neither see him nor hear him—not until he was way beyond the canal zone and his sonic booms began rattling their cages. They would have to get used to it. For little did they know that their cozy little world on the Panamanian isthmus was soon to be turned upside down. When that happened, sonic booms were going to be the least of their troubles.

Now, back at his home away from home, Hunter took a deep sniff of the high mountain air. The smells were all still there. The jungle, the rain, the jet exhaust. All of it felt good going into his lungs and out. Even the perpetual night mist was a welcome addition, muggy as it was.

In all the time he'd been away from the peak, he could honestly say Sara had never left his thoughts. Despite his rowdy week in Dallas and his intense time at Area 52, he'd always tried to think of her at dusk and at dawn, the times she would be just getting ready to go out on patrol or just coming back in.

After all was said and done, he realized he'd missed her.

Missed being with her. Missed talking with her. Missed sleeping with her.

He'd wondered many times if she had missed him as well.

And that was the real reason he'd returned to Xwo.

He was here to find out.

He walked down the flight line, keeping to the shadows, passing the bombers and the support planes and the Mustangs of Sara's squadron. Thank goodness her fighter was here, or this whole unauthorized pit stop would have been a huge failure. His heart began beating very fast.

Further down the line he noticed the airplane that had carried the network reporter to Xwo mountain was still on hand as well, a gaggle of TV insta-film cameras, transmitters, and things still set up and waiting nearby. Hunter guessed the news maven and her crew wouldn't return to the U.S. until they got a story to bring back with them. If that was the case, he would have to avoid them at all costs.

He finally reached the barracks area where Sara and her female squadron slept. Sara's billet was at the rear of one building, isolated from the rest. Hunter knew this area very well; he'd gone through her window many times under darkened conditions such as these. The getting-in part would be a snap.

He reached the magic portal and laid his helmet and gloves aside. There was a faint light flickering from within the room. This too was a good sign. Many times when they were together at night, Sara would light a candle and keep it going while they made love or just slept. Now, to Hunter, the flickering light told him she was awake, or possibly had just gone to sleep. This would be perfect for his surprise.

He reached the window and like a cat burglar returning to the scene of the crime, lifted it gently, one centimeter at a time. Once open, he went in smoothly, silently. The candle was indeed flickering. In the unusual light it cast, he saw Sara's form beneath the sheet. He took a deep breath. This was a strange thing he was doing here. And a big step he was taking.

He began to walk toward her . . . but then suddenly, he stopped.

There was another form under the sheet too. The whole mattress was moving. Hunter's breath caught in his throat. His heart plunged about 50,000 feet. His head felt like some cartoon character had just whacked him with a ninety-pound sledgehammer.

All this from the knowledge that he'd just made a huge mistake.

Sara's hand reached out from the covers and fumbled with the night light. Finally it came on and there she was: hair longer now, her face a little more tanned, her body, so shapely and pert. She was more beautiful than before. And here he was, like a phantom, looking down at her, wearing a confused smile.

"Hawk . . ." she whispered.

He stood there mute, and once again, time stood still for him. He needed the pause. A million things were running through his head at the moment. He would have to figure out at least a few of them before everything started moving again.

Yes, he had made a huge mistake here. Bigger than huge. It was actually gigantic or even colossal. He had made an assumption of his relationship with her and obviously it had turned out to be very wrong.

The next question was: who was the other form under the sheet with her? It could be anyone, Hunter realized. There was no shortage of bomber pilots at the base, all of them working hard at maintaining their hunk status. There were a number of eligible bachelors among the staff officers too. Even the enlisted ground crew guys were known to sniff around Sara's squadron every now and again, even though any liaison between an officer and a noncom was strictly forbidden.

So who would it be then? Hunter's mind blazed with the question. He had to know. He had to see the face of the person who he was sure would soon be his rival.

So with the blink of his eye, everything started moving again. That's when the form beneath the sheets moved and finally a head popped out. Hunter was shocked again.

It was the female network reporter.

She looked up at him and smiled too.

"Well, if it isn't the famous Sky Ghost," she cooed. "Ready to do that interview now?"

The sun was already coming up when Hunter finally made it back to the flight line.

His ground crew was still on hand. They'd spent the time topping off his fuel tanks and admiring his switch-blade of an airplane.

They stared at him strangely for a moment, though, when he arrived. He looked uncharacteristically ruffled.

Hunter checked his fuel tanks and did a quick diagnostic on the *Stiletto*. Then he donned his flight suit and climbed in.

The ground crew strapped him down and oversaw the starting of the airplane's mighty engines. They flared with characteristic bombast. Hunter was ready to leave. Dopey made sure he was snug in the cockpit, then gave him a whack on the helmet and a salute.

"Tell Major Payne I'll see him next time I come through, OK?" Hunter asked Dopey.

"You got it, sir," the ground man replied.

With that, Dopey descended the access ladder and stood by as Hunter closed the canopy and taxied away.

Within a minute the Z-3/15 was rocketing down the

runway, through the LSD screen, and out into the early-morning air.

The mechanics watched the airplane until it finally disappeared into the high clouds overhead. Only then did they speak.

"Man, what was the matter with him?" Sneezy finally asked. "He looked a little shook."

Dopey just shrugged his shoulders; of the three, he knew Hunter the best.

"I don't know," he finally replied. "Maybe it was something he ate."

The *Stiletto* soared straight up for nearly two minutes. It rose above the clouds, above the dawn, until it finally reached 82,000 feet.

Up here the moon was still out, still full, still burning bright white. The stars were still out too. Cold fire mixed with the planets; specks of color in the vast black and white sea.

The needle-nosed Z-3/15 could carve through the clear air up here almost effortlessly. Hunter was fully aware of the plane's capabilities now. Not quite its limits, but definitely its jack. The plane was incredibly fast. Close to Mach 7 fast, and that was with only two-thirds of the double-reaction engine power fully engaged.

Hunter didn't want to open the plane up all the way, because fuel was at a premium and he really wanted a closer look at the power plant before he went burying the speedometer.

At the moment, though, for this flight to nowhere, Mach 3.5 was just fine.

His mind was not quite numb, yet not quite engaged, as he rocketed above the mid South American continent. If he closed his eyes for more than a second or two he saw the image of Sara propped up in bed, looking sexy, looking beautiful—with the equally-erotic equally-topless network reporter snuggling beside her. That image was emblazoned indelibly on his memory now.

A loved one will surprise you. It was another bingo for the crazy street psychic. Already he was wondering just how long it would be before he'd be able to get back to Xwo Mountain.

But now it was 0510 hours—ten minutes past five in the morning. Time to get to work.

He had his own MVP now, and it was plugged into the *Stiletto's* control panel. A numeric readout was counting down to 0515, the magic time when he would receive his next set of orders. With them, he would finally learn exactly where he was to pick up the Bomb. The Z-3/15 was so loaded up with fuel—and topped off at Xwo Mountain—that he had a current radius of nearly 6,000 miles, meaning he could probably go to where he was going and get back to a friendly base without loading up on fuel again.

But he was flying over the middle of South America—where could he possibly go from here? Antarctica? Africa? Easter Island?

Three minutes to go.

There was a massive break in the clouds up ahead and Hunter suddenly had a clear view of the central part of Bolivia and northern Paraguay. These too were Japanese puppet states and even from this height the Nippon influence was apparent.

In among the trees and mountains and rain forests— places that had been inaccessible for thousands of years— now were dots of towns made up of luxury-style homes and huge pagoda-like structures. Roads had been plowed through the dense forests and highways built to tie them together. Many small but capable airports were in evidence as well. As vile as their motives may have been, the Japanese had done to South America what no one—not even its inhabitants—had ever been able to do: Tame it. Exploit it. *Civilize* it.

In less than a year.

Quite a feat.

Too bad it was not long to last. Of this, Hunter was sure, as he zoomed over dozens of new villages and settlements, all of them bearing an Asian imprint in design. Because here and there he would come upon a city, and there would inevitably be firebomb damage somewhere within it. This was the evidence of the relentless bombings from Xwo Mountain. Soon, when the other three hidden air bases became active, this bombing campaign would quadruple in intensity. Then, if Brazil really did come into the war . . .

But was that going to happen now? Was the Brazil operation still on? Hunter wasn't sure. If the upcoming Panama invasion plan was simply a massive deception to cover for his upcoming secret mission, then what the hell was the massive buildup in Brazil all about? Again, he didn't know, and something inside him was telling him he really didn't want to find out. He had to concentrate on the matters at hand here. Get the Bomb, drop the Bomb. Whatever else was going to happen, it would have to happen without him.

So he flew on.

Two minutes to go. While he wasn't quite clear on many things from his time Back There, he had a feeling that wars were not fought in the same way as they were Here. In both this conflict and the last war against Germany, there never seemed to be any middle ground. One side was usually destroying the other. One side was always on the verge of victory, only to be tripped up by some quirk or incident, and then see the scales tipped all the way back to the opponent again.

Just a few months before, it appeared that Japan was unstoppable in its conquest of South America. Now, while the conquering of the land still went on, and Japanese citizens were still pouring into the country for the repopulation programs, it was not like landing in some foreign paradise anymore. Hunter and the people atop of Xwo had made sure of that. They had turned the place into a battleground, and that had changed everything. Now the pendulum was swinging very quickly in America's favor. Hunter knew—and he hoped the OSS realized—that they would be wise to take the momentum and end this thing before the inevitable swing happened again and they were all looking back down the wrong end of the Japanese sword.

He was sure his whole secret mission was the first step in that kind of plan. In fact, maybe it was the only step. . . .

At exactly thirty seconds to go, Hunter came out of a cloud bank at 80,000 feet. Once again it was just him, the moon, and the stars.

The mission screen began blinking green at ten seconds out, red at five seconds out, and then it finally went all white.

Slowly, the animation began to form. It was a map, outlining the lower half of the South American continent. A little cartoon version of his airplane appeared and began moving south. He was being told to proceed to a coordinate shown on the map's grid as Tango Point Charlie, a location just off the coast of southern Argentina. From there, he was to head in an easterly direction for nearly 500 miles. At that point he would intercept a homing beacon which would lead him to an airport. Here he would land and go AFI—await further instructions.

At first the directions off the coordinate seemed simplistic. Basically the MVP was telling him to get down to the tail of South America and take a left. Then fly for a few hundred miles. But what exactly was out there?

Hunter pushed the grid map extension and got his answer right away. Two oddly shaped islands riding amidst the high waves of the South Atlantic.

Yes, he had heard of them. They were actually infamous in a way.

They were called the Falkland Islands.

Twenty-three

Nevada

Agent Y was sitting in a control room in the heart of the Area 52 command center.

Before him was a bank of six TV screens. His ever-present MVP was plugged into the console beneath these screens and connected to an interface which tied into the room's gigantic Main/AC computer. The thinking machine was whirring away, blinking and burping as usual. On the six TV screens there was a small clock in the right-hand corner counting down to 0100 hours mountain time.

This was a big night for Y, a big night for this audacious plan which had Hawk Hunter flying somewhere down at the bottom of the planet, thousands of soldiers sitting on the border of Brazil, thousands more getting ready to jump off for the Panama Canal—and Y sitting here alone in a TV control room.

This was Phase 3 of the Big Plan; in Y's own language, the Gathering of the Associates, possibly the strangest part of all.

At that moment, there were six OSS "hit squads" scattered across the country. Each one was waiting for the small clock in the corner of their MVPs to click down to 0100 hours. Each group was equipped with an insta-camera which would feed live visuals to the control room monitors arrayed in front of Y.

Y didn't smoke cigarettes, but if he did, he would have lit one up now. Trying to pull all these strings—while the Main/AC was pulling his—was a nonstop juggle. The multilevel diversion plan, Hunter's suicide mission, this mysterious Bomb.

It was strange, though, because in all this, it was the odd disappearance of his estranged colleagues, Agents X and Z, that kept coming back to him. In some ways it made everything that much stranger.

Where were they? Alive or dead? Free or imprisoned? On the inside or on the out? The fact that the agents were missing was the best-kept secret on a planet overloaded with top secrets and intrigue. Could they have been kidnapped by Japanese agents? Y doubted it. His colleagues were not so foolish as to leave themselves exposed to a snatch. Were they dead? Assassinated maybe? By a enemy hit squad? Y doubted that too. The cosmos just didn't feel like X and Z were gone.

So where the hell were they? At this, the most critical time in the country's history since the last critical time in the war with Germany, two of the most valuable spies around had decided to go underground. It was all so very odd. . . .

Y checked the time again. It was the last minute of the countdown. He really didn't have time to worry about X and Z's whereabouts now. He had more important things to do.

The clock finally ticked down the last few seconds, then instantly the six TV screens came to life.

Y immediately activated his microphone and was talking to Squad A. They were located in a section of northeastern Pennsylvania known as the Endless Mountains. They were in front of a nondescript, pleasant-looking house.

"OK, go," Y told them.

Two agents got out of their car, one carrying the insta-cam with him. Whatever was to happen next, Y would see it in real time.

The agents approached the front door and hesitated a moment before knocking. There was a noise in the background. A high-pitched whining. Electrical. Possibly a power tool of some kind.

They rang the doorbell and a pleasant-looking Asian woman answered the door. Two young girls were in the background watching TV. The agents identified themselves. The woman looked over their ID cards.

"We'd like to speak with your husband," one of the agents told the woman as politely as possible. She showed them in, they passed through the living room where the two young girls politely said hello. They proceeded down a set of stairs to the basement where a workshop was located. The husband, wearing a protective mask, was leaning over a large power saw, cutting a length of very thin material, half plastic, half wood. Before him was a large, incomplete—well, something. Y could not tell what it was from the camera's angle.

The two agents walked forward and finally the wife got the man's attention. The power saw stopped. The object he was working on came into better view. It was an airplane—a small one, but one that looked to be jet-powered and highly advanced in its stunning design.

The man lifted his protective mask; he was slightly startled, slightly confused. The agents showed their IDs. The man read them and relaxed somewhat.

Finally one agent spoke.

"Is your name Ben Wa?" he asked.

At nearly the exact moment, Squad B was approaching the door to a teachers' residence on the campus of J. Kathryn College, outside of Chicago.

The pair of agents, camera running, went through the main door, up two flights of stairs and stopped at Room 1333. They knocked twice. The door eventually opened, but very slowly.

Watching TV monitor 2, Y got an unexpected eyeful. The dormlike room was filled with young coeds, all in various states of undress. Some were awake and engaged in animated conversation; others appeared to be napping. Four were playing cards in one corner. Another pair were kissing and fondling one another nearby. One side of the room had been turned into a photography area with a large white backdrop, low-intensity lights, and an expensive portrait camera set on a tripod. Here, a group of semi-naked beauties were taking pictures of each other.

In the midst of this harem sat one man. He was in his mid twenties, fashionably if comfortably dressed, with tussled hair and a professorial beard. This is a teacher's residence; he is the teacher.

He is also the man the two agents have come to see.

The agents make their way over to the man, show their ID cards, and ask him a single question:

"Are you J.T. Toomey?"

On TV monitor 3, very nearly the same sequence was playing out.

A pair of OSS agents were walking toward a bar located in the northernmost city of New England, a place called Loring, Maine.

The weather was so cold the vapor was fogging the lens of the insta-camera, even in the few seconds it took for the agents to cross the street and go into the saloon. The place was loud and rowdy, but warm. A pool game was going on in one corner. Many dancing girls were in evidence. Many patrons were carrying firearms. From Y's point of view, it looked like the Old West, except it was really the cold Northeast.

The agents threaded their way through the crowd, finally coming to a table where a man sat counting out huge stacks of money.

Beside him were two enormous female bodyguards, armed with shotguns, hand-cannon pistols, and dressed entirely in black leather.

The man looked up at the OSS agents, and like the previous two subjects, greeted them with a facial expression that was a mixture of surprise and bemusement.

"Trouble with your bill, gentlemen?" he asked with a thick Canadian accent.

The agents ignored the jibe and got right to business. "Mr. Frost, we presume?"

Oddly enough, the fourth TV monitor was broadcasting from a place that Y had just left.

It was in a squad car parked outside the Visiting Players entrance to the huge Dallas football stadium.

As always, there was a crowd of fans and general street partiers passing by, even though it was fairly late in the evening.

The agents left their car, going quickly through the merry crowd and gaining access to the Visiting Players door via a door-unlocking tool carried by all OSS operatives.

They walked down a long tile corridor and finally found themselves looking at the door to the visiting team's locker room. The temporary sign on the door read: NEW JERSEY GIANTS. NO ADMITTANCE.

The agents went in without knocking and were confronted by what appeared to Y to be an entire professional football team, all suited up, just seconds away from running out onto the field. There were about fifty people in all. Some stared blankly into the insta-camera lens. Most ignored it entirely.

The agents approached the man who was obviously in charge of the team. He was surrounded by five other coaches. They had their names sewn into their workout shirts: Matus. Palma. Cerbasi. Vittelo. Delusso. McCaffery.

The agents showed their ID badges to everyone, then came face to face with the man in the middle.

"Coach Geraci?" one asked. "May we have a word with you please?"

Hit Team Five was slightly late in finding their subjects.

The contact point was in the isolated foothills near Santa Fe, New Mexico, and the ride out had been a long, dusty, dirty affair for the OSS men. When the agents finally did arrive, they were certain they were at the wrong place.

It was not a bar or a suburban house or a college harem or a football team locker room. It was a monastery—out in the middle of nowhere.

The agents checked back with Y that they were indeed at the right location, and he confirmed that they were. They got out of the vehicle, went through the main gate, and quickly spotted a room in the courtyard from which a faint light was coming.

They knocked on the door and were greeted by a nun, young, fresh-faced, but heavily garbed in a white habit.

The agents had a few words with her, apologizing for the late hour. She led them into the main dining room. Here a small group of monks was just beginning a late meal. They all looked up—again a look of bafflement on their faces.

Oddly, the monks were wearing name tags: Brother Miller. Brother Snyder. Brother Higgens. Brother Maas.

The agents walked over to the monk sitting at the end of the table. They flashed their ID cards.

But the monk spoke before they could.

"I am Brother Jim Cook," he said. "May I help you with something?"

Y had been privy to a confidential information message concerning the subject of Hit Team 6.

For whatever reason, the Main/AC was expecting the sixth person to be the hardest to track down, the hardest to contact, and possibly the hardest to convince of what his country expected him to do.

Finding him did turn out to be a bitch. It took all of forty-eight hours, which was forty-seven hours and fifty-five seconds longer than it took to locate all of the other contacts combined. The sixth man was finally tracked down to a small military outpost in the wilds of the Florida Keys. It was a reserve naval station, a place that was always on the cusp of deactivation. It held a complement of exactly sixteen men.

The station had a seaplane—a small, two-engine recon thing—and the man the OSS men had to track down was its pilot.

They found him in the operations hut, writing a report and drinking a huge cup of mud-black coffee.

The agents walked in and took stock of their subject. Back at the Area 52 command hut, Y was doing the same.

The man was in his mid thirties, with slightly graying hair. His face was red, his nose redder. He was, as they would say, a fireplug of a man. But, in his defense, there was an air of slight sophistication about his face.

He was rugged, tough, and obviously very strong. Yet he smiled broadly when the agents appeared. There was no look of confusion or befuddlement here. This man *knew* something.

As Y watched, the agents introduced themselves, pulling out their ID cards and then showing them to the subject.

But the man barely read their names.

"How strange is this?" he asked, a slight brogue in his voice. "I dreamed this would happen and now it is."

"Sir?" one agents replied.

"You're OSS, I know," the man continued. "And your computer selected me as one of a bunch of people for a secret project. Right?"

The agents were startled, so much so, one looked directly into the insta-camera and shrugged. Y was fairly astonished too. How could the strange little man possibly know this, unless he was telling the truth and *actually* did dream it?

He stood up and began packing his bag—that's how ready he was to go.

Finally Y just sent the agents a voice message. "He's so willing, looks like you will have no problems at all."

The agents on the other end agreed. Then one turned to the man and said, "For the record sir? Your name is . . ."

The subject smiled again and then looked directly into the camera.

"Mike Fitzgerald," he replied.

Twenty-four

Hunter arrived at his first coordinate less than twenty minutes after receiving his orders.

His grid map indicated he was over a point in Argentina called Punta Norte. It was a coastal city, thick with cargo ships and tankers bringing in supplies for the Occupation Forces. Someday soon, he imagined, it would feel the sting of an American firebombing.

It was now 0530 hours, and way off in the distance Hunter could see the beginnings of the new dawn.

He punched his present location into the in-flight system and waited while the MVP agreed with his selection. Then he made a long turn to the east, set his throttles to supercruise, and felt the *Stiletto* accelerate smoothly through the clean air.

The ocean horizon stretched out before him now, and he detected no less than six storms within his visual range. To his right, where the reaches of Antarctica could be found, a large white blizzard was in full blow. To his left, whipping off the coast of Uruguay, a tropical storm was beginning to stir. But the largest disturbance of all was right in front of him. It was an enormous tempest, black and gray clouds twirling in a counterclockwise motion, like a slow-motion tornado, tearing off the Argentine coast and heading east, out to sea.

Hunter checked his coordinates with the MVP and they

came back as OK. He wondered, briefly, what the Z-3/15's characteristics would be in bad weather. The plane was built to carve through clean high air with the greatest of ease. How would its needle shape, short wings, and enormous fuel tanks take to the bad atmospherics? He decided to find out.

He reduced speed to barely Mach 1 and took a long, deep breath of oxygen. The storm clouds were topping 55,000 feet—he held at about 53,000 and dove in.

There was a little buffeting, and his needle nose began oscillating slightly. But Hunter simply pushed the throttles ahead a notch and everything smoothed out. He took another deep breath of Big O in celebration. This airplane was simply amazing. . . .

Suddenly, everything began shaking again.

Hunter immediately checked the aircraft's instrumentation. The cockpit of the Z-3/15 was an elegant array of buttons, push pads, and switches. At the moment, all of them were lit and normal. This proved one thing: It wasn't the airplane that was shaking. It was him.

He checked the MVP. Maybe this vibe was a prelude to some kind of wacky message coming in from the mother-hen Main/AC?

But no. The MVP was clear.

Whatever was making him shake was local. He scanned the skies above and to the sides—maybe there were some unfriendly fighters lurking in this soup? If any enemy aircraft were close by and he had to fight them, he would at least see what the *Stiletto* could do in a shoot-out. But both his radar screens were clear: the one installed in the aircraft and the more efficient and accurate one located between his temple lobes.

So why the shakes? he wondered.

Purely on instinct, he began to dive. Through the thick clouds, through the swirling winds, through the rain itself.

The needle-nose airplane was down from 55-angels to barely a mile high in less than twenty seconds.

That's when he saw them.

Warships. A small fleet of them. Right below him. Two destroyers and two cruisers, escorting six cargo ships. There was no guessing here; these cargo humpers were troop carriers. Leading the fleet was an aircraft carrier. Not one of the mammoth subs that Japan had recently used in its conquests, or a megacarrier of the type the U.S. Navy favored. This was medium-sized for this world, and thus, odd in its own way. But still it could carry at least 200 aircraft.

Just who these ships belonged to seemed very apparent. All of them were flying the huge red ball flag of the Japanese Occupation forces. No wonder his entire body was vibrating.

But worst of all was the direction of these enemy warships.

Like the storm, they were heading east.

Right toward the Falklands.

There were two working airports on the Falkland Islands.

One was at Stanley, the capital. It had a 6,500-foot runway, capable of handling small fighters and cargo airplanes. Neither made any regular trips there however.

The larger airport was actually a somnambulant RAF base located at McReady Bay on the northwestern tip of East Falkland.

This base boasted no less than seven runways, two of them 20,000-foot giants capable of handling just about any plane flying, save the latest supermonsters. McReady had been built in 1983 during the war with Germany to interdict German supply routes coming around Cape Horn. When the war switched phases and all action left the area, the base was all but mothballed. The maritime and defensive airplanes were moved out, and now the base supported a single C-330 Hercules S&R plane, a few prop observation planes, and an ancient Beater.

The base did not even have an operational early warning system. No base emergency alarm, no long-range threat radar. Its entire defensive package was made up of exactly two 188-mm triple-barreled flak guns.

For the two dozen people assigned to the base and those citizens living in the village of Hampton nearby, the first warning that anything was wrong came from three miles across Falkland Sound. It was a coded message sent by a detachment of the Special Tank Services commandos which were in charge of protecting the small farmhouse on the hill near Summer Point.

Their mobile attack-threat radar had detected an unknown aerial force heading east toward the Falklands. This urgent message had been sent at exactly 0600 hours. But by the time the people at the McReady Air Base received the message, decoded it, understood it, asked for confirmation, and then decoded *that* message, it was too late.

Fighter-bombers bearing the red ball markings of the Nipponese Occupation Army had already appeared overhead.

Two and a half miles away, across the sound which separated East and West Falkland, the detachment of STS soldiers who had sent the warning message were perched on a high cliff which looked out on the water and East Falkland itself.

They were inside the huge armored vehicle known as the Roamer. From this high ground, they could clearly see McReady air base and the enemy planes that were now circling overhead.

It was these soldiers who first realized something bad was on the way. On a security patrol around the tip of West Falkland, a routine drill performed as part of their protection duties for the farmhouse on the hill, the soldiers had set up their mobile long-range aerial threat and surface-radar array. The exercise was performed more to test the equipment than anything else. The STS commandos had been astonished when they had turned on their screens and seen a ten-ship task force heading right for them.

The ships and their size indicated they were not friendlies. One of the vessels was an aircraft carrier of medium size and as they watched on their radar screens, this ship had commenced launching airplanes. Most of those attack planes were now circling above McReady Air Field.

There were seven STS soldiers inside the Roamer, which was a kind of half tank, half personnel carrier that came equipped with many warning devices and communications equipment. Thirty-five feet long, fifteen feet wide, and weighing in at twenty-five tons, the Roamer also had a small but lethal antiaircraft weapon on board. It was a guided rocket array which could launch up to sixteen small, semi-maneuverable HE projectiles at an airplane, hoping that one or more of the rockets would hit something. It was the shotgun approach to antiaircraft artillery.

The problem was that the rocket array could only be effective inside a three mile range—the Roamer's current position was two and a half miles away from McReady, nearly at the edge of the AA weapons envelope. The STS men would have to pick their targets very carefully, and be fully prepared not to hit a thing.

They had already messaged back to the farmhouse, of course, and the tank crews back there were at that moment going into high alert, mode one. This meant the threat to the farmhouse and the facility below was at the highest point possible. The orders back from the STS commanders was for the Roamer crew to aid the defenders of McReady air field in any way they could, even if the sky was about to fall in on them. Gaining this vantage point at Point

Curly and studying the situation was the first part of the Roamer crew's carrying out of this order.

By the time the sun broke the far, stormy horizon, the full enemy aerial force had arrived over McReady. The aircraft were of two types. Roughly half of the fifty airplanes were SuperKate attack craft. Large two-man jet bombers, these planes had been instrumental in the sneak attack on Panama almost a year earlier. Each plane was weighed down with eight 2,000-pound Hiki bombs known for their building-busting as well as their runway-cratering capabilities.

The other two dozen airplanes were SuperZeroes, the powerful, highly maneuverable jet fighter of choice of the Nipponese Occupation Forces.

There was another airplane out there as well—bigger than the others, and slower too. It was a multiengined affair, a unique aircraft known for its ultra-long range, its relatively lightweight construction, and its bug-eyed appearance. It was orbiting out to sea, about twenty-five miles north of McReady. Out of visual range and for the most part flying below radar, the STS commandos could only guess what its purpose was.

Once the attacking forces were set, the SuperKates began to dive on McReady. Screaming down from a height of 15,000 feet, they dove in pairs, their first target the base's second-longest runway.

The first pair swept in, laying their 2,000-pound bombs in a line across the field's north-to-northwest runway, a 9,000-foot strip. The bombs hit hard and exploded like a line of gigantic fireworks. The plumes of smoke, flame, and concrete went straight up in the air, nearly clipping the tails of both attacking airplanes—that's how precise these pilots were.

As the second pair of SuperKates came down, their bombs heading for the same runway, the base's defenders finally opened up. The two AA guns, one located at each end of the base, began valiantly firing away at the attack planes. But it was a rather pathetic sight. The air was filled with swirling aircraft, bombs were falling, engines screaming, and in the middle of it all was the rather weak *pop-pop-pop* of the two small, antiquated AA guns.

Somehow word about the defenders' weapons reached back up to the SuperZeroes, who were circling the attack area in carousel fashion at about 8,500 feet. Two of them broke off from this orbit and came screaming out of the cloud layer. It was obvious they were going in to strafe the AA guns.

That's when the STS men went into action.

One AA gun was located at the northwestern edge of the base, and, at about 3,000 yards, the closest defenders' position to the STS team's Roamer. One of the SuperZeroes came down to nearly wavetop level and began a run across Falkland Sound, heading straight for the AA gun which was still popping away at the SuperKates.

This flight path took it right past the cliff where the STS Roamer lay in wait. With the 'Zero slowing in speed and its pilot obviously powering up his electric guns, the STS commander sighted his hot engine and launched a half-barrel barrage of AA guided rockets. The eight projectiles went spiraling away from the hidden cliff position, turning swiftly if uneasily as their primitive radiation-seeking nose cones followed the warm electronic heartbeat being emitted by the attacking SuperZero.

Their paths might have looked uncertain, but the timing of the barrage couldn't have been better. Five of the eight rockets hit the 'Zero and a sixth clipped its tail. There was a series of quick explosions as the tiny HE warheads blew up. A second later the SuperZero began to come apart.

First there was smoke. Then flame. Then many swirling pieces of metal, bone, and skin. Another explosion shook the morning air. After that, there was nothing left of the

'Zero or its pilot except tiny pieces of debris falling into the cold, choppy waters of the Sound.

Scratch one SuperZero.

But now the STS crew had a problem. It had revealed its position. Still, when the second SuperZero came in, mimicking its partner's path, the Roamer opened up again, this time launching its eight remaining guided rockets. Only two of the projectiles hit the target this time, but it was enough to sheer off the unsuspecting 'Zero's wing and send the plane careening into the sound, right after its partner.

While all this was going on, the SuperKates continued their systematic cratering of the base's northwest runway. Several control buildings had also been hit and now long plumes of smoke were beginning to rise above the airfield.

The Japanese planes were going about their job in a very leisurely fashion. The base's AA guns were still firing, but now a swarm of 'Zeroes came screaming down and, avoiding the lethal approach over the sound, began mercilessly strafing both AA guns from the opposite direction.

Even worse, a six-pack of SuperZeroes had located the Roamer's position and were now coming out of the sky, cannons powered up, intent on destroying it.

The crew of the Roamer locked up tight and began moving off the cliff. Its commander knew he had to get to a less exposed position, but such a maneuver would be difficult. The terrain all around Point Curly was wide open, rocky, with barely a tree or a bush in sight to hide behind. Their only chance, and it was a slim one, was to make a mad dash for the bottom of the cliff, where heavy beach foliage and some convenient rock outcrops could be found.

Two 'Zeroes came in just as the huge tracked vehicle had backed out onto the roadway from which it had come. Both 'Zeroes opened up with electric guns and cannon, both missing the Roamer cleanly, but not by a wide margin.

A second pair of 'Zeroes were right on their tails. Their aim was true, and in seconds heavy machine gun rounds began pinging all over the Roamer's turret.

It was at this point that the Roamer's commander sent an urgent message back to the command hut at the farmhouse, telling them they were under attack, that there was little they could do about it, and to please dispatch "any and all" aid or recovery forces—STS lingo for, send some body bags for us. So desperate was this message—sent as a third pair of 'Zeroes were homing in—the Roamer commander ended it with the even more fateful words, "God Save the Queen."

All did seem rather bleak inside the Roamer at that moment. They were about to be torn apart by cannon shells, McReady airfield was about to be bombed out of existence, and a substantial naval force was on its way to invade the island, all of which would put their main responsibility—the operation at the farmhouse—in dire straits indeed.

To a man then, the STS troopers believed that they had fucked up royally and that by failing to protect the secret at the farmhouse, they'd triggered a widespread, global event of historic proportion.

That's why it was so strange that in that last dark second when they were convinced only a miracle could save them, that's exactly what happened.

Their first indication was that the expected barrage of armor-piercing, skin-ripping, bone-crunching cannon fire never came. They heard the 'Zeroes bearing down on them—but they heard another sound as well. This one was deeper on the mechanical end, yet higher in pitch.

The noise, and the strange echoing that accompanied it, led them to think that whatever was making it was going very very fast.

They did hear the unmistakable sound of an aerial cannon going off—this was the last sound many a soldier had heard, and it was terrifying. But the fusillade did not hit the Roamer. Instead the Roamer just kept on going, at full speed, twisting and turning down the steep road off the cliff.

The commander was pounding his driver on the back to go faster, and the driver was trying to comply. But in the confusion and the sheer elation of not being dead yet, the commander did not realize the vehicle's power plants had no more rpm left in them.

About hallway down the hill they heard more cannon fire, more screeching engines—but still, no gut-wrenching cannon barrage came. The driver was now eyeing a small forest at the bottom of the hill, hard by a frozen bog and next to an outcrop of thick granite rocks. It would be a perfect place to hide.

He made for it quickly. Through more noise and engine screeching and cannon rattling, the big vehicle somehow skidded its way through the trees and under the protective granite top.

Only then did the commander order all stop and told his men to stay fast and in place.

Then he lifted the turret hatch and had a look out.

Jet engines were still screaming and cannons were still rattling and the bombing of McReady field was still booming in the background, but the commander wasn't paying much attention to any of it. He was looking straight up into the clear cold sky above them.

For the first time ever, his men actually heard him curse.

"Goddamn!" he yelled excitedly. "What the hell is *that?*"

Across the sound at McReady, the crew manning AA gun emplacement #2 was running out of ammunition.

It had been years since they'd fired their gun, it was a small wonder it was working at all. They had been hitting targets since the terrifying aerial attack began five minutes ago. The sky was so full of Japanese aircraft, it would have been hard *not* to hit anything.

So they had destroyed three SuperKates and had damaged at least three more. But again, it didn't make any difference. There were so many enemy airplanes roaring about, killing three and banging three would have little effect. There was no doubt who would ultimately prevail in this battle.

But the gun crew had been firing away madly nevertheless and now they were running out of ammunition. Once they ran through their last magazine, what would happen? They didn't know. . . .

Meanwhile, the enemy airplanes were so systematically attacking the air base, it was easy to see what their plan was. The main north-to-northwest runway was destroyed by now, as were the two smaller east-to-west strips. But this still left four major runways unscathed, three big enough to handle fighters, one that could handle everything but monsters.

It was the same with the hard targets. The attackers had blown up the half dozen support buildings at the base, along with the main access road, a bridge, and the water desalination plant. Left untouched were the weather rooms, the control towers, the main radar station, the fueling facility, and the backup communications hut.

So the intentions were clear: The attackers were seeking to disable the air base but not destroy it. In other words, they wanted to take it over.

And kill everyone on the ground in the process.

That's what happened to Gun Crew #1, far across the base. They and their gun had gone up in a huge explosion about a minute before, courtesy of a double pounce by a pair of SuperZeroes. Now Gun Crew #2 was all that was left between the attackers and giving up the ghost. Though valiant and loyal, none of the six men in the crew wanted

to die here, in the lonely northwestern edge of East Falkland Island, literally out in the middle of nowhere.

But that's what was going to happen. The crew let off
its last ammo tube, and tore a good chunk off the tail of
a SuperKate—and then the gun went dry.

The gun crew had rifles, but it would have been pathetic
to try to fight off the huge fighters and attack planes with
small-caliber ammunition. Not that the gun crew would
have any chance to do so. Now that the first gun crew was
gone, no less than eight SuperZeroes were diving on the
#2 gun position. Each plane had four machine guns and
a cannon. Combined, one plane could spit out nearly 300
rounds in three seconds. Multiplied by eight, that's the
fusillade that awaited the hapless gunners.

It was odd, then, because the British soldiers did raise
their rifles at the first SuperZero coming in. They all knew
they were just seconds from death in this godforsaken
place. The SuperZero was coming right across the tarmac
at them, five yellow splashes of light emanating from its
nose and wings. The air was suddenly filled with fire and
hot, piercing lead. A couple of the men began praying. A
couple began shooting back. . . .

And then, something very strange happened.

To the men in the guncrew, it looked like a white
streak—a bolt of lightning from the cold, smoky sky.

It went by them so fast, it really *was* a blur. No sharp
edges could be detected at all. A second later, the SuperZero that had been bearing down on the gun crew was
gone. There was some smoke, some flame, and a few pieces
of wreckage, but nothing else remained. Instead of a barrage of deadly cannon fire and machine gun bullets, the
gun crew was covered in a small cloud of cinders.

The men looked at each other in disbelief. The bombing
of the field was continuing, jet engines were still screech-

ing, explosions were still going off. Yet somehow, they were still alive.

Now the second SuperZero was coming in low and slow and firing all its guns at once too. Suddenly the white streak was back and the attacking enemy airplane went up in a ball of fire and smoke as well. The same thing happened to the third 'Zero, and then the fourth.

Lying on the ground, hands over their heads at this point, the members of the gun crew looked up and saw this strange flying thing above them again. The white streak was taking on the image of an airplane, but it was still going terribly fast. Attacking planes were falling out of the sky all around them. Crashing, exploding, disintegrating—suddenly the gun crew was more in danger of getting killed by a piece of falling wreckage than by the bombs and cannon rounds of the attackers.

A SuperKate, totally in flame, came crashing down no more than fifteen feet away from the depleted gun, so close it had actually burned several gun crew members slightly. At that moment the crew got up as one and ran toward a cement embankment next to a burning maintenance shed nearby.

From here they had a better view of what was going on above them. But still it was a fantastic, confusing scene.

The white streak was a fighter aircraft. They could see it better now. Its wings and nose were emitting huge streaks of muzzle flame—much bigger than those of the attacking Japanese planes. It was shooting down the enemy aircraft as if they were standing still. Its pilot was making his way through the attackers, weaving a tapestry of flame and jet exhaust in his deadly wake. No shot was wasted, no movement of the airplane superfluous. Every bullet hit, every cannon round exploded, every attacker caught in its gun sights went down.

But this airplane—it just didn't seem real. It was going too fast, flying too low. It was performing aerobatics that seemed to defy physics itself. The attacking airplanes tried like hell to get out of its way, but once before its gun barrels, the white streak would simply emit a few well-placed cannon rounds and go on to the next attacker. The plane hit would invariably go down in flames.

This all lasted less than two minutes, but as the gun crew watched in awe, it seemed to go on for hours.

Finally, the scream of jet engines began to fade. The sound of gunfire drifted away, and all that was left was the wind whipping off the sound and the crackling of flames all over the heavily damaged base. Those Japanese planes not shot down had turned tail and were running for home.

The gun crew saw the white streak roar overhead and out to sea to a point about fifteen miles offshore. Here they saw a glint of yellow and a large puff of black smoke. This grew larger and closer and the gun crew saw that it was actually another airplane. A recon plane of some sort, bug-eyed in appearance, with six engines, all now trailing smoke. The white plane had somehow spotted it, had shot it up, and now its pilots were desperately trying to make a crash landing on solid ground. To crash at sea, in the cold South Atlantic, meant certain death to everyone on board.

It took about thirty seconds for the recon plane to reach the shoreline, its wings smoking, its fuselage in flames. It suddenly veered off to the right, went across the sound, and crashed onto a small island about hallway between East and West Falkland.

After that, it got real quiet. Just the wind could be heard.

Then the white plane landed.

The gun crew joined the dozen or so survivors of the air base in running across the burning tarmac, toward the long runway where the white plane had set down. At that same time, the Roamer, recovered from its ordeal on West Falkland, had forded the sound and was climbing up onto the long runway from the other side.

The white plane finally came to a stop and simultaneously was surrounded by the base workers, the ecstatic gun
crew, and the members of the STS squad.

After a few moments, the canopy lifted off the needle-
nosed airplane and Hawk Hunter stood up and stretched
his tired legs.

He looked down to see two dozen faces looking up at
him, and a few gun barrels too.

Finally one of the STS soldiers stepped forward, his pistol pointing directly up at Hunter.

With a thick English accent, he asked, *"And who the hell
are you?"*

Twenty-five

Near Summer Point

The man in the farmhouse had never worn a battle helmet.

There had never been a need before. He was not a soldier. Not Here. Not There.

But he had a helmet on now and his wife did too. And their front lawn, where they had so laboriously tried to grow green grass for the past twenty years, was now all mud, churned up from tank treads. Indeed, an enormous SuperChieftain tank was sitting right outside their front door, its crew at their battle stations, its three gigantic 188-mm antiaircraft guns pointing skyward in three different directions.

Another SuperChieftain, just as big, its treads just as destructive, was sitting by their back door. A third was firmly implanted in the cabbage patch next to the house. A fourth was hidden in the apple orchard.

Down by the front gate, a series of trenches had been blown out of the rocklike peat by the Special Tank Service commandos, using rubber explosives. These trenches were now bristling with two-man cannons, recoilless rifles, and antipersonnel rocket launchers. All of them were pointing down the east road, the barely paved path which led to the beach. There were so many heavy weapons on the front lawn of the farmhouse, it seemed like there were more guns than soldiers to man them. In fact, this was the truth.

The man and his wife were sitting on the living room couch watching all this out their huge picture window. They were at a 2,197-foot elevation; the height gave a good view of the surroundings for miles around. From here, down the hill and beyond the stunted scrub trees, was the beach, and beyond that, Falkland Sound. Three and a half miles beyond that was McReady airfield. At the moment, it was nearly obscured by clouds of billowing smoke.

They had watched the titanic air battle from their living room, nervously sipping their morning tea. Against the typically gray skies, it had looked like a fireworks display going off. Red and yellow explosions above the air base. Millions of sparks spraying everywhere. The battle had seemed time-delayed, though. They would see a flash and then the fire and smoke—and the sound and concussions would arrive half a minute later. The same was true for the scream of the jet engines and the multitudes of sonic booms. Some of them had been so strong, they'd rattled the farmhouse down to its many foundations.

The battle had ended about thirty minutes ago and now all was quiet—except for the noise of the tank's engines running in the cold air outside the front door. Still, the smoke continued rising above McReady Field, and some major fires were raging out of control across the sound as well. The heavy winds were whipping these flames everywhere, blowing some of the thick black smoke all over the normally peaceful Falkland Sound.

The man had no idea what had happened, but it seemed very apparent an enemy had come to the Falkland Islands. Now, his main concern was for his wife's safety. He had to protect her, no matter what the cost. That much was a given.

But he was also responsible for the lives of the men working in the facility deep below the farmhouse: the scientists, the technicians, the support people. Colonel Asten, the STS unit's overall commander, had sent two soldiers down into the Hole to bolster the pair of guards permanently stationed down there. But he knew, should the situation get critical, all four of these commandos would have to come back up top and fight in the trenches along with the rest of their unit.

The man shuddered to think how bad the situation would be if that turned out to be the case.

The man poured his wife another cup of tea, then strapped his helmet down and walked out onto the front porch.

Colonel Asten was there, huddled over a field-size Boomer, trying to get a clear radio channel to an RAF base on Ascension Island and not having a good time of it. The radio transmitter at McReady had been destroyed in the air battle. It was this transmitter the STS used to "steal" from. That is, feed off of without the people at McReady knowing about it. With that line of communications gone, the STS unit was suddenly very isolated. The commandos had been trying to get a message out since the first plane appeared over McReady. They had not come anywhere close to succeeding as of yet.

Asten saw the man come out the door. The STS commander told his radio man to keep trying, then walked up to the front porch.

"Any further news, Colonel?" the man asked him.

The STS officer's face looked uncharacteristically pained.

"No, sir," he said. "No news at all, I'm afraid. McReady's radio transmitter is knocked out. The base is being abandoned and we are taking the survivors over here."

"What are you expecting next exactly?" the man asked him.

"I'm not sure," Asten replied truthfully. "The air attack on McReady might have been an isolated event, or it might

be the prelude to something—though it did end rather
unexpectedly. The airplanes were definitely of Japanese
origin. They have been making lots of noise over on the
continent, as you know. But I'm afraid that's all I can tell
you, sir."

The man just shook his head. That was enough.

"It is best then that you and your wife stay inside, sir,"
Asten went on. "In fact, you might consider joining the
others down below."

"Do you have a gun for me?" the man asked him unexpectedly.

Asten was stumped for a moment. It was a rather strange
request, considering.

"If it comes to that," Asten finally answered. "I'll see
what I can do."

With that, the man nodded numbly and went back inside the house.

His wife's usually pleasant face was now thick with worry.

"What is it?" she asked him, hoping he would report it
was all just a plane crash or a false alarm. But his own
worried features betrayed him.

"They may be expecting some . . ." he stuttered, grop-
ing for the right word, *"uninvited* company. But I'm certain
they can handle it."

Still the man did not want to take any chances that his
wife might be in danger. Instinct was telling him it might
be best to go below immediately. He helped her off the
couch and together they walked toward the closet door
behind which lay the hidden elevator.

"Let's go make some doughnuts," he told her softly.
"Together."

Twenty minutes later, the Roamer appeared.

Crawling up the south road, its crew was hanging all
over the sides, its twin exhaust tubes spewed large clouds

of black smoke. The approaching vehicle was traveling as fast as it could, its engines screaming in response. Still, it was coming up the hill, very slowly.

It topped the crest and squealed to a stop next to the huge SuperChieftain tank positioned at the front gate of the farmhouse. The Roamer crewmen jumped off, exhausted from their adrenaline-packed experience against the Japanese planes.

The Roamer's driver killed his engines and now the commander of the vehicle climbed out of the front hatch and down the access ladder. He was a lieutenant, his name was Ponch. Behind him was the driver, his hands and face covered with sweat and grease. Behind him, led out by two privates, was Hawk Hunter. He was blindfolded.

Colonel Asten greeted Ponch with a silent salute. Ponch had radioed him right after the air battle had concluded. He told the STS CO that he was bringing someone back from McReady, someone that the colonel absolutely had to talk to.

Now this man was standing before him. Asten took a long look.

He was a pilot, his uniform was a flight suit. He was a very strange sort; that was Asten's first impression. He looked different, but in a way the STS commander could not describe, not even to himself. He looked familiar too; Asten had been stationed in the Falklands for four years. He didn't see much from the outside world. But this man's face he might have caught on a TV report, or perhaps in a newspaper at some point.

Asten walked Ponch a few paces away from the Roamer, out of earshot of Hunter.

"OK, who is he?," Asten asked the Roamer commander.

"He's the pilot who saved us and the airfield," Ponch replied starkly "He's the guy who iced all those Japanese airplanes."

Asten had seen the white blur twisting and turning

through the attackers. The carcasses of more than two dozen SuperKates and 'Zeroes were still burning over at McReady or in the waters nearby. There was no doubt that through his amazing aeronautics, this man had saved the people at the base from certain doom, at least temporarily.

But heroics aside, Asten still had a big question to ask. He turned back to Ponch.

"So what the hell is he doing here?"

Lieutenant Ponch just shrugged. "He said something about a weapons pickup. Says he was supposed to come here and await further orders. Did we ever get any word of that, sir?"

Asten shook his head no. He hadn't received any such report. But that didn't necessarily mean that he'd have *seen* such a message if such a message had been sent. This was a place of many secrets. Asten's job was to protect the people in the farmhouse and those in the facility underneath. He didn't know what went on down below, or even how many people were actually down there. Nor did he need to know. His job was to watch the door. That was all.

"I heard nothing like this," he finally told Ponch. "Maybe he's in the wrong place."

"Well, if that's the case, we're damn lucky he was," Ponch said. "He saved our arses. And the people left over at McReady too."

There was a huge roar. From behind the hill came the enormous old Beater from McReady. It was carrying the survivors in its expansive cargo hold. What's more, dangling from a chain attached to its belly, was Hunter's Z-3/15.

Asten just stared at the strange plane as it went overhead.

"Look at that, will you?" he exclaimed. "I've never seen an airplane like that in my life!"

"I've never seen anyone *fly* an airplane like he just did." Ponch said. "I just knew you would want to see him, sir."

Asten looked back at the pilot.

"What has he seen so far?" he asked Ponch.

The lieutenant just shrugged. Hunter's blindfold was still in place.

"Nothing over here," he replied. "Yet."

One of Asten's radar men ran up to him.

He was holding a long sheet of yellow paper. It was a readout from the unit's surface radar set. It showed a detailed impression of the sea for 100 miles around West Falkland Island. Clearly at the western edge of this limit there were twelve blips.

"What are they?" Asten asked the radar man to interpret.

"Can only be one thing, sir," the man replied quickly. "Warships. Twelve of them."

"This guy said he flew over them," Ponch reported. "Those Japanese planes came from one of those ships."

Asten crumpled the yellow paper into his fist. West Falkland was home to so many secrets simply because it was out in the middle of nowhere; two mere specks of land at just about the last point on Earth. Now, though he sure didn't want to believe it was happening, it seemed like the day they had all trained for but never expected to come, had indeed arrived.

"So this isn't any isolated thing, this attack on the air base," Asten said, more to himself than to Lieutenant Ponch. "It's a prelude to an armed landing."

Ponch just shook his head in disbelief.

"Who would be crazy enough to invade the Falkland Islands, sir?" he asked Asten incredulously.

"That's a very good question," Asten replied.

Asten thought for five seconds, then began issuing orders. His men were to go on Alpha One High Alert. This meant an invasion of the island was imminent. They would bring some of their forces down to the beach in case this invasion was by the sea. They would leave several tanks up top, to protect the farmhouse, in case the attack came from the air.

Already Ponch was barking Asten's orders out to his men in short, clipped British bites. Soon the commandos were running this way and that, moving tanks, cranking up guns. It was a study in organized chaos.

That's when Ponch looked back at Hunter, still standing alone at the side of the road, waiting patiently.

"It may get a bit 'airy around here, sir," Ponch said. "What shall we do with him?"

Asten took another long look at the man and then just shook his head.

"Give him a rifle and put him down on the beach with the others," Asten finally replied. "Whoever the hell he is, he's just as stuck here as the rest of us."

Twenty-six

Agent Y was waiting out on the runway when the huge transport plane roared in.

It was escorted by two Mustang-5 fighters. Their pilots waited until the transport was down and braking before they broke off and landed on a shorter runway nearby. The very precious cargo they'd been protecting had arrived safe and sound. Their jobs were done.

Three buses appeared on the tarmac and met the huge transport plane as it finally came to a stop at the end of the runway. The rear of the airplane opened and a small army of passengers trooped out. They were directed to the three buses by the crew. Once full, the buses headed back across the Bride Lake air base to an isolated hangar which had been set up as a reception center.

As the buses passed close by his jeepster, Y took his MVP pad from his pocket and punched in a coded message. Its rough translation: "The Associates have arrived. More later."

Then he put his jeepster in gear and moved into position at the end of the small convoy. Slowly, they all drove toward the hangar.

It was a typical dry, windblown morning. Already scorching hot. Already very unsettled. Questions were going through Y's mind as quickly as the desert wind. When would the upcoming Panama Canal action really begin? What would happen on Brazil's border when it was time to move? Were both of these things really just feints to cover the real mission, the one involving the colossal bomber? Or was the bomber mission just a ruse to divert attention from something else?

Y just didn't know.

Other things were troubling him as well. There was still no word on the missing Agents X and Z. From everything he could determine, it was as if the two agents had simply vanished into thin air. Though there was a report that a very unusual plane was also missing from its berth at Maryland, no one he'd talked to was connecting these two events—yet.

There had been no word from Hunter yet either. He'd left on his bomb retrieval mission very late the day before—and not a word had been heard from him since. According to Y's MVP readout, the Sky Ghost had received his last vector order, and the location where he was to pick up the Bomb. But there had been nothing but silence since.

This was war. Y was in special operations, and it was the nature of special ops that when agents go out, they sometimes go out for a long time. Some come back. Some don't.

As far as X and Z, who knows what they were up to. But if Hunter turned up missing for any length of time, it would certainly put the kibosh on the War Department's very secret Big Plan.

All this gave Y an odd feeling. The world of special ops was treacherous, true. But it was also very exciting, intriguing. And suddenly he felt like he was stuck in the wrong part of the world. At that moment, someplace else, he knew things were happening. Important things. Historic things.

Yet he was stuck here.

In the middle of the desert.
Missing everything. . . .

He finally arrived at the reception hangar and slipped
in the back door.

The group of passengers were seated in the middle of
the huge barn, about a dozen Area 52 security people lining the edges. The passengers were reading a briefing paper which had been distributed to them as they came in.
This had been Y's idea. The reason these people had been
brought here was so unusual and so unexplainable, he
thought it best if they read about it first.

He watched as the fifty-six individuals scanned their mission papers, their heads moving back and forth in an almost choreographed fashion. Gradually, Y made his way
to the front of the hall, where a slightly raised platform
with a microphone and podium had been placed.

By the time he reached the platform, many in the crowd
were just finishing the mission paper. To a man, they were
now looking up at him, their faces masks of absolute confusion.

Y looked out at them for a moment. They were a dispa-
rate bunch. Forty-four of them were dressed in football
warmup gear; these were the New Jersey Giants. Eight were
in monks' robes; these were the Brothers of the Living
Desert. In the front row were the four individual targets
picked up in the sweep. Y knew their names by heart now:
John Thomas Toomey, Benjamin Wa, Jacques-Ivan Frost,
and, sitting on the end, a beaming Mike Fitzgerald.

Seeing them for the first time, Y found something
slightly unnerving about this bunch, especially those in
front. The reason they were all called here was simple:
Hunter believed that these people were connected to him
somehow. They, or people exactly like them, had been colleagues of his, back wherever the hell he came from. They

were the Associates. Looking at them, studying their faces, Y realized something else.

They all looked familiar to him too.

He waited until the last person had finished reading the mission paper. Then he tapped the microphone and asked, "Any questions?"

They came like a torrent.

One man stood up. He was Geraci, the head coach of the New Jersey Giants.

"Excuse me, but I think a huge mistake has been made here," he began politely. "According to this, you are looking for people who know about building airplanes and flying combat missions. We're football players. We don't know squat about any of that stuff."

A second man stood up, Jim Cook, the head monk.

"It's the same situation here," Cook said. "We are men of the cloth. We know nothing of what you are looking for."

"Same here!" the man named Wa called out.

"And here . . ." said Frost.

"And triple here. . . ." Toomey yelled.

Only the guy named Fitzgerald remained quiet. He just kept on smiling.

Y raised his hands and politely asked for quiet. Then he recited something he'd been practicing all day.

"We realize this is highly unusual," he began. "And we realize it's highly extraordinary. But no mistake has been made. Your government needs you—all of you, for this very special, very secret mission. We are hoping you will serve willingly."

That last word sent a chill through the room, as it was meant to.

"You mean, we still have to do this, even if it's unwillingly?" Geraci, still standing, asked. "You will make us?"

"Your country has called on you to serve it in wartime," Y said. "It is your duty to serve. We at the OSS hope you do so."

With that a silence descended on the room. Y had said the three magic letters: OSS. No one wanted to be on their bad side.

Y saw the resistance crumbling and spoke quickly again.

"Your families will be notified. They will be told you are safe and working for the war effort—but nothing more. Hopefully, you'll all be back with them very soon."

One hour later, the three buses were pulling up to the huge isolated hangar called Building 2A.

The fifty-six men were led into the hangar. They were all now wearing nondescript work coveralls, boots, and gloves. Each man had been give a personal field pack which included a one-man tent, a foam mattress, bathing items, snack food, cigarettes, and two changes of clothes.

The inside of the hangar had been reelectrified and now a series of bright halogen lamps bathed the place in a deep golden light. The colossal bomber took on a particularly eerie glow in this illumination. It really did look like something from someplace else now.

Twenty-four air mechanics from the Bride Lake base had accompanied the Associates here. They too were carrying personal field packs. They were at the disposal of the Associates. They would do the heavy lifting; they would do whatever the fifty-six men found they could not do. To aid in this task, the mechanics were lugging boxes of manuals on the gigantic airplane with them, and trunkloads of tools. They too were in awe of this monstrous aircraft.

As the small army began to fan out over the hangar, looking up at the huge plane from all sides, Y corralled Fitzgerald, Toomey, Frost, Wa, Geraci, and Cook and asked them to step to one side. These men had been designated as leaders for the group.

"This is it gentlemen," Y told them. "Everything you might need is here. Now you know the problem. You know what we want you to do. My advice is to just stick with your instincts and see what happens."

But the guy named Toomey was scratching his head. The college professor seemed to be the most confused of the bunch, and also the loudest.

"OK, let me get this straight," he began. "You have a little bomb and you have a big plane, but the little bomb creates such a big blast that if the big plane drops it, the big plane won't be able to get out of the way in time. So you want us to figure out a way to adapt this plane to a mission that can only be described as suicidal? And you want us to do this even though none of us has had an ounce of experience in this area?"

Y thought about what Toomey had said for a few seconds and then finally nodded his head.

"Yes," he said. "That's *exactly* what we want you to do."

Twenty-seven

The South Atlantic

The storm hit West Falkland Island just after noontime. It was a typical December gale—high winds, sheets of rain, lots of sideways snow. Once it was upon them, an enormous frozen fog bank enveloped the island like a cumulus cloud.

As uncomfortable as it was, however, the bad weather provided perfect cover for a rather desperate operation.

By 0100 hours, four of the STS SuperChieftain tanks were being positioned along a spit of sand near Point Curly called Tenean Beach. Sixteen heavy machine guns, four antipersonnel rocket launchers and a pair of recoilless rifles were being placed on the beach too. Manning all these weapons were some very cold, very anxious STS commandos.

The weapons were being placed inside a series of trenches which had been dug into the hard ice-encrusted sand along the half mile-long beach. The first trench was filled with pieces of wreckage claimed from the cratered runways at McReady airfield and carried here by the ancient Beater. Jagged and charred, they made for good low-tide water obstacles. Placed in the thick sands way out on the sandbar, they could prove a hindrance to any troop-bearing landing craft, though not a very large one.

Behind the beach obstacles was a line of light machine

guns. These posts were manned by twenty STS soldiers spread out in a pathetically thin line that stretched more than a quarter of a mile. Behind them was a second trench bearing twelve more commandos and eight survivors from McReady airfield. They were manning the rocket launchers and the remaining AA guns salvaged from McReady. Despite their heavier firepower, they were stretched along the beach in ranks even thinner than their comrades in the first slit.

Behind them were two more STS tanks. They were being partially dug into a sand dune, the bent branches of a grove of scrub rag trees providing convenient covering for their very long gun muzzles. Behind them were two more tanks and the last of the rocket launchers. These were manned by a squad of remaining troopers.

This was the defense force that would face the twelve warships of the approaching invasion fleet.

On the highest part of the tallest dune stood Hunter. He looked down at the fortifications he and the other commandos had carved out in the last two very uncomfortable hours. Shovel in hand, digging madly along with a handful of commandos, he tried like hell to remember back to a time Back There when he'd faced such overwhelming enemy odds. But there was no memory of anything quite so lopsided as this. He figured from the size of the troopships he'd seen, each one was carrying at least 300 troops, probably more. This meant that within an hour or so, as many as 1,800 enemy troops could be splashing ashore—and there would be less than seventy people here on the beach to stop them.

Hunter looked up and down the trenches again. It would be nothing less than a slaughter.

It was strange, because the only thing of which everyone was absolutely sure was that the invaders would come ashore here, at Tenean, simply because, between the rocky northern shoreline and the perpetual ice and snow, this small beach was the only place where landing craft could get a clean passage to shore. But for this twist of topography, they would have been hard-pressed to land at all.

Helping to dig in one of the recoilless rifles, Hunter had gained much admiration for the STS commandos. They were as cool as the situation would allow, and certainly responding well to the dire turn of events, while at the same time not giving any indication at all what such an elite unit as their own was doing here on this very desolate South Atlantic island.

Of course, it wasn't a hard question to answer. A certain amount of deduction told Hunter a few things: Obviously the STS was here to protect something highly secret in nature—and what else could that be than the same facility from which Hunter was supposed to pick up the Bomb.

By backtracking, he could also assume that, the Main/AC being as timely as it was, the message that Hunter was on his way to retrieve the Bomb probably arrived some time during the attack on McReady, where the main radio transmitter was located. Once the main radio shack had been bombed, all hope of the message getting through had been lost. With his MVP totally out of juice, and the STS's Boomer not reaching very far, any hope of getting any kind of SOS message out to anyone was practically nil.

So Hunter was stuck here. The Z-3/15 was sitting up in a cow pasture near the farmhouse. There was nothing even resembling a runway anywhere on this island, so in effect, his jazzed-up airplane was useless.

Try as he might, there just wasn't any scenario he could come up with that had this coming battle turning out any other way but disastrous.

But even darker were Hunter's premonitions about this invasion, now probably less than one hour away. The question was a simple one, and it was on everyone's lips: *Why?* Why were the Japanese invading the lonely Falklands?

Expansion of their South American empire would seem to be the logical conclusion—but there was something cockeyed about that notion. Hunter knew firsthand the true state of affairs of the Nipponese Occupation Forces in South America. They were on the defensive just about everywhere. They were confused. They were paranoid. They feared Brazil coming into the war. They were frightened to death of the nightly firebombings. Not exactly the time to be going off on some wayward adventure, trying to capture two empty islands nearly 600 miles off the coast of the very tip of their very shaky South American empire.

No, it didn't add up—that is, if one looked at the attackers' motives as being purely military. But if not military, then what would their motives be? Clearly they wanted control of McReady airport—and soon they would have it, because it would be impossible to defend it again. Clearly they had thousands of men with which to take the islands. But why? If not a military exercise—what was this then?

A special operation? That really was the only other answer. A massive covert act. But again, why the Falklands?

There was only one answer there too: They were coming here for the same reason Hunter had. Somehow they had found out about the Bomb; somehow they had divined its location in the Falklands.

There really was no other explanation.

Hunter kept digging into the rock-hard frozen sand, at the same time scanning the work being done on the trenches in front of him, as well as behind.

The STS commandos were doing their work well, and with amazing pluck, considering what awaited them when the Japanese finally landed. A cold wind blew across Hunter's face as he turned west, looking for the first sign of the invaders.

Is this really how it is going to end? he asked himself gloomily. On some small beach in the middle of nowhere? A heroic death would be hard to manage here. There were no components in place to show much courage. With the odds running nearly 50 to 1 in manpower alone, there probably wouldn't be any medals won today. Hunter chuckled grimly to himself. It was darkly funny. After nothing less than a transuniversal journey, he'd thought the cosmos had bigger plans in store for his demise.

But Hunter would soon discover the Cosmos had one last joke to play on him.

Just as he checked the horizon again, Hunter heard a mechanized noise coming down the beach. It was the Roamer, the gigantic half tank, half trailer truck, slowly making its way down the shoreline. Inside, Hunter knew, were the dozen or so civilians evacuated from the small fishing village of Summer Point nearby. Colonel Asten had decided that they would be safer inside the farmhouse, where the last of the tanks and a reinforced squad of STS soldiers were holding fast. These particular commandos and their equipment would be the very last line of defense against the invaders, and the fact that Asten had them stationed around the farmhouse told Hunter something else too. As odd as it sounded, what he had come for—the Bomb—and maybe other even more secret things were probably inside the little structure.

The Roamer stopped nearly in front of him and began discharging its civilian passengers. From here they would walk up the hill, gaining the road and the way to the farmhouse. The first to come out were two old-timers, retired fishermen in their eighties. They were followed by a bevy of elderly women, then two middle-aged couples.

The last person out was a young girl. Hunter took one look at her—and suddenly he couldn't move. He was frozen to the spot. He couldn't have lifted his shovel, spoken a word, blinked his eyelids, even if he had tried.

This girl. Blond. Young, fresh face. Beautiful skin. Beautiful eyes. Beautiful everything. She was dressed like everyone else: old jeans, heavy wool overcoat, waders, and a thick wool hat. Yet somehow she actually looked sexy, alluring, erotic even, in that getup.

But it was not this miracle of fashion that had turned Hunter to stone. No, it was her eyes when she glanced up at him. Yes, she was beautiful. Yes, she was the last ounce of beauty in this desolate cold place that might very well soon be his grave.

But it was more than this.

Much more.

Because he was shaking again. And it was with the feeling he'd experienced whenever he saw people in this place that somehow reminded him of people Back There.

And while it usually came to him with the ferocity of maybe a sneeze, or a cough, right now his body was absolutely vibrating with the sensation, so much so, his teeth were actually chattering.

Now looking down at this young girl and she glancing up at him, everything just froze. In his mind's eye he saw a lake, shimmering. Cold. Mountains all around. He was in the Swiss Alps. He was walking along the shore, and he saw her. She was in the frozen water, bathing. Completely nude.

Flash forward. He was at the top of a mountain, peering into a building that looked like an artificial igloo. Inside were three men, armed, dangerous. Inside as well, this beautiful creature. Gunshots. A scream. A laugh. He'd rescued her from them.

Flash again. They were in the cockpit of a huge airplane, almost as big as the monsters that fly here. Flash again. They were kissing. Flash again, they were sleeping close. Flash again they were in prison. Flash . . . they were out. Flash . . . they were on another mountain, this one in the Himalayas. Flash . . . they were kissing. Flash . . . then there were tears.

Yes, that face. That hair. Those eyes. Those curves.

He knew them well. And he knew who she was, because even a trip across universes could not erase this memory.

It was Chloe.

Then a pull came on his shoulder and he looked away and saw it was Colonel Asten. He was pointing out to the horizon. Twelve ships. Dotting the horizon. Smoke pouring from their stacks, wide white wakes behind them. They were heading their way at top speed.

Another jolt went through Hunter and he knew it was time to switch into his desperate-last-battle mode.

He took one more moment to turn back, to look at her again.

But Chloe was gone.

The word went down the trenches that all weapons should be powered up.

The Japanese ships were moving very fast. The storm clouds behind them seemed to be pushing them along. There was a line of three destroyers in front, then came the small aircraft carrier. Next were the six troopships. Flat, squat, and plying through the water as opposed to sailing on its surface, they looked more like seagoing barges than warships. Bringing up the rear were a pair of cruisers, both heavy with guns and rocket launchers.

Hunter was flattened out atop the sand dune now, a pair of binoculars glued to his eyes. There was no activity that he could see on the aircraft carrier. All of its planes were either on deck or below. He was sure of this simply because his psyche would have been buzzing wildly if there had been any enemy aircraft about.

The fleet was now about four miles offshore, and sure enough the ships were slowing down perceptibly. Hunter tried to conjure up a vision as to how the invasion would proceed. He could see the capital warships slow to a crawl, then the troopships turn toward the beach. The troop carriers looked to have shell doors in their bows—from here Hunter could imagine dozens of amphibious vehicles heading for the long, thin strip of sand.

The only hope the defenders would have—and it was a slim as well as a temporary one—would be for the landing craft to bunch up while sailing into the small bay. Here they would make economical targets for the tanks and the big guns. And maybe the initial wreckage would block off the rest of the bay. But it would only take a little while for the Japanese to either clear it or find another place to land nearby, one which the STS had no hope of defending.

So, this was it. The invaders would come into Tenean and here they would be met by the motley crew of defenders and there would be a short, bloody fight—and then, they'd all be dead. And whatever secrets were up in that farmhouse would be gained by the enemy. Then the world would probably turn upside down for real.

Oddly, in this rather desperate moment, Hunter found his thoughts going back to the young girl he'd just seen. *What would happen to her,* he wondered.

Colonel Asten was running the thin defense line one more time, taking a moment with each small group of STS men, bucking them up before their world came to an end. Hunter was checking the M-18 the Brits had given him. It was a long-range combat rifle, with a five-shot auto feature and a long belt of ammo. It was a powerful weapon, but this last firefight would be a particularly frustrating one for him. For any battle, his place was in the air. That would not happen here. The Z-3 was useless where it was, in the cow pasture, three miles and a large body of water away from any appropriate runway. No runway, no takeoff. The plane was useless.

It was strange because just as the storm clouds joined

completely over their heads and the cold rain began to fall and the troopships grew closer to the shore, Hunter felt another odd sensation go through him. It was familiar too. Its meaning was not quite as clear though. It was almost like the cosmos was telling him to stand by, watch what happens next.

Whatever the meaning, the vibration rang true.

Because just as the defenders were beginning to count their last minutes, just when it seemed they would soon be overwhelmed by a tidal wave of heavily armed amphibious troops, just as it seemed like the troopships were ready to stop and start discharging troops, something very, very odd happened.

The ships just kept on going. The destroyers, the carrier, the troopships, and the cruisers went right by the entrance to Tenean Beach, right by the sandbar, by the rocks at its tip, and kept on sailing.

There were gasps of disbelief and no little relief from the slit trenches. Asten was immediately on his radio, shouting at a squad of lookouts he'd posted on the hill.

"What's happening?" he was yelling into the mouthpiece. "Where are the ships going?"

Hunter had already scrambled up the highest dune and he now had the Japanese ships in sight as well. He watched as they went right by West Falkland point, and into the middle of the sound. They all bore to starboard and soon they were steaming down into the sound itself. Only then did the ships begin to slow down. Hunter and Asten jumped into the only jeepster available to them and tore up the road to the nearest cliff. From here they could see the whole sound and the coast of East Falkland beyond.

Over the next few minutes they saw the ships stop, throw out anchor, and begin to discharge in their landing craft. These amphibs were heading southeast and entering a place that according to Asten's map, was called San Carlos Bay.

Asten and Hunter stayed on this cliff for the next two hours, watching the invaders dislodge their troops and supplies, not quite believing what was happening.

But after awhile it was clear.

A miracle of some sort *had* happened.

The Japanese had invaded the wrong island.

Twenty-eight

The place was called Casket Island.

It was a small piece of land located in the middle of Falkland Sound, nearly equidistant from West and East Falkland.

The island was not much more than sand, rocks, and a few scrub trees. An ancient wind sock erected on its northwest edge provided the only evidence of human contact. In years gone by, the directional aid had been used by pilots flying into McReady field, one mile to the east. Now the sock was ripped and tattered, its pole barely winning the battle against the constant gales which swept up the sound.

The island was usually home to thousands of seabirds—terns and gulls mostly. But they were nowhere to be seen now. They had scattered during the brutal air battle at McReady the day before. At the end of that battle, an odd six-engine long-range-type aircraft had been shot down and crashed on Casket Island. Since that happened, the birds had yet to return.

The wreckage was fairly intact. The left wing had been partially ripped from the fuselage and the tail had separated after coming down. But the flight compartment was still in one piece. Indeed very few of the large array of window-panes in the craft's bug-eye nose were even cracked. More importantly, the insides of the airplane had not been too seriously damaged.

This was one reason that Hunter and six of the STS commandos were now approaching Casket Island in a small rubber boat. There were things inside the airplane they might need.

Hunter had spent the day secreted atop a Point Curly cliff looking across the sound at San Carlos Bay where the Japanese were still unloading their invasion troops and provisions. The invaders could be clearly seen fanning out over the rugged landscape of East Falkland, setting up command posts, cutting slit trenches, installing weapons. Watching them for hours on end through his binoculars, Hunter's intuition was that the Japanese were looking for something—but having a hard time finding it. He wasn't sure how he knew this. There just seemed to be an air of desperation and frustration emanating from the Japanese beachhead.

Too busy invading the wrong island, the Japanese had not paid any attention to the plane wreck on Casket Island. There was a chance they didn't even know it was there. The way the plane had come down, the wreckage could be seen more clearly from West Falkland than from the east. But it was probably just a matter of time before the Japanese did find the wreck. Hunter wanted to beat them to it.

The defenders of West Falkland all knew that the reprieve they'd received earlier in the day would be a temporary one. Eventually the Japanese would realize their mistake, and come across the sound to West Falkland. At the moment, the defenders needed every piece of weaponry they could get to bolster their defense. Hunter was fairly sure the bug-eyed airplane had intended to land at McReady in advance of the seaborne invasion troops. If that was true, then there probably were some special ops troops on board and these people would have weapons and ammo that the STS defenders on West Falkland could use. He'd convinced Colonel Asten of that fact; thus he was made lead man of this special mission.

There were other things inside the airplane that Hunter thought they could use too. Besides weapons, he hoped the airplane was carrying a radio, possibly one powerful enough to get a message to a friendly base and tell them of the suddenly desperate situation unfolding on the Falklands.

But most of all, Hunter wanted to examine the bodies on board.

Ever since he'd first spotted the invasion fleet heading for the Falklands he'd had a strange feeling about the whole thing. Things just didn't add up, especially the motive for such an operation. If he was able to get to the wreckage of this plane, and get a look at the people who were flying in it, his gut was telling him he might uncover some answers.

The rubber boat made landfall right where they wanted to be: on the edge of a rocky beach about 300 yards from the plane wreck.

The STS commandos silently moved into the high shore grass, weapons up, heads low; like Hunter they were wearing black smudge camouflage on their faces and hands. It was a waning moon this night and the shadows were stark and bare. Still the STS men managed to make themselves invisible. They were so good at this, Hunter could barely see them and he was only a few feet away!

Once everyone was up on the beach, two troopers went ahead to scout the area in front of the crashed plane. The word came back that it was clear. Hunter and the others took their cue and ran the final 100 yards to the airplane. They made it with no problem.

Hunter was the first to reach the wreck. It was still smoldering in places. The crash was now about twenty hours old, yet some parts of the crumpled fuselage were still warm.

Hunter kicked in a side access door and immediately saw the first goal of this mission had been a success. The airplane was full of rifles, machine guns, and firebomb rocket launchers. It was also full of bodies.

The STS commandos immediately began hauling the cache of weapons out of the wreck and running them back to the waiting boat. Hunter stepped into the gory hold and made his way up to the mid fuselage. Here he found the plane's long-range radio and receiver. The device was a total wreck, split in several places in the crash, impossible to repair. Next to it was a computer which looked a little like a Main/AC, all lights and knobs and buttons and things. But it too was smashed beyond repair.

Disheartened, Hunter began moving forward. He appreciated the small irony here. It seemed as if he'd spent much time in his life crawling through plane wrecks, looking for clues. The last time was up in Iceland, literally the other end of the planet, when he searched a huge German air transport he'd shot down. This wreck was smaller, more cramped, and nowhere near as damaged. But clues sometimes fall out of the sky, he recalled thinking back then, and he'd been right. He wondered if it would be the same case now.

He and some STS men came upon the first clutch of bodies; these were twelve special ops soldiers, Japanese shock troops who'd been riding up at the front of the airplane. They were well equipped and heavily armed. Right away the STS men started stripping the weapons from them.

One of the commandos reached out and tapped Hunter's arm. He was shining his flashlight on the face of one of the dead men. The man was badly cut, with many broken bones. He was probably in his mid thirties, with bad teeth, and several scars crossing his face. He looked Asian.

But was he, really?

The STS man rubbed his fingers along the dead man's cheek and came up with a startling discovery: The man was wearing makeup. The STS man wiped some more and sure enough his fingers were turning dull orange from the makeup.

Hunter pulled out a kerchief and rubbed the man's face clean. This was a little too weird. Makeup? On a special ops soldier?

It was true though. Once the makeup and eyeliner and other powders and paints were gone, there was no doubt the man lying before them was a Caucasian.

The STS men rolled over another body and wiped its face. The same was true here: The man had been made up to look Asian, but was in fact white. They all were; these twelve special ops troopers as well as the other dead soldiers further back in the plane. Not Japanese regular troops, but white men made to look Japanese.

The Brits were simply stunned. As was Hunter.

What the hell was this?

Then it got stranger.

There was a yell from the rear of the wreck. Hunter immediately began crawling back toward it. Two commandos had found another clutch of crash victims. They weren't soldiers and no one had tried to make them look Asian. But they *were* wearing eyeliner, blush, nail polish, and lipstick. There were females—four of them. They were young, shapely, but dead—or at least three of them were. The fourth one was still alive.

Not for long though.

Hunter got to his knees and propped her up in his arms. She was dressed in the clothes of a hooker.

"What are you doing here?" he asked her.

"It was a job," she began. "These two guys hired us to take an airplane ride with them. We thought it was a two-day trip. You know, a party. Well, it lasted three weeks. And these two guys were crazy—crazy and drunk all the time. There was a computer up front, they were always asking it stupid questions. They were also looking for someone they kept called the Third Guy or something like that."

Hunter gave her water from his canteen. She drank greedily but then coughed most of it back up.

"One day they asked the computer some very hard question," she went on in a gasp. "And it took so long for the answer to come back, these two assholes thought they'd broken the thinking machine. Finally it spits out an answer that just drives these two weirdos even more crazy. Right away they forget all about looking for the Third Guy. Now they wanted to go get whatever it was that the computer had told them about. I think it was a bomb or something."

She gasped again and Hunter tried to give her more water. But it was not going down at all.

"We stopped in Bermuda," she went on, her voice now no more than a whisper, "and they kicked off the regular crew and hired these soldiers. They made them wear this weird makeup and clothes to make them look Asian. They also bought all these weapons for them. Finally we headed south. We landed and met up with some real Asians—I think they were Japanese—and they made a deal. A deal to come here and attack this place."

She coughed and what came out was mostly blood.

"Where are these guys now?" Hunter asked her.

"The cowards," she said with her last ounce of strength. "They jumped out, with the only two parachutes on board, just before we got shot down. They knew it was going bad, so they bailed. I'll see them in Hell, I suppose."

"Do you have any idea who they were?" Hunter asked her, even though he knew she was fading fast.

The woman shook her head no. "They never said. But before they went out the door I pulled this off of one of them. It was hanging around his neck, like it was a religious medal or something. . . ."

She put something in Hunter's hand. Then came another cough, and a series of convulsions.

"I don't want to die here," she said, looking up at Hunter. "I don't even know where I am . . ."

She clutched his hand tightly and then let go. He tried mouth to mouth on her, but it was too late. She was gone.

Hunter gently lowered her to the crushed cabin floor and closed her eyes. Then he looked at what she had given him. It was an ID card. For the Office of Strategic Services, the OSS.

There was no name on the ID, no address, rank, or personal information. All it had for the man's sole identification was a single letter.

That letter was X.

Twenty-nine

West Falkland
The next morning

The trenches protecting the beach at Point Curly looked the same as the day before except they had twice as many weapons sticking out of them.

Thanks to the raid on Casket Island, the small force of defenders had twice as many rocket launchers, twice as many heavy-caliber triple-.50 machine guns, twice as many fire rockets.

But bulked-up as the defenders were, it didn't change the overall situation. They were still outnumbered more than 50 to 1. The enemy also had at least fifty aircraft still operational over at McReady. *Plus,* they had two cruisers and two destroyers at their disposal, each with plenty of long-range naval guns and sea-launched artillery rockets.

Even worse, now the Japanese knew where they were. A pair of SuperKate recon planes had been flying over West Falkland all morning, undoubtedly taking photographs and paying particular attention to the defenses at Tenean Beach. It was no longer a hiding game for the defenders. The Japanese probably knew more about their positions than they did themselves.

What stealing the extra weapons might accomplish could only be measured in time. Because of the extra guns and ammo, the fight that everyone knew was coming might last a little longer. The defenders might enjoy a little longer life span. But that was it. The extra rockets, bullets, and fire shells would not affect the ultimate outcome of the battle. It would just delay its arrival.

His head thick with these thoughts and a million others, Hunter was in the third beach trench, helping dig a hole in which the last stolen rocket launcher would be placed. The day had dawned with routinely awful weather. Heavy rain mixed with snow. High winds. The waves were crashing on Tenean Beach with the impact of disrupter shells. For the defenders, these were the perfect atmospherics for a cold dark battle that would ultimately be the death of them all.

What a perverse joke all this was, Hunter thought now as he began packing icy sand around the launcher's legs. He'd been handed a suicide mission which, if anything, would have given him the opportunity to go out as a very big hero, not that it meant very much to him. But still, after all the deep think and anxiety and philosophizing about it, fate or something had determined that he was actually going to die here, on this crummy cold and dirty beach. Nothing more than a piece of sand, going out like a match goes out. One-trillionth of what he'd been imagining.

It *was* kind of funny, he thought, as he hefted his millionth shovel full of wet sand. Yes, the cosmos *did* have a sense of humor. A cruel one.

It was also particularly ironic, considering the circumstances, that he would die on the ground. Whether it was going to be the soft mushy sand of Tenean Beach or the hard ice-packed bogs of inland West Falkland, Hunter knew now that he was definitely going to give it up with his two feet firmly entrenched on terra firma. That too was funny. The least God could do was allow him to die while airborne, preferably while battling the fifty or so jet aircraft the invaders still had at the ready.

But that was just impossible. The Z-3/15 was still sitting up in the cow field, gas in its tanks, ammo in its guns, and absolutely fucking useless.

If only . . .

A radio began buzzing. The electronic sound ran a cold chill through all the troops in the trench with him; it froze him for a moment as well. This buzz could very well be the death knell for all of them. The Roamer crew was up on the cliff nearby, looking over at San Carlos Bay where enemy troops had been massing all night and morning long. They'd been told by Asten to call down to the beaches when the invaders made their first move. Now the radio was vibrating with its warning buzzing.

The radio man clicked his set to receive and turned up the volume for everyone to hear. The Roamer crew's message was simple. To the point. Chilling.

"Here they come. . . ." was all it said.

The word went down the trenches in a matter of seconds.

Another report from the Roamer came in a minute later. It said the Japanese were pushing off the northwestern tip of San Carlos in landing craft disgorged from the troopships earlier. This was an interesting piece of news. It meant the invaders would have to travel several miles up the sound, make a wide turn to the west, go around a natural jetty known as Ashmont Rocks, turn south, and finally make for Tenean or "Tin Can" beach, as the defenders were now calling it.

That was a lot of sailing to do in what were basically landing craft built to run in from the big boat to the beach and little else. The awful weather would play havoc with the landing crafts as well. The waves presently breaking on Tin Can beach were huge, irregular, driven by the rain and snow. Many were over six feet at the crest and some even higher than that, possibly the worst weather conditions imaginable for a huge amphibious landing.

But all this meant little to the defenders on the beach. It would not be a gentle ride for their executioners. So what? There was a chance some of the Japanese troops might be swept away before they even reached the beach—but again it didn't much matter. Whether the defenders faced 40 to 1 odds, or 35 to 1—what difference would it make? At the end of the day, they would all still be just as dead. Maybe it would only be a matter of how many bullets were riddling their bodies.

There was another thing: If the invading troops were on their way, that meant their air support, the fifty SuperZeroes and SuperKates over at McReady, would soon be in the air.

True, the defenders were stretched out so thin, the enemy aircraft would have to try to kill fifty people with fifty separate attacks. But all that meant was the inevitable would simply take a little longer, and the enemy pilots would be slightly more exhausted at the end of the day. Perhaps they would all be rewarded with naps.

Ten minutes went by.

The Roamer crew reported that the invasion force was now four miles away from San Carlos and moving northward fast.

Hunkered down in his trench, trying for some reason to keep dry, Hunter was continually checking his rifle's magazine and sorting though what was left of his last thoughts.

It seemed like he would die with a real mystery on his hands. Or maybe just a set of totally screwy events. What they had found over on Casket Island had haunted him ever since returning to West Falkland. Like everything else lately, it didn't make a whole lot of sense. Somehow the two OSS agents—both, he believed, were colleagues of his friend Y—had gotten wind of the powerful bomb Hunter had been sent to pick up. They had obviously decided to make a play for it first, but had gotten cold feet and bailed out when things got tough.

But now, even though they were gone, the invaders—whether they were real Japanese or not—were still going ahead with the invasion. Did the people behind all this even know why they were attacking West Falkland? Or were they just fulfilling a deal made with the OSS? And why would the OSS pay the Japanese to attack a place that the OSS had sent Hunter to on a highly secret mission? The more he thought about it, the less it made sense.

Not lost in all this was the dying woman's reference to the OSS agents' original quest: to find the Third Guy. Could this be Viktor Robotov, the man who fell into the Atlantic Ocean that day along with Hunter and Elvis Q? Hunter didn't know, and would probably never know—not unless they had network news broadcasts in the afterlife.

The fact that he was going to die with all these unresolved notions was irritating. But what was really pissing him off was the fact that when the Japanese airplanes did come into play, they would be able to attack with impunity. He had an airplane. It was better than theirs. He had ammunition and the gas to fly rings around any of the Nipponese clowns.

All for want of a runway.

Or was it . . .

You will fly this way and that, and that way and this . . .

Hunter froze again. He'd heard those words so clearly just then, it was like someone was standing next to him, whispering in his ear.

That's what the psychic had said. And damnit if her nonsense just suddenly made a lot of sense to Hunter. But was it real? Or was he freaking out because certain death was so near? He didn't know.

Suddenly he was running.

Up and out of the trench, down a dune of icy sand, toward Colonel Asten's command position. He reached it less than a minute later to find Asten directing a squad of soldiers who were putting the finishing touches on a fire rocket launcher position.

Just by his sudden appearance, Hunter interrupted them.

"Excuse me, Colonel," he began, "but is the man who flew the McReady Beater over here with you?"

Asten looked at Hunter like he had gone daft. But then he turned around and searched the trench.

"Yes, there he is," Asten said. "Fifth man down. Duggen, I think his name is."

Hunter didn't stay long enough to hear any more. He was scrambling down the icy trench until he reached the man in question.

"You Duggen?" he asked the man.

"Yes?"

"What is the lift capacity of your Octo?" Hunter demanded of him.

Like Asten before him, Duggen looked back at Hunter as if the American pilot had gone mad, which, in a way, he had.

"I don't know," Duggen finally replied. "On a day like this, not very much."

"Can you lift twenty-five long?"

Duggen was startled. This was a strange conversation to be having when death was about to sail into the bay. But Hunter continued to press him.

"Twenty-five thousand pounds?" he replied, astounded. "With this wind, and that bird's shitty engines? That would be a stretch."

That's when Hunter literally picked the man up and out of the trench.

He turned to Asten who had walked up behind him, and made a strange request: "Permission to take this man from the line, sir?"

Asten was totally befuddled at this point, as was anyone within earshot. As if to add to the chaos, the Roamer teams' latest message was blaring from the radio.

"Thirty-six invasion craft confirmed heading your way," the dire report came through, washed in static and nearly drowned out by the howling wind and the driving rain. "At least five hundred troops. More like seven hundred. . . . Estimate time to your position is about twenty-five minutes. Tops."

There might have been another army that, upon hearing those words and knowing their implications, would have simply given up, and fled. But not these people. If anything the people in the trenches began working more furiously, not less. Death was less than half an hour away. They didn't want to go with a whimper.

Neither did Hunter.

Somehow the STS colonel sensed this.

"Permission granted," he said with a plucky clip. "But what on Earth are you planning to do? Lift us all out of here with that beast?"

Hunter stopped in midstream. Lift everyone out? On the Beater? . . . "Not a bad idea," he finally replied. "But I think I've got a better one."

The Roamer crew hiding atop of Point Curly cliff had the best view of what happened next.

They were still sending back reports on the enemy's methodical progress up Falkland Sound. Battling high waves and wicked winds, the small fleet of landing craft was nevertheless moving slowly but surely to the other side of the three-mile-wide waterway. After that, they would have to round Ashmont Rocks in order to face Tin Can beach. But this would take only about ten minutes to do once the invasion force was fully across the sound. They were about halfway across now.

Worse still, a long line of Japanese aircraft was waiting along the longest runway still intact at McReady air base. This parade was made up of approximately thirty SuperZeroes and twenty SuperKates, the survivors from the previous day's disastrously costly air raid. The fact that there were more fighters left than bombers was a telling reminder just how brutal the air battle over McReady had been. It also showed just how badly the fighters had failed in their duty the day before. Despite the fact that McReady was eventually claimed by their forces, the fighters had not protected the bomber force as they had been charged to do. They had run away at the first sight of the strange white airplane which had seemed to come out of nowhere and shot down half their number. Their cowardice would have a big effect on today's operation as well: The Japanese were lopsided in favor of fighters when, according to the book on amphibious invasions, if one was attacking a beach, one should have as many bombers in the air as possible.

But in this case, common military sense was not too important. There was still a substantial force waiting to take off at McReady, no matter what kind of airplanes they were. And it certainly seemed more formidable considering the defenders of West Falkland Island had no air power of their own to challenge the Japanese.

The Roamer crew continued to send back its dire reports, trying to stay hidden while battling the extrahigh winds and rain up on the cliff.

They had just reported that the Japanese landing crafts were about two-thirds of the way across the sound when suddenly, they heard the most ungodly sound. It was loud enough to blot out the scream of the wind, the splattering of the rain, and the roar of fifty jet engines being warmed up three miles away.

The Roamer crew turned as one and in time to see a very strange thing coming over the top of the hill.

It was a Beater—it was making this hellish sound. But not just any Beater. This was the absolute shitbox, which had spent the last ten years rusting away over at McReady airfield before being moved to West Falkland the day before.

It was a fright to see. Only seven of its eight rotors looked to be actually turning—and two of them were in flames! But the Octo was somehow flying, somehow clawing its way into the stormy icy skies with a bansheelike squeal that seemed multiplied more than just seven times.

But that was not all. The Octo was carrying something— and this was the really strange part. Hanging by a three-strand set of heavy chains below the enormous, slightly banana-shaped fuselage, was Hunter's Z-3/15.

The Beater went over the Roamer's position so low, the bottom of the Z-3/15 actually scraped the top hatch of the Roamer's turret. Just the closeness of such a maelstrom of wind and exhaust and electricity and electronic junk caused all the juiced-up systems inside the Roamer to blink on and off several times before settling back down and staying on, though almost reluctantly.

Once the Beater topped the peak of Point Curly though, it suddenly found about 800 feet of flying space underneath it and its strange cargo, a welcome development. Still, its engines were smoking heavily and its noise only grew louder as it moved offshore. The Roamer crew simply didn't know what to think. They watched open-mouthed as the Beater slowly made its way—sideways— toward enemy-held East Falkland island, its strange aerial cargo swinging wildly beneath it.

"What are they going to do?" someone inside the

Roamer cried out. "Drop the needle-nosed airplane on the Japanese?"

No, not quite.

But close. . . .

They continued to watch in amazement as they saw the Beater close in on McReady field. Incredibly, because of the angle of its approach and its relatively low altitude and the masking wind and rain, the Beater was actually sneaking up on the unsuspecting Japanese.

Once it made landfall over the east island, it got even lower. It was heading right for the runway where the fifty enemy warplanes were waiting, engines turning, their pilots effectively deaf to what was happening outside their canopy windows.

The Octocopter was now down to a breathtaking seventy-five feet and was really pouring on the coals. The Z-3/15 was swinging so madly beneath it, surely the chains would break at any moment. The aircraft tandem looked so bizarre, that if anyone at the enemy-held field *had* seen it, chances were they'd have been too astonished to react.

Whatever the case, the Octo had closed to within 100 yards of the line of waiting jets when someone inside the big flying can unleashed something and suddenly the front strand of chain holding up the Z-3/15's nose began to go slack. The plane's needle snout fell perilously by forty-five degrees before the chain caught again. Now the airplane's needle nose was pointing nearly straight down. By their own eyes, everyone in the Roamer crew was certain that the forward chain had given out somehow, and then had caught again, maybe just temporarily, saving the strange white airplane from falling off completely.

There was no suspicion among them that this desperate maneuver was all part of the plan.

This became apparent a few seconds later when the Beater, the white jet still hanging precariously off its bottom, finally reached the line of unsuspecting jets.

Suddenly the Roamer crew saw a flash of light pour out of the nose of the dangling, sleek white jet.

What the hell was this?

At first they thought the airplane had suddenly caught on fire. After a second or two, it was clear that what was actually happening was the Z-3/15's cannon was going off. Each time it did, the recoil would cause the plane to swing even more wildly under the Beater, which in turn was swinging wildly on its own, driven crazy by the action-reaction of its strange payload.

Impossible though it seemed, the Beater went right up the line of waiting aircraft, the Z-3/15's cannon firing non-stop, hitting some taxiing aircraft, missing others, but causing an incredible amount of damage, considering the way it was delivering its punches. From the Roamer crew's point of view, this was happening almost in slow motion. With great amounts of wind and rain and snow blowing between them and the action, it all had an almost dreamlike quality to it.

The Beater finally reached the end of the line of waiting aircraft. Before anyone at the base could react, the Octo-copter started to climb, the Z-3/15 still swinging crazily, its cannon still firing and hitting targets on the ground.

Below, it had left at least ten aircraft in flames and maybe another dozen damaged in some way. What's more, a major portion of the all-important longest runway was now blocked by several piles of burning fighters or bombers.

In all, the strange attack had lasted only fifteen seconds.

Hunter was dizzy.

Not just a little, not with just a speck of disorientation.

He was dizzy to the point of nausea. The fact that he was now being hauled straight up by the flying Beater was compounding his distress exponentially.

If all this swinging didn't stop soon, Hunter was sure

he'd blow lunch—that is, if he had any lunch in his stomach to blow.

Now *this* was desperation. Possibly the most desperate thing he'd ever done, in this life or the last. And for it to be based on what some crazy if beautiful fortune-teller had imparted to him on the morning after a drunken spree—well, it was just too stupid to think about.

But the defenders of West Falkland Island were looking certain death right in the eye, as was he. He had a perfectly good airplane, half full of perfectly good gas and perfectly good ammunition in his possession—just no runway to get it from point A to point B.

So he had this plan. If the Beater could lift him high enough and then drop him, maybe he could start his engines in enough time to attain flight. If this happened, then maybe he could shoot down some Japanese planes now taking off from McReady and help out the guys on the beach once the invaders finally reached Tin Can beach.

Additionally if his engines started, maybe he could get enough juice to charge up the MVP and get a goddamn call for help out to the world. And then, maybe . . .

Well, there were already too many maybes, he knew. But something had to be done and so now he was doing it, maybe for no better reason than to avoid dying on some frozen beach. Or maybe not.

He was counting on the Beater to fulfill a fundamental part of this desperate design and at the moment he was sure this very big link in the chain would eventually fail him.

He had no instruments to tell him how high he was. And the fact he was swinging so violently back and forth gave him little opportunity to get a good reading. His guess was that the tincan already had passed 7,500 feet and was still climbing. Below him, in a blur, Hunter could still see the burning wreckage at McReady field; that had been an improvised thing, to tear up some of the waiting airplanes before they started their long climb up. Hunter had literally yelled the hasty plan up to the Beater pilot just seconds before their crazy tandem left the ground.

Had it failed, it would have been a very stupid, lethal move. But it had played out, and he had killed ten airplanes on the ground that he wouldn't have to kill in the air—plus, he had fucked up the field's main runway for a while, which was really a good thing because he and the Beater would be sitting ducks for any Japanese plane that could take off and fire at them.

That's why he was urging the Beater silently to climb as fast and far as possible. The more air they got between them and the ground, the more of a chance this gigantic gamble could work.

But this brought up another question: How high was high? Or better yet, how high was *high enough*?

Starting the engines in the Z-3/15 usually took a minute or so, leaving time for oil pressures to build up and the double-reaction process to take full effect. Hunter figured he could probably cut that time down to thirty seconds just by shutting off half the shit on his control panel. But a six-ton airplane could drop a long way in half a minute, and if the engine balked at all on the way down, well, there wouldn't be any second chance to try it all over again.

If the engine was as nauseous as he was, or if the damp Falkland air had fouled something in the firing system, or if the flight computer didn't snap in on time, or if a million and one other things had happened to the power plant since his time at the bottom of the world, then he would fall his three or four miles and just keep on going. . . .

He might just die on a cold snowy beach yet.

He had no radio contact with the Beater, no way to tell Duggen when to drop him and how. That would have made it all too simple. The manual said a Beater could go up to 30,000 feet, Duggen had claimed before takeoff. But that was a figure for a brand new Octo. Judging by the rusting hulk above him, Hunter guessed that making it up to 15,000 feet would be a strain it probably couldn't take.

But still they kept going up. Through the low clouds, through some rain and snow. After a while, the Z-3/15 stopped spinning long enough for Hunter to look down and get a reading on how high they might be. He was surprised—they were maybe as high as four miles already.

Yet the Beater kept on climbing.

Now he started to spin again and ice crystals began forming on the Z-3/15's canopy, creating a kaleidoscopic effect that did nothing to improve his unsettled stomach. Lots of clouds were getting between him and the ground. Thick ones, thin ones, rain clouds, and more snow. Still, the Beater kept climbing.

Hunter knew the ancient Octocopter couldn't take much more of this. It was time for him to either throw up or get his shit together. He decided to go with the latter. He began pushing buttons on his control panel, some to ON, some to OFF. At the same time, he set the flight computer to *preactivate* and killed all the weapons' displays. His plan was to prejuice the engines with some reserve fuel, set everything to *standby* and then when he was finally dropped, throw everything into *activate*.

Then hope for the best. . . .

The problem was, the best hadn't been happening much for him lately.

Was there any reason for it to start now?

The actions of the Beater and Hunter's plane dangling underneath it were being watched with great interest and curiosity by the soldiers on Tin Can beach.

They knew the desperation in the plan mirrored their own, here on the beach. Still, they looked up into the cold windy sky and watched as the Beater and the Z-3/15 became smaller and smaller until they just about disappeared altogether.

It was at this point that the Roamer crew up on the cliff radioed down another chilling report. The Japanese landing craft had reached the west side of the sound and were now making for Ashmont Rocks. After that, it would just be a matter of minutes before they would be steaming onto Tin Can beach itself. After that, and following a valiant fight on the beach, no doubt some sort of slaughter would ensue.

"About a mile from the rocks now," came the Roamer crew's next report. "We can see the troops checking their weapons. They appear to be taking the weather-protection gear off their rifles."

The Japanese troops were getting ready for action. It was time for the defenders to do the same.

The call to ready weapons went from Colonel Asten's lips to his men's ears. But the troops were spread so thin, it took several minutes to repeat the message enough times for everyone to hear the order. By that time, the Japanese landing craft had reached Ashmont Rocks. Now all they had to do was turn into the bay and make for the beach. There really wasn't very much to stop them.

The Roamer crew was ordered to return—every gun would be needed now. Colonel Asten's plan was simple, really. It would be defense in depth. They would fight the Japanese on the beach and then gradually fall back to the real site they were protecting: the farmhouse on top of the hill. The occupants of the house and those who worked inside the underground facility were all now deep down inside the sixteenth-level laboratory, along with the civilian occupants of Summer Point, who had been evacuated earlier. But this would offer only a temporary refuge, Asten feared. To some extent the invading Japanese knew what was here and their aim was to get it. Once they reached the farmhouse area it wouldn't be too long before they would find and gain access to the underground lab.

After that, no less than the whole world would change—and not for the better.

Asten planned to fight to the last man all the way up to the front porch, if that's what it took. No Japanese was going through that door, he vowed. Not while any of his men were still alive.

Another tense minute passed. The waves were hitting the beach very hard now, then rain sounded like the crash of a million cymbals. To make matters worse, from across the sound they could hear the roar of jet engines once again. First two, then four, then six Japanese airplanes were heard taking off. Moments later, they could be seen rising through the low clouds above the sound. More were following right on their tails. All of them seemed weighed down by multitudes of bombs hanging from their wings.

The first line of Japanese landing craft came around Ashmont Rocks and were now heading for the beach. Asten gulped out another order, and this one didn't take but a few seconds to make it up and down the thinly spread line.

"Activate weapons. Be prepared to fight for your life. . . ."

With all this going on, someone on the beach finally remembered to look up. When he did, it gave him cause enough to shout to his comrades, and now everyone was looking up.

Way, way up, in a patch of clear sky past 35,000 feet, the tiny speck of the Beater could still be seen. Beneath it, still spinning like crazy was the Z-3/15. But something was happening. Faint puffs of smoke were sprouting from the back of the sleek white jet. These were clear-out bursts—prerequisites to starting a double-reaction engine.

"Damn! He's going to do it!" someone yelled.

Sure enough, a second later, the chain beneath the Beater let go, and the Z-3 started falling—very quickly.

Right away, the people on the beach could tell something was wrong. The airplane was falling and spinning and tumbling, all at the same time. Many puffs of black smoke could be seen coming out of the rear of the sleek jet, but not any telltale streaks of clean yellow flame. It was obvious to all those on the beach that Hunter was trying frantically to start his engines—and so far, failing miserably.

With all the trepidation of a circus crowd watching the tightrope walker fall, the soldiers on the beach followed the Z-3/15 as it tumbled, end over end, spitting out desperate puffs of black smoke, but not even the spark of a flame. Their hearts fell along with the struggling airplane.

Hunter's valiant if bizarre attempt to get airborne was about to die a violent death.

And soon after that, so would they.

Not every member of the Special Tank Service unit was down on the beach.

Third Squad, made up primarily of the unit's mechanics, were in place around the farmhouse. These twelve men were positioned inside the trenches which were blown out of the small house's front lawn. They had two antipersonnel rocket launchers, three .50 caliber triple-barreled machine guns, two heavy mortars, and one SuperChieftain tank with only its driver and a single gunner on board.

These men represented the STS's last line of defense. If and when the enemy made it off the beach, only Third Squad, and their surviving comrades, would stand between them and the farmhouse.

Because they were up on a hill, the members of Third Squad also had an excellent view of Tin Can beach, about 2,500 feet away, as well as Point Curly bay, Ashmont Rocks, the sound, and McReady field over on East Falkland. Third Squad had a front row seat for the events unfolding this desperate morning.

What they would see they would not soon forget.

The Japanese landing craft had all rounded Ashmont Rocks by now. They were approaching the beach in two waves, one behind the other. It was a distance of about 1,500 yards and the invasion craft were opened to full throttle. Meanwhile, the first squadron of Japanese jets to take off from McReady had formed up about two miles offshore and were now coming in low over the water. Four Japanese warships, two cruisers, and two destroyers had steamed up Falkland Sound and were now in position about three miles off Tin Can beach. Already their gunners had lobbed several smoke shells onto the beach in order to give them aiming points when it came time to fire.

In all, 2,237 Japanese troops, fifty jet aircraft, and fourteen major naval guns would be used against the seventy or so defenders of West Falkland. There was no reason to believe that the battle would last more than an hour.

The men in Third Squad, watching from the farmhouse trenches, would see it all.

The first noise that reached Third Squad's position was the scream of the Japanese warplanes roaring toward the beach. At almost the same moment, the naval guns offshore opened up. The landing craft were about one-third of the way to the beach. The Japanese soldiers were hunkered down in their flat, open boats, crouching as low as they could go. There was lots of lethal stuff flying over their heads at the moment, some of it so low they could hear it sizzle as it went by.

The first three Japanese warplanes roared over the beach. They were SuperKate attack jets. They let loose two bombs each, and all six missed their targets. The naval gunfire increased, the disruption shells plastering the shallow waters off the beach, sending tremendous shock waves out in all directions and creating even larger waves, but not causing any causalties among the defenders.

There was even machine gun fire coming in from the approaching landing craft themselves. On the beach, the defenders were holding their fire. When the real shooting began, every shot would have to count. There was no sense in wasting ammunition now.

Up on the hill, the members of Third Squad found the noise beyond deafening. Jet engines, booming naval guns, disruption shells exploding, the screaming wind, the pounding rain. Like a gigantic fiery monster with huge steel jaws, the incoming Japanese force was about to tear through their friends down on the beach without mercy—then move on them as well.

When it really seemed that all hope was lost, another noise was heard above all else.

From the low clouds hanging drearily over the beach, there came a bright flash of white-hot light. It crackled like lightning. There was a huge clap of thunder. From the bottom of the cloud, a gleaming white aircraft appeared. It seemed to hang in midair for the longest of moments, as if everything on Earth had stopped for one eternal second.

Then, surrounded by fire and smoke, another roar shook the entire island. It was the unmistakable screech of a double-reaction engine finally kicking in. In a snap the ball of light turned into the Z-3/15 *Stiletto*. A cheer went up from the defenders. It was Hunter! He had somehow gotten the engine to kick in just seconds before he would have impacted on the beach. There was another roar and then the sleek jet took off like a shot. The people on the beach were now startled. One moment the white jet was there, the next it was gone. The sonic boom it left in its wake was louder than all the other noises going on around them combined.

Now the defenders of West Falkland watched in awe as the Z-3/15 went to work.

It might have seemed strange that the first target of the white jet was one of the warships off shore. However as soon as it had attained forward flight, the blur went three miles out to sea and began a murderous strafing pass on one of the two cruisers. This particular ship had more radar antennas and communications gear sticking out of its mast, and that was the clue why it was the first to feel the *Stiletto*'s sting. For this operation, the cruiser was serving as the command and control ship, the brains of the attack. It was important to knock it out of action first.

The *Stiletto*'s first pass severed all the electronic trees sprouting from its mast. A three-shell burst from the white jet's cannon also found the massive communications room right below the bridge and set off three explosions, killing all its communications technicians as well as half its crucial radio gear.

The white jet then climbed, looped, and came back down again, this time lining up its needle nose with the stern of the ship. Its guns opened up again at about fifty yards out. A string of cannon shells walked along the deck and up the superstructure, each one perfectly placed to destroy something vital on the ship. One naval bombardment gun, one antipersonnel rocket launcher, and one antiaircraft array were knocked out—in less than two seconds.

The white jet veered off and climbed again. By this time the cruiser's forward sections were smoking heavily. Huge clouds of sparks could be seen emitting from its rear end. Electrical short circuits of explosive magnitude were running throughout the ship, starting many secondary fires. It was soon going dead in the water.

But the Z-3/15 had already moved on. It was now climbing through the low cloud cover, the unearthly screech of its superengines sending out sonic waves so intense that even the soldiers protecting the farmhouse had to plug their ears for fear of going deaf.

The needle-nosed plane cut into the low clouds like a knife. A short series of machine gun bursts could be heard—and a Japanese SuperKate suddenly fell out of the clouds, like a bird that had been killed on the wing.

The plane came down about fifty yards off Tin Can beach, its flaming wreckage creating an instant water hazard for the incoming landing craft. Another sonic boom, another series of machine gun bursts, and a SuperZero came down right behind it. Just like that, two enemy airplanes were gone and nearly one-fifth of Tin Can beach was blocked.

The white jet was then seen streaking back out to sea. Flying low, its nose lit up in yellow flame, a destroyer was its victim now. The fusillade from the airplane concentrated on the destroyer's naval guns and its bridge. Twisting wing over wing as it bore down on the suddenly swerving ship, the airplane's cannon rounds once again went up one side of the destroyer's hull and down the other. Another twist and suddenly the jet was firing directly into the ship's bridge, where all the officers were. There was a two-second delay, and then a huge explosion shook the destroyer's entire superstructure. In one stroke, its entire command staff had been killed, along with all its controls and weapons systems. The white jet climbed, its engine emitting another terrific sonic boom. Very quickly the destroyer went dead in the water too.

By this time, the Japanese landing craft were just 1,200 yards off Tin Can beach. The defenders had still not fired a shot—this surely would be a whites-of-their-eyes situation. Above the beach the clouds were literally shaking with sonic booms and jet engines screaming. The rain and wind had also increased, adding much to the confusion.

Now another SuperZero came down out of the clouds. It was on fire, its pilot desperately trying to pull up before hitting the water, but failing miserably. His left wing fell off about 200 feet above the waves and that put the big fighter into a mighty spin. It corkscrewed itself into the beach not 250 feet from the front trenches. It was heads-down for the defenders, as a cloud of burning jet fuel went right over the trenches. The wreckage itself exploded once more as it buried itself near the low water mark, creating yet another obstacle the invaders would have to get around.

The white jet disappeared again, but not for long. More sonic booms ripped the morning air. Then it was back, turned over, streaking below the clouds, its machine guns glowing, two streams of tracers ripping into the three leading landing craft.

These new targets were especially vulnerable. The warships and the Japanese airplanes at least had the means to defend themselves, as ineffective as they had been. But the landing crafts were defenseless. They had no real guns, no AA capability. They were big open boats with 300 soldiers crammed inside. Like fish. In a barrel.

The white jet tore into the first three landing craft in such mechanical fashion, it was gut-wrenching to watch— even by the defenders. The three landing crafts were suddenly on fire, suddenly out of control, their helmsmen dead, the steering systems destroyed. Two boats immediately collided and began spinning around wildly. The third turned 180 degrees and then perversely headed back out to sea, its hold on fire, the flames searing the flesh of the unlucky Japanese soldiers trapped inside.

The white jet pulled up, twisted around, let out another sonic boom, and disappeared again.

The survivors in the first line of landing craft were now making their way around the burning wreckage; some were within 500 yards of the beach. The words went down the trenchline. "Ready . . . aim . . . *fire!*"

A great puff of smoke roared off the beach and headed for the landing craft. While many bullets pinged off the raised front ramps of the landers, many more made it over the sides, hitting the crouching soldiers in their heads and necks. Blood and brains were suddenly flying into the winds.

Still the landing craft kept coming.

Another fusillade erupted from the shore. This time it was joined by HE rounds fired from each of the four SuperChieftain tanks. Again the combined wall of fiery metal and lead went through the invasion craft, killing more soldiers and causing one boat's engine to explode.

Still the landing craft kept coming.

Another sonic boom echoed as another SuperZero came down in flames out of the sky. The white jet was right behind it, finishing it off with a quick burst of machine gun fire. The jet lifted itself nimbly over the tumbling flaming wreckage, leveled off and its machine guns began chattering again. This time the targets were the landing craft closest to the beach. Again, every tracer bullet spitting from the sleek jet's gun found a target in an enemy soldier's brain or heart. Once again the landing crafts' helmsmen were the first to be killed. Once they were gone, the landing craft went out of control.

The white jet streaked by in less than two seconds, firing off nearly 300 rounds, and ripping through soldiers on five landing craft.

But still, they kept coming.

Now the defenders fired again. Bullets, antipersonnel rockets, tank shells, firebombs. The wall of death hit the landing craft just 100 yards off the beach. It took out three boats and heavily damaged three more. But still, the remaining landing craft kept coming.

More than half the landing craft of the first wave had

been destroyed. But this still left six afloat and nearly 300 Japanese troops still alive. These men were now splashing through the high waves, trying desperately to get onto the beach. In their throats their screams were stopped madly as they ran into yet another wall of fire from the defenders.

All this was playing out to the soldiers on the farmhouse hill like a surreal movie, with all the lights, the sounds, the explosions. But suddenly the cries of the dying became very real.

Someone else was watching the battle too. Standing on the front porch of the farmhouse, his battle helmet strapped on, the man was following it all. His eyes were continually locked on the white jet and the impossible maneuverings of its pilot. Whenever the needle-nosed airplane was not visible, the man searched the cloudy skies frantically until he saw it again.

In all this time, he could only say the same words, over and over again, for he knew more about the white jet's pilot than the pilot did himself.

"My God," the man kept repeating. "He's an angel. . . ."

Hunter was doing six things at once.

He was flying the airplane, hands on the throttle and stick, feet on the pedals. He was firing his guns, his thumb going numb from tapping the firing button on top of the control stick. He was following his airborne radar, looking for Japanese planes hiding up in the clouds. He was also looking at his surface radar and trying to find the best angles from which to fire on the landing craft.

He was also banging his MVP mercilessly, swearing at it, punching it, spitting on it, he was so furious with the thing. It wasn't working. It was full of power, but it was refusing to clear itself. Its screen was a jumble of numbers and letters, confused and confusing, just like most of the crap here in this advanced yet still tube-happy world.

The destruction he and his jet plane were wreaking was happening almost by remote control. See the target, aim at the target, shoot the guns. Simple as that. Flying the plane was simple too, no matter what impossible twist or turn he was performing, it was like second nature to him. It was trying to get the fucking MVP to do something that was draining most of his energy—and that was very frustrating.

For despite what was happening below, it was still absolutely critical that they get a message to the outside world. That had been Hunter's real objective in getting his plane working and airborne again. To charge up the MVP and send an SOS. But now the damn thing was charged to the max and still it wouldn't even burp for him.

While he was screwing around with it, he'd put the white jet into a long elliptical orbit; this was the most efficient way for him to fire his guns and hit targets. The fact that he was doing it just 300 feet above the ground and a speed approaching Mach 3 gave it all that unreal blurry image. In one second, he would find himself over the beach, firing on the landing craft. The next, he was over McReady, tearing up a few taxiing warplanes. Turning continuously to the left, he was suddenly over the warships, raking the second cruiser with cannon fire. A few seconds later, he was back over the beach again.

It was a crazy carousel of speed and fire and death and all the while he was banging the goddamn MVP and screaming at it to do something. Anything.

Finally, after his third pass over McReady, the MVP screen cleared itself and began blinking: *Send Message Now.*

It was as if the sun and the moon came out at the same time. Suddenly, there was light before Hunter's eyes where since he'd come to this haunted place, there had been nothing but darkness. He passed over the second destroyer, pumping a barrage into its foredeck, and kept screaming left. He began punching words into the MVP—a long, yet concise message. He'd been rehearsing it for a long time, so he wasted no time now. The words began spitting onto the MVP screen faster than he could turn the jet.

He was sending the priority message burst to Agent Y and OSS headquarters simultaneously. He was telling them his current position, the situation, and how dire it all was. It took him just one pass over the beach and another over McReady to complete the message. He was sure anyone receiving it would recognize the circumstances right away and send help—quick.

But, after he scrambled the message and hit the Send button, the usual screen-blink from green to white did not happen. The screen blinked blue, and then came back as all red. The words it was showing now were: *Access Not Possible. Overload situation. Try later.*

Hunter was barely able to contain his fury. Calm down, he told himself. Stay cool. Stay tight. After all, this might be a temporary thing. He tore up two more landing craft and hit the MVP's send button again. Again, he got the overload message. He tried again, but to the same result.

He just couldn't believe it. He was getting a fucking busy signal!

He tried again and again and again—to no avail. He imagined every goddamn Main/AC computer in the United States was plugged in at the moment, everyone feeding off the thing on the eve of the great American counterstrike and thus causing the electronic logjam. But the fools were cutting their own throats because down here, where it was all happening, the one message that *had* to get through wasn't going anywhere.

He tried again and again and again—and finally the screen began blinking with a new message. It repeated the overload problem again, and then, in big red letters, it informed him that the next possible access wouldn't be for three hours. Then it blinked off for good.

For Hunter, that's when the sun went down again.

Colonel Asten knew the time had come.

Despite the grand heroics of his men in the trenches and the slightly frightening performance of the crazy American in his slightly unreal jet, the reality of the situation was now quite clear.

At least 200 enemy troops were now firmly established on the beach. Dug-in on the soft sand or using the many wrecked landing crafts littering the beach as cover, this vanguard was hanging on, at great cost, for the second wave of the invasion to come in.

The landing craft of that wave were no doubt still within the belly of the Japanese troopship which had just appeared offshore. Called up from San Carlos Bay at the first sign of things going badly, there was no reason for Asten to believe it contained anything less than another 1,000 or more heavily armed Japanese troops.

His men were preparing to fall back. Behind the beach was a small forest of scrub trees, then a large peat bog, then the east road. About a third of a mile up that road was the farmhouse they'd all been sent here to protect.

There was a series of booby traps and mines set in the woods behind the shoreline. Defending the road to the farmhouse would give Asten's men an advantage, as they would be in possession of the high ground at all times. But these would simply be delaying actions. It would be just a matter of time before the enemy overcame them and marched up the hill to the farmhouse itself.

The problem was a failure to communicate, the cause of most major defeats. All attempts by Asten's radiomen to get a message out on their field Boomers had been fruitless. Asten was sure that Hunter's communications gear was not working either. They were all isolated here at the bottom of the world, fighting a battle which could literally turn the current war and perhaps affect history for decades, even centuries to come. Yet they were losing simply because there was no way to get an SOS out to any friendly ears.

At least no way that Asten knew of.

But maybe there was someone else on the island who knew of another way. . . .

The STS commander figured the enemy was less than an hour from overwhelming his small force. It really was time for desperate measures. He left the defending force in the hands of his seconds, and jumped into the unit's only jeepster. Ducking bullets that were pinging off his bumper as he slammed the vehicle in gear, he was off the beach, through the woods, and roaring up the road to the farmhouse in a matter of seconds.

The men of Third Squad were startled to see him coming; even more so when he crashed the jeepster into the farmhouse's front gate, he was so much in a hurry.

He jumped out of the vehicle unhurt and ran up the path to the farmhouse. Gaining the front porch, he stopped before the front door, took a deep breath, and then began knocking loudly.

The man answered right away. Helmet in place, a look of concern was drawn on his face.

There were none of the usual pleasantries between them now. Asten got right to the point.

"Sir, we have about one hour left and . . ."

The man held up his hand. He'd been watching the battle from the porch or from inside. He knew how desperate the fight was becoming.

"I know you're doing the best you can," he told Asten.

"Sir, I must ask you an important question," the STS commander went on. "Even if it breaks every security rule in the book, I must ask it anyway."

The man nodded. "Go ahead. . . ."

Asten cleared his throat. A series of huge explosions from the beach rocked the small front porch.

"Sir, do you have in your possession," Asten began, "any method of communication—maybe a highly classified one—that we might use. We *must* get a message out for help immediately, sir, or . . ."

Asten let his voice trail off. He didn't want to say the final words—and from the look on the man's face, he didn't have to.

The man steeled himself. This really was a desperate act. The facility beneath the farmhouse held many, many secrets and there was a means of communication he could use. But it was most unusual and he had sworn he would never resort to it, no matter what. But now, he had the lives of so many people in his hands, it would have been sacrilege not to attempt it. Though he doubted he would ever have peace again, once the deed was done.

There was another round of explosions from the beach. These sounded louder, closer. A Japanese SuperZero streaked directly overhead; Hunter's Z-3/15 was right on its tail, firing madly. They disappeared into the low cloud cover an instant later, like they were phantoms fighting some other distant war.

Both Asten and the man had to hang on to the porch railings now, the vibrations all around them were so intense.

Settled that he was going to go ahead, the man had to ask the STS commander a very strange question first.

"Colonel, among your men, is there someone who is an orphan? Who has no family? No wife, no children?"

Asten just stared back at him. "Excuse me, sir?"

The man nearly lost his nerve. This *was* a hard decision to make.

But he repeated the question. Asten took in the words, thought about them, then replied: "Yes, sir. Private Andi

McShook. He just came in three months ago. I happen to know he has no family. No relatives. He was raised as a ward of the state."

"And if he should die," the man went on, "the impact would be less than if it happened to one of your other men?"

"Yes, I believe that's true, sir," the STS commander replied.

The gunfire was getting closer.

"And Colonel, is it your opinion that *all* of your men will be killed within the next hour? Every last one of them, if something isn't done?"

Asten didn't even have to think about that question.

"Yes, sir," he replied truthfully. "They will be dead. We all will be."

To which the man nodded gravely. A tear was beginning to glisten in his eye.

"All right, Colonel," he said. "Send Private McShook to me."

Thirty

Five minutes later, Private Andy McShook was knocking on the farmhouse door. The sound of gunfire was very close now. Just before McShook was called off the line, the Japanese had landed another 100 troops or so on the beach. And more were on the way.

That's why he was very surprised when Colonel Asten got him out of his trench and told him to report to the farmhouse immediately. McShook knew better than to ask why. He'd double-timed it off the beach and up the hill in a matter of minutes.

The man answered the door after the first knock. McShook saluted him smartly. The young soldier had never seen the man close up before. From what he'd heard about him, McShook expected him to be much older. But the man was nowhere near as ancient as the soldier had imagined him to be.

The man told him to come in, so McShook stepped gingerly into the living room. He and the other commandos had speculated about what the inside of the farmhouse might look like; now McShook was getting an eyeful of the real thing.

It was just as he imagined a typical family home would look like, nothing he would know about. It was simple, homey. Pictures on the walls, books on the shelves. A checkerboard on the dining room table.

The man bid him to follow. McShook walked through the kitchen and through the closet door, to the elevator chamber beyond.

His mind was racing now. He was being shown the inner sanctum, the place that was so secret. Suddenly McShook feared some kind of huge mistake had been made. He didn't have any security clearances past the one needed to be a member of the STS team here on West Falkland Island.

"Sir," McShook said as the man called for the elevator, "I think I should warn you. I only have a level-one security clearance. I might not be able to . . ."

The man held up his hand just as the elevator arrived and the door slid open.

"Don't worry about that, my friend," he said.

They took the elevator down to the sixteenth level. The guard station was empty as the soldiers were up top, fighting.

They walked down the long corridor and the man sprung the door into the lab chamber. They both stepped inside.

McShook looked around, his eyes wide in awe. What he saw was indescribable. It was a laboratory, but to the layman's eye, it was much more than that. There were machines, huge devices full of buttons and lights and switches and levers, and McShook had not the faintest idea of their function. Electrical bolts running from here to there. Huge tanks bubbling with unidentifiable liquids. Even the hum of the place sounded otherworldly. This place *looked* like an inner sanctum, McShook thought, as portrayed in a comic book. As the secret places of all of secret places, it really fit the bill.

Again, he felt like an enormous error had been made. Instinctively he knew he should not be seeing any of this.

"Sir, again, I must tell you," he stuttered, "I am not cleared for . . ."

But the man again waved his concerns away.

"It really doesn't matter now," he told the private.

He brought the young soldier to a table and sat him down, telling him to take off his helmet and to get as comfortable as possible. No one else was in evidence, though McShook thought he could hear voices coming from the next room.

The man sat down next to him.

"Private," he began. "You are going on a very special mission. One that will save the lives of everyone else here. I want you to understand that from the start, OK?"

McShook nodded slowly. A chill went through him. It was not what the man was saying exactly, but how he was saying it.

"Yes, sir. I understand," he finally replied.

The man talked to McShook for the next five minutes. They consulted a map of the nearest American allied military installations. The man told the soldier what would be expected of him in the next hour. McShook's eyes went wide, first filling with terror, then filling with tears as he listened to the man's instructions.

When he was finished, the man gave him a document to sign. It had one section that served as a last will and testament, and another for any last statements.

McShook sniffled as he spent a few minutes writing down what he wanted. Because of his background, it was brief.

The man asked McShook to stand.

"Do you fully know what you are about to do?" he asked the soldier. "Do you understand your mission completely?"

McShook nodded, tears streaming down his face.

As he was doing this, the man had moved behind him.

Now he asked McShook to close his eyes and hold his breath. The soldier did so.

The man pulled a very long, very thin, very sharp knife from his desk and, without hesitation, plunged it into the soldier's back.

The knife went directly through McShook's heart. The heart exploded instantly. He slumped into the man's arms and the man lowered him gently to the floor. He checked McShook's pulse. The young soldier was dead.

The man wiped a tear from his eye and let out a long troubled breath.

They didn't call him God for nothing.

Xwo Mountain

Major Payne was working alone in his office.

The mountain base was nearly deserted. It was a very cloudy, stormy day, and the bombers and fighters had been gone for two hours and weren't expected back for another three.

Anyone who could be was inside now. The ground crews were huddled in their barracks. The staff officers were in their billets or in the mess hall.

Payne was the only person inside the dark, dank operations building at the moment.

Things were happening up north. Payne knew it unofficially. He was not privy to many classified messages. His MVP hardly blinked at all. But he was in constant touch with officers of his own level and rank back in the U.S., and just from their idle gossip, Payne knew that at least two major operations were supposed to be launched against Japan very soon.

One, he was sure, was to going to happen here in South America—and it didn't take a military genius to figure out that it was probably an invasion from Brazil. A second push was probably going to come in the Panama Canal Zone. Again, no deep thought needed there.

But his grapevine of officers had also hinted, because they had heard it hinted themselves, that yet *another* highly secret operation was up. Though no one had a clue as to what it might be.

There was also some rather disturbing information. One chilling report said that the two top OSS operatives had been captured and assassinated by a Japanese hit squad. Others said they'd heard only that the two operatives were missing. There was also a strange report that the airplane carrying the New Jersey Giants football team had either crashed or was missing.

Strangest of all, and most disturbing, Payne had heard that Hawk Hunter, sent on a secret mission several days earlier, was overdue or had not been heard from. This was typical Hunter stuff—dropping out of sight for days at a time to get the particularly hard jobs done right. But Payne had a bad feeling about this one.

Payne tried to go back to his mountain of paperwork, but suddenly he felt very uneasy. A chill went through him. Beads of sweat appeared on his brow. It was suddenly very dark inside the ops building. And he felt very, very alone.

That's when he heard the noise come from the outer office. He wasn't expecting anyone to come see him. With the weather, his huge workload, and the general gloominess of this place, he didn't expect to see another living soul for at least three hours.

So who was out in the other room?

Payne called out. "Yes, who is that, please?"

There was no reply.

Payne tried again. "Is there someone there?"

Once more, there was no response.

Payne finally got up and walked over to his closed office door. He stopped just before his hand reached for the doorknob. He could hear movement on the other side, maybe a faint murmuring as well. On a whim, he reached into his holster hanging from the coat rack and took out his gun.

Then he opened the door—and was transfixed.

The person on the other side was transparent. He was wearing the combat uniform of a British commando. A small patch of blood stained his breast. But the man wasn't really there. Payne could see right through him.

He was a ghost. Not all that unusual in this world. But absolutely frightening nevertheless.

"Major Payne?" the ghost spoke, his voice sounding like it was coming from someplace else. "My name is Private Andrew McShook. I have an urgent message for you."

Thirty-one

The Battle of Tin Can beach went on for another thirty minutes.

Using superior fields of fire and well-situated positions, the defenders had been able to kill more than 1,200 Japanese troops. This death toll was helped greatly by the white jet, making strafing runs continuously up and down the beach, while neutralizing the ships offshore and halting, at least temporarily, any aircraft taking off from McReady field.

The beach was littered with dead Japanese soldiers, many burning landing craft, at least a dozen crashed warplanes—and surprisingly few STS casualties. The problem was, while the defenders had done a heroic job, there was another wave of Japanese landing craft soon to come in. It would contain at least 750 fresh troops, with plenty of ammunition. The defenders were spent, both physically and in their ammo belts. Already many men were into their reserves, and the recoilless rifles had exactly two shots left in them apiece. All four tanks were down to the last six shells, as were the mortar men and the antipersonnel launcher squads.

Worse yet, their protector on high, the man and the airplane which had kept them all alive this far, was running out of ammunition too. Even more dire, he was running out of gas.

Hunter had tried every trick in the book to conserve his fuel. Shutting off all unnecessary electronics, jettisoning his empty fuel tanks, even shutting down his oxygen supply.

But the fuel problem was a finite thing. Once he was out, he was out for good. What would happen then, he didn't know. He would have about a five-minute warning before his reserve tanks went completely dry, then he would have to make a big decision. Either bail out and let the plane crash, or try to bring it down somewhere soft and preferably not in the hands of the Japanese, or—a third choice—crash it into one last enemy target, riding it down all the way.

He decided to put that third option on the back burner for the moment and concentrate on the first two. He didn't want to bail out and watch the best airplane he'd ever spanked go in with a fiery crash. It was the setting-down-someplace-soft choice that proved the most appealing.

While he was contemplating these things, he was still circling low over Tin Can beach, taking potshots at the troopship currently cruising about two miles out at sea. Inside was yet another wave of Japanese landing craft. Hunter didn't have enough ammo to take on a whole big ship. He would have to wait for the wave of landing craft to float out of the mother hen and then try to pick some off individually. The problem was, the longer the Japanese waited, the longer he would be burning gas. He checked his fuel readout and asked the computer for a time-link. He had about twelve minutes of flying left. Then it would be time to come down, no matter how, no matter where.

He'd given up on the MVP a long time ago. Given up on getting any kind of message out. Right now his energies were concentrated on keeping the commandos below—on the beach and in the woods—alive for as long as possible. Some Japanese had gained the lower beach and now he could see the large troopships opening their front doors and letting out the next wave of troops.

Damn! There had to be another 1,000 or so invaders heading for the beach. There was no way the men on the ground could possibly fight them off, no matter how much protection he gave them.

The defenders opened up early on these new landing craft, firing on them from 500 yards or more, a sign they were close to running out of ammunition too. Hunter checked his own ammo supply. He was down to fifty rounds in his four machine guns and twelve rounds in his cannon. There was no need to be selective here, he thought. He broke from his protective orbit above Tin Can beach for the first time in an hour, and dove on the landing craft just as they were coming out of the troopship. He walked a line of tracers across the first three boats, getting major hits and putting two out of commission. Hunter circled around and sprayed the next line of boats with machine gun fire. Again, he hit good targets. But halfway through his third strafing run he heard the disturbing *pop-pop-pop* sound that meant his machine guns had just run dry.

He passed back over the beach and saw that the last of Asten's men were now pulling back. Those Japanese alive behind the barricades finally managed to wade to shore. One fool among them set up the Nipponese flag, which someone firing from the woods instantly cut down. Hunter looped back around and fired off six of his twelve cannon shells, hitting a small command post the invaders had hastily established, but pulling up and away before he blew his entire cannon load.

For this he turned his attention back to the incoming landing craft, lined up the first one, and let loose his last six shells. They hit the landing craft straight on, igniting its fuel tank and blowing it out of the water. It was a spectacular explosion and the wreckage that came back down served to further block the entrance to Tin Can beach.

But that was it. Hunter was out of ammo. He could do no more. . . .

Now what? he wondered. *Look for a soft spot? Or a target?*

The question was answered for him. Everything just started shaking. At first he thought it was the airplane. Was he running out of gas sooner than he'd calculated? No— the plane was still flying, his control board was still all green.

It was his body that was shaking so violently. This could only mean one thing: Enemy airplanes were close by. Very close.

Hunter turned in his cockpit and saw first one, then two, then four Japanese SuperZeroes coming down out of the clouds at him. They'd been cruising high above, waiting for him to run out of ammo. Now they were going finish him off.

Or so they thought.

He hit the throttle and shot ahead of the four fighters. But these were the stripped-down, faster version of the SuperZeroes, the so-called F/U-machines. They could get up to 1,200 mph in bursts, and at this low altitude, and with Hunter's dwindling fuel situation, he was loath to go to 100 percent on his own engines. If he did, he'd be out of fuel in a matter of seconds, rather than minutes.

So he did the next best thing: He went even lower, two of the 'Zeroes right on his tail. They opened up with cannons at 300 feet out. Hunter just let his psyche take over. He began twisting the airplane this way and that, getting it out of the way of everything being shot at him. The lines of fiery streaks going by were almost blinding. But not one enemy round hit his Z-3/15.

He was back over the water now—and down to twenty-five feet. The 'Zeroes were still with him, their pilots shooting wildly as he zigged and zagged mere inches above the water's surface. He turned sharp left and headed directly in toward the beach. He could see the last of Asten's men falling back through the woods and up the hill toward the farmhouse. The 'Zeroes turned with him, their sights set on his very vulnerable tail. At the very last instant, Hunter yanked the control stick and put the *Stiletto* on its tail. The 'Zeroes could not mimic this maneuver. Before them now was a wall of burning wreckage: the last two SuperKates Hunter had shot down. The 'Zero pilots tried to peel off, but they were going way too fast. Both went into the wreckage full force, slamming into a pair of hapless landing craft chugging toward the beach. Everything inside of 500 feet went up in one big ball of fire and smoke and metal.

Meanwhile, Hunter turned over at 150 feet. The two other 'Zeroes were on his tail in a second. But that was OK. That's how he'd planned it. He streaked over the hill where Asten's men were falling back. He was so low, his tail was actually ripping off treetops. Greedy for a kill, the 'Zeroes went right down to the deck with him, the lesson their colleagues had just learned the hard way apparently having little impression on them.

Hunter turned hard right, as a steep hill was coming up. The 'Zeroes were firing madly at him, but could find no place to hit on his speedy white jet. He went even lower, the 'Zeroes followed. At the exact right moment, he pulled back on his stick and was soon looking straight up into the cloudy sky. Neither 'Zero could match such a radical maneuver. They saw the hill coming, but there was nothing they could do. One actually turned into the other, colliding with it and creating a massive ball of fire and metal that went cartwheeling over the hill and across the frozen bogs.

Four enemy airplanes, four dead ducks. And Hunter had done it all without firing a shot. But he had paid in a different way. He looked at his fuel gauge and felt his heart drop. The wild ride had sucked almost 100 gallons of fuel from his reserve tank. He now had twenty-five left—or about one minute of flying time. For what it was worth, this ride was coming to an end.

He started looking for a soft place to set down simply because the only good targets for a kamikaze dive—one of the warships offshore—were so far away, he wasn't sure he could reach them. He flew back around one last time over the farmhouse and saw Asten's men fighting the mass of Japanese soldiers which were now moving up the east road and toward the farmhouse.

Hunter's throat got thick with emotion. The STS guys were brave and loyal—but soon they were all going to be dead. They were fighting without quarter, taking a massive toll of enemy soldiers before giving up a yard, but it was simply a question of numbers and ammunition. The three tanks on the beach had been set afire by their own crewmen. Out of ammo, out of gas, they'd abandoned them, very reluctantly he supposed. The other tanks were firing point-blank into the approaching Japanese soldiers as they climbed the cold and bloody hill, but it was just a matter of time before their ammo ran out too.

Now going less than sixty knots, Hunter could see some of the STS soldiers up on the front porch of the farmhouse itself, firing madly back at the swarm of Japanese troops. There was a man down there on the porch with them. He was not dressed as a soldier, though he had a helmet on. He was motioning for the soldiers to come inside the farmhouse. Hunter let out a grim laugh. As if the thin walls of the tiny cottage would actually offer some protection from the guns of the oncoming mass of enemy soldiers!

Hunter was over the farmhouse, over the next hill, and heading south away from it all. He had to get serious about where to set down. The frozen waters of Falkland Sound were always a possibility, though, once immersed, the Z-3/15 would most likely sink like a stone. A field with high grass might do—the longer the grass, the more he might be able to cushion the blow. Trouble was, there *was* no high grass on the Falklands, at least none that he could see. It was always so damn cold here, few things made it over a couple of inches in length. If only he could find . . .

Suddenly, his body was vibrating again. . . .

Damn!! He swung around and saw three more 'Zeroes on his tail. In a heartbeat, bullets were zipping by him like fireflies. They were so close he imagined he could smell the cordite smoke. He looked at his fuel gauge. It simply read *Empty*. He was now officially flying on fumes. There'd be no fancy maneuvering now. No escape at all.

This time, *he* was the dead duck.

Well, he thought, *so this is the way I'll go. Quick, maybe painful, but at least airborne.*

Still, he did not want to go so gently. His survival instinct took over. He yanked back on the throttle, at the same time banging the flaps and exposing his landing gear. All this proved the equivalent of hitting the brakes. The Z-3/15 seemed to come to a stop in midair. The change was so dramatic, Hunter whacked his head mightily on the control panel. It was like hitting the windshield in a car accident. Even with his helmet on, the impact on his cranium was so severe, he literally saw stars. Constellations. An entire galaxy of them swirling in front of his dazed eyes.

Two of the 'Zeroes fell for it though. They overshot him by a factor of ten, and were suddenly so out of position only a long, slow, hard climb and turn could put them back in their former dominant positions.

But the third 'Zero had hit the brakes at the same time as he had. Now this plane began pumping bullets into the air. As soon as the first barrage went by Hunter's canopy, he heard the faintest of warning buzzers emit from his control panel. He looked down at the fuel gauge and saw it was blinking red. He ran out of gas two seconds later.

The third 'Zero was right on his ass now. Hunter

couldn't zig; he couldn't zag. He couldn't do anything at all. It was only a question of seconds before the enemy's bullets found him.

It has been a short life in this world, he thought, *and a damn strange one.*

Then he actually closed his eyes and waited for the final blow to come.

But it never did. . . .

Suddenly the 'Zero was no longer shooting at him. He spun around and saw the enemy plane was no longer there. What happened? It was as if it had simply disappeared. He shook his head, trying to clear it, but to no avail. His vision was blurry, his lips were bleeding. The bumps growing out of his forehead from his double whack felt the size of baseballs. Were they making him hallucinate as well?

He turned again, and now he saw the 'Zero was definitely gone. Instead there were three other airplanes in its place. Not 'Zeroes. Not Kates. But American Air Corps Mustang-5s!

Hunter couldn't believe it. Was this a dream? A nonsensical vision that happened at the moment of death? Hunter blinked and made sure he was still among the living. He was. A second later, one Mustang roared by him and he saw a very familiar face looking back at him. The person was waving at him.

It was Sara!

She wagged her wings at him and then was off like a shot, the two other Mustangs right on her heels. They disappeared quickly into the clouds overhead. Hunter just shook his head again.

Did that *really* happen?

He didn't know—but one thing was for sure: the 'Zeroes were gone, and as dazed as he was, he knew he suddenly had a new lease on life. He had to take advantage of it.

He looked frantically for something below him that was

flatter than scrub hills. He was totally gliding now, and the Z-3/15 wasn't an airplane that liked flying without power. Finally he was able to finesse it up and over one last hill—and on the other side he saw something soft. Very soft.

It was a muddy swamp, one that was about five miles from farmhouse hill and maybe half a mile from Falkland Sound. It was big enough and wet enough, and do or die, this was where he was coming down. He lowered his flaps again, locked his landing gear in place, and even raised his canopy, doing anything he could to slow the plane down.

Somehow he succeeded in getting the aircraft into an almost floating mode. Nose up, ass down, he was just ten feet above the ground. He leaned on the stick for a microsecond, then pulled back on it as hard as he possibly could. He hit the mud an instant later.

It was messy, and it was smelly, but it was damn soft, and it took the full weight of the empty Z-3/15, thank God. Hunter was thrown forward as the plane came to a sudden stop. Once again, he whacked his head on the console, then was whiplashed back into his seat. His knees buckled and cracked in unison. His right elbow was instantly crushed.

But he was down, and he was alive. That was all that mattered.

He sat there for a long moment, trying to catch his breath. A few seconds ago, he'd been sweating and flying. Now he was standing still, covered with mud—and still sweating.

He finally managed to climb out of the Z-3/15 and half walk, half swim to the edge of the mud pond. Reaching the shore, he dragged himself up on fairly dry land, and collapsed. He was suddenly very cold. He closed his eyes for a second and tried to think. *What just happened?* Had he really seen Air Corps Mustang-5s? Or had it been an illusion? Was that really Sara that had streaked by him? Or was this yet another punch line in this long-running cosmic joke?

He heard a low rumbling sound. He opened his eyes and there were more airplanes above him. Not 'Zeroes or friendly fighters, but bombers. B-17/36s and B-24/52s. There were eighteen of them. Flying right over him in a prebombing chevron formation.

They were the bombers from Xwo Mountain. He could tell just by looking up at them. Why were they here? What kind of message could have possibly gotten through to them?

Hunter somehow found the strength to get on his feet and scramble up the next hill. From here he could see the bomber formation turn sharply and begin a long slow turn over West Falkland. The biggest question now was not how or why, but what.

What were the bombers going to do?

He got his answer a few seconds later. They began breaking into combat formation, the flock of Mustang-5s riding on their flanks. Two by two the huge bombers screamed down from 5,000 feet. Hunter's breath caught in his throat. They were going to bomb the Japanese on farmhouse hill. But this was crazy! Hunter knew there was no way the bombers could hit the invaders without hitting the defenders as well. He let out a scream as the first of the flying monsters swooped in and began dropping their loads of firebombs on farmhouse hill, right where Asten's men had been fighting a minute before.

The whole horizon lit up in flames and smoke. Two more bombers came in; they too dropped their loads on farmhouse hill. Again a wall of flame rose up five miles away. Hunter let out another long, agonizing scream. Two more bombers came m. Then two more, and two more.

He watched, tears in his bleary eyes, as the bombers unloaded tons of firebombs on Tin Can beach, the east road, and especially on the hill where the farmhouse was.

In seconds, this whole section of West Falkland had been turned into a forest of flames and black smoke.

It was over in less than a minute. Eighteen bombers, thousands of pounds of firebombs. Their work done, the bombers formed up again and quickly turned northwest. Hunter could just barely hear the scream of their engines as they roared away, over the horizon, going back to from where they came.

He just stood there, looking up into the smoke-filled sky. The world suddenly became very quiet. Only the crackling of the flame could be heard, five miles away.

A terrible mistake had been made. The last he'd seen of Asten's men, they'd been retreating right into the farmhouse itself. And judging from the flames leaping into the sky, Hunter knew there was absolutely no chance the farmhouse—or anyone inside—could have survived.

Thirty-two

It took Hunter nearly four hours to walk the five miles to farmhouse hill.

His legs were not broken, but they felt like they were. His right elbow was throbbing with pain, but he hardly noticed it. He'd whacked his head with such force, his helmet had two dents in it, one in the front, one in the back. He was still suffering from a five-star case of woozy.

He was covered with smelly, sticky mud. Never before in his life could he remember being in worse need of a bath.

When he finally topped the next hill over from the farmhouse, he had a real desire not to look. *Just keep your eyes closed and keep on walking,* he told himself. Past the devastation he knew was there, through the burned-out woods, out onto Tin Can beach. Eyes closed, just keep on walking, right into the water, and maybe swim his way back to South America.

At least then he would get his bath.

But he never was one for denial. He knew his eyes would have to see the truth eventually. So why not now?

Besides, maybe it all had been a illusion. . . .

So he finally staggered to the top of the next hill and opened his weary, dazed, muddy eyes.

There was nothing left. No woods, no beach. No farmhouse. Everything was black. Burned to a crisp. Tanks. Big guns. Bodies, everywhere. Dull black skeletons were all over the scorched hillside, some with the rifles still in their hands, like ghostly warriors still trying to take the hill.

He knew this was what the ground's-eye view of a massive firebombing looked like. For once, he was on the other side.

He trudged down into the small valley between the hills and reached the periphery of the square half mile of smoldering soot.

What was the sequence of events here? Somehow the bombers at Xwo had gotten word of the battle on Tin Can beach. That much was clear. Hunter even guessed that they had probably been on their way to another bombing mission when a divert order got to them somehow—thus making their time to target very short. As well as their time *over* target. That's why all the airplanes had departed so quickly after the conflagration.

But why would the normally pinpoint firebombers lay down such a wide swath of destruction? Had something been missed here? Had the bombers been mistakenly told that only enemy troops were on the ground?

He didn't know, and at that moment he felt he would never know. Now, looking up the scorched hill, even the smell of death was not in the air. Like everything else, it had been burned away.

Hunter collapsed, falling in a heap onto the seat of his pants.

This was alone, man. *Really* alone. He was here in the middle of nowhere, probably the only living person left on West Falkland. Or maybe even on the pair of islands.

Alone, in the middle of nowhere. A wave of gloom came over him. Not only was he absolutely isolated here in this world—he was actually an entire *universe* away from where he was supposed to be. You couldn't get more isolated than that.

His head sunk into his hands. His stomach turned itself up into knots. The glum feeling was hitting him with double punches now. When you really got down to it, even Back There, he'd been all alone. He didn't have any family in the last world. His mother and father had been lost in a plane accident when he was just a kid. He had no brothers, no sisters, no uncles, aunts, or cousins. Back There he was as alone as one could get, as far as the family tree went.

Here, he was even more so.

It was strange then, that at that moment, when he was just sitting there, dejected by a factor of a trillion or so, he heard someone calling his name.

"Major? Major Hunter?"

Hunter shook his head at first—he was so sure it was his bruised brain playing tricks on him, he didn't even bother to look up. It was the wind, he told himself, sounding like a voice calling his name.

"I say . . . Major Hunter? Is that you down there?"

Finally he did look up. And he knew that if this was an illusion of some kind, it was a dandy.

He scanned the unburned hill. Nothing. He looked down toward the water. Again, nothing.

Then he looked up at the pile of smoldering rubble that once was the farmhouse.

There was a man up there, holding up a cup in one hand and smiling broadly.

It was Colonel Asten. He looked no worse than if he'd just come home from a brisk walk. He was holding a white cup and saucer in his hand and beckoning him with it.

"I say, Major Hunter," he yelled down to the man some people called the Sky Ghost. "Why not climb on up here and have a spot of tea?"

Ten minutes later, Hunter was sitting at one end of a long table.

In the other chairs around it sat six men, all in lab coats, all wearing glasses, all with the same haircuts and the same facial expression.

On the table in front of them, next to Hunter's cup of tea, was the Bomb.

It was small. Smaller than he'd ever imagined. Smaller even that the six he'd hauled out of Germany. This was in fact one of those bombs, but it was in a different, more diminutive casing and its shape had been altered.

The men in the lab coats were trying to explain something to him about ions or quarks or quakes—or quacks. Did they really call subatomic particles "quacks" in this world? Hunter wasn't sure, and he wasn't going to ask. These six scientists might have been the most earnest collection of people he'd ever seen in one place at one time. To ask them a question such as that just wouldn't be cool.

So he sat and listened about the little bomb with the big bang, and whenever he could, he would steal a glance at this fantastic place he'd just found himself in.

Sixteen levels below the earth. No wonder all of Asten's men had lived through the firebombing. As intense as it had been, the STS men—only one of whom had died during the battle, remarkably—had been drinking tea by the time the carpet bombing up above had reached its full intensity. This was one time that calling in an air strike on one's own position had actually worked.

But all that seemed oddly secondary now. The place he was in looked like a movie set—a common impression, he was sure. It had everything Frankenstein's lab had, but all of it much bigger and much scarier looking. Electrode tubes. Strange bubbling liquids. The cranking sound of weird machinery.

"More secrets here than anywhere else in the universe," was how Asten described it to him as they rode the elevator down into the belly of the Earth. The lift's solid metal casing was the only thing left standing of the farmhouse.

It would hold secrets still. The first thing Hunter asked

Asten was how in the world word had gotten back to Xwo Mountain to send the cavalry.

"I asked them that very same question down here," the STS man confided in him. "They told me it was classified."

Hunter sipped his tea and went back to staring at the Bomb.

"So you see, Major," one of the lab coats was telling him, "the warhead has an ultrasensitive magnetic targeting device in it. It is keyed to vibrations in the Earth's inner core. Therefore the Bomb will go to the exact spot it must go to *only* if it is released at exactly the right height and exactly the right moment. It's a sort of an intellectual process we've been able to build into it. We like to call it the world's first intelligent bomb."

"Do you mean 'smart bomb'?" Hunter asked.

"Whatever," the coat replied.

"Thus the transpolar route you and your airplane must take," another scientist began telling him. "The timer built into the warhead must take a full global reading to arm itself properly. It's really a matter of basic magnetism and . . ."

Hunter wasn't listening anymore.

His eyes were wandering again—his ears, too. He was certain there were more people down here than just those he could presently see. All of Asten's men were jammed into a room with heavy glass windows nearby, drinking gallons of tea and reveling in the fact that they were still alive.

Hunter had the definite impression that other souls were close by as well, maybe just a door or two away. The people from the fishing village at Summer Point. He'd seen them being evacuated. Where were they now? And the girl, Chloe. What had happened to her?

There was another strange thing tugging at his psyche, too. Far down at the other end of the lab, there was a door that looked like it should be protecting all the gold in China, it was so big and thick and its locks were so elaborate. What lay behind it? Hunter strained his battered ears and listened very hard, his scrambled brains thinking that he could actually hear something coming from behind the thick door.

But the only sound that reached his ears—or seemed to—made no sense. To him, it just sounded like the blowing of the wind.

". . . so as you see, Major, timing on this will be everything. Any questions?"

Hunter just looked up at the lab coats again.

"Well, just one," he said. "If I'm really flying this weapon back to Area 52, then I need a plane to do it in. If you want it back there as *quickly* as possible, then I will need *my* plane. The problem is, it's stuck in a mud hole about five miles from here."

"No, it's not," one lab coat told him. "Your friend, Mr. Duggen, has already picked it up with his Beater and carried over to McReady—which is completely abandoned, by the way. The savages ran like dogs after the bombing. Mr. Duggen reports your airplane is in very good shape. You'll be ready for takeoff as soon as you like."

Hunter just shook his head. He was still somewhat convinced this was all just a dream. So why not play along?

"OK—well, then what about fuel?" he asked. "I can't imagine there's any extra aviation gas over at McReady, is there?"

The lab coats seemed worried for the first time. But then one stuck his finger in the air and actually said, "Ah!"

He disappeared into a workroom for a moment and reemerged with a small steel box. He put the box on the table and opened it. He took out what looked to Hunter to be a big, thick, white antacid pill.

"Fill your tank with water," the lab coat said, giving Hunter the pill. "Drop this in. Wait five minutes and you'll have a full tank of gas."

Hunter stared at the pill then back at the lab coats.

"You sure?"

They all nodded as one.

"Trust us. . . ."

They all checked their watches at the same time, and came to the same conclusion.

"It's really time for you to get going, Major," one said.

Hunter didn't want to get going. He wanted to stay here and discover the secrets behind all the secrets and drink some more tea and look for the girl he thought was Chloe.

The lab coats had other ideas. They brought out a large metal pod which had two hooks on it. It looked similar to the fuel tank that he'd carried on his airplane, only much smaller.

They picked up the Bomb, not at all bothering to handle it gingerly, and put it inside the pod.

"This should fit nicely on your wing pylon," one coat told Hunter. "You should have no problem transporting it safe and sound from here."

Hunter kind of shrugged. His head was still spinning, he felt almost high. Maybe it was the tea.

"So, if there are no further questions, then . . ." one coat said. It was obvious they wanted Hunter on his way so he could deliver the bomb in a timely fashion.

"OK, one last question, then I'll go," Hunter said.

"Ask away. . . ." two scientists said at once.

Hunter studied the six of them again. "You guys are all Americans, right?"

The scientists nodded their heads as one.

"And this is a very secret place, correct?"

They all nodded again.

"Then how come the Brits are defending it?"

The men laughed, all six of them. "Who do you suggest we get?" one asked.

Hunter just shrugged.

"I don't know," he said. "The OSS, I guess. They could certainly . . ."

But Hunter's words were interrupted by the six men laughing again.

"The OSS?" one lab coat said. "With all the stuff we got here? Who the hell would trust *those* guys?"

Hunter visited the men's room—it too looked like something out of a sci-fi movie. He washed his face and hands. He put his ear to all four walls, thinking again he might hear a voice or a sound or anything. But all he could hear—or *thought* he could hear—was the wind blowing.

He finally reemerged to find two STS men were waiting for him, as was his friend Duggen, the Beater pilot. He had watched the wild battle from the air, thinking that he might somehow help again.

"I thought I might catch you in flight—when you ran out of gas," he told Hunter.

Hunter just stared back at him. Was he kidding? He didn't want to ask.

Colonel Asten was suddenly there too. He shook Hunter's hand.

"Thanks for everything, Major," he said. "I understand you're a famous one, back in the real world. Maybe we'll see each other again some day."

Hunter gave him a salute and fell in step behind the two STS men and Duggen.

Maybe we will, he thought.

They walked back toward the big door which would carry them out of the lab and down the long corridor to the elevator.

As they reached the big door, Hunter was able to catch a glimpse of another room, one that he hadn't seen on the way in. This room too was glass-encased and sound-proofed, he was sure. And that's where he saw her. The young girl, Chloe, was sitting in this room with the other civilians from Summer Point.

Hunter stopped. She looked up. Their eyes locked again. Her face lit up. So did his. He broke ranks and walked over to the window. She stood up and put her hand to the glass. He touched it—and damned if he didn't feel the warmth of her skin through the thick pane. It was as if there wasn't any glass at all.

She smiled. It was like she was recognizing him too. The other civilians were looking at this little display with a mixture of humor and confusion, but the two of them didn't even know they were there.

She mouthed four words: "Is your name Hawk?"

Hunter nodded enthusiastically. Few people called him by that name here. But why had she? By cosmic design? Or had she simply read a newspaper sometime in the last nine months?

He didn't know.

One of the STS men nudged him, at the same time looking at his watch. The meaning was clear; Hunter had to go.

He pressed his hand closer to the glass, and the sensation of touching real skin never left. She smiled again and he smiled and said, "I'll be back someday."

Then he turned and resumed walking with the STS soldiers.

In all that had happened to him here in the cold, cold Falklands, that encounter might have been the strangest of all.

They rode the elevator back up top, the smell of the scorched earth reaching them even before the doors opened.

They all stepped out. Duggen had landed the shit box Beater very close by. A chill went through Hunter at his first glimpse of it. What if he had made it this far, only to go down in a Beater crash during the short four-mile hop over to McReady?

Could the cosmos be *that* cruel?

The STS men loaded the pod onto the Octocopter, shook hands with Hunter, and bid him farewell.

At that moment, Hunter realized two other people were nearby. They were picking through the ruins of the farmhouse. They seemed overjoyed at the moment because they had found two framed pictures in the smoldering rubble. Somehow these two items had survived the massive firebombing.

They all looked up at one another at the same time and again it was like Hunter had been hit by a lightning bolt. The two people—a man and a woman—were both middle-aged, both pleasant of face and sturdy looking.

They looked damned familiar too.

But just as Hunter was about to call out something to them, Duggen revved the Octo's eight very noisy engines and after that, all thoughts of communication were lost. Hunter just stood in the open cargo bay door watching the pair as the Beater began slowly and unsteadily to rise into the sky.

And then the man and the woman waved to him.

And then Hunter waved back.

Thirty-three

Only one of the Japanese warships taking part in the Falklands campaign was able to make it back to South America under its own power.

It was the command cruiser, the vessel first attacked by the sleek white jet at the beginning of the battle for Tin Can beach.

It had lost more than half its crew. It had no communications ability left. It could only move at half power, and was riding with a fifteen-degree list. The chances of it making port safely were only about fifty-fifty.

Still, this seemed of little concern to two of the three men presently ensconced in the ship's captain's quarters. The pair was more interested in getting drunk, or more accurately, getting drunk on something drinkable.

It was X and Z, the two wayward OSS agents. They had watched the strange battle for Tin Can beach unfold from the relative safety of a gun mount on the cruiser, after have been picked up by a Japanese rescue boat, as so hastily planned, shortly after the attack on McReady Field.

Watching the Japanese attempt to invade West Falkland had been an exercise in frustration for the two rogue agents. They had learned about the Bomb from the thinking machine on their German-built *Nacht-Sputnik* airplane. There was a high probability that some kind of weapon of mass destruction was being kept on the Falkland Islands and that this weapon could literally change the balance of power in the world. This was too good of an opportunity for the pair to pass up—at the time even their search for the all-important Third Guy had been suspended.

Getting into a deal with the Japanese to attack the Falklands had been easier than they'd figured. Characteristically, they went right to the top in presenting their dirty deal with America's current enemy and initially found a responsiveness which they were certain would insure their success.

But fate came back to bite them on the ass. Little did they know that Hawk Hunter, the Sky Ghost, the only other guy on the planet whose very presence could alter events, was also in the Falklands. What were the chances of *that?* These two had asked themselves that question over and over again. They never did come up with the right odds, but both knew as soon as they saw the white jet in the sky that their plan to snatch the Bomb and use it for whatever they could dream up, was lost.

They had watched the battle from a gun turret, a guest of the ship's high commander, and had narrowly escaped the brutal strafing the white airplane had delivered on the vessel.

Now as the ship made its way slowly west, the men were scouring the cabin for anything mildly alcoholic, but having a hard time of it, much to their dismay.

The third man in the cabin however had had no problem getting and staying inebriated. He may have needed to be in such a state even more than they. They were simply discouraged. He was devastated, his failure to succeed in the operation had reached new lows of shame for him. He could hardly speak, he was so depressed.

It was, of course, High General Hilo Wakisaki, the man who was responsible for the Japanese invasion of South America in the first place, slumped in the chair across from the two agents, simply staring out into space, not talking,

hardly breathing. His loss of face following the embarrass-
ing Battle of Axaz plain on Xwo Mountain and the overall
failure of the Night Brigade had affected him greatly. It
was like a knife had been thrust in his heart and become
stuck there. He was no longer the darling of the population back on the Home Islands, he was no longer regarded
as Japan's greatest general. His triumph had so quickly
turned to failure, it was almost surreal.

When the pair of OSS men had approached him
through back channels to make a deal on invading the
Falkland Islands, Wakisaki had jumped at the chance, hoping to regain his previously lofty reputation.

But now with the dismal failure of this operation, Wakisaki was running out of options.

"You would think the highest bug on the Japanese food
chain would have something decent to drink," X said to
Z as he ransacked the captain's cabin once again, looking
for some liquor.

Z just shrugged. He was tired. The last few weeks had
been a bitch for him.

"Why do you expect this guy to have taste?" he replied
nodding toward the nearly comatose high general.

X went right over to the Japanese commander, got down
in his face, and, in perfect Japanese, asked him: "If you
were going to hide something like brandy or bourbon,
where would you put it?"

Wakisaki simply grunted. In his eyes one could see he
was reliving the triumphs that had become him until recently. His eyes were watering. He was hardly alive. X re-
sisted the temptation to slap him across the face. Instead
he reached inside his gun belt, drew out a revolver, and
placed it in Wakisaki's hand.

"Here you go, pal," the OSS man told him. "Do the
right thing."

Finally Wakisaki moved. He looked down at the gun,
then back up at the two OSS men.

"That man in the white jet," he began asking in halting stuttering Japanese. "He was this Sky Ghost?"

X slumped back onto the couch beside Z.

"That's right, pal," the OSS man told him. "He was the brick wall we were unlucky enough to slam into."

"There was no way it could have gone in our favor no matter what we did," Z said, more to himself than to Wakisaki. "Damn, that guy is a pain in the ass."

"A valuable pain in the ass," X moaned.

But Wakisaki wasn't listening to any of this. He was staring down at the pistol in his hand. Before his eyes flashed many, many final scenes. Strangely, the last one was his memory of his favorite vase, the one he'd smashed that morning in his suite in New Lima. It seemed like things just never got any better after that.

"If only I could have that moment back," he whispered. "And a bottle of glue."

Then he put the gun to his head, pulled the trigger and blew his brains out.

The cloud of blood and brain mist stained the far wall of the cabin, but X and Z hardly moved a muscle.

Z reached down to the only bottle they could find in Wakisaki's supply cabinet and took a swig, but spit it all out just as soon as it touched his tongue.

"*Grape sake!*" he said with disgust, wiping his mouth. "Who the fuck would ever drink this stuff?"

Thirty-four

Hunter took off just as the sun was going down.

Bomb-pod finally attached to the bottom of his aircraft, fuel tanks filled to the brim with something, he left McReady field, climbed to a mind-numbing altitude of 101,000 feet, and turned northwest.

Timing was everything, he knew. For this plan to finally reach its last stage, Hunter would have to make the 7,500-mile trip to Area 52 in record time.

Luckily the Z-3/15 was just the airplane to do it.

The events of the past few days ran through his head now like a movie reel set to replay. The cold, cold Falklands. The battle at McReady. The strange tale of the hooker in the crashed airplane. The battle on Tin Can beach. The world beneath the hill. Seeing Chloe—and the man and woman glimpsed briefly in the rubble of the farmhouse.

It all seemed unreal, and so intense it made what he was about to do—his "suicide" mission—almost seem dull by comparison.

He reached optimum height and booted in the *Stiletto*'s double-reaction engines to 93 percent power. Whatever was feeding his power plants definitely had a kick to it. Previously he had shied away from opening up the plane's throttles all the way, simply because he wasn't sure it could take the strain. But now was not the time for caution. Now was the time to get from one lonely, secret spot on the Earth to another as quickly as possible.

So he pushed his throttles ahead and watched the air-speed indicator begin spinning madly around the dial.

Mach 5. Mach 6. Mach 7. . . .

Once again the needle-nosed airplane cut through the air like a knife. The steamy green of the South American continent was soon in view, even though Hunter was barely two minutes out of the Falklands. He nudged the throttles ahead further. Mach 7.5. Mach 8. . . .

The g-forces were pinning him against his seat with an intensity he could not ever recall, at least not in this world. It made it hard for him to move, to breathe, to blink—but he didn't care. He loved the feeling, loved the pressure he felt on every square centimeter of his body. Why? Because he knew it came as a result of ultimate flight. Fast, faster, fastest. That's all he ever wanted to be.

But the feeling had a downbeat to it as well. As soon as he reached his destination, he knew the chances that he would ever fly this beautiful, if slightly muddy airplane again, were practically nil. He had to enjoy it while he could.

So he hit the throttle again and now the engines were burning at 110 percent, and he was approaching Mach 9, close to 5,500 miles per hour. Below him, the entire South American continent looked like a green blur. He sucked in a long breath of oxygen and let it out very slowly. He knew it would be wise to savor this.

His control panel began blinking just a moment later. It was not a warning light or a trouble indicator that was flashing—it was the MVP, coming back to life. Hunter lifted his oxygen mask and tried to spit at it again, but the saliva simply rocketed back into his own face. This gave him a laugh. The aerodynamic properties of a loogie. Interesting thesis, he thought.

He strained his sore elbow lifting his finger to push the

MVP activator button. Once engaged, the screen immediately came to life. It was filled with the routine jumble of numbers and letters and computer codes at first, blinking at him like it was happy to be back on, and flushed out and working and what have you been doing Mr. Hunter since we last spoke? Finally the message screen went all white and then purple, an indication that an animation was forthcoming.

Hunter did a check of his aircraft's vital signs and everything looked fine, despite the fact that he was traveling more than a mile a second.

He turned his attention back to the MVP screen and was surprised by what he saw. It was not the long list of instructions and inquiries he'd half expected, but rather the same cartoon he'd viewed when he first received the orders for the top secret bombing mission.

Well, at least the OSS wasn't wasting time getting him back into the game, he thought.

The cartoon showed the huge hangar out in the middle of the Nevada desert, the one containing the colossal airplane. The first time he'd seen this visual, the briefing animators had showed it shaking slightly, giving the impression that work was being done inside. Now, in a very bizarre comic fashion, the hangar was shaking again, but even more so, and puffs of smoke and steam were emitting from the windows and the doors. The whole building was shaking at its foundations. Slowly the huge hangar doors were beginning to open.

It looked ridiculous, but the meaning of this comical animation was crystal clear: Much work was going on inside the huge hangar. The doors opening told him that, incredibly, the project was nearing completion. *In three days?*

The implication for him was clear as well. He had to get back to Area 52 as quickly as possible.

This deflated him again. The urgency of the animation was pressing on him like the monstrous g-forces. It meant at least one diversion he'd been toying with was now impossible. He wouldn't be able to stop at Xwo Mountain.

That meant he would probably never see Sara again.

He let out a long slow breath and sucked in another one. Maybe that was the way it was supposed to be.

He reached forward and managed to hit the throttle again and now the Z-3/15 was going full out at Mach 9.2.

At this velocity, he'd be in Area 52 in less than two hours.

Nevada

Mike Fitzgerald was exhausted.

He'd been up for three straight days now. In that time, he'd drunk more than five gallons of coffee, six gallons of highly caffeine-enriched soda, had eaten 35 candy bars, and eighteen bananas.

After all that, and with the strange excitement within the big hangar, Fitzgerald's sugar buzz had him high as a kite.

Which was good. Because if he fell asleep, he had no idea what would happen to the others. They'd been following his lead since they were brought to this fateful place. This enormous hangar with its colossal airplane. The place called G-2. He'd become the project foreman. The mother hen. His main fear was that if he lay down and went to sleep, the rest of them would too.

And that would be a disaster.

So Fitz continued gobbling Snuckers bars and draining huge mugs of coffee.

If it was up to him, he'd never have to go to sleep ever again.

Probably the most startling thing about the past forty-eight hours was how smart the New Jersey Giants turned out to be.

Fitz had always held the impression—and he knew he wasn't alone here—that most football players were basically big and dumb. But not these guys. These guys were wizards. They had performed engineering feats way beyond anyone's expectations, the OSS included. They had provided the backbone and the muscle for this bizarre project. They had contributed a lot of the reasoning too. True, the majority of this inspiration was coming from Coach Geraci and his assistants. But the players themselves—the linebackers, the defensive ends, the linemen, and both backfields—had contributed some outstanding ideas in the reconfiguration of the colossal airplane, and once approved, implemented them by way of some frighteningly efficient time-saving dictums.

As a result, the project was miles ahead of schedule—almost as if that's how it was meant to be.

They were presently in the process of rebuilding the colossal airplane, all fifty-seven of them, plus the small army of Bride Lake mechanics. Rebuilding was the key word here, because they had spent the first twenty-four hours *un*-building it.

The mission statement had posed this problem to them: This gigantic plane had to deliver a bomb whose blast would be so big and so quick, the plane would virtually have no chance of escaping it. There was no other way to deliver this bomb because it had to hit a certain spot at a certain time per the calculations in its warhead, and no rocket on Earth was accurate enough to deliver it. So the little bomb with the big blast had to be dropped from an airplane that had the size and the staying power to fly around the world, literally, via the transpolar route.

It was an extremely large order, especially since the people who the government was convinced could fulfill it had all just been plucked from their relatively simple lives and plunked down here in the middle of a vast secret project with nearly zero experience in things aeronautical. It made no sense. But that's what had happened.

The strange thing was, it was working.

At first there was an element of shock involved, but as soon as they'd spent some time all together in G-2 building, people thought they started recognizing each other. Football players knew monks. Monks knew hedonistic college professors. People became instant compadres. It was as if all of them had known everyone else before—yet no one could remember when or how or where or why.

Still, it was massive, rather instantaneous bonding. Everyone was so stunned by it that they began thinking that maybe the real spooks inside the OSS—the Psychic Evaluation Corps—were on to something bringing them here.

Buoyed by this feeling, real or not, the Associates got to work.

Fitz believed it was one of the monks who first suggested that if they were forced to work with an airplane that was too slow to get out of its own bomb blast then perhaps the emphasis should not be on the plane's performance, but on something else. It was clear that they weren't going to make the airplane any faster, or the bomb blast any smaller. So what then became the most important thing? It was, of course, the survivability of the crew. So the focus changed a little. Not in how to prevent the plane from coming apart when the blast hit, but on what could be done to protect the lives of the crew *before* that happened.

Once that truth had been realized, they really got down to it.

What had followed was two straight days and nights of disassembling, torch-cutting, hammer-banging, and lots and lots of screw removal. Then the reconfigurations were begun. Again, more on guesswork than science, more on instinct than any known set of rules or values, they

changed the airplane as they all thought it should be done.
They had added several important components as well,
got rid of some that were deemed unnecessary. They even
had extra stuff brought in from Area 52.

Now, they were putting it all back together again.

Through all this, Y had watched them. He was always at
a distance, always keeping one eye on his MVP pad. He
was a man who seemed worried about many many things
at once. In the few times that he'd spoken to them, he'd
alluded to the fact that the pilot of this flying beast would
be arriving at any time and that everyone, from the president, through the War Department, to the OSS, and on
down was hoping that the giant airplane would be ready
to fly by that time.

Incredibly, even though they still had much work to do,
it seemed like it would be.

Xwo Mountain

The huge B-17/36 bomber roared through the LSD
screen and set down with a puff of smoke and a mighty
screech as six dozen wheels hit the hard rocky runway all
at once.

The fire crews raced out toward the bomber and sprayed
Purple-K flame retardant on its outermost engines. The
forty-four-man bomber crew quickly exited the plane just
seconds after it had stopped rolling at the end of the runway—standard procedure. They had just completed a mission over northern Argentina, the firebombing of a new
Japanese settlement named Okodoko, which was close to
the ancient Argentine city of Tazco.

The bombing mission had been long and arduous, the
skies full of Japanese fighters, and the flames from a previous firebombing had licked the underbelly of this air-

plane, as well as the others, as they went in ultralow to drop their bombs.

But the airplane had come through it in one piece, and to a man, the crew knew the person responsible for that was the plane's COA, the Commander of the Aircraft. He was the most senior bomber pilot on Xwo. His name was Captain PJ O'Malley.

Crewmen fought to be part of O'Malley's crew simply because it was believed anyone flying in his airplane had the best chance of making it home alive. Invariably O'Malley was a bombing mission's leader; many times the rest of the group dropped their firebombs on targets already marked by O'Malley's pathfinder aircraft. It was heard later that the Japanese actually had a price on O'Malley's head, they feared him so much.

O'Malley was that good.

That's why it seemed so very strange when he reached the debriefing room after securing his airplane at its hardstand to find a set of orders waiting for him. They were enclosed inside a red envelope.

Every American serviceman operating overseas knew what a red envelope meant: It was standard War Department practice to put home-return orders inside red envelopes. Anyone who got one was usually being told that he was going back to the States. Seeing the red envelope then was usually cause for a great amount of joy.

But in O'Malley's case, it simply caused a great amount of confusion.

"Going home?" he blurted out when first handed the red envelope. "Me?"

It *was* strange because O'Malley actually took the red envelope as an insult. He was not completely devoid of ego. He knew he was playing a pivotal role on Xwo Mountain. A crucial one even. He'd come to regard any notion that he would actually be transferred out of the mountain ops to be nonexistent. This was certainly true after the wing's recent hurry-up mission down to the Falklands. It had been O'Malley who'd taken the divert order first and changed the overall flight plan of the group. It was because of his leadership and innovation that the unexpected bombing raid on West Falkland was now considered an enormous success.

So why then was he being sent home?

The red envelope was handed to him by the officer of the day, the man running all the debriefings in the absence of Major Payne.

"Congratulations, Captain," the officer had said to him. "You deserve it."

But O'Malley never heard him. He was just too stunned. Going home? Why? Or more to the point, why now?

He opened the red envelope.

Then he understood.

The knock on Major Payne's billet door was quiet but direct.

The chief operations officer for Xwo Mountain was awake, lying still, intravenous tubes sticking out of his arm, resting quietly in bed as the doctors had ordered.

The lights were on in his room though; he had insisted upon that and his doctors, considering his condition and what he'd just gone through, finally said OK.

The last thing Payne wanted to be was alone in the dark.

He was a little shy about blindly answering the door too.

He called out: "Who is it?"

"It's O'Malley, sir. May I come in?"

"Are you alive, O'Malley?" Payne called to him in all seriousness.

"I am, sir," O'Malley replied from behind the closed door.

"OK," Payne finally said. "Come on in."

O'Malley found Payne looking very pale and drawn. The

bomber pilot knew Payne was under the care of a psychic evaluation officer long-distance through an MVP, and even now he could see the mission pad on Payne's nightstand, blinking messages to him. Much care had to be taken in what O'Malley said then. He did not want to upset Payne in any way.

Payne sat up a little on the bed and shook O'Malley's hand. The bomber pilot hoped his facial expression wouldn't show it, but Payne looked awful to him.

Of course, he was the first person O'Malley had ever met who had actually seen a ghost.

"How are you, Major?" O'Malley asked him.

"I'm alive," Payne replied wearily. "They tell me I'll be OK, someday. I can't ask for more than that."

"Well, if it's worth anything," O'Malley told him, "you're considered a hero around here—and in other places as well. If it wasn't for you . . ."

If it wasn't for Payne then the enemy invasion of West Falkland Island would have been a success and the Bomb, which was now heading toward Area 52, would have wound up in some very nefarious hands.

"I mean, no one I've talked to really understands what was going on down there," O'Malley went on. "But I can tell everyone thinks you took the full brunt of this thing, and as a result a lot of people on our side are still alive and a lot of people on the other side ain't. . . ."

Payne smiled for the first time in a long time. The psychic eval guys told him the shock of actually communicating with a ghost would wear off in time. Maybe a week. Maybe a month. Maybe a year. But a smile or two wouldn't hurt the process.

"I'm glad for that," he finally told O'Malley. "So is this strictly a cheer-up visit? You didn't smuggle me any brandy from the OC, did you?"

O'Malley just shook his head. "They'd shoot me if I got caught," he said, and they both laughed.

"Actually, I got orders to ship out," he told Payne. "Leaving in an hour. I've just come to say good-bye."

Payne's face went slightly pale again.

"You? Leaving? Why?"

"My exact questions," O'Malley confessed. "But then I read the orders, and now I get it. I think."

"Anything you can tell me?" Payne wanted to know.

O'Malley drew a little closer to the man's bed. "It's all classified," he began. "But I'll let you in on a little bit, seeing what you've been through."

He lowered his voice to a whisper.

"I've been ordered to help pilot an airplane on a very top secret mission," O'Malley began. "The rest of the crew are a bunch of unknowns and exactly what I'll be doing, what I'm flying, and where we are going, I don't know."

"Typical," Payne responded. "The OSS is behind this I suspect."

"Good guess," O'Malley told him. "But there is something I will tell you: I think or at least it was hinted in the orders, that there is another pilot going along as well, and it's someone who I think you should know is still alive."

Payne's left eyebrow went up a notch.

"Really?"

O'Malley nodded. "The way this whole thing was laid out to me in my orders," he said, "I'm sure Hawk Hunter is involved. In fact, this will sound crazy, but I think he was flying around down in the Falklands when we arrived to do our bombing run. Someone had been driving a crazy-looking jet all over the sky just before we got there."

Payne settled back down into his bed. The smile returned a little to his face.

"So he's still among the living?"

O'Malley nodded. "I'm almost positive of it. I know he's a friend of yours, so I thought I'd tell you."

Payne smiled fully now. "Well, that is good news then," he said. "Thanks. I appreciate it."

O'Malley got up and shook hands with Payne. "Got to get going, sir," he said. "Take care of yourself, OK?"

"You too," Payne told him. "And tell Hawk he owes me a drink."

O'Malley smiled. "If I get to see him," he said, "I'll tell him he owes both of us."

With that, O'Malley saluted and went out the door.

Thirty-five

The crane that was used to reattach the large section of the left wing of the gigantic airplane was so big, they had to cut a section out of the G-2 hangar roof to allow its tip to poke through.

Even with the help of this hydraulic giant, it took all the muscle power that could be mustered among the strange group inside the hangar to get that last wing section attached.

It took four hours of nonstop pushing and pulling and grunting and groaning, but finally the wing was reconnected and an army of rivet-fastener men went to work making the attachment permanent.

With that, the reconfiguration of the B-2000 "Colossus" was complete. In a stunning achievement, the football players, monks, college professors, and aging soldiers had done exactly what their country had wanted them to do. At least now, when the huge bomb blast went off, there was a chance that the crew didn't necessarily have to go up with it.

Now, all they needed were the pilots.

It might have been described as fate, or as a cosmological initiative, or simply the way it happened.

But no sooner had the last fastener been put in place

on the huge airplane than the hangar door opened and the man charged with flying the colossal airplane walked in.

Hunter had landed at Area 52 two hours before, the Z-3/15 running out of fuel the exact moment his wheels touched down.

The next thirty minutes were spent in the delicate operation of taking the Bomb off its belly-mounted rack and getting it ready for transfer to the colossal airplane.

A briefing with Y followed, taking another hour or so, and again Hunter could only give him the highlights of his adventure in the Falklands, including the evidence that the notorious agents X and Z were involved. It would be left to a later time for Y to explain exactly how word of the dire situation on West Falkland had reached Xwo Mountain. At the moment, those circumstances were still highly classified.

While this debriefing session was going on in Y's office, his MVP began blinking. A burst message from OSS Central was beaming in. According to the shadowy Psychic Evaluation Corps, the time to begin the mission in the big plane was looming very near.

The airplane was ready, the bomb was in place, and most of the crew was too. The airplane should take off no later than midnight, the MVP declared.

It was now 1800 hours. That gave them just six hours to pull the last strings together.

The trip out to the huge hangar ate up another thirty minutes, but Hunter needed the long ride in the desert to cool him off. The last thing he wanted to do was take an Octocopter out. If he was just hours away from leaving on the most dangerous mission he'd ever accepted, he didn't want to waste what could be some of his last precious minutes of life getting sick on a Beater.

So Y agreed to drive him out to the big barn and Hunter tried to enjoy each mile of the long, quiet journey.

When he walked through the door of the place, it was as if the world had stopped for him again. Yet this time it was more than just an illusion. This second time he stepped into the place, everything and everybody came to a stop.

Staring back at him were fifty-seven sets of eyes. They belonged to such a mélange of people, Hunter nearly burst out laughing. They *did* look like football players and monks and ordinary Joes, just as Y had told him. But there was something different about them as well. Hunter knew them. Every last monk, every last New Jersey Giant. He knew who was a soldier and who wasn't. He knew all these men. From Back There. These were his "associates."

Everything began moving again when one of these people finally approached him. It was Mike Fitzgerald. He walked up to Hunter and stuck out his hand.

"Hi, Hawk," he said simply. "Welcome back."

Hunter felt frozen to his spot. He'd already seen a few ghosts since coming to this world. But this one was different. Back There he and Mike Fitzgerald had been tight. When he was killed at the Battle of Football City, Hunter had wept as though he had lost a brother.

But now, here he was—again. Same guy. Same red nose. Same powerful build. Same sophisticated graying of the jet-black hair. The same guy he had seen briefly before shipping out to Iceland.

Mike Fitzgerald. Back from the dead.

"Hey, Fitz," Hunter said, shaking his hand. "Good to see you . . . again."

What followed was a guided tour of the airplane that the Associates had just rebuilt.

Hunter was astonished at what they had done. It was the same airplane. It looked the same, had the same number of engines, same gigantic size, same gigantic capabilities.

But it was a different beast.

Radically so.

Fitz gave him the tour and laid most of the praise on the New Jersey Giants. When Hunter first came to Y with the crazy notion as to where he might find his "associates," he had recalled working with a large group of engineers back in the other world. Combat engineers. He'd been able to recall just about all their names and those were the ones fed into the Main/AC. That all these people would be together here in this world—not as a combat engineering unit but as a pro football team—was mind-blowing enough. That they would be able to be put into a situation which by all rights, should have been totally alien to them and work the miracle they just had worked, was nothing short of well, *miraculous.*

Hunter spent the next two hours going over all the modifications the Associates had made. It was the monks' idea to hang five of the rogue squadron fighters from the bottom of the huge airplane. The Bantams were hanging way out near the wingtips. The VTOL planes were hanging about halfway in toward the fuselage. The swing-wing ugly was attached to the forward belly. As for the big Z-16 ultrarecon plane, it couldn't be attached to the gigantic airplane because its wings were too long and they would have interrupted the airflow coming off of the colossal fuselage. So they were going to tow it, on a long tether sticking out of the back, right around the planet.

It was Frost's idea to defend the colossal airplane with more than just machine guns, of which there were no less than a hundred lining both sides of the fuselage. Frost's notion was to take as many antiaircraft rockets as they could find and install them under the leading edge of the bomber's wings, similar to where a fighter would carry such a weapon. In the Air Corps inventories they'd found a type of AA rocket known as the Rattler. They'd put a call out for these weapons, and in one day were able to secure

200 of them, plus their attendant launching packages. Frost had overseen their installation and now the wings of the monster bomber were heavy with dozens of air-to-air missiles.

Ben Wa had come up with the sticky solution to the question of what to do with the flight compartment of the colossus when the moment of truth came. The people who would be in the most peril right as the bomb was being dropped would be the primary flight crew. Hunter looked over the work that Wa and his crew had done. It was nothing short of brilliant. The survivability factor of the airplane had been increased at least threefold.

Fitzgerald was obviously the one who had pulled it all together. That left only the man named Toomey. He had worked just as hard at reconfiguring the airplane—helping Frost with his idea, helping Ben Wa with his, and so on.

But what had his own personal contribution been?

It turned out he'd suggested they put an ice cooler on the airplane. A place that would be stocked with beer for the long trip awaiting them. For some reason, the rest of the group agreed. So there was now a fully stocked beer cooler down near the navigator's station. Hunter realized this was the strongest confirmation that what he was working with here was real. There was a long possibility that if you put forty football players in a room long enough, they might build you an airplane. And if you took a bar owner from northern New England and asked him how best to defend that airplane, he eventually might come up with the idea of stringing 200 air-to-air missiles along the plane's wings. And if you asked eight monks how to make an airplane more survivable in light of where it was going and what it would be doing, maybe they would come up with the rogue-squadron attachment idea.

But it took a certain kind of mind to suggest that they install a *beer cooler* for the long ride toward Armageddon. The J.T. Toomey Hunter recalled from Back There would have suggested exactly that. The one here did too. This was proof to Hunter's mind that the two universes he'd inhabited were, in fact, parallel. And now, they had connected.

At the end of this long day, and at the beginning of what would prove to be a very long night, it was that fact that warmed him greatly inside.

Thirty-six

Many searchlights had been brought out from Bride Lake to illuminate the enormous hangar known as G-2.

The doors to the barn had finally been opened and the nose of the gigantic B-2000 bomber was barely sticking out.

No less than twenty vehicles—tractors, trucks, even a few jeepsters—had lines attached to the monster's wheels and wings, and on one call, they began the long task of pulling the Colossus out of what had been its home for many years.

Once the plane was clear of the barn, another long process commenced: starting the giant's twenty engines. Just to get each one of them running up to pitch would take an hour. It would prove to be a very noisy sixty minutes.

Watching all this from the sidelines was Agent Y, his MVP in hand as always, its screen going absolutely crazy with messages.

The forces that would be in motion this night were mind-boggling. From Area 52, down to Panama, down to the Brazilian jungle, everyone was waiting for word to proceed. That word would only come when Y sent a message to OSS Central that their secret flying beast was finally on its way.

It was this strange scene that the chugging, smoking, jittery Beater came upon—long beams of light playing on an aerial monster in the middle of the Nevada desert.

The Octo came down with a bang not far from where Y was stationed. The side door opened and the sole passenger fell out, coughing from the internal exhaust.

Y greeted him, checked his ID, and gave him a good looking over. The man was familiar to him. His name was PJ O'Malley. He'd just arrived from South America.

O'Malley's eyes had gone as wide as half dollars at first seeing the gigantic plane; they had not decreased in size yet.

"You want me to fly in *that* thing?" he asked, totally in shock.

"Your government has called on you to perform a special duty," Y replied, giving him the standard line. "The OSS is hoping you'll accept."

But that veiled threat wasn't working with a veteran like O'Malley. There was no way he was getting aboard this beast. Not unless . . .

"Who is piloting this plane?" he asked Y.

Y actually smiled. It was his ace in the hole.

"Want to see for yourself?" he asked the bomber pilot.

O'Malley had already started walking toward the plane. It got bigger with every step. The noise from the engines was not only deafening, it was disrupting the air all around the monster. A veteran of untold combat missions, O'Malley actually felt his knees begin to quiver as he got closer to the big plane.

The side front door was open when he arrived. He stepped in only to find it was actually a small elevator. It carried him to the flight compartment, four stops up. He stepped out onto this tier and found it nearly five times as big as the flight suite on a B-17/36, which in itself was huge.

There were at least twenty people inside. They all glanced at him, and he thought he saw a lot of familiar faces—he just couldn't place any of them.

"Who's the skipper of this mother-effing tub?" he asked the room.

The guy sitting in the left-hand pilot's seat turned around and gave him a friendly salute.

It was Hunter.

"Hello, Captain," he said. "We've been waiting for you."

The engines were finally warmed and ready by 2315 hours.

No less than six MVPs had been installed in the plane's flight suite, and it took some time getting them all in sync. Then a special squad of armorers came over from Area 52 and installed the single bomb in the monster's gigantic bomb bay. A few tests went well. By 2345 hours, the plane was ready to go.

There were no speeches. No last-minute prayers or sentimentality. Y shook every man's hand—the entire group of Associates was going on the mission—then left the airplane and secured the outer hatch himself.

Anyone who was in the immediate area was cleared to 1,000 feet away. The shock wave from all twenty engines revving at once would be strong enough to break eardrums, so the manual said. Therefore everyone was also equipped with industrial-strength earplugs.

At exactly 2345 hours, the plane started rolling. It moved so slowly at first, Y was sure that something was wrong with it, that it would never get airborne, that this whole thing had been a colossal waste of time, and that Japan would eventually prevail in this damn war.

But slowly and surely, the beast began to pick up speed. By the first mile of the ten-mile-long runway, it was moving at fifteen knots. By mile two, it was up to twenty-five. Mile three, maybe thirty-five.

By mile five, it was up to nearly seventy knots, but it was

clear that all ten miles of asphalt would be needed to get the giant into the air.

Y watched in awe, one eye on the departing monster, the other on his MVP, counting off the seconds and the miles. Finally, at about 9.5 on the mark, Hunter pulled back the controls, and the gigantic bird began climbing into the air. It went so slowly that Y, watching now through nightscope binoculars, was convinced it was going to crash.

But up it went, the scream from its engines masking the groan made simply by such a large mass getting airborne. The large-enough Z-16 recon plane, in tow behind the monster, looked puny in comparison.

Y watched for a signal from Hunter telling him all was OK. It came about a minute into the flight, when the plane had achieved a somewhat miraculous 500 feet in altitude. Hunter simply blinked the huge array of navigation lights hanging all over the B-2000. This was the high sign. They were go for the mission.

Y dutifully punched this message into his MVP and told it to send the word immediately to OSS Central.

When he looked up from this operation, he was disheartened to see the big plane was fading fast from view. It was a clear but moonless night, and soon the only evidence that the giant was in the air were those fading navigation lights.

After five minutes or so, they disappeared completely.

At 0100 hours, exactly sixty-five minutes after the B-2000 had left the ground, two squadrons of Air Corps attack bombers swooped in on the eastern edge of the Panama Canal and began bombing Japanese gun emplacements. At the same time, Navy warships, including the USS *Chicago* megacarrier, the only survivor from the Pearl Harbor sneak attack nearly a year ago, began striking at Japanese positions on the western entrance to the waterway.

Several hundred miles to the south, three entire armies—made up of twenty divisions, or close to 400,000 men, crossed the Brazilian border into Peru and moved like a juggernaut to positions west.

By 0500 hours, the monster airplane, flying at 85,000 feet and at a speed of an incredible 1,400 knots, was approaching the outer coastline of Antarctica. If all went well, it would pass over the south pole by 0730 hours and begin its long polar suborbital trip back up the other side of the planet. Always drifting to the west, it was intent on topping the north pole and coming down right above Japan itself.

On West Falkland Island, the man they called God was all alone.

He was in his lab. Everyone else was topside by now. The civilians were back at Summer Point, and his wife was helping them get settled. The STS commandos were already over on East Falkland, starting the rebuilding process at McReady airfield.

The fight was over. It had been a close call. But they had survived. Until next time. Still, he had learned many things from the strange little war. He'd learned about heroism and cowardice. He'd learned that valor had no bounds. He'd seen just how far some men would go to save their comrades. He learned that he might have a son. . . .

These were the thoughts going through his mind as he sat in the room behind the big thick metal door. Yes, there were many secrets down here, near the middle of the earth. Big bombs. The secret of ghosts. Other things.

But nothing like what was behind this second door.

Now the man put his ear to the door and could hear the wind blow, even though he was 250 feet down in the middle of the hill.

He hit a few buttons. After all that had happened, he felt like looking on the other side today.

He unlocked the portal and waited for it to swing open. He had to be very careful here. Sometimes this could be a little unpredictable. He strapped on a safety harness which was attached to chains on the opposite side of the wall. One could never be too cautious, he liked to think.

Beside the door was a box of rocks he'd collected from the nearby beach just for this occasion. The door finally opened, and sure enough, there was a thick cumulus cloud rolling by.

The man inched his way over, testing the safety harness with every step. To fall now would be disastrous. Or at least he believed it would be.

He finally reached the door's open edge and felt the vapor of the cloud on his face. It left his forehead and nose covered with hundreds of tiny water droplets.

The man leaned further over the edge and looked at the deep blue North Atlantic below. The sea was especially churned-up today.

He picked up a handful of rocks and threw them over the edge. He watched as they fell exactly 1,865 feet to the ocean surface below, landing with a barrage of splashes.

Then he smiled. And he felt better, and the cloud came into the room again and drenched the man they called God, but he didn't care.

It was windy Back There today.